KILL ZONE

A Lucy Guardino FBI Thriller

CJ Lyons

PRAISE FOR NEW YORK TIMES AND USA TODAY BESTSELLER CJ LYONS:

"Everything a great thriller should be—action packed, authentic, and intense." ~#1 New York Times bestselling author Lee Child

"A compelling new voice in thriller writing...I love how the characters come alive on every page." ~New York Times bestselling author Jeffery Deaver

"Top Pick! A fascinating and intense thriller." ~ 4 1/2 stars, RT Book Reviews

"An intense, emotional thriller...(that) climbs to the edge of intensity." ~National Examiner

"A perfect blend of romance and suspense. My kind of read." ~#1 New York Times Bestselling author Sandra Brown

"Highly engaging characters, heart-stopping scenes...one great rollercoaster ride that will not be stopping anytime soon." ~Bookreporter.com

"Adrenalin pumping." ~The Mystery Gazette

"Riveting." ~Publishers Weekly Beyond Her Book

Lyons "is a master within the genre." ~Pittsburgh Magazine

"Will leave you breathless and begging for more." ~Romance Novel TV

"A great fast-paced read....Not to be missed." ~4 ½ Stars, Book Addict

"Breathtakingly fast-paced." ~Publishers Weekly

"Simply superb...riveting drama...a perfect ten." ~Romance Reviews Today

"Characters with beating hearts and three dimensions." ~Newsday

"A pulse-pounding adrenalin rush!" ~Lisa Gardner

"Packed with adrenalin." ~David Morrell

"...Harrowing, emotional, action-packed and brilliantly realized." ~Susan Wiggs

"Explodes on the page...I absolutely could not put it down." ~Romance Readers' Connection

KILL ZONE

A Lucy Guardino FBI Thriller

CJ Lyons

EDGY READS

Dear Reader,

This book would not have been written without your constant emails asking for "More Lucy, please!" or shouting out, "We love Lucy!" As always, I am most grateful that you have fallen for Lucy, a character who unlike so many thriller heroes is "just" a normal mom juggling work and family, trying to do it all as best she can.

I must warn you that in KILL ZONE the stakes have never been higher—and neither has the body count. When I came up with the idea of a cartel invading Pittsburgh I thought I'd have to work hard to make it seem possible.

Boy, was I wrong! As I researched, not only did I find that there already was cartel activity in Pittsburgh (and many other US cities) but that I would have to *lower* the level of violence by at least 90% in order for readers to accept it as realistic.

How often do you hear a thriller writer saying they had to portray LESS violence so the audience would believe a story? The more I read about the cartels in Central America and traffickers in the Middle East, the more horrified I was...especially as I realized that my scenario could actually happen.

The majority of details included in KILL ZONE, even the cartel's favorite method of body disposal, are all true. I actually did view the covert DEA video mentioned and still have nightmares about it.

If you'd like to learn more about the real life facts that create Lucy's world, I've set up a webpage listing the most relevant research as well as a dictionary of FBI and law enforcement terms and other info. You can find it here: http://cjlyons.net/extras/lucys-world/

Those links and articles are just a small fraction of the research I do for each book. Most of it involves talking to experts and KILL ZONE was no different. I'd like to thank my law enforcement, tactical, explosives, and weapons experts including: Robin Burcell, Joe Collins, James Faris, Adam Firestone, Finn Jackson, Lee Lofland, Wally Lind, Bob Mueller, and the others on the CrimeScene Writers' loop.

Any errors are mine, not theirs. I'd also like to point out that I did rearrange some of the geography of Pittsburgh, creating fictitious streets, housing projects, churches, and even a zoo. No animals were harmed in the making of this story.

Thanks for reading!
CJ

PROLOGUE

JIM FROM DIAMOND Security double-checked the directions on his GPS. The alarm's address was off his usual beat. Diamond specialized in expensive home protection systems. Their usual Pittsburgh clients lived in upscale Shadyside or fancy lofts downtown or out in Fox Chapel. Not here in Point Breeze North.

It was late enough on a December Friday afternoon that he didn't have to worry about school buses slowing him down as he drove his Blazer, with its flashing amber lights, to the address. Mr. Rashid Raziq. He practiced saying it, hoped he had the name right. At Diamond, it was all about customer service, especially as 99% of these alarms were homeowners forgetting their key code.

According to his records, this system had been installed only a few weeks ago, making it even more likely that this was a false alarm. The Twelve-Carat Package: interior and exterior motion sensitive cameras and lights, remote viewing via any Internet enabled device, 24/7 monitoring. Pricey.

Jim didn't think it was worth the money, himself. Nowadays two hundred bucks could buy you a decent camera you could set up yourself with alerts going to your email and phone. Probably faster response time than any company could promise.

But you wouldn't get the handholding. That's what people coming to Diamond were really buying. The reassurance that a real live person would come when you called, day or night. That peace of mind they got when Jim rang the doorbell and told them everything would be okay.

Like many Pittsburgh neighborhoods this one was a contradiction. A block north, near the Busway, was lined with warehouses, auto repair shops, abandoned small-time wholesale operations. A few blocks east were yellow brick row houses and run down single-family homes crowded together.

Jim drove past Westinghouse Park—once upon a time there used to be mansions in this neighborhood. Westinghouse and Henry Heinz, the ketchup guy. The Raziqs' street seemed to have retained some of the stately elegance inherited from Westinghouse and Heinz. It was a wide boulevard lined with mature trees at least a century old. Adding to its charm was a central grassy median, wide enough that he imagined kids running along it, flying kites when the weather was nice. The houses were mostly large, stately brick homes on nice-sized lots, evergreens forming natural privacy fences between neighbors.

The homes were in various states of disrepair or gentrification, reflecting their owners. Young couples buying cheap, pouring their sweat into renovations—

those were the houses with the older Fords and Toyotas parked in front. The driveways with dumpsters parked on them belonged to remodelers knowing a bargain when they spotted it, flipping homes for a tidy profit. And the houses with the mid-sized sedans and crossover SUVs: people with enough money to buy a flipped house but not enough to live in one of the tonier sections of town.

He pulled to the curb several houses down from the Raziqs' address and decided they belonged in the final category. The house was a white frame Colonial—which made it stand out among the brick houses on the block—otherwise, totally unremarkable. Two stories, porch too narrow for his taste, bonus room above the attached garage.

"Dispatch, I'm at the location. No signs of anyone present or any disturbances. Have you raised the homeowner?"

"Still no answer."

"Okay, I'm going to check it out." Jim grabbed his large D-cell Maglite, closest thing to a weapon that he was allowed to carry, and exited the SUV. According to the customer profile, the Raziqs had three children. Probably one of them came home from school and tripped the alarm before becoming immersed in their milk and cookies and afternoon cartoons. He climbed the porch steps. No welcome mat or any holiday decorations. Not even a porch swing.

He rang the doorbell. No answer. Rang it again. Nothing.

The front door was solid and the drapes were drawn tight across the windows to the front room. He keyed the radio on his phone. "Dispatch, no answer. I'm going around back."

"Okay, Jim. Let me know if you need me to alert police." Since 99% of their alarms were not true emergencies, Diamond had a hands-on policy of sending their own people to respond before calling the authorities on routine calls. It saved the police unnecessary calls and their clients' unnecessary embarrassment. In the rare case of a true alarm, what was the rush anyway? If there'd been a break in, the crooks would be long gone before anyone arrived.

He climbed down the porch steps and walked behind the garage to the rear of the house. The back yard was quiet, reminded him of his own out in Swissvale: swing set, turtle-shaped sandbox, flagstone patio. Mature hemlocks lined the property boundaries, giving the yard a feeling of privacy. An oasis, the sounds of the city barely audible. At some time in its life, the house had been expanded, and now boasted a large, eat-in kitchen with a wide bay window to the left of the door.

Jim climbed the stone steps leading from the patio and looked through the window. Oak table, six chairs, one with a baby seat strapped to it. Nothing out of place. The only window on the working side of the kitchen was up high, over the sink. But, if he flattened against the door, he could just see past the edge of the counter.

A splash of color against the white tile near the sink caught his eye. His first thought was, *spilled ketchup*. At least that's what his brain tried to tell him even as his stomach twisted in revulsion.

He blinked once, twice then forced his gaze to move past the blood and focus on the body it had come from.

A little girl, maybe three, maybe four, just a little girl, almost as pale as the tile she lay on.

Except for the slash of blood across her throat.

CHAPTER 1

THE LAST FRIDAY before Christmas, all of Pittsburgh seemed intent on careening down the same stretch of highway, pushing and shoving and wielding their middle fingers as gestures of Peace on Earth and Good Will to Men.

"See if there's any update from Burroughs," FBI Supervisory Special Agent Lucy Guardino told her partner as she drove through traffic leading from Downtown. Pittsburgh drivers were immune to lights and sirens, but she used them anyway.

Isaac Walden waited until he had Don Burroughs, the city detective who'd requested their help, on the line before putting the phone on speaker.

"Raziq's still not talking," Burroughs reported. "Except to ask for the Feds—you, the DEA, CIA, I don't think he cares. Says he can't compromise his safety, won't deal with us locals. I'd be offended, except this one has fucking crazy written all over it, so I'm glad to have you on board."

The last came out in an almost conciliatory tone—for Lucy's benefit, she was sure. She and Burroughs had worked together before. They'd had their differences, but he was a good cop.

Local law enforcement officers didn't call the FBI for assistance except as a last resort. Not even for two dead girls.

Except the victims' father's name had shown up in the NCIC database with a note to call a DEA agent named David Haddad. No reason why, no label, no sign that Rashid Raziq was in protective custody, just a cryptic flag. Burroughs was savvy enough to know a lose-lose situation when he saw it.

Walden was working his own phone. "Only thing I can find on Raziq is that he's here on a State Department-sponsored visa. From Afghanistan. Everything else is behind DEA firewalls."

"Nice to know us locals aren't the only ones being kept in the dark," Burroughs said. "Happy to hand this off to you before word gets out."

"I take that to mean you want us out there as targets for the press if things go wrong," Lucy said.

"Not to mention the DEA. Only things are already about as wrong as they can get." Burroughs sounded jovial. "Just the way you like them, Guardino." She had the feeling it was payback time after she'd gotten him involved in a case that almost got him killed a few months ago.

"The ME release the bodies yet?" Walden asked.

"No." Burroughs grew serious. Two kids dead on his watch: a four-year-old and a fifteen-year-old. Close in age to Burroughs' own sons, Lucy realized. "They're taking it slow so we can process the scene fully. You can jump on board the crazy train with everyone else once you arrive." He hung up.

"Still nothing from this DEA Agent, Haddad," Walden said before Lucy could ask. Federal agents' cell phone numbers weren't shared readily, not even with fellow agents, not without a supervisor's permission. "I left a message with the call center."

Exactly why Lucy liked working with the man. Walden was her Rock of Gibraltar, his logic a good counter-balance to her more intuitive methods of investigation. She could trust him not to undermine her, even when she wasn't playing as close to the FBI protocols as the brass upstairs would like. Plus, it was a whole lot of fun working with him. There was nothing like seeing the look on a subject's face after being questioned by a big scary black man only to have Lucy with her petite Italian frame walk in acting even crazier and scarier than Walden. It usually sent them scurrying back to Walden for protection, ready to give it up.

"Two kids dead and a father refusing to talk to the locals. Why is it the crazies always come out at Christmas?" she asked.

"No idea." Walden shifted in his seat as she edged the Tahoe into the lane beside them, sliding into a vacancy that hadn't existed when Lucy began the maneuver. "Maybe just to piss you off?"

"Then they'd better watch out. Nick is surprising me with tickets to *The Nutcracker* tonight and there's no way I'm missing it."

"*The Nutcracker?* You do know it's a ballet, right?"

Lucy smiled—not at him but at the driver who moved out of her way without her even needing to show him her weapon. "Yeah, I know. My mom told him I was in it when I was a little girl. I was one of the extras, those kids opening presents in the background, barely even remember it myself—but now he thinks I like ballet."

"Wait a minute. After fifteen years of marriage, Dr. Nicholas Callahan, the man with a doctorate in clinical psychology, who has taken advanced training in behavioral analysis and specializes in untangling the dark recesses of the mind, this man thinks you like the ballet because your mother told him so?"

"Isn't it sweet? Good thing I found the tickets so I can act surprised."

They hurtled down the parkway—well, *crawled* would be more like it, as they approached the Squirrel Hill Tunnel. Why the hell did everyone slow down just because they were driving beneath a mountain? If you were worried about the damn thing collapsing on top of you, shouldn't you go faster?

"Mom had ulterior motives," she continued. The radio cut out as they entered the tunnel, leaving only the tires humming against the concrete pavement as background noise. "Gives her an excuse to take Megan for the weekend."

"Your mother would have made an excellent hostage negotiator."

"I'm actually looking forward to it. It's three hours long and you have to keep your cell phone off, so I'm thinking it's going to be the best uninterrupted sleep I've had in a long time."

"Still worrying about Morgan Ames?" His voice dropped as if someone could be eavesdropping.

Morgan was a teenaged girl-slash-psychopath whose homicidal tendencies had been instilled in her by her serial killer father. A serial killer father who'd kidnapped Lucy last month and tried his best to kill her before she'd been able to turn the tables on him. Now he was in maximum security, locked down twenty-three hours a day, awaiting trial.

"Yeah," she admitted grudgingly, not wanting to talk about Morgan, Morgan's father, or last month. She hadn't told anyone the entire truth, not even Nick. He specialized in treating posttraumatic stress disorder and wanted her to see one of the FBI headshrinkers, but no way was she going to let one of the Employee Assistance goons rattle around inside her brain. Not when she had the best guy for the job sleeping beside her every night. "But it's getting better."

Walden gave a small grunt. "Still owe you for not taking me on that one. What a nut case."

They emerged from the tunnel, the mountain's shadow casting them in darkness. Lucy goosed the accelerator and they took the exit onto Braddock Avenue, narrowly avoiding running down a car ogling the Christmas decorations adorning Regent Square.

The address Burroughs had given them was on a quiet street in Point Breeze North, not far from the Allegheny County Police Headquarters where the 911

Communications Center was housed. Lucy tended to navigate by law enforcement landmarks since part of her job as leader of the FBI's Sexual Assault Felony Enforcement Taskforce was coordinating the efforts of over two hundred municipal, county, state, and federal law enforcement agencies.

Unlike the narrow streets north and south of it, the Raziqs lived on a wide boulevard off the major thoroughfares. It was a few blocks west of Westinghouse Park and another couple of blocks south of the ravine that carried the railroad tracks and municipal Busway. The street felt isolated in both time and space. A safe haven.

Until tonight.

They pulled up to the modest white frame Colonial and parked in front of the ME's van. Walden went to gather witness statements and get the lay of the land from the city detectives. Lucy paused beside the Tahoe to take in the scene.

The houses on this block were uniformly old, most a century at least. Some looked newly renovated, others in various stages of disrepair. Scattered across lawns and front porches were holiday decorations in an international festival of light celebrating Christmas, Kwanza, and Chanukah.

Except this house. No decorations here. Not even a pink flamingo on the neatly mowed lawn. The shrubs were carefully bundled beneath burlap to shield them from the Pittsburgh winter, although it looked like they weren't going to have a white Christmas, not this year. The only color came from the flashing amber lights on top an SUV parked haphazardly across the driveway, one tire trespassing onto the grass. Diamond Security, the logo read. Their reporting witness.

Burroughs' unmarked white Impala was a few doors down the street along with two marked radio cars, one on each side of the street.

She felt stares from the surrounding houses, but no one was bold enough to come out and see for themselves what disaster had landed at their neighbor's doorstep. Interesting. She wasn't sure if it said more about the Raziqs or their neighbors.

"How's Kim?" Lucy asked Burroughs as he approached the Tahoe from the house.

"Good. I think we're going to make it this time." He and his ex-wife had reconciled a few months ago. It suited him. He'd added a few pounds to his six-foot frame, filled in the hollows beneath his eyes. Even his wardrobe had undergone a face lift: instead of a variety of suits and shoes all in shades of brown matching his hair and eyes, today he wore a navy blue suit and black shoes. And his wedding ring, a definite good sign.

"The boys?"

His eyes lit up. "They're great. Kevin made the traveling hockey team."

"Thought we were trying for a low profile?" She nodded to the lights on the SUV sitting across the drive.

"Security guy saw the youngest, and ran back for his car, thought maybe he could get her to the ER." Burroughs shook his head at the security guard's naiveté. "He's over there," he jerked a thumb over his shoulder to the shrubs shielding the driveway from the neighboring house, "puking his guts out, you want to talk to him."

"When did the father arrive?" Raziq, the gentleman insisting on making life difficult for the investigators trying to work his daughters' murders. She couldn't wait to hear what the story behind that was.

"He got here right after I did. Screaming and cussing when we wouldn't let him inside. Literally ripping his shirt. Threatened us in three different languages then demanded we call the Feds. Guess us local yokels weren't good enough for him."

"Where's he now?"

Burroughs nodded to a patrol car across the street. "Back of a squad with a patrolman. Only way to shut him up and keep him out of our hair. Still haven't heard back from the DEA."

Lucy sighed, hoped this didn't turn into some kind of pissing contest with the cowboys over at Drug Enforcement.

Burroughs read her expression effortlessly. "This one's a ball buster. And I have a feeling it's only going to get nuttier."

———•———

TEXT MESSAGE RECEIVED 16:24
TRES: POLICE TOOK BAIT. HAVE RAZIQ.
Z: MAINTAIN CONTACT. INTERCEPT ON SIGNAL.
TRES: POLICE?
Z: KILL THEM ALL.

CHAPTER 2

"RUN IT DOWN for me," Lucy told Burroughs.

"Rather you see it for yourself."

She glanced toward the squad car parked beneath a street lamp across the street. Shadows from a barren sycamore scratched the roof of the car like a skeleton's fingers. Thankfully the vehicle pointed away from the house. The father sat in the back, alone. As far as she could make out in the faint light, the man sat facing front, away from the crime scene activity. "You made notification?"

"Told him as little as I could. Enough to let him know his girls were gone."

"How'd he take it?" Death notifications were the worst part of a policeman's job, but they also provided an opportunity to observe subjects at their most vulnerable. There was a damn good reason why cops were cynical: they had to be in order to separate true reactions from superb performances.

Burroughs shrugged one shoulder, glancing over his shoulder towards the patrol car. "After his initial hissy fit, after it sank in, he choked up, tore the top button off his shirt trying to get air. A few tears, lots more shouts, then… nothing. Just shut down. Could be cultural, I don't know."

She wished she knew more about Raziq, and why his name had popped up with a DEA flag attached. "They're from Afghanistan?"

"Right. The dad speaks English. British accent, kinda."

"Been here long?"

"A little more than a year."

"We brought them here. Any idea why?" she asked, trying to get a handle on the politics and the DEA involvement.

"Not sure. Once a Taliban, now a Yankee Doodle Dandy, or something like that. Here to help the good ole US of A with its war on drugs, I guess."

She thought about that. DEA, Afghanistan… the two together meant drug violence. Could that violence have traveled halfway around the world to Pittsburgh, targeting two little girls?

"No signs of drugs in the house?" It wouldn't be the first time the DEA had allied with a dealer. One of the problems working drugs: often you were forced to choose the lesser of two evils.

"Nope. Clean as a nun's habit. A few weapons, but they're mainly antiques. Showpieces."

They walked past the SUV blocking the driveway, Burroughs pausing to reach inside and turn the flashing lights off, and continued up the path to a uniformed officer standing guard at the front door. Lucy showed him her credentials, which he duly noted on a clipboard. There was a cardboard box of surgical booties, hair caps, and gloves waiting at the threshold.

"It's bad, Lucy," Burroughs murmured as they stood side by side, awkwardly donning the protective gear. "I mean, what those girls—" He gulped, looked away.

"Are you thinking the father, Raziq, is our guy?" Lucy bent to slip shoe covers over her Reeboks. It wasn't a court day for her, so she'd dressed in khakis and a fleece sweater—the Federal Building was always cold, no matter the time of year. The lightweight hair cap fought with her thick, long hair, but she managed to get it all tucked inside. She straightened, putting an extra pair of the Nitrile gloves into her parka pocket. Never hurt to be prepared.

"I'm not thinking anything until I get forensic data and finish all the witness statements." Good man. The more emotional a crime was, the easier it was to jump to conclusions too soon and close off avenues of investigation.

She opened the door.

Gasoline and burnt flesh mixed with metallic scent of fresh blood. Primitive reflexes made her gag and swallow. The smell of feces and urine wove their way into the olfactory mix. Burroughs waved a tube of menthol cream her way, but she declined. She'd experienced much worse; knew in a few minutes she'd cease to notice it.

There was a living room to their right, dining room on the other side of the foyer, staircase leading up, and a narrow hallway leading to a kitchen at the rear of the house; a layout almost exactly like Lucy's own home across the river.

She pushed the thought aside and focused on reading the scene. Men and women worked throughout the house. Camera flashes going off upstairs, the medical examiner's team in the living room waiting for the crime scene techs to finish documenting evidence. It was strangely hushed compared to most scenes. No banter, no gallows humor. Professionals concentrating on getting the job done as best as they could.

The first bloody handprint was on the cream-colored wall of the staircase in front of them. It was low on the wall, below the banister. Tiny, smaller than Lucy's. A child's.

"We think the girl interrupted our actor." Pittsburgh slang for unknown subject, or Unsub in FBI parlance. No one called them perpetrators outside the movies and TV. "The little one, I mean. The older girl, she was the real target. He started with her—" Burroughs gestured for Lucy to enter the living room.

Here the smell of burnt flesh was worse. There was more furniture than the room could comfortably accommodate: two couches, a coffee table, several smaller tables that appeared to be antiques, three boxy chairs with intricately carved teak backs and brightly upholstered cushions. Blood spatter fanned out in all directions from the center of the room where the brass coffee table had been knocked off its wooden base. The thick wool rug had a dark gold and burgundy print with the brighter scarlet of fresh blood sprayed across it like unholy confetti.

Crime scene techs had unrolled plastic sheeting in a two-foot wide ribbon, skirting the evidence they had flagged, giving Lucy and Burroughs a safe path to walk across. She glimpsed the body behind Burroughs, but forced herself to stop and focus on the rest of the scene. One step at a time.

Burroughs said, "ME said at least a dozen stab wounds, and from the arterial spray, hands cut off while she was still alive."

Lucy blinked away the thought of how much the girl must have suffered. Focus. "Restraints?"

"Hard to tell, but none at the scene and no obvious ones left on the body." He turned toward the large stone fireplace that took up the entire outside wall. It was tall enough that if Lucy ducked her head she could have stood inside it. The girl didn't have that choice. She was curled up in a ball surrounded by partially burnt logs. Her flesh was black in some areas, angry red in others, in a few spots the skin had split from the heat. Lucy couldn't tell if she wore clothing or not—if she had, it had fused to her flesh.

"He shoved her inside, doused her with gasoline, lit her up."

"Still alive?" Lucy asked. Somehow her voice emerged in a neutral tone, as if the answer to that question didn't matter.

Burroughs swallowed hard, pivoted to face away from the fireplace as the ME's team prepared to move the body. "Preliminary exam says yes." He cleared his throat, obviously working hard to maintain his own neutrality. Working cases like this you learned to distance yourself. You had to, both to ensure that the investigation remained unbiased and to protect your sanity. "ME hopes he's wrong. The autopsy will tell for sure."

Lucy forced herself to look. Her daughter Megan was thirteen, not much younger than their victim.

Framed photos stood across the mantle, arranged with military precision. Most were of men carrying rifles or Kalshnikovs, a mountain range in the background like a serrated knife speared into hard-packed earth. Everything was muted grays and browns, the only color the men's red embroidered caps. The buildings were mud-slab huts, the men dressed in long tunics and pants. Afghanistan, the Raziqs' home country. Other photos featured men in sky-blue fatigues, American soldiers in camouflage, and bearded men in khaki uniforms. They were grinning, raising their weapons in triumph.

The centerpiece was a larger photo, a family shot in an expensive silver-plated frame. In the background was the Washington Monument and people in shorts and T-shirts. In the foreground was a man, mid-forties, a woman a decade younger, two daughters ranging from waist-high to shoulder high, and an infant held in the mother's arms. They smiled for the camera but looked stiff, posed, their bodies angled towards the father as if he were the center of their universe. The mother and daughters all wore long dresses with long sleeves, bright scarves over their heads, faces uncovered for the camera. Similar family photos—all of the entire family, none of individual members—crowded the end tables as well.

"Raziq, wife Fatima, the two girls, and baby's name is Ali," Burroughs told her.

"Any problems since they've been here?" Lucy asked.

"Nothing major, far as we know. Neighbors report a few domestic squabbles between him and his oldest." He nodded to the girl in the fireplace. He hadn't said her name out loud since his initial call asking for her help.

"Mina." Lucy was a firm believer in personalizing victims. Resurrecting their humanity. "What were they arguing about?"

"Typical teenager stuff. She met a guy."

"American?"

"Jewish kid from Squirrel Hill. Mom and Dad disapproved."

"So, possible honor killing." Now she understood why Raziq was sitting in the back of a squad car. Definitely a person of interest in addition to being the grieving father. Plus an official guest of the US government. Any statement he made needed to be recorded three ways from Sunday, free of any coercion. "And the other victim?"

"The other daughter. Badria." He beckoned to her to follow and led her into the kitchen. "She was four."

More blood here in the kitchen, but instead of being sprayed all over, it was concentrated in one area. Around a little girl's body, her skin unnaturally pale in contrast to the blood. She lay on her side on the white tile floor, hands curled up in fists as if fighting off Death. Her throat was slit.

Lucy crouched low, avoiding the blood. "No hesitation marks." She looked around. The furniture, a large oak table with six chairs, one of them with a colorful high chair strapped to it, appeared undisturbed. "And no struggle."

"Such a tiny thing, it wouldn't have mattered."

"Yeah, but he hadn't planned on killing her, was caught off guard. Was she even supposed to be at home?"

"No. Mom took Ali to visit a family friend in Cranberry who'd just had a baby. I sent a squad for them, should be there soon, give or take with rush hour traffic. The little girl was supposed to go with them but had a cold, so mom left her with the oldest girl at the last minute."

"And the dad?"

"Supposedly at his office. We'll confirm with receptionist and assistant."

"Where's that?"

"Shipping company near the Mon wharf. They handle barge traffic, tugboats, that kind of stuff."

"Must pay okay," she murmured, thinking about the antiques and hand-crafted Middle Eastern heirlooms that cluttered the living room. A desert dweller in the shipping industry. Maybe Raziq had wanted a fresh start here in the States, leaving his desert roots behind. Cut all ties to his former life.

"Used to be some big shot with the Afghan National Drug Police. Lots of those positions are bought rather than earned, so maybe he brought his money with him from the old country." Burroughs sounded like he already resented the guy. Lucy forced herself to keep an open mind until she had more facts.

"No forced entry?" She looked across the kitchen to the back door. No signs of any obvious damage.

"No evidence of it. New security system but it was off during the action."

"Wait, I thought it was tripped—wasn't that how the guard got here?"

"Tripped, yes. But as they left. They went out the back door, left it unlocked. Only thing caught by the cameras was the back of one guy running through the trees. Worthless."

"They were smart enough to disable it or talk one of the victims into turning it off, yet stupid enough to trip it on the way out?" Made no sense. "Unless they wanted us to find the bodies. Didn't want to wait for the parents to get home."

Burroughs shrugged one shoulder. Lucy filed the thought away for further consideration once they had more to go on.

She stood and pivoted back towards the living room. "If Mina was the primary target, there was a lot of screaming, a struggle. Blood… Badria heard it, came in, got blood on her hand—"

"And her feet," Burroughs pointed out. "You can see her trail if you angle the light against the carpet."

They used the protective plastic sheeting the crime scene techs had put down as a path and crossed through the living room. Burroughs squatted and used his high-intensity pocket light to show her the tiny footprints.

"She runs," Lucy continued. "He stops what he's doing, grabs her, subdues her, and slashes her throat with one swipe of his blade. Why doesn't the older girl, Mina, run out, get help?"

"Maybe she can't. Too weak from blood loss. He cut her hands off while she was still alive, she would have collapsed, been in shock."

"Did we find the hands?"

Burroughs took a second, his gaze moving beyond her, before answering. "No. Actor must have taken them with him."

Lucy paced the distance back and forth between the two rooms. "How about the accelerant he used on the fire?"

"Gone." Burroughs watched her from the foyer. "The knife, too."

Lucy stopped in the middle of the living room, realized what was wrong. "The coffee table is the only piece of furniture knocked out of place."

"So?"

"So, you're one man subduing a teenaged girl, holding her down as she fights for her life, stabbing her, slicing off her hands, then chasing after her little sister—don't you think there'd be more signs of disruption?"

"What are you getting at?"

"We have more than one Unsub here. At least two."

Burroughs frowned. "Doesn't mean Raziq can't be one of them."

"If it wasn't him, do we have a motive?"

"No signs of anything missing, but we'll go through the house with Raziq and his wife to be sure. There's a floor safe in the master bedroom closet, but it doesn't appear to have been disturbed. If it was more than one killer, then I doubt it was the boyfriend in a crime of passion."

"Anyone talk with the boyfriend yet?"

"He's at a hockey tournament. I've got a uniform picking him up."

"Pretty cold, killing your girl and her baby sister then going to play hockey."

He shrugged. They'd both seen worse.

"Point is, Burroughs, I'm not seeing anything that makes this my jurisdiction." She was juggling close to two hundred open cases, and with court dates approaching for several of her team members, her ability to put bodies in the field was dwindling. As the Bureau moved its focus and resources to counterterrorism and financial crimes, Lucy's Sexual Assault Felony Enforcement team was perpetually overworked and undermanned with an ever expanding list of crimes—internet pornography, human trafficking, high-risk missing persons, and crimes against children, to name a few—falling under their purview.

Burroughs led her back across the slate foyer to the dining room, which appeared untouched. "Could be a hate crime. Anti-Islamic. That would be yours."

"Could also be the boyfriend or a home invasion or the father. All of which would be yours."

"If it's the father, it'd be an honor killing. Wouldn't that be like a hate crime?" He tried a coaxing smile. "Two out of three, I win."

"You suck at math, Burroughs."

"Look, Lucy."

Oh, no, he was using her first name. Next would come the dimples and the boyish charm.

He surprised her. He got serious—something Burroughs rarely did. "If Raziq's gonna bring in the DEA and the State Department and Lord knows who else from alphabet city, I need some back up. Otherwise those two girls are going to end up in the fridge."

The fridge was the Pittsburgh nickname for their cold case files. Lucy frowned, glancing beyond Burroughs to the foyer, her gaze fixed on the tiny handprint.

Bloody handprint coming out of the living room. Instead of answering Burroughs, she moved past him and crouched at the edge of the living room carpet where the floor transitioned into slate. Below the handprint a bloody child's footprint fell half on the carpet, half on the slate.

Burroughs hovered behind her, watching. He knew better than interrupt. She grabbed her high intensity LED flashlight and craned her face down parallel to the slate as she shone it across the foyer and down the hall beside the stairs to the kitchen.

"There isn't any more blood."

"No. He must have grabbed her, carried her to the kitchen through the living room. That's where all the blood is."

"But there weren't any bloody footprints in the kitchen." She didn't wait for his answer. Spinning on her heels, she directed her attention back to the living room, focused on the carpet and the rug. Immediately inside the entrance to the room, across from the fireplace, a chair had been moved about four inches from where the indentations of its legs had sunk into the carpet. Not tossed or turned in the midst of a struggle. Deliberately moved to have a better view of the killing.

It was an upholstered chair, boxy and Middle Eastern in style with beautifully carved legs. And on the floor near the left hand side, was a long ash. Cigar.

"Does Raziq smoke cigars?"

"I don't know. We'll check." He motioned for a crime scene tech to photograph and process the chair and area around it. "Would have gotten there sooner or later. Why is it so important?"

She stood, knees popping, reminding her that she'd skipped her last few workouts. Thirty-seven and already creaking, that couldn't be good.

In an effort to answer his own question Burroughs retraced Lucy's steps, examining the handprint and footprint just beyond the edge of the living room and then the chair.

"The little one saw her sister, turned and ran. One of the actors chased her, caught up with her, took her to the kitchen—" His face cleared and he nodded, slowly, enlightenment dawning. "You were wrong."

"I was wrong," she admitted. "There were three of them, not two. Two to do the dirty work and one to watch."

"Except they weren't counting on the little girl."

"Right. So the watcher, Mr. Fancy Cigar, grabbed her and took her to the kitchen himself. He didn't have blood on his shoes, that's why no prints in the foyer or kitchen."

"He killed Badria. Guy must have some experience. It was a clean strike, no fuss, no muss. Was he trying to save the little girl pain? Some kind of warped mercy, taking her out so fast?"

She closed her eyes for a moment, blocking out the room with its grisly contents. Sighed and opened them again. "No. He wanted to get back to the main event."

Her voice tightened with anger. It was hard work not letting her cases get personal—but how could she when so many came across her desk? Her job as a supervisor wasn't like Burroughs'; she didn't have the luxury of putting everything she had into one case. Across the room, the ME's men were finally moving Mina's body.

The smiling girl from the photo on the mantle tugged at her heart.

Lucy continued, "He killed Badria fast, but not out of mercy. He did it because her sister was still alive and he didn't want his entertainment interrupted."

Although her voice was low and no one except Burroughs heard her, everyone in the room stopped what they were doing. All eyes followed the ME's men as they removed Mina's body, now triple wrapped in a sterile sheet, plastic, and a body bag.

Good, hardworking men and women, standing silent out of respect for what the girl had endured. Their eyes were hard, not out of apathy, but because they cared about their job, cared about the victims who were their job. They would do whatever it took to find the men, the monsters who'd preyed on these innocents.

Lucy's hands curled into fists. Useless reflex, but she couldn't help it. Mina's smile in the photo above the fireplace caught at her again. All she could think of was her own daughter, Megan.

Like many law enforcement officers, Lucy was secretly superstitious. Magical thinking, her husband Nick called it. By doing her job, throwing everything into her fight for the victims, she blackmailed the universe into keeping her own family safe.

Silly, maybe, but it was the best she could do: hope that Someone, Somewhere, was Up There, keeping score.

She didn't take her eyes from the photo on the mantle as she told Burroughs, "I'm in."

CHAPTER 3

STANDING IN THE front hall of his grandmother's Ruby Avenue row house, Andre Stone stared at the brass knob on the front door. Outside. Panic sang like electricity through his veins at the thought of touching the knob, of turning it. Twenty-seven years old, eight of them spent serving his country, the last two from behind the doors of sterile hospital rooms the size of prison cells.

How many doors had he gone through with his men in Kandahar? Hundreds. And he'd never felt the fear inspired by this one. More than fear. Terror.

Difficult for a Marine to admit. But when he was in the burn unit and got his first glimpse in the mirror, Andre had decided the one thing he wouldn't run from was the truth.

"You ready, Sergeant?" Dr. Nick Callahan's voice sounded in Andre's Bluetooth earpiece.

"I guess." Andre hated the uncertainty that haunted his voice. So different from two years ago when he led a squad in Afghanistan. Or from eight years ago when he ran these lawless streets intent on mayhem and impressing his homeys.

The memory of his old bad-assed cretin self stopped him. Did they even use the word "homey" anymore? Showed how far he'd come from the streets of Pittsburgh's most gang-ridden neighborhood. How far he'd fallen by returning here, the only home he had left after the Marines. A home where he didn't dare show his face in broad daylight.

Andre took a deep breath and opened the door. The sun had dwindled to a faint smudge in the sky, leaving the daylight murky. Not dark, yet not light. Perfect time for a monster to roam.

The cold air stung as he breathed through his nose. A good thing. It meant he could wear his mask without attracting attention. Lord only knew what he'd do once it got warm outside. The mask covered his entire head with special openings for where his ears and nose used to be and was a shade of brown not found anywhere in nature. It was going to be impossible to conceal.

"Maybe this isn't such a good idea," he hedged.

"I can drive over and we can do it together."

"Don't know how I feel about a shrink with a death wish," Andre quipped. Watching out for his redheaded, paler-than-pale trauma counselor on a Friday night in this neighborhood was more than Andre could handle right now. Only thing worse than chickening out by himself would be failing the Doc up close and in person.

Callahan chuckled. "Let's do this."

Stretching for every ounce of courage in his body, Andre stepped over the threshold and onto the porch.

"Outside the wire," he told the Doc. No one seemed to notice: no women screamed, no children cried, no gunshots rang out. First time out alone in daylight—okay, dusk, almost-night—and so far, so good.

He took a step forward. Across the street a bright jumble of Christmas lights blazed to life. Andre jumped, rattling the bars on the screen door blocking his escape back inside where it was safe. Making enough noise to wake the dead—or Grams, napping in her room. She slept in the old dining room, fixed up with a special hospital bed his docs had ordered to help his skin grafts heal better. But she was an old lady blind with diabetes and had already lost a few toes to the disease as well. She needed it more than Andre. Besides, the egg crate mattress he'd gotten for his old twin bed was way more comfortable than the wooden pallet he'd slept on in Hajji Baba.

"Breathe, just breathe," Callahan coached.

Thanks to modern technology and the heart rate monitor Andre wore, they both could see Andre's vitals on their phones. The Doc wore one as well and, as soon as they began to run in earnest, Andre was determined to set a pace that would send the shrink's pulse into overdrive. Only fair given what Callahan was making him go through. Facing reality, rejoining the world, all that bullshit.

"I'm fine." Andre scowled at how difficult it was to talk when your jaws had locked shut with panic. His fist tightened around the Beretta M9 in the pocket of his hoodie. Callahan didn't know he had it, but no way in hell was Andre going to be the only unarmed black man prowling Ruby Avenue.

"Your turn to pick the tunes," Callahan said.

Andre chose a driving hip-hop beat, mainly because he knew Callahan hated the dirty lyrics, and sprinted down the porch steps. They'd done this before, running together but not together, but always on their treadmills, never outside where people might see Andre.

"Just an easy run over to Holy Trinity, up the bell tower, ring the bells and back down, right Doc?" Andre joked.

"If you say so, Quasimodo." The Doc never flinched at Andre's warped humor.

Still, Andre kept trying. After all, his black—pun intended, given that he was a black man who'd had most of the upper half of his body scorched black, haha—humor had a 99% success rate, having driven away his friends (the ones still alive), most of his nurses and doctors, all of his family except his blind grams, and of course, his wife. No, couldn't forget Darynda, could he? Bitch ditched him just when he needed her most, leaving him to come home from rehab to an empty apartment with three months rent due.

A wave of despair flooded over him, his pace faltering as he began to hyperventilate again. His footsteps faltered, fallen soldiers—empty drug vials—popping and cracking beneath the soles of his shoes.

"You're not breathing," Callahan chided, his Southern accent sounding out of place against the background sound of the Ying Yang Twins. "Got your bag handy?"

The bag was an airplane sickness bag—handy if you had to barf, which Andre felt like he might, or were hyperventilating and needed a bag to breathe into. It was nestled in Andre's waist pack along with Andre's inhaler, keys, med-alert info, knife, and water bottle. The burns had healed but the resulting scar tissue (pale and grey and pink heaped-up ugliness that honest to god Andre would have traded for the charred skin any day) didn't sweat like it should, so Andre had to stay hydrated while exercising, even during a Pittsburgh December.

"Don't need it," he gritted out, pushing his pace fast enough to leave pain and memories behind. He was goddamn Dog Company, used to pounding the desert carrying fifty kilos on his back. No one could ever take that from him. Plenty of men lost their women, left bits and pieces of their bodies behind on the battlefield. Faces of his squad danced before him. Dead, all dead.

Stop your bitchin. Their voices filled his mind. *Wanna trade places, Sarge?*

Problem was, most days the answer to that question was: *Yes.*

A truth he'd never shared with the Doc, but Callahan was smart enough to figure out for himself.

Of course Andre wanted to die, rejoin his squad. He'd let them down in the worst way imaginable. By living, by surviving Hajji Baba, he'd failed them. Yeah, he'd tried his best to die, but his damn body just refused to give up the fight.

Andre focused on his pounding steps, his Beretta a comforting weight even as it pressed against the scars on his belly, pain crackling like lightning across his flesh.

The echo of his first drill sergeant's bellow rang through his mind: *Good thing you're not a Marine yet, dog meat. Because a real Marine only quits when he's dead!*

Slowly the pain and panic subsided. He could do this. He would do this. Because, goddamn it, there was one truth he couldn't deny: He wasn't dead yet.

———•———

TEXT SENT 16:47

Z: STATUS REPORT.

SEIS: MOVEMENT FROM HOUSE. MAN LEAVING.

Z: CONFIRM IDENTITY.

SEIS: DESCRIPTION MATCH.

Z: ALERT LOCALS TO INTERCEPT. CONFINE UNTIL MY ARRIVAL.

SEIS: LOCALS PREPARED. FORCE?

Z: LETHAL, IF NECESSARY.

CHAPTER 4

LUCY WANTED TO go through the house, get a feel for its inhabitants, before interviewing Rashid Raziq. She didn't want Burroughs or Walden to think she was naive, but she'd never had any personal exposure to Islamic culture beyond basic training sessions at Quantico. Hell, she'd never even traveled outside the country except for a long weekend with Nick to Toronto.

She climbed the stairs to the second floor where the bedrooms were located. How would Raziq react to the monstrous way his daughters were killed? If he was responsible, he might even be proud that he'd restored his family's honor by butchering his wayward teen. The thought sickened her, but she couldn't ignore the possibility.

Her heart lurched at the sight of Mina's bedroom with its teenaged-girl-blossoming-into-womanhood mix of stuffed animals and photos of pop icons torn from magazines and pasted together into a collage of young male hunkiness. Lucy wondered how Mina's parents felt about that—or about the collection of religious and philosophical books lined up on her desk including a Christian Bible, the I Ching, and a Torah. She saw a typical teenager exploring their options and boundaries, not unlike her own thirteen-year-old, who pushed those boundaries every chance she got.

Would parents raised in a fundamentalist atmosphere see it that way? Or would they see Mina's small rebellions as betrayal?

Walden caught up with Lucy as she rifled through Raziq's desk in the downstairs study behind the dining room. Burroughs had a warrant to search the entire crime scene for physical evidence, so anything in quasi-plain sight was in bounds. Anything she happened across that wasn't in plain sight, well, it might not be evidence but if it could give her any insight as to why Mina was targeted, and if Raziq's past in Afghanistan had anything to do with it, then at least it was a starting point.

It was one of those many gray areas when an investigator was expected to use their "best judgment" even though the ultimate decision would be made much later by the pundits in the press and lawyers arguing before a judge. That's when the breakthrough that "blew the case wide open" could just as easily turn into the fuckup that "sank it all." Hindsight was a bitch.

"Any word from Agent Haddad?" she asked Walden as she paged through Raziq's passports. Turned out he and his family were Pakistani citizens but Raziq alone also had an Afghan passport. Paperwork in that corner of the world was less regimented than here. Made her wonder what documents might be inside his safe.

"The DEA duty agent says he hasn't returned his messages."

"How about the neighbors?"

"Quiet family, kept to themselves, only disturbances were when the daughter and father got into it. Once after her boyfriend dropped her off, and once when the daughter was attempting to leave and the father physically restrained her."

"Mina was how old?"

"Fifteen. Enrolled at the Schenley Academy over in Highland Park."

"Nice school. Expensive." She glanced around the study again, searching for insight into its owner.

Like the living room, it was filled with tasteful handcrafted furniture, and a variety of expensive-appearing pieces including a mahogany display rack that held an assortment of antique guns and swords. Family heirlooms or trophies of war, she wasn't sure. Maybe bought on eBay. She needed more on Raziq to see how deep his roots went. It said a lot that a man in his position had left his home country—countries—so easily. Big question was why?

"What about the mom?" she asked as she twirled a curved ceremonial dagger, balanced its intricately carved hilt across her fingers.

"The neighbors never see her except when she's coming or going. Doesn't drive, uses a car service when she goes out. They're not sure if she speaks English or not."

"Isolated." She thought about that. Stared at the computer monitor hooked into the security system. Tons of bells and whistles yet no help since it hadn't been on during the attack. The setup was pretty fancy and expensive for the neighborhood or a modest, unassuming house like this. More paradoxes. "Cultural? Or because Raziq is afraid of someone?"

He shrugged, studying an antique map hanging on the wall. "We working this with Burroughs? How about the DEA, stepping on their toes?" His voice held a tone of caution. With good reason. Walden knew a clusterfuck waiting to happen when he saw one.

Lucy didn't answer him. Instead she propped herself up on Raziq's desk, the dagger still in her hand. "No pictures of his family. Out in the public area they're arranged like trophies. But here, in his inner sanctum," she gestured with the dagger, "nothing of them. He's surrounded himself with items that prop up his ego and his family isn't part of that."

Walden shrugged. "Different culture."

Maybe. But she'd gotten the same vibe when inside the homes of serial killers and child predators. Living a lie with a public facade very different than who they were in private. She pushed off the desk, returned the dagger to where she'd found it. "I want to talk to Raziq, and before I do I need to learn as much about him as possible. What exactly he did back in the old country, why he came to Pittsburgh, is he working for the DEA, who his enemies are, who his friends are."

"Only one place to find all that."

She sighed. "I know. The DEA."

"What about the girl?"

"Burroughs' guys will handle that." Homicide 101, learn everything you could about the victim's life. "The locals can do a better job of tracing Mina's footsteps than we can. But this doesn't feel like a crime targeting a fifteen-year-old girl. This feels like a message. A big, neon light, horse head in the bed kind of message."

"Speaking of messages," he said. "There was one from Jenna Galloway on Raziq's machine. And I found this on the refrigerator." He handed Lucy a card bearing Jenna's contact info.

Jenna Galloway had been temporarily assigned to Lucy's SAFE team and worked a case with Lucy last month. Morgan Ames, the teenaged daughter of a serial killer, had captured Jenna, almost burning Jenna alive before escaping arrest.

Lucy had never told anyone of those last moments before Morgan disappeared when Jenna had her weapon aimed at the unarmed girl's back, ready to pull the trigger until Lucy stopped her.

Turned out Lucy didn't need to address the issue of Jenna potentially shooting an unarmed juvenile. Jenna had been transferred off Lucy's squad after failing her psych eval. As far as Lucy knew, Jenna was back working Nigerian mail fraud.

"Why would the DEA be working with the USPIS?" Lucy didn't wait for an answer. Instead, she dialed Jenna's number. It was a good excuse to check in with Jenna, see how she was dealing with being back to work after what she'd suffered at the hands of Morgan Ames.

She'd tried to reach out to Jenna a few times since Morgan's escape, but Jenna had rebuffed her. Lucy had a feeling Jenna resented the fact that Lucy had seen her so vulnerable: first outwitted by a teenager, then almost burned alive before Lucy rescued her. Or maybe she just didn't like it that Lucy stopped her from shooting Morgan in the back.

"Galloway."

"Jenna, it's Lucy Guardino. I'm at a homicide scene. Family name is Raziq. We found one of your cards. The father, Rashid, was flagged by an Agent David Haddad of the DEA. Want to fill me in?"

"Shit. Did you say homicide?"

"Raziq's daughters."

"Was it another mail bomb? The first one was a dud—planned that way. A warning. Our profile said this guy would escalate. But Raziq declined protective custody." That explained the Postal Service's involvement: investigating and profiling letter bombers was their territory.

"No. Not a mail bomb. Raziq refused to talk to the local police and I haven't interviewed him yet."

Jenna grunted. "He won't talk to you. Maybe Walden if he's with you. Guy doesn't trust women. Or local cops. Will only deal with David Haddad."

"We haven't reached Haddad yet. He's the case agent?"

"No. He's a victim. Both he and Raziq have been getting threats via the mail as well as Internet. We've chased leads from Afghanistan to Iran to China. Between the two of them, they have a lot of enemies overseas. Still not sure who's behind them, but I'm narrowing things down." She said the last on a superior note as if waiting for Lucy to congratulate her investigative brilliance. Typical Jenna.

"Haddad's working the case and he's the victim?" Lucy put the phone on speaker as she and Walden headed through the dining room to the front door.

"The threats are my case, my jurisdiction, but Raziq is David Haddad's pet project. Guy's providing DEA with tons of info, bringing down smuggling routes across Asia and the Mid East. Besides, you know the DEA. Bunch of hotshot control freaks. I'm lucky David shares anything with me on my own freakin' case."

Lucy really didn't care about the complexities of interdepartmental cooperation as long as they pointed a finger to the animals who'd butchered two young girls.

Leaning against the door, she slipped her shoe covers off, her gaze once again caught by the small bloody handprint. "You'd better get over here. Bring everything you have."

She expected Jenna to balk. But even Jenna knew the murders of two innocent girls took priority over the Postal Service case. "I'm on my way."

Lucy hung up. "I think it's time I met Mr. Raziq."

———— • ————

JENNA GALLOWAY THREW her cellphone to the kitchen countertop of her Regent Square loft. Damn, she'd just walked in the door from work and had plans for this evening. Didn't Saint Lucy know it was a Friday night? There were drinks to be drunk, men to be fucked. Not necessarily in that order.

Swearing under her breath, she glanced around the wide-open living space of the brick-walled loft. She was tempted to keep Saint Lucy waiting. After all, the woman had gotten Jenna kicked off her squad with that rigged psych eval, then had the gall to call and order Jenna to do her bidding, like Jenna was some kind of peon. Never asked, *Hey, how you doing after that psycho-bitch Morgan Ames almost killed you?* Never apologized for dragging Jenna into that damned case in the first place.

Just, *get your butt over here.*

But two girls. Dead. She'd seen their picture when she visited the Raziq household last week. Cute kids. She'd warned David and Raziq. Arrogant prick—Raziq, not David. David was okay, just sometimes not as with it as she'd like. No wonder the DEA had him on babysitting duty.

She put her coat back on and re-pocketed her phone. It rang again just as she was grabbing her bag with her laptop inside. The caller ID read: Lucy Guardino. "I said I was on my way."

A young woman's voice answered. "Sure you don't want a drink first? I left one out for you—it's on your dresser beside your lipstick. Too bad you won't have a chance to wear the outfit I picked out. I made sure it was easy on, easy off."

"Morgan." Jenna bit back expletives along with the urge to hurl the phone against the living room's exposed brick wall. The bitch always spoofing familiar numbers to get Jenna to pick up at all hours of the day and night. Last night it'd been a call at three-thirty in the morning, supposedly from Jenna's mother.

She'd just added a security system—nothing too fancy, she actually hoped to some day catch the darling little psychopath in action—thinking she'd have a few days privacy away from Morgan's prying eyes and ears and hands all over Jenna's stuff.

"Don't you ever get tired of watching?" Jenna asked as she walked into the bedroom. As promised, Morgan had left a tumbler of bourbon on the dresser and Jenna's favorite low-cut black dress and fuck-me heels on the bed. "I'd think a girl like you would want to come out and play in person."

"Don't worry, you're on my to-do list. Just not at the top. Besides, I'd miss our little chats."

Little chats that came day and night, interrupting Jenna when she was working, sleeping, eating. And people wondered why she'd started drinking and picking up men. It was the only way to get Morgan out of her head for at least a little while.

Jenna carried the tumbler out to the kitchen, dumped its contents—who knew what fun stuff Morgan had added?—and rinsed it out before putting it in the dishwasher.

"We can chat all you want as soon as I have you behind bars," she told Morgan in a falsely chipper tone.

It was damned hard work trying to track and trap a psychopath like Morgan. She might not be very old, but she was cunning. A few times Jenna had come close to nabbing her while Morgan was stalking Lucy, but every time Morgan had slipped away.

Saint Lucy didn't have a clue Morgan was obsessed with her. But Jenna knew Morgan would never let Lucy go—not after Lucy had caught Morgan's serial killer father and ended Morgan's fun. Jenna had watched Lucy for almost two weeks before she spotted Morgan.

Unfortunately, Morgan had also spotted her and pulled Jenna into her web of deceit.

In addition to tormenting Jenna day and night with phone calls and text messages, Morgan invaded Jenna's home on a routine basis. She also sent Jenna anonymous photos of Lucy and Lucy's family, daring Jenna to warn Lucy and send Morgan on a killing spree.

Jenna had forged a desperate pact with Morgan: the teen psychopath looked without touching while Jenna hunted her without telling Lucy the truth about the danger she and her family were in. It was a race to the finish. The only question was: who would be left standing in the end?

"Don't you feel guilty?" Morgan asked as if she could follow Jenna's thoughts. "Using Lucy as bait? She's your friend, right? I never had a friend like that. Her daughter is almost my age, I'll bet she'd make a good friend."

"We talked about this," Jenna said, her tone reminding her of her own mother's. She hated when Morgan got all adolescent whiny on her, but it was better than when she acted superior and played power games. Everything was a game with Morgan, you just had to understand what the rules were. Playing the game was the only leverage Jenna had with Morgan, which didn't leave her much in a way of trump cards. "You go near Lucy's daughter, I'll end this. You'll never get near Lucy then."

Lucy could take care of herself. But no way would Jenna jeopardize Megan. Even if Megan's mother had almost gotten Jenna killed.

"Maybe." Morgan's pout carried through the airwaves loud and clear. "But I get so bored just watching you trying to find me. Really, Jenna, you're a trained federal agent. Can't you find one little girl? I think you *have* been drinking too much. And all those men, a different one every night. Did you tell Lucy's husband about them at any of your sessions? He's so dreamy. I wish he were *my* doctor."

Jenna's stomach clenched. She'd begun seeing Nick Callahan after failing her psych eval as a way to keep tabs on him—and through him, Lucy. He thought he was treating Jenna for Post Traumatic Stress, but really, Jenna was treating herself with booze and sex. Dangerous, spontaneous, anonymous sex. So much better than talking. Especially about her feelings.

Now Morgan was taking that away from her. "You want me to stop going out?"

"I feel so lonely. If you don't start paying more attention to me, I might need to visit those men you hook up with. Show them my pretty knife collection."

"Okay." Jenna hated giving in to Morgan's manipulations but what choice did she have? "If you promise to stay away from Lucy's daughter." For some warped reason, Morgan prided herself on her integrity. She'd once told Jenna her brutal honesty was what separated Morgan from the rest of the world. It was the only weapon Jenna had to use on her. "Promise?"

"Yes. I promise. If you hold up your end of the bargain." Morgan paused and Jenna could sense she was deciding which tactic to torture Jenna with next.

"I really need to go." She tried a pre-emptive strike. "Lucy's waiting for me."

"I heard." Morgan didn't sound upset by Jenna's attempt to regain control. Always a bad sign. "Your letter bomber. Think you'll catch him? Finally make your grandfather proud?"

Jenna sucked in her breath, caught off guard. Her grandfather had been dead for fifteen years. And if Morgan had linked him to letter bombs, then she must know the whole story. How an anonymous bomber who was never caught had targeted the Judge. The fact that he hadn't died right away, it had taken over a year for him to finally succumb after being left in a persistent vegetative state.

It was all a matter of public record, Jenna told herself. Didn't mean that Morgan had any real insight. Just a bunch of facts she could wield like scalpels, re-opening old wounds.

Jenna passed the mirror in her foyer, automatically checked her hair and make up. Her eyes looked puffy, her red hair dull, and her cheeks sunken—probably not a bad idea to cut back on the all night partying. Not that she'd get any more sleep playing Morgan's game, but she'd be one step closer to ending all this.

At first she'd been content fantasizing about Morgan behind bars, locked up for life. Lately though, her fantasies had been of the moment when she had Morgan in the sights of her pistol, finger on the trigger, ready to shoot her in the back before she could escape.

In her dreams Lucy didn't stop her. Jenna pulled the trigger. Over and over and over again, emptying the gun. Morgan's body jerked like a puppet with its strings cut, arms flailing, crumpling to the ground, a stream of crimson pouring from her. The fantasy was beginning to feel more real than this sleepwalk existence the rest of the world called life.

Jenna slid her hand in front of her face, blocking out her blue eyes and most of her hair in the mirror. She lowered her hand like closing a blind, blanking her expression to a professional neutral. Better. Saint Lucy could see way too much when she read a person's face. Jenna grabbed her coat and bag.

"I've got to go," she told Morgan, setting boundaries. Or trying to. "We'll talk later."

"Of course. I can't wait to hear *all* about your grandfather. Tell Lucy I'm thinking about her." Morgan hung up before Jenna could manage a retort.

Jenna slammed the door behind her, double checking the locks and alarm. Morgan was always thinking about Lucy. But her words held new menace tonight. Plus she'd said she was bored—not a good combination.

Jenna sighed, shoulders hunched as she ran down the stairs to her car. At least she'd be with Lucy tonight where she could keep an eye out for Morgan.

Then maybe this would all be over. Morgan caught—*or killed*, a quiet voice whispered in Jenna's head—Lucy safe thanks to Jenna, Jenna a hero.

Was that too much to ask?

CHAPTER 5

LUCY WALKED ACROSS the street and down the block to the patrol car holding Rashid Raziq. Curtains rustled in windows of houses as she passed—homeowners wondering how violence had come to choose their street. Worried if their families were safe. Or maybe it was just plain morbid curiosity, that primal instinct to turn and stare at danger even as you ran from it.

She introduced herself to the patrolman watching over Raziq. Burroughs must have cleared her because he nodded as soon as she said her name. Or it could be that her reputation preceded her—she'd been a bit unlucky these past few months, receiving a lot of unwanted media attention. "Has he said anything?"

"No. Wanted to make some calls but Burroughs had me take his phone before he could. After that, he just kinda sat, rolling those prayer beads between his fingers, mumbling in Arabic or something."

He opened the car door and gestured for Raziq to get out. Raziq looked up, eyes sharp, jaw set, as if expecting an attack. But then he focused on Lucy and his expression softened.

He was in his forties, dressed in an expensive suit, black or navy blue, she couldn't tell in the limited light, with a white shirt and conservative dark tie pulled tight to hide the missing top button. Dark hair, neatly trimmed beard, dark eyes that wouldn't meet hers at first. When he stood he was only a few inches taller than her own five-five, yet his posture was one of a man accustomed to intimidating others, being obeyed.

No sign of the distraught out of control man Burroughs had described. Except for the tearstains, wet against the collar of his otherwise impeccable shirt. His hand was fisted tight around a set of ebony prayer beads.

Contradictions. Just like inside his home. Not a man easily understood.

Lucy offered her credentials, hoping to build some trust. "Mr. Raziq, I'm Supervisory Special Agent Guardino from the FBI. I'm very sorry for your loss. What did Detective Burroughs tell you?"

He nodded. Not to her but to the official seal on her ID, as if satisfied she was high enough rank to be worthy of his attention. She stood so he had his back to his house and he never once tried to turn to look at it. Instead he faced her, square on.

"The police told me nothing. Other than my daughters were dead."

Interesting. Already using the past tense. "Yes sir. I'm afraid both Badria and Mina are dead."

"Who did this to my family? Have you caught the man yet?"

"No, sir. Do you have any ideas? Is there any one who might want to harm your daughters?"

"Only that boy she took up with." He spat out the words, looking away and down at the ground as if he might physically spit as well. Lucy noticed he didn't use Mina's name.

"We're looking into that. I understand you've been receiving some threats lately?" Funny how Raziq immediately blamed the boyfriend instead of whoever was behind the threats and mail bomb. Guilt? Or deflection?

"Yes. They're nothing."

"I was told one of them was a letter bomb?"

He glared at her. "In my country, if we send you a bomb you are not alive to discuss it afterwards. This man, he is a coward, a fool. He had nothing to do with this, this attack on my family."

"Do you have any idea who this man sending the threats could be?"

His elaborate shrug took a beat too long. "Who knows. Isn't that your job? To find him?"

She tried changing tactics. "Sir, who else had the code to your security system?"

"Just my wife and I. And our daughter. She was always turning it off when that boy came over—" His jaw clenched and his face grew red. "Was it that boy? He dishonored my daughter, my family."

"No, Mr. Raziq. We do not have any evidence at this time that it was Mina's boyfriend."

"He wasn't her boyfriend. That mongrel, that—" He changed to a language she couldn't understand, harsh syllables that didn't need translating. "This is all his fault. She wouldn't have turned off the security for anyone else. Deceitful girl. She thought she could hide him from me."

If it was Mina who'd turned off the cameras and alarms. "And when did you get to work, Mr. Raziq?"

"Eight o'clock. My usual hour. Of course." He turned a scornful gaze on her. "You aren't suggesting—"

"I'm not suggesting anything. I'm just trying to see where everyone was so we can better determine who this crime was aimed at." That sobered him. "You were at your office all day?"

"Yes. Of course."

"Until when?"

"Until I left." She waited. "Four o'clock. I came directly home only to find—" He spread his arms, palms up. "To find, this, you people, this, this…" His shoulders slumped as words failed him.

For the first time his gaze focused on her face. Gauging her reaction? Or was it another cultural difference she couldn't translate?

"My wife, my son. When can I see them? We should be together."

"We sent a car to pick them up." Strange, he never asked about the girls. Most parents would have endless questions, wanting to know the details of their deaths, what would happen to their bodies. She decided to push a little. "The medical examiner will need to examine your daughters' bodies." He flinched and looked away. Lucy waited, expecting him to request special treatment or religious observations in preparing the dead.

He shook his head, looked at his hands then sat down heavily onto the cruiser's rear seat. "Please. Please. I need my wife. My son. I can't—"

He buried his face in his hands, the prayer beads dangling between his fingers. His body shook with silent sobs.

Lucy left him with the patrolman and walked back to the house, more uncertain than ever. Was Raziq acting? Or was he a father in mourning? How much of what she saw was personality, cultural differences, the truth, or lies?

He wasn't telling the whole truth, that much she knew. But in her experience everyone lied, even grieving loved ones of murder victims.

The question wasn't: Was he lying? It was: What was he lying about?

CHAPTER 6

AFTER A FEW MINUTES Andre and the Doc settled into a nice, comfortable pace, running up the hill past Holy Trinity. Nowhere near Andre's old six-minute miles, but fast enough to leave him focused on his breathing rather than the world around him.

"Tell me what you see," Callahan said.

"What's to see?" Andre fought to keep his voice steady. He really didn't want to look past his feet pounding the cracked sidewalk. Too afraid he might see someone… or someone might see him.

The Doc, as usual, out-waited him.

"It's Ruby Avenue. Busted up sidewalks, busted up street. Boarded up businesses and houses. Vacant lots. Damned Terraces down at the bottom." He hated the squat garish yellow brick public housing units all clustered together like they were RVs at a campground. They reminded him of the cargo containers Dog Company squatted in before they were sent to build the outpost at Hajji Baba. Or worse, of Hescos, the hollow rectangles they'd shovel load after load of sand and gravel into to create defensible perimeters. "A couple of places still in business if they let the Rippers gouge them for protection money. A few nice old homes with that curly wood trim—"

"Gingerbread."

"Yeah, gingerbread. Like once upon a time this was a fairy tale place to live." To hear Grams tell it, that wasn't far from the truth. His great-grandad had bought their row house way back when, between the world wars, when Homewood had been a nice "Colored" neighborhood. He'd chosen the house because it was on the same street as Holy Trinity church and he'd liked the idea of nuns and priests watching over them. What could go wrong on a street with a house of God on it?

Poor old man would have a stroke if he saw the hood now. Every block with its own set of gangsters dealing. All run by the Ruby Avenue Rippers. Constant turf wars to protect their territory from outside gangs. Got so bad, the school buses wouldn't even come down here; parents had to drive their kids down to Penn Avenue, meet the bus there. And Holy Trinity? The priest and nuns remained hidden behind their thick wooden doors and stone walls, too damn stubborn to leave a lost cause, too damn weak to do anything about it.

"Any people on the street?" Callahan's voice interrupted Andre's thoughts.

"A few cars. I dunno." He really didn't want to know. He was perfectly content to stay inside his little bubble of anonymity—just a black man in a mask and hoodie out for a run. Any other neighborhood in the city and he'd be the center of unwanted attention. But not here, not on Ruby Avenue.

"Let's slow down a bit. Take a breather."

Pride let Andre fool himself into thinking it was the Doc who needed to catch his breath. He slowed down. This was the block where the war between the Rippers and Gangstas had broken out last summer. The tenement they'd torched still stank of burnt wood. The smell gagged him as memory ambushed him.

"Talk to me, Andre. Your heart rate just spiked."

Andre couldn't talk. He was too busy breathing, gasping for air, air that wasn't super heated, filled with flames, there were flames crawling everywhere, his face, his head… God, where was his helmet, how had he lost his goddamned helmet, shit, now he was really screwed… Flames down his arms, down his chest, heat scorching between his body armor and his shirt, the fabric melting into his skin, oh God, oh God, he was burning, he had to let go of the girls, put the flames out, but he couldn't he couldn't he couldn't…

"Andre! Breathe, breathe. In, hold it, now out, hold it. Good. You're okay, you're okay." Callahan's voice was a metronome, slowly throttling Andre's panic.

Andre looked up. He'd turned and run back towards home. By now he was just a few blocks away. His chest hurt, his arms ached, his hands were cramped into tight fists he couldn't open, but he was almost home, almost to safety, and he was alive.

"Gotta go home, Doc. Can't do this."

"Stop. Use your bag if you need it. It was just a panic attack. You've been there, done that—"

"Got the T-shirt," Andre finished the corny joke. He pressed his gloved hand against the barred window of a barbershop closed for the day. Leaned his weight against it, realizing the Doc was right. He was okay. He'd survived. Again.

"What was the trigger?"

"Place burned down, the block where the Rippers and Gangstas torched most everything."

"You were still in the hospital then—"

"Yeah, but I read about it. Then tonight, ran past and smelled that—"

"It was the smell. Most powerful memory activator there is."

"You're so sexy when you go all scientific on me, Doc."

Callahan laughed. "Glad you appreciate it. My wife usually falls asleep. Let's get you home and wrap this up. I have a hot date."

"Right. You said. I never got that whole *Nutcracker* shit. I mean who takes their kid to see a bunch of scary toys come to life? I'd have nightmares the rest of my life."

"Good thing I'm not taking you."

"Good thing. 'Coz I'd be the one giving them nightmares." He felt the Doc's disapproval radiate through the phone—smack talk and jokes were one thing, but Callahan didn't like it when Andre used his humor to mask self-pity. Neither did Andre. But it was time for him to face his new reality. A life where everything was off the table: a wife, trips to the ballet—hell, trips to the grocery store.

Andre pushed away from the barbershop window in time to see three guys with red Ripper ball caps staring at him as they crossed the street. He shook his head to drop his hoodie back, freeing his peripheral vision. Panic vanished as adrenalin sang through him. The hum of impending battle. This, this he knew. This didn't frighten him. No, this feeling was an old friend he'd last seen half a world away. God, how he'd missed it.

He tightened his grip on the Beretta M9. "Doc, we might have a little trouble here. I'm going to ditch the ear piece and put you on speaker."

"Need me to call the police?"

"No. Not yet." The Rippers were close enough that he recognized the one in the middle. Maddoc, "affectionately" known as Mad Dog or MD. He was older than the other two, the same age as Andre, twenty-seven, and from his swagger he'd moved up the ranks since Andre left Ruby Avenue eight years ago.

Andre palmed the Bluetooth, slid it into his pack, switched the phone's speaker on, and muted it. He kept his back to the storefront. It was as good of a place to make a stand as any. His right hand was on his Beretta. But he didn't draw it. Not yet.

Calm settled over him. He assessed the three men approaching with cocky swaggers. Layers of flannel, sweatshirts, and parkas were between their hands and the semi-automatic pistols shoved into the waistband of their baggy jeans, aimed at the family jewels. Idiots wouldn't last a day with Dog Company.

They'd only taken four steps towards him and he'd already catalogued their vulnerable spots—throat, eyes, spine—and killed them several times in his head. One good thing about PTSD, its hyper-vigilance gave him an edge.

Not like he needed it, not with eight years of combat under his belt, not with fools like these. But it was nice to know that although he was literally afraid of his own shadow, much less anyone else seeing it, although it took more courage these days to leave his house than it had to race into a burning building, although his mind was fucked up and his nerve had deserted him, despite all that, he still had what it took to step into battle.

A tiny whisper scuttled through his mind faster than a scorpion crawling under a rock: If he played it right, maybe this time he'd get his wish. Maybe this time he would die.

CHAPTER 7

LUCY HAD JUST rejoined Walden on the porch when a black Suburban with its four-ways flashing stopped in the middle of the street. A tall man in his late thirties, Middle Eastern coloring, wearing a black trench coat over a gray suit jumped out of the driver's seat without closing the door behind him and ran across the yard.

"Where is he? Where's Raziq?" the man shouted at the uniformed cop who intercepted him.

"Sir, I need to see—"

He pushed past the cop and rushed up to where Lucy and Walden watched, attempting to move through them like they weren't there. Walden crossed his arms over his chest and stood, implacable, while Lucy closed the door to the house, barring the newcomer from getting a glimpse inside.

"DEA?" she asked. "Agent Haddad?"

"Yeah. Out of my way."

"Not until we have a little chat."

He gave up trying to outstare Walden and finally deigned to glance down at her. "Who the hell are you?" Despite his appearance and name, his accent wasn't Middle Eastern. Midwest. Maybe Detroit?

"Supervisory Special Agent Guardino and Special Agent Walden."

"What's the FBI doing here? Raziq is my guy. Let me through. I need to see—" He stopped as the door behind them opened and the medical examiner's team came through with the second body.

Lucy pulled the DEA agent out of the way. His eyes went wide and a hand flew up toward his face when he saw how the tiny body on the stretcher didn't take up all the space in the body bag. "It's one of the kids?"

"The youngest daughter," Lucy said.

"Little Badria? Oh no, oh…" He turned away, leaned over the porch railing as if he might vomit. Not the reaction she'd been expecting.

Walden shrugged and watched closely as he gave her space to comfort the agent. Lucy put her arm around his shoulder. "I'm sorry. Her sister was killed as well."

"Mina?" His voice was choked with tears. "Where's Raziq? Fatima and Ali? Are they okay? What happened here?" He straightened abruptly, spun around. "Home invasion? Did you get the guys?" Then he frowned and stared down at Lucy. "Why the hell is the FBI here?"

"The locals called us. When they ran Raziq's name through NCIC they saw your flag." The National Crime Information Center was the fastest way for law enforcement agencies to share data.

"They should have called me. I'm the agent of record." Sounded like he was a lot more than that to Raziq and his family.

"We did. We've been waiting for you—"

He stared at the ME's van as it pulled away from the curb. No hurry, no lights or sirens. But somehow the entire block got quieter as if taking a deep breath.

"I got a message to report here, but I was already on my way—" His voice trailed off as the van turned the corner and vanished.

"How long have you known the Raziqs?"

"Two years," he answered distractedly, his gaze still following the path of the van. "DEA eradication operation in Kandahar. He was one of the few local cops who took our efforts seriously. Introduced me to the tribal chiefs and village elders, arranged *sharias*, meetings, gave me whatever assistance he could. Raziq saved my life. Taliban ambush," he said in a defiant tone, sounding more like a defense attorney than a DEA agent.

"That's where I got this." He rubbed a scar above his eyebrow with his thumb. He sucked in his breath, still staring out into the night. Lucy had the feeling he'd forgotten she was there. "Fatima, she'll be devastated. I was on my way here for dinner. I should have been here, should have gotten here sooner, I could have—"

His words spun into a confused silence and she realized he was in shock. Babbling. Strange. Very strange. Raziq was obviously more than a cooperating witness or confidential informant. This was personal to Haddad.

"Take me inside," he said, his tone grim.

Lucy and Walden exchanged glances.

"I need to see," Haddad said.

The bodies were gone, only the blood remained behind. She nodded to one of the uniforms who opened the door, waited for Haddad to don his protective gear, and escorted him into the scene.

Once the door shut behind Haddad and the uniformed officer, she motioned to Walden. "We need to get Raziq and Haddad to the Federal Building. Have Burroughs bring Fatima and the baby there once he locates them. Protective custody until we understand what these threats are all about."

"Our offices?"

"No. Let's use the DEA's. We'll get more cooperation from everyone involved if we keep this on their territory." Why was it whenever she had to deal with the DEA she always felt like she was wrangling a bunch of testosterone-addled adolescents? Not even the ATF was as bad. Thankfully, since the SAFE unit was multi-agency, encompassing local, state, and almost every branch of federal law enforcement, Lucy had plenty of experience in negotiating interagency cooperation. "And get me Haddad's supervisor. I'll need to let him know what's going on."

"On it. Want me to call in Taylor?" Taylor was their youngest team member and their best computer analyst.

"Good idea. Get him working on piecing together Raziq's background, family connections, any Afghan political involvement. He can help Jenna with the threats as well." She thought about the weapons collection in Raziq's study. "I can't get over how personal this all feels. Some of the tribes over there still carry out vengeance killings. If Raziq's helping the DEA, maybe they tracked him here."

Walden grimaced. Not only because it was a long shot, but because juggling local law enforcement, the DEA—including an agent who obviously took anything involving the Raziq family very personally—and a possible motive stemming from a country half a world away was like walking through a minefield blindfolded. "Burroughs was right. This case has crazy written all over it."

As if on cue, Burroughs came running from the rear of the house, his phone to his ear. "Are you fucking me?" he was shouting. "Get to the car service, I want that driver in my office with GPS records. Get a warrant, call the goddamned cell company." He hung up and turned to Lucy. "Patrol just called. Wife and son weren't at the friend's house. Friend says they left around one o'clock, right after lunch."

"That's hours before the 911 call," Walden said.

"No sign of them here. And the car service can't raise their driver." His phone rang. He listened for a moment. "Fuck an egg. I'll send CSU and the ME. I'm on my way."

"They found the driver," Lucy said. She wasn't asking.

Burroughs nodded. "Driver's dead. Car's empty. No sign of the mom or baby. Looks like we have a double kidnapping in addition to our double homicide.

CHAPTER 8

BURROUGHS LEFT TO check out the second crime scene. Lucy cursed silently, keeping a professional tone as she and Walden worked their phones to hammer out an Amber Alert and mobilize their team for a high-risk abduction.

She glanced at the patrol car where Raziq waited. She had to let the father know what was going on. To keep him in the dark any longer was inhumane. The dining room was clear but, no, that smell... She sighed. It'd have to be in the vehicle.

Walden met her at the street. "Troops are on their way into the office. We should get moving."

"You go with Haddad. I'll move Raziq to our vehicle and let him know about Fatima and Ali." Both Haddad and Raziq were potential witnesses as well as victims; she needed to keep them separate.

"You get anything from him the first time around?"

She shook her head. "He's a hard read."

"Want me to take a crack at him? Jenna said he might respond better to a man."

The cultural differences were just one more complication in an already tangled mess of a case. She thought about it. "You're right. You take Raziq in our vehicle and I'll get what info I can from Haddad."

He nodded and moved to the squad car. She watched for a moment, noticing Raziq's stiff posture as he scrutinized Walden's credentials, the way he finally bowed his head the slightest bit in agreement and went with Walden to the Tahoe. She'd just turned to retrieve Haddad when he came walking out.

"Hurry up," she called to him. "We're headed out."

"Where's Rashid? I need to talk with him. He shouldn't be alone—"

Lucy stood her ground between him and the SUV as it passed them. "Walden is taking him to your offices. We need to go as well. How about if I drive?"

His gaze jerked from house to house along the quiet street, as if searching for answers in the holiday displays. "No. I can drive."

She phoned Walden who stopped the Tahoe at the end of the block to wait for them. Best to keep everyone in sight. She climbed into Haddad's Suburban, moving a heavy leather bound book from the front passenger seat as she did. A *Quran*.

He got in, saw the book in her hand, and took it from her, placing it carefully on the backseat. He turned back, looking a bit embarrassed and defiant. "I was never religious until I met Rashid. My parents weren't observant, although my grandparents were—they came from Syria."

She nodded, interested in the relationship the DEA agent had with Raziq. "You study with him?"

"Yes. Friday nights." He looked over his shoulder as he did a quick U-turn using a neighbor's driveway. "Over there, so far away from anything that made sense, almost dying… it was a real comfort. Finding something to believe in."

He cleared his throat, looked away. They hadn't gone far before Lucy spotted Jenna Galloway's bright yellow Mustang at the next intersection. She dialed the postal inspector's cell and put it on speaker.

"Jenna? Change of plans," Lucy said. "We're headed to the Federal Building."

"What happened?" Jenna asked.

To Lucy's surprise David leaned forward and said, "Jenna, it's worse than we thought."

"I was afraid of that." Jenna hung up and took the turn, the Mustang ending up as the lead vehicle in their tiny convoy.

"What did you mean, it's worse than you thought?" Lucy asked the DEA agent. "Haddad, you'd better fill me in. Now."

———◆———

JENNA LED THE way down Thomas Boulevard. Slipknot blasted from the Mustang's stereo, but she clicked it off, wanting a few moments of quiet to think. Two girls dead. Her fault? No. She'd warned David and Raziq that the bomber might strike again.

The DEA had insisted the threats were international in origin. But Jenna's use of geographic profiling and some magic with traffic cams had narrowed their target area to a few blocks around Ruby Avenue, right here in Pittsburgh. If she was able to catch the subject in the process of sending a threat—either physically by mail or electronically via the Internet—she could nail the bastard.

She'd hoped to take him in custody in the next few days and so erase the blemish of the failed psych eval from her record. Prove to everyone that she was fine.

Sure, maybe she had night terrors and day terrors and some anger issues—along with sleep deprivation and overdrinking and screwing total strangers just for the chance to sleep in the safety of a man's arms. Not to mention a touch of obsession over catching Morgan. But she was still damn good at her job.

Two girls dead. The words hammered through her mind, unrelenting. Not her fault. Not her fault.

Her phone rang and she answered it without looking. "Galloway."

"I think my amygdala is three sizes too small," Morgan whined. "You know. Like the Grinch's heart."

"His grew."

"Only after he stole Christmas. Did the worst thing imaginable."

"Morgan, I'm in the middle of something." Jenna jerked the steering wheel to miss one of Pittsburgh's infamous car-eating potholes. "Just this once could we cut the bull? What do you want to do and how can I stop you?"

Morgan's sigh whispered through the phone followed by an ominous silence.

Jenna regretted her words. "Okay, okay. I'll play along. You want to steal Christmas? What does that mean?"

"Guess you'll find out. Gotta go, he'll be coming soon."

"No. Morgan, wait. Who's coming? Morgan—" Too late. The bitch hung up.

Had Morgan sacrificed her damned integrity and reneged on her earlier promise to go after one of the guys Jenna had slept with? If so, they were shit out of luck, because Jenna barely remembered what they looked like, much less their names.

Damn, Morgan was right. She needed to cut back on the drinking. Start facing reality. She needed help.

Not just for herself. To save Lucy. And stop Morgan. Before it was too late.

Jenna focused on the road in front of her. At least she could do the first, keep Lucy safe. But she had a sinking feeling Morgan was more than one step ahead of her and it was already too late.

———•———

TEXT MESSAGE RECEIVED AT 1804:
TRES: ON THE MOVE. THREE CARS. R IN MIDDLE SUV WITH ONE MAN.
Z: ADVANCE TEAM READY. TEXT WHEN IN POSITION TO CLOSE OFF ESCAPE.

CHAPTER 9

LUCY PAID THE price for giving in to diplomacy and letting Haddad drive. The DEA agent was distracted and it showed as he followed the cars in front of them, almost ramming Walden's rear bumper at the first stop sign they encountered.

"What did you mean it's 'worse than you thought'?" she repeated when Haddad remained silent.

"We figured the threats came from Rashid's work back in Afghanistan. Saber-rattling, old enemies frustrated because he was out of their reach. Well," he blew out his breath, "I had it pegged that way. Jenna was worried the threats would escalate. But we never dreamed—"

"You think the person behind the threats killed the girls?" Lucy wasn't quite ready to make that leap of faith. Not until she saw the evidence. "You said Raziq was helping the DEA back in Afghanistan," Lucy continued. "Is he still working with you?"

"For the first few months he worked with us as a civilian advisor. But budget cuts—" He shrugged. "He isn't working for us now, but he still has contacts in that part of the world and lets me know if he hears anything."

"Mina had her hands cut off. And then she was burned. Could it have been some kind of tribal custom from Afghanistan? Someone settling an old score?" She didn't mention the possibility of an honor killing. No sense pushing too hard.

He jerked the steering wheel as he turned to face her. "Burned? Alive?"

She hoped not. "We won't know until the autopsy. Can you think of anyone who'd have that kind of personal grudge against Raziq?"

A pause. "There's one guy, but last I heard he was in a VA burn rehab. Marine. Blames Rashid for the fire that burned him and got his men killed."

He touched his forehead, the scar there.

Fire. Burned alive. Like Mina. "Was it the same attack you were injured in?"

"Yeah. That entire mission was one huge SNAFU— there was no way either Rashid or I could have prevented it. We played it by the book, given the intel we had."

"Start from the beginning," Lucy told Haddad, wanting to explore the DEA agent's relationship with Raziq. There had to be something she was missing, something that would explain the level of venom she sensed in these crimes. "Tell me more about the mission that went wrong."

"It was almost two years ago. I was in Afghanistan working a FAST mission."

"Fugitive Apprehension Strike Team?" Lucy had worked a few alongside the Marshals and local LEOs.

"No. DEA Foreign-deployed Advisory and Support Team. We were there to help the Afghans, teach them methods to stop the opium smugglers, perform search and seizures, that sort of thing."

"What happened?"

"One day we got a tip about a Taliban opium cache hidden at a school."

"I thought the Taliban were gone from power."

"Doesn't mean anything. You have to understand, in Afghanistan drugs fuel everything. Insurgents use them to raise funds to topple the government and fight our forces. The militias and local police are under the control of provincial governors who use drugs to keep their jobs and line their pockets. Then there's the Taliban who use drugs to keep locals under their control. If your only way to get money to feed your kids is to grow poppies for the Taliban, you have no choice, even if you don't agree with their ideology. The average guy on the ground over there is stuck between a rock and a hard place with a sledgehammer swinging down aimed right at his head."

"Okay, so the Taliban hid their drugs in a school?" Seemed awfully risky.

"A school for girls. Last place on earth we would have looked for Taliban opium. Rashid and I did the initial recon. Couldn't barge into a girl's school with the whole squad, would have been a PR nightmare, destroyed all the trust we'd worked so hard to win."

His voice grew rushed as if he was out of breath. "I tripped an IED. Thing was rigged with a delay to get whoever triggered it plus their teammates behind them.

Rashid pulled me out just as it blew. I was knocked out for a minute or two, by the time I came around the entire place was in flames."

"What about the girls?"

Haddad shook his head, focused on the vehicle in front of him. It was a moment before he replied. "There was a Marine squad working with us. They saw the flames, heard the girls screaming, but it was no good. One guy managed to get two girls out but he was burned real bad himself. I don't think the girls made it. The whole thing was a Taliban set up—the other Marines were ambushed while they tried to protect our escape route. They all died. If it wasn't for Rashid, I'd be dead, too. And you know the worst of it?"

Like a school full of girls and American Marines killed wasn't bad enough? "No, what?"

"There weren't any drugs present. They'd either already been moved or we'd gotten a bum steer."

"After that you arranged for Raziq and his family to come to the States?"

"Rashid ended up with a bounty on his head over there. He almost got killed; there were a few assassination attempts. Relocating him seemed like the least we could do. It paid off, too. He's been invaluable, helping us dismantle smuggling routes across Asia and Eastern Europe."

"So this Marine who was upset. He blamed Raziq for the bad intel?"

"Yeah. But how would he know where to find Rashid? Plus, I can't see him coming after Rashid's kids. And after all this time…" His voice trailed off.

Lucy dialed Taylor. "You at the office yet?"

"Just got here, or should I say *back* here. Walden has me working background on Raziq. Most of it I'm still waiting for the DEA to release." Taylor's tone of disdain made it very clear what he thought of the DEA hogging intel.

"Give me what you can on——" She turned to Haddad. "What was the Marine's name?"

"Stone. Andre Stone."

"A Marine named Andre Stone," she told Taylor. "And talk to the DEA about any unusual activity here in Pittsburgh. Ask Homeland Security to send over the foreign arrival data for the past few months."

"You focusing on an Afghanistan connection?"

She remembered Raziq's multiple passports. "Yeah, but don't rule out Pakistan or any other countries in that area."

"That's going to be a lot of names."

"Cross check them all with Raziq's cases with the DEA. I'll call if I think of anything else." Lucy hung up and turned back to Haddad.

"You said Mina had her hands cut off?" Haddad said. His voice was flat, distant, as if willing himself to remain professional. "Sounds more like Mexican cartel style of violence than the Middle East."

Talk about your remote possibilities. "Why would Mexicans target an Afghan——and in Pittsburgh of all places?"

"I don't know. I was just thinking. It's kind of our doomsday scenario: if the cartels south of the border ever teamed up with the Afghans, they'd control virtually the entire world's production and distribution of heroin. Talk about global domination."

85

Given Haddad's personal allegiance to Raziq, Lucy wondered if the DEA Agent was trying to deflect suspicion from Raziq. After all, most of the time, in crimes like this, a parent was involved. Sad but true. "You think a Mexican cartel would come all the way to Pittsburgh to target a former Afghan DEA informant's daughters?"

"No. You're right." He blew his breath out. "As horrendous as it is, killing two little girls is small potatoes to the cartels. They'll take fifty-sixty people in a day—civilians, not even fellow narcos—chop off their heads and hands, hang their bodies from highway overpasses just as a friendly warning."

That fit with the briefings she'd read on the violence south of the border.

"It's just that we've heard chatter about the cartels looking for new routes to expand east of the Mississippi. Detroit, Philly, and Baltimore top the list of potential operation centers. My bet was on Detroit. With the kind of money a cartel has, they could buy the PD and police union, fire all the honest cops, and run the entire city within a week. The way things are up there, the citizens might even be better off."

"Detroit, Philly and Baltimore are all port cities."

He nodded at her like she was an exceptionally bright student. Lucy decided to let it pass. They had more important things to worry about than her ego. "Right. Control one of those ports and a cartel would have a backstage all-access pass to the entire Eastern seaboard."

Pittsburgh wasn't exactly a "seaboard" city. It had three rivers and tons of barge traffic that went from the

Ohio River to the Mississippi and Missouri rivers. But she doubted that counted.

Haddad continued, "All that bullshit about tunnels and submarines filled with drugs? Just the tip of the iceberg, believe me. They've already infiltrated California, Arizona, New Mexico, Texas, moved up into Colorado and the Pacific Northwest. But the real prize is east of the Mississippi. Own that real estate and you've hit the jackpot as far as the cartels are concerned."

"Let's leave exotic narcoterrorist schemes aside and concentrate on the threats you and Raziq received." Lucy said.

He shrugged. But his detachment didn't make it to his face. He looked worried, as if he'd missed something. Something that had left two girls dead and the rest of their family in danger. "We've been through all this with Jenna. There's no one."

He wasn't giving her much to work with if she wanted to get Fatima and the baby back alive. Lucy ground her teeth together, a bad habit. Still too many possibilities, too many directions the threats could have come from.

Then Haddad asked the question she'd been dreading. "Do you think Fatima and Ali are dead already? Or would they keep them alive, use them as bait to get Raziq?"

———•———

TEXT MESSAGE RECEIVED AT 1812:
CINQO: READY.
Z: BRING IT DOWN.

Another text, this time to his man following the federales: Close the trap. Bring R to me.

He tapped the last character and smiled. Ten men had brought the city of Mumbai, a metropolis of twenty million, to its knees during the terrorist attacks of 2008.

He had twice that many, plus the gangbangers to use as cannon fodder.

Pittsburgh didn't stand a chance.

CHAPTER 10

"NICE TO SEE some familiar faces," Andre said when Mad Dog and his two boys were half way across the street. More to let the Doc know he had things under control than anything else.

Funny thing was, for the first time since being evac'd from Hajji Baba, Andre actually did feel in control. No panic, no dread apprehension as he waited for the pain of the next procedure or the next person who looked at him like he was less than human. Most of all, no sense that anything Mad Dog or the Rippers said or did could affect his life.

He'd finally done what Grams had urged him to do all those years ago when he first began running with the Rippers. He'd risen above them and become a better man.

Not a good man, never that, not with the voices of seven dead Marines and twenty-three dead schoolgirls rattling through his brain. But better than these street dogs? Hell yeah. Roger that.

Mad Dog stopped a safe distance away and tilted his head, staring at Andre's mask. Then he flashed a grin, complete with gold grill spelling out his initials. Did he have any idea how stupid he looked?

"Wasn't sure you'd remember yo' old friends," he said, his tone one of rebuke. "Sho haven't shown us any love since you been back."

"Busy. Grams needed taking care of." Andre took two steps towards home, gauging their reaction. He didn't want anything they were selling, so best to just part ways here and now.

"Well, we's gots somethings need takin' care of, too. Darius wants to see you."

"Sorry, Grams is waiting." Darius had brought Andre into the Rippers when he was twelve. Taught him everything he needed to know to stay alive on the street—including how to take a fall for the OG's like Darius when the cops came knocking. When he'd left the Rippers eight years ago, first to Juvie then to the Marines, Darius had run this block. From the way MD talked, it sounded like Darius had moved up in the ranks to major shot caller.

Mad Dog jerked his chin and his two boys sidled to block Andre's path. "She needs to wait a little longer. You don't want to keep Darius waiting. No sir."

Andre didn't move. He simply blinked at MD. He realized the advantage there was in facing another man while wearing a mask. Andre could read every emotion that crossed MD's face but Mad Dog got nothing in return. Andre's finger caressed the Beretta's trigger guard.

He could take them all out—*pop, pop, pop*—and be halfway home before their bodies hit the ground.

Easier than taking out the trash.

He actually considered it for a moment—a fleeting pleasure, a quiet fantasy. Most of his time at war was made up of so many moments like this: more about imagining what could be rather than actual doing. Because when the shit rained down, the doing was so automatic there was no thinking. No time for anything except remembering to breathe between the bullets and for doing whatever it took to keep his men safe.

Seeing Mad Dog and the other Rippers, he was tempted. So damn tempted. What was the worst anyone could do to him? Lock him up? Solitary confinement? Hell, he was already there.

No. He needed to keep the peace—couldn't put Grams in the crossfire.

"Where's Darius at?" No way was Andre getting into a vehicle with these punks.

"Just across the way at Kujo's."

Kujo's was an old three story house—once white, now painted Ripper red with that gingerbread trim the Doc was talking about—that the Rippers had taken over from an old man after his wife had died, literally forcing the poor guy out of his own home. Back when Andre had been with them it was a stash house, but Darius always talked about making it his own. His "HQ" he'd called it, like he was Ruby Avenue's answer to Donald Trump.

"Ten minutes," Andre said as he slid his finger away from the Beretta's trigger. "I'll give Darius ten minutes."

The three men crowded and jostled against Andre as they pushed across the street. Like they were still on the school playground, vying for the title of King of the Hill. Andre just shrugged it off.

Darius had fortified Kujo's with metal shutters and two guards on the porch. Mad Dog nodded to them and they were granted entrance.

The interior of the old Victorian style house had been redone in classic Ripper fashion: spray painted graffiti, disco ball spinning where the dining room chandelier used to hang, antique dining room table now serving as a catwalk where two naked women, one black, one white, danced as jeering men watched. The dining room chairs had been removed to make more room for men to stand.

Across the hall the front parlor was jammed with sofas and chairs of every design where Rippers relaxed, getting lap dances, blow jobs, cleaning their guns, smoking meth or crack with the women, or playing video games on the large plasma screen TV that blocked the front of the fireplace.

Different music blared from each room, competing with the gunshots from the video game and making Andre's teeth ache. All the women were naked, even the one who greeted them at the front door like a hostess at an upscale restaurant and ushered Andre and Mad Dog to the only interior room with a proper door still on it.

"Darius is waiting for you," she said, eyeing Andre with open curiosity. She was gorgeous. Light skinned black or dark skinned Hispanic or some delicious mix of both. Generous breasts, thick lips and wide smile, black hair flowing down to her waist except where she had it pinned up in curls and braids and what-not to frame her face. "Can I get you gentlemen anything?"

"Nah, Giselle, we good." MD opened the door, motioned for Andre to go before him.

Andre hesitated, letting his eyes adjust to the dim light and taking a look before committing. The room was a library—or had been in a past life. The floor to ceiling oak shelves were still filled with books, there was a large fireplace and elegant velvet drapes. The couch was squared-off and modern; black leather and chrome— Darius' idea of style—and in the center of the room was a round glass-topped table with two black leather upholstered chairs. Darius waited in one chair, sipping champagne from a gold-rimmed flute. He nodded to the other chair for Andre.

"He strapped," MD told Darius. Andre wasn't surprised he knew; it wasn't like the M9 was small enough to conceal. Andre stood tall, daring Mad Dog to try to take the Beretta from him.

"That's okay," Darius said dismissively, as if he were bulletproof.

Andre stepped into the room. Mad Dog followed and closed the door behind him, leaving his goons on the other side. Giselle moved to refill Darius' glass and poured one for Andre, bending over as she set it down, a well-practiced seductive pout crossing her features.

She started to sit on Darius' lap, but he shooed her off and she sat on the couch instead, stretching her long legs in their six-inch stiletto heels along its length.

"Andre," Darius said without standing. "Good to see you back." His gaze ranged over Andre's body. "In more or less one piece."

Andre couldn't answer, not right away. Giselle had distracted him. It'd been a long time…too long. She smiled and blinked slowly at him, the light from the chandelier sparkling off her eye makeup. Then she reached behind her and brought out a glass pipe that she lit with a rhinestone covered lighter. Crack or meth. No wonder she was so bright and eager to please. Just a strawberry, whoring her body for another hit.

"Who knew the trick to keeping the women in line was so simple?" Darius said as Andre stared. "Keep 'em naked. I'm making almost as much money off the ho's as the dope these days. 'Cept of course for the product they inhale and the freebies for the crew. Still, not a bad business model."

Darius fancied himself an entrepreneur. No wonder he'd graduated to the head of the Rippers' food chain. Andre slid his gaze from Giselle to examine his former mentor. Darius had brought Andre into the Rippers when Andre was just a kid and taught him everything he needed to know to survive... right up until the moment when Darius had betrayed him, and left Andre to rot in jail for something Darius had done. But that was just Darius being Darius. Nothing personal.

Unlike the bangers outside, Darius was dressed in a designer suit. He wore gold rings on each finger, a gold silk shirt unbuttoned almost to his waist, gold chains draped around his neck. A cross between the Godfather and a pimp. Probably exactly the look Darius was aiming for.

"Before we get started Andre," he said, in a condescending tone that made Andre itch to pop him a good left jab just on basic principle. Darius was only a few years older than Andre, but always talked like he was the shot-caller and Andre was a know-nothing punk. "I

don't do business with men except face to face. Take off
the mask."

Giselle sat up in anticipation, eyes wide as she took
one long drag on the glass. Mad Dog made a snickering
noise and shifted to the side so he could watch as well.
Darius leaned back in his chair and sipped champagne.

Andre suddenly understood what a zoo animal must
feel like, all those humans gawking. Except Darius and
the others weren't human. They were monsters just like
he was. But where Andre's humanity had been stolen
from him, scorched away inch-by-inch, Darius and his
crew had surrendered theirs willingly. Sold their souls.

Anger seared through Andre and he wondered if the
Doc was still watching his vitals. He wished he'd never
left the phone on. Too late now. But this rage he felt was
very different than the shame and fear and humiliation
that kept him from leaving the house because he couldn't
bear for people to see the monster he'd become.

There was none of that shame here.

"I said take off the mask," Darius repeated. "Now."

He thought he was ordering Andre. It almost made
Andre smile. Because as soon as the mask came off,
Andre would be the one set free.

He nodded to Darius and peeled off his gloves. They
were made of the same special compression material as
his mask and the long sleeved shirt he wore. Back in Hajji
Baba his Nomex shooting gloves had protected his hands,
so they weren't too badly damaged. Lost the left pinky
finger, but thanks to a few surgeries and a lot of intensive
rehab, both hands functioned. He folded the gloves into
his pocket then raised his arms to carefully undo the
mask.

It had taken five months of PT and three surgeries to release scars and muscle contractures enough to allow him to raise his arms above his shoulders, but Andre's audience didn't appreciate the feat. They were waiting for the finale.

The compression mask was custom fitted to his face and head. It couldn't be put on or removed quickly. Andre felt like a stripper teasing the crowd as he slowly, careful of the sensitive nubs of tissue where his ears used to be, inched the mask off.

Giselle gasped, a high-pitched noise that echoed through the room. He didn't blame her. It was the same noise Andre had made when he'd first caught a glimpse of his reflection. MD stepped back, his gun in his hand, looking down at it as if he didn't know how it'd gotten there. It was pure defensive reflex. You see Frankenstein's monster, you grab a pitchfork.

Darius leaned forward, elbows on the table, eyes gleaming. The man actually licked his lips as he imagined the hell Andre had survived. It took everything Andre had to meet his gaze—it felt like Darius was some kind of vampire, wanting to devour Andre's pain.

Sick SOB, that was Darius. He'd used to tie M80s to the tails of alley cats when they were kids. Laughed when Andre tried to save one only to almost get burned himself.

"Have a seat." Darius gestured to the champagne flute waiting for Andre.

Andre slid into the empty chair. Darius took his time, examining Andre's face up close. The missing ears. The mouth, half the size it used to be, carefully reconstructed from muscles re-routed from Andre's shoulder. The nose with its nostrils fused to Andre's cheeks. The heaped up scars, like ugly pink worms, that crisscrossed Andre's scalp. The shiny skin with no hair where they'd used shark cartilage to grow artificial skin when the original grafts failed.

The face that would make Frankenstein's monster look like a beauty queen in comparison.

Darius nodded and raised his glass. "To coming home."

Couldn't argue with that sentiment. Andre raised his own glass, touched it to his lips but didn't try to drink— he did best with a straw, otherwise he tended to dribble. "Coming home."

"You eating, Andre?" Darius asked. He wasn't concerned about Andre's diet, he meant was Andre earning money.

"I do okay." Gram's house was paid off and the VA took care of his medical bills. Between his pension and Gram's social security, he was able to keep food on the table and the heat on for the two of them. Didn't need much else, and it was more than most folks around here had. Honest folks, at any rate.

Andre pretended to sip his champagne. The bubbles tickled the sensitive skin the surgeons had used to create his new lips. It was a weird feeling, painful, yet not painful, kind of like an electrical tingling.

"Government should give you a million dollars. You risked your life for their little war and they send you home looking like that—I were you, I'd sue or something." Darius sensed Andre's attention drifting and snapped his fingers at Giselle, who slithered off the leather couch to join them. She stood over their table, her breasts at Andre's eye level, her expression blanked by the drugs as if she wasn't really even there.

Andre was used to going without a woman for long periods of time. Stationed in remote combat outposts with a few dozen men, sex and death the main topics of conversation, no running water, no electricity, long boring duty followed by short bursts of intense live-or-die adrenalin, there was no choice but learn to endure it. But he still hadn't gotten used to the idea that he might never have a woman again. At least not without paying one to sleep with a monster. And he hadn't gotten that desperate, not yet.

As Giselle leaned over him, refilling his glass that didn't need refilling, he raced past desperate to outright surrender. Ready to beg. His mouth went dry and all the blood in his body seemed to rush below his belt. He shifted his weight, sliding his chair forward, to hide his obvious erection. Felt like a goddamned schoolboy who couldn't control himself.

Darius chuckled. "What do you say, Giselle? How much money and crank would it take for you to go down on Andre here?"

Giselle's gaze caught Andre's and her expression turned to pity mixed with revulsion. She blinked and stood up quickly, turning to attend to Darius.

Pity. Quick fire way to smother any arousal. From her jerky movements and the way she brushed up against Darius, he could tell she was trying to distract him. Afraid he'd order her to fuck Andre, knowing the consequences if she refused. Her entire body trembled and a line of sweat slipped down the length of her spine.

Andre felt sorry for her. At least he could defend himself against Darius and the Rippers. She, like the other women here, was trapped. By addiction. By weakness. By the very fact that she was a woman and the Rippers treated all women the same: as objects to be used up and cast aside once they were done with them.

"What did you want, Darius?" Andre broke the tension by asking. He was tired of the damn power games.

Darius blinked, glanced at Andre then Giselle as if considering, then finally jerked his chin, dismissing Giselle once again. Andre caught her arm. She flinched, but he didn't let go, instead pulled her to him. She glanced over at Darius in panic, but Darius smiled at her fear.

"We each build our own prisons," Andre whispered into her ear. He hoped the Doc didn't hear it—it was Callahan's favorite homily.

He released Giselle. She hurried back to her spot on the couch, this time hunched in the corner where she sucked greedily on the glass pipe.

Darius rapped his knuckles against the table, commanding Andre's attention. "Got a job for you. Remember how good you were building those bang-bangs for us back when?"

Pipe bombs. Incendiary devices. Andre had a gift for making them, setting them in just the right spot. Big enough to scare whoever the Rippers wanted scared, aimed so they wouldn't kill. The Rippers weren't afraid of killing, but in this city gang killings were noticed big time, bringing the wrath of the cops, the media, and worst of all, the old ma'ams.

When you had grams raising not just one but two, sometimes three generations, nothing got them hot and bothered more than an "innocent" getting killed. The old ma'ams did not believe in collateral damage and when they hit the pavement the Rippers' income stream would dry up for weeks.

So the Rippers learned to play the game. Kept their trigger fingers in check, mostly, in exchange for free rein to run Ruby Avenue. It was a win/lose situation in the long run, but with so many mouths to feed and clothe and raise up, the old ma'ams only had so much energy to spend on a fight.

"I'm out of that." Andre set his glass down a bit harder than he needed to.

"Things have changed around here. We're partnering with the Mexicans now."

What kind of fools were they? Andre wondered. Mix in the Mexicans and all of a sudden you got bodies hanging from streetlights. No one wanted that kinda shit on their streets. Not for the first time he wished he could find a way to get Grams the hell off Ruby Avenue. But she'd never go, never leave her home. "Never surrender," was how she put it.

Andre shrugged. "What's it gotta do with me?"

"We need men with your talents. We're gonna deal with the Gangstas. Once and for all."

He did not like the sound of that. Last time the Rippers and Gangstas went to war an entire block burned down. Andre frowned, his facial muscles bunching. Frowning hurt as much as smiling. It used too many muscles, stretched too many raw nerve endings, so he tried not to do either. He stood. "You got plenty of soldiers. You don't need me."

Darius smiled, the kind of smile you didn't turn your back on. "You're right. You're right. Only reached out to you because we go back and I wanted to give you a chance to get right with us. Do what you'll probably end up doing anyway."

"What the hell you talking about?" Andre was tired of this riddle-me-this bullshit. "All I intend to be doing is taking care of my Grams and minding my own damn business." He turned and stalked toward the door.

"Raziq."

Andre froze. Every muscle in his body quivered as adrenalin and fury sliced through him. He turned back. "What did you say?"

"Raziq. Towelhead working with the DEA. Busting us right and left. Mexicans want him dead and gone." He raised his glass to Andre. "Could be the start of a beautiful relationship."

Andre's stomach churned with the urge to run away from this madness. But every other part of him, parts long numb to any feeling, parts he thought were dead, they fired to life at the thought of revenge.

"*Rashid* Raziq?"

Darius nodded. Again with the smile. He slid Andre's champagne glass towards Andre. "Word is he's the same guy set that school on fire, killed all those girls and your soldier buddies. Same guy that left you looking like something the dog chewed up and crapped out."

Andre downed the entire glass, half of it running down his chin and onto his shirt. He couldn't think. All he could do was feel flames licking his skin, hear the roar of the fire and the screams and his own blood-curdling cries of pain, and all he could see was Raziq's face, smirking as his men mowed down Andre's squad.

Andre sat the empty glass down, his fingers clenched around it even as his mind raced half a world away. "Raziq," he whispered. He raised his eyes, met Darius' gaze. "I'm in."

CHAPTER 11

THEY WERE ALMOST to the County 911 Communications Center. Lucy fumbled with her phone, calling Nick, avoiding Haddad's question. It was way too early in the case to start assuming the worst about Fatima and the baby.

Nick's phone went to voice mail. Probably in the shower getting ready for their date night. Damn, she'd rather tell him in person that she had to cancel. Leaving a message was easier, but she knew how much Nick was looking forward to *The Nutcracker*. It didn't feel right, taking the easy way out, so she simply said, "Call me when you get this. Thanks, love you."

Haddad hunched over the steering wheel, easing closer to Walden and Raziq in the Tahoe. "They're slowing down," he muttered as they approached Lexington. "Why are they slowing down?"

Lucy dialed Jenna in the lead car to see what the problem was.

"The road's blocked," Jenna reported. "Propane tanker. It's taking up the entire intersection so we can't go straight and can't turn down Lexington. Not sure what the problem is. We're going to have to—"

Before she could finish, gunfire cracked through the night. Red lights filled Lucy's vision as the Tahoe jammed on its brakes. Haddad stopped the Suburban inches from the Tahoe's rear bumper. Lucy heard more gunfire, mingled with the sound of tires squealing, as Jenna tried to turn her Mustang around.

"Holy shit!" Jenna yelled over the open line. Then it went dead.

Lucy rolled down her window, craned her head out, and was able to see a large black SUV roll up on the south side of the intersection, coming to a stop beside the propane tanker. A man was standing up through the sunroof, aiming at Jenna with a submachine gun.

"We have to give her cover," Lucy shouted. Haddad was already backing up to gain them room to maneuver.

"Tell Walden to get out of here with Raziq." Haddad cranked the wheel hard, driving the Suburban up onto the curb and down the sidewalk.

Lucy called Walden. "We'll run interference, you and Jenna get out of here."

"On it," Walden said.

"Weapons?" she asked Haddad. This was his personal vehicle, but she hoped he was prepared.

"In the back."

She squirmed into the rear of the Suburban to see what armament they had. The cargo compartment was nicely stocked: a ballistic vest, which she slipped into even though it was too large, a Colt M4 submachine gun with spare magazines, a Remington 870—her own weapon of choice—spare ammo, night vision goggles, and a Kevlar helmet and second ballistic vest, both in camouflage and bearing the insignia of a skull impaled on the tines of a three-pronged pitchfork. Haddad's personal armor from when he led the FAST squad in Afghanistan. No radios. Damn. But at least they weren't rushing in without protection and firepower.

Bumping along the sidewalk, they passed the Tahoe as Walden reversed it back the way they'd come. The man firing the gun turned his weapon on the larger target, giving Jenna the chance to pull out of the kill zone using the Suburban as cover. To Lucy's surprise, Jenna then made an abrupt right turn into the parking garage on the north side of the street.

She didn't have time to wonder whether Jenna was abandoning them or simply planning a strategic retreat to get help via the 911 Communications Center that was on the other side of the parking garage. Headlights filled the street behind Haddad's vehicle: two Escalades, one in each lane. One of them was equipped with spotlights on a roof rack. Men leaned out the windows of both vehicles and fired machine guns at the Tahoe.

"Walden, get out of there!" Lucy yelled, not even sure if her call was still connected.

The Tahoe lurched from reverse into drive as it stormed into the parking garage, following Jenna's route. Haddad made a wide U-turn, angling their larger SUV crossways to block the narrow entrance to the garage from the oncoming Escalades.

By blocking Lexington to their east and the cross street behind them to the west, the shooters not only cut them off from any help, but they'd also cut off the 911 Communications Center. The ravine with the train tracks and Busway was on the other side of the 911 Center, leaving no escape except through the shooters. It was a perfect ambush.

Gunfire pinged against the Suburban's passenger side. The front window cracked, then shattered, but Haddad was already sprawled out on the floor below the back seat. Some of the shots must have gone past them into the garage because the air filled with the whoops and beeps of car alarms.

"They must want Rashid," he shouted over the noise. "But why also target the county cops' offices?"

"Not the cops," Lucy said. "The communication center. It handles all the 911 calls and dispatch for county first responders." This time of night, most of the personnel in the 911 Center would be unarmed civilians. No help there. "It won't be down long. Not once they get the NIMS system up." The National Incident Management System was the emergency preparedness communication system in place for mass casualty and terrorist attacks. Pittsburgh also had a RED—Rapid Emergency Deployment—team that would respond as soon as word got out about the attack on the 911 Center. Plus, all the federal agencies had reactive teams that would be rolling.

The five of them just had to hold out until somebody responded.

She handed Haddad his ballistic gear and the M4, then tumbled forward into the rear seat to join him as the SUV rocked unsteadily. One of its tires had been hit. The Suburban wouldn't be going anywhere. For better or worse, they'd have to make their stand here in the garage. "You go, I'll cover."

They crouched by the door, ready to move. The sounds of car alarms and sirens and gunfire all faded from her awareness as Lucy concentrated on the task at hand.

"Now!" she shouted. She sprang from the vehicle and took up a position behind the engine block, providing cover fire. Automatic weapons spit a barrage of bullets her way and she only got off two shots before being forced to duck for cover. Haddad sprinted towards where Walden waited, the Tahoe backed into a strategic spot behind a concrete pillar.

Walden had grabbed the M4 from the Tahoe. Once Haddad was in the clear, he and Walden began firing to cover Lucy's escape. She backed away, zigzagging between the garage operator's shack and support beams on the right-hand side. The Escalade operator fired up a high-powered spotlight, aiming it in her direction.

A sudden flare of light filled the air, followed by an explosion. Inside the cover of the garage, the blast wasn't very powerful, but it caught Lucy off guard. The spotlight from the Escalade centered on her and more weapons' fire flew her way. She dove to the ground, rolling beneath a vehicle and out the other side.

Haddad reached a hand to help her back to her feet.

"What blew?" she asked.

"Propane tanker," he answered.

The fire would block any hope of rescue or escape. They were cornered.

Lucy shook her head to clear the ringing in her ears then backed away with him, her gaze and aim on the entrance while Haddad watched her back.

"Who are these guys?" she shouted over the din of car alarms.

"Wish to hell I knew," he shouted back.

———•———

OPERATOR 14: 911, WHAT IS YOUR EMERGENCY?
CALLER 234513: THERE'S BEEN AN ACCIDENT. A TRUCK—I THINK IT'S A PROPANE TRUCK—JUST BLEW UP. CORNER OF LEXINGTON AND THOMAS.
OPERATOR 14: SIR, ARE YOU SAFE?
CALLER 234513: YEAH, YEAH, I'M FINE. BUT I CAN SEE THE SMOKE. GOD, I HOPE NO ONE WAS IN THERE.
OPERATOR 14: SIR, STAY AWAY FROM THE WINDOWS. THE FIRE DEPARTMENT IS ON ITS WAY.

OPERATOR 23: 911, WHAT'S YOUR EMERGENCY?
CALLER 234515: THERE'S A BOMB. FORT PITT BRIDGE AND TUNNEL. YOU HAVE TWENTY MINUTES.
OPERATOR 23: SIR, ARE YOU STILL THERE? SIR?

OPERATOR 34: 911, WHAT'S YOUR EMERGENCY?
CALLER 234519: IT'S GONE, IT'S JUST GONE!
OPERATOR 34: WHAT, MA'AM?

CALLER 234519: The police and fire station on Northumberland. There was a car. Then—oh my God! Everything exploded. Send help. It's on fire, everything's on fire. Oh my God, I can't, I need—help, please, help.

CHAPTER 12

THE GUNFIRE STOPPED. For now. Outside the garage, men shouted to each other as they regrouped. No need to rush. Their quarry was cornered.

Lucy pulled her shirt collar up to cover her mouth and nose as thick oily smoke from the burning tanker roiled through the open walls of the garage. She tried her cell. Couldn't get a call through. Stupid parking garage. "We need to get to the Tahoe so we can radio for help," she told Haddad.

They moved from the cover of one vehicle to the next, the smoke provided a bit of concealment, but not as much as she'd like. If the shooters had the numbers, they could climb over the retaining walls and easily surround them. Walden joined the two of them behind a minivan two vehicles from the Tahoe. He handed Lucy and Haddad each a radio.

"Is Rashid okay?" Haddad asked, coughing.

"He's fine. Jenna's covering him. But we're screwed. No one's coming anytime soon."

"Why not?" Lucy asked.

He nodded to her radio. "They took down Zone Four. Car bomb." The Squirrel Hill police station was in a small building it shared with a fire company. It was their closest back up. "There are bomb threats all over the city. 911's overloaded. Locals are going nuts trying to respond to the calls that can get through."

"What the hell?" This couldn't be a coincidence, and that kind of attack took precise timing and coordination. "Did you see anything to ID these guys?" It would help to know who they were up against.

"I saw a couple of guys wearing Ripper colors," Walden said.

"This is way too sophisticated to be a gang hit. And why the hell would the Rippers want to target Raziq?"

They both stared at Haddad. He was hunkered down, scanning the perimeter for signs of movement.

Suddenly, an amplified voice thundered over the car alarms. "Give us the Arab and we'll leave you alone. All we want is Raziq."

Right. Like the Rippers were known for keeping their word or sparing cops' lives.

Lucy angled the van's side view mirror up and out to get eyes on the speaker. He stood above the smoke, on the running board of an Escalade just beyond Haddad's stranded Suburban at the garage entrance behind them. Early thirties, shorter than her own five-five, Hispanic, dark hair, arrogant set to his jaw, designer suit, no weapons. He left that to the men ringing him, all of who wore full body armor and carried automatic machine pistols and AK-47's.

"That's no gang banger," she said. The spotlight from the second Escalade made him a perfect target if only they could get close enough for a clear shot. It wasn't going to happen. Not without exposing their position. The Suburban blocked the Rippers from coming after them in their vehicles, but it also made it damned difficult to fire back. They needed to find higher ground with better cover.

Haddad pivoted to take a look. "Shit. That's Victor Zapata." He said the name like a curse.

"Who's Victor Zapata?" Walden asked. Lucy had a feeling they wouldn't like the answer.

"Youngest son of Marco Zapata, leader of the Zapata cartel. Victor's a real psycho, always trying to prove himself a badass. He once torched a nightclub full of kids just to send a message to one of their dads who was blogging about Victor's business. Made a few rap songs about it, put the videos on YouTube."

Lucy swallowed. She'd thought dealing with pornography and child predators was ugly. "You said the worst case scenario was the Mexicans teaming with the Afghans. Is that why they're after Raziq?"

"If they have Rashid, they could learn everything they need to cripple the Afghan operations, force them to partner with the cartel. Not to mention intel on DEA ops." Haddad used the back of his hand to slick the sweat from his forehead. "We can't let that happen."

"A Mexican cartel here in Pittsburgh?" Walden said in disbelief. "No way. Homeland Security will fry their asses."

"Like the combined forces of the Mexican Army, Mexican Police, DEA, ATF, and ICE have in Mexico?" Haddad said bitterly.

"Yeah, but this is Pittsburgh. What the hell would they want here?"

"They want to own the streets. The Zapatas only need one night—less than that, a few hours—to stake their claim. This isn't like conventional warfare, fighting over a grid on a map. They're fighting for control of hearts and minds. For that split second of indecision every cop and first responder will have next time they're called out. For the fear that will make normal people stay home and hunker down. And as soon as news hits that a cartel was able to cripple a US city, even for one night, they've won."

Lucy couldn't waste time on speculation. Right now Pittsburgh first responders would be headed here, thinking only a vehicle fire awaited them, and speeding right into the Zapatas' trap.

She raised the radio Walden gave her. It was set on the local police channel. Unfortunately there was overlapping chatter from officers trying to help their comrades at the bombed out Zone Four station house. Half of the radio calls were garbled as everyone rushed to get through. She switched to the central dispatch channel. "Dispatch, this is FBI Supervisory Special Agent Guardino. Please advise all units responding to the tanker explosion and gunshots on Lexington and Thomas that we have multiple gunmen armed with automatic weapons and wearing body armor. All units should proceed with extreme caution."

The channel was also crowded; she wasn't sure she got through. Infuriating since the operator was less than a hundred yards away in the 911 Center. The scream of approaching sirens reverberated from the concrete walls. Not police, fire. The Shadyside station responding to the tanker fire.

Either the dispatcher didn't get Lucy's message or she hadn't gotten one out to the firefighters fast enough. Lucy clicked through the channels on the small Motorola handheld. "Walden, what channel is Fire on? We need to warn them off."

Too late. The sound of automatic gunfire was followed by another explosion, this one smaller. Grenade? The sirens were drowned out by men screaming and shouting.

Jenna skidded over to Lucy, wearing one of the ballistic vests from the Tahoe. Lucy realized Walden must have given Raziq the second one, leaving himself unprotected.

"We need to get out there, protect those guys," she said, raising an AR-15 assault rifle in her hand.

Lucy didn't waste breath asking where Jenna had gotten the rifle favored by SWAT operators. It must be hers because she and Walden hadn't brought it in the Tahoe. "They've got the exits covered. Only way out is on foot. We'll have to climb over the rear retaining wall and sneak past their men at the end of the block. Then we'll be in a position to help."

"Okay, then." Jenna's cheeks were flushed and her eyes sparked with adrenalin.

"You've got to be kidding," Haddad put in. "Those firemen will have taken cover or retreated. Either way, we can't do anything for them. We need to get Rashid out."

He was right. Raziq was the cartel's target. Lucy rethought her plan of action. "Jenna, I need you and Walden to protect Raziq." She glanced at Haddad, hoping he had some brilliant military strategy he'd picked up in Afghanistan, because other than a suicide run in the Tahoe, she didn't see any way out of this. "We'll provide a diversion."

"They want Rashid alive," Haddad said. "That should buy us a little time."

"Okay. Walden, you and Jenna get Raziq and make your way to the rear of the garage. When you hear all hell break loose, you run for it." Lucy gave up on using her cell to get assistance—the towers were either jammed or simply overloaded with all the 911 traffic, and she couldn't get through to either the Federal Building or to Burroughs. The radio was no better. The police channels were crammed with overlapping calls as officers all over the city responded to the multiple calls for assistance. From the newly charged chatter, it sounded like Zone Five, their best remaining bet for backup, was now under sniper attack.

The dispatchers in the 911 Center calmly routed units to support their brothers in blue and cover firefighters and EMS under attack both here and at Zone Four, and sent special response teams to the multiple bomb threats all over the city: hospitals, mosques, synagogues, tunnels, bridges, even a high school hockey tournament.

Zapata had left nothing to chance.

The cartel had declared war on Pittsburgh and Lucy and her team were caught right at the heart of it. She blinked away smoke. At least Megan was safe with her mother in Latrobe for the weekend. And Nick would be home, wondering where the hell she was, but safe.

"We'll use the training channel, that should be clear." Lucy switched her radio channel and clipped the radio to the inside collar of her vest where it would be close at hand.

"What are you going to do?" Walden asked.

Lucy studied the layout. Entrance at their six o'clock, exit leading out onto Lexington Avenue at three o'clock. It would be covered by Zapata's men and the Rippers, of course, and physically blocked by a gate. If they drove around the garage's outside lane, built momentum, and came through it fast enough, they'd break through the gate, scatter the cartel shooters, and hopefully lead Zapata's men on a chase that would divert attention from the others. "We're going to take the Tahoe for a little spin."

"It's suicide," Walden protested.

"It's our only chance of saving Rashid," Haddad argued.

"Then I'll go—"

Lucy shook her head. She wasn't about to send someone else in her place. That was the price she paid for being the boss. "You have your orders. Get any gear you'll need from the Tahoe and start moving."

Jenna and Walden duck-walked back to the Tahoe while Lucy and Haddad covered them.

"Send the Arab out, now!" The voice on the bullhorn sounded impatient.

"He's not an Arab, you ignorant bastard. He's Pashtun. And he's not going anywhere with you," Haddad muttered, his voice barely audible over the din of car alarms.

Before Lucy and Haddad could make their own move to the Tahoe, Jenna popped up in the aisle, her red hair gleaming in the fluorescent overhead lights. Shots rang out. Jenna dove to the floor as a barrage of bullets pinged against the cars and impacted the concrete beams.

"Rashid's gone!" she shouted.

———•———

THE CHAMPAGNE BURNED, the final drops sliding down the wrong way. Andre choked and coughed, turning away from Darius, covering his mouth before he could bring it all back up again.

As he bent over coughing, he fumbled for his waist pack and grabbed his inhaler. Mad Dog stepped forward, as if worried Andre was reaching for the M9, then laughed as Andre straightened and puffed on the albuterol. Andre caught Darius's expression in the mirror: smug. Satisfied. Like Andre was a puppy who'd finally learned to heel.

"Need to get home," Andre choked the words out as he fought for air.

"You're not going anywhere. Not until you do the job." Darius' tone was final.

Eyes tearing as the coughing spasm continued, Andre gasped, "Bathroom?"

Darius waved his hand at Mad Dog who took Andre's arm, then flinched as if Andre was contagious. "This way."

Andre got his breathing under control once the albuterol hit his system, but he continued to make fake wheezy gasps as MD led him up the stairs to a bathroom off the landing. Best if they didn't know he was okay.

At least the bathroom had a door. He rushed inside, retching, leaning over the sink like he was going to be sick and MD shut the door with a bang. Andre started the water running to drown out any sounds, and calmed his breathing. The champagne really had irritated his lungs. He still felt its burn, so he took another hit from the inhaler.

The room was all black and white tile, tiny little octagonal ones that fit together like a puzzle. One of those old-fashioned claw tubs, no shower, tiny window above the tub too small for him to even dream of fitting through.

He grabbed his phone. "You hear all that, Doc?" he whispered.

"I did. Who was that man? Andre—"

"I know, I know. It was the only way I could get away without someone getting hurt." Liar. Part of him wanted to do what Darius asked. Nothing would give him more pleasure on this earth than to see Raziq suffer the way Andre's men had.

"Where are you now?"

"In the bathroom. They won't let me leave. Something's going down, something big. And it's happening tonight."

"I'm trying to call the police, but I'm having a hard time getting through," Callahan said.

"I'm all right for now. Just have to figure a way out of this so the Rippers don't come after my grams."

"Or you."

Andre made a grunting noise. "Let them try."

"You need to get out of there, Andre."

"Not sure that's an option. Not without a firefight. Doc, if you're serious about helping, I need you to get Grams." The first thing Darius would do if he thought Andre was double-crossing him would be to grab her. "She knows you, she'll listen to you. Take her someplace safe. Can you do that for me?"

"Yes, but——"

Silence filled the line. "Doc, you still there?"

Nothing. The call was dropped, the Doc gone. Probably for the best.

"Andre, you fall in or what?" Mad Dog shouted, pounding the door.

Andre took his time, flushed the toilet, washed his hands, then opened the door and glowered. Mad Dog backed up. Fast.

Still got it, Sarge. Just had to play along long enough to see what their plan was, try to stop it if he could. Now that he knew the Doc would get Grams to safety, he had nothing to worry about.

Except getting out of here alive.

At least that's what the Doc would want him to focus on. But Andre couldn't stop thinking about Raziq. About wrapping his hands around the man's neck, tightening slowly, watching his eyes bulge as Raziq realized he was dying… If Darius gave him the chance to do that, Andre wasn't sure he'd be able to refuse.

Ooh-rah, the voices of his dead squad cheered.

———•———

OPERATOR 17: 911, WHAT'S YOUR EMERGENCY?

CALLER 234518: THERE'S A FIRE AT THE HOCKEY RINK. SMOKE EVERYWHERE. OH MY GOD, JASON, HOLD MY HAND.

OPERATOR 17: MA'AM, WHICH HOCKEY RINK?

CALLER 234518: SCHENLEY ACADEMY. THE HOLIDAY TOURNAMENT.

OPERATOR 17: STAY CALM, HELP IS ON THE WAY. PLEASE EVACUATE THE BUILDING AS CALMLY AND QUICKLY AS POSSIBLE.

CALLER 234518: WHICH WAY? I CAN'T SEE. WHAT IF WE'RE RUNNING INTO THE FIRE?

OPERATOR 17: DO YOU SEE FLAMES?

CALLER 234518: NO, NO, JUST A LOT OF SMOKE. HEY, DON'T SHOVE. JASON, STAY CLOSE. WHICH WAY SHOULD WE GO? HELLO? ARE YOU STILL THERE? HELLO? THAT'S FUNNY. THE LINE WENT DEAD.

CHAPTER 13

"WHERE IS HE?" Haddad shouted at Jenna, ignoring the bullets flying above them. He craned his neck, trying to spot Raziq.

"I don't know," Jenna yelled back.

The gunfire stopped, but echoes kept drumming through Lucy's head in time with the blasted car alarms. Thankfully a breeze had started to clear some of the smoke so she could at least breathe. She crawled between the cars, meeting Walden on the near side of the Tahoe. He'd grabbed one of the tactical medic kits and was bandaging his calf. Blood spattered the floor around the Tahoe.

"I spotted Raziq over there, third row from the entrance," he pointed a bloody finger towards where the Escalade and Zapata were. Lucy looked but couldn't spot Raziq.

"How bad is it?" Lucy took over bandaging his wound.

He grunted as she tightened the pressure dressing. "Not bad. Ricochet off the floor. I told Jenna to keep her head down."

A high-pitched whine of feedback from Zapata's bullhorn shrieked through the air. Jenna and Haddad joined them at the Tahoe.

"Give me the Arab or everyone in the 911 Center dies," Zapata announced. "Listen to your colleagues."

He held a radio to the bullhorn. Gunfire, sounding tinny and faraway as it echoed through the bullhorn, followed by a man shouting: "Down, down, everyone down!"

There were screams, a few more shots then a woman's voice. "Active shooter, repeat, we have an active shooter in the Lexington Avenue 911 Center. Two—no, three gunmen, carrying machine guns, wearing body armor." Her voice was calm although hushed. Dispatchers were trained to deal with chaos. There was the sound of a scuffle and then the smack of a fist striking flesh.

"Tell them we have bombs," a man demanded. "Tell them if they come near, you all die."

"They-they say they have bombs," she repeated. The sound of a muffled blow was followed by a scream choked short. Lucy flinched as if she'd been the one struck instead of the anonymous 911 operator.

"No one is to approach," the operator said with a gasp.

A single gun shot. Then silence.

Lucy exchanged glances with Walden. She swallowed hard, her mouth dry. "Think that was for real?"

He nodded grimly, his grip tightening on his M4. Now they had more than just one civilian to protect— they were the 911 operators' only hope. No other responders could get close, not with the streets blocked by Zapata's men and the Rippers. She marveled again at the degree of planning and coordination that had gone into the blitz attacks.

But no matter what, there was no way in hell she'd give them Raziq. She waved Jenna and Haddad over to the Tahoe then craned her neck trying to see if there was a place where they could use Jenna's AR-15 to get a clear shot at Zapata. Two rows over, if she could climb up onto the exit ramp, might work. But she'd be exposed—

Over near the entrance to the garage, Raziq rolled out from between two cars and stood, hands in the air. His expression was grim, but determined.

"Don't shoot. I surrender," he called out as he walked toward where Victor Zapata waited. "Just let my wife and son go free."

Haddad moved as if to rush after Raziq, but Walden grabbed his arm. Lucy craned her head around the Tahoe's bumper in time to see Zapata's men shove Raziq into the back of the Escalade. Zapata climbed down from the running board and into the passenger seat.

Haddad shook Walden free and stood to fire at the Escalade as it sped away. Return gunfire shook the air around them. Lucy yanked him down so hard his helmet flew into the aisle where it was hit by a bullet, skittering beneath a car.

"We have to go after Rashid. We'll go out on foot, find a car. They don't have that much of a lead on us," Haddad told Lucy, his voice hoarse from shouting above the car alarms and gunfire.

The gunfire stopped. Bad news. It meant the bad guys would be closing in. Now that Lucy's team had lost their only bargaining chip, there was nothing to slow Zapata's men.

"One man or a building filled with civilians?" Lucy shook her head. "Sorry, your man has to wait."

"Don't forget his wife and son." Haddad sounded as frustrated as she felt.

"Believe me, I'm not." How could she? Her team would be the only ones even thinking about Fatima and the baby. But they had to wait as well. She couldn't abandon the 911 operators.

"They got Raziq," Jenna protested. "Why aren't they just leaving?"

No one wasted time explaining the obvious to her.

"Change of plans," Lucy said. She knelt at the Tahoe's rear hatch and collected the rest of the gear. She distributed spare ammo for the two M4's to Haddad and Walden, stuffed the pockets on her vest and parka with shotgun shells, found two flash bangs and a night vision monocular that she kept.

"You any good with that?" Lucy asked Jenna, nodding to the AR-15 rifle Jenna clutched.

Jenna opened her mouth, ready to ask another question, but instead closed it, and nodded. "Yes."

Lucy debated. Decided to take Jenna at her word. "Head up to the roof, we'll need sniper cover."

"Zapata will have a man up there already," Haddad said. "To cover the 911 Center entrance on Lexington. Maybe another to cover Thomas Street."

"Right. Jenna, wait by the door until you hear us. We'll distract them and you can take them down." She turned to Walden who was monitoring the radio frequencies. "Anything?"

"Nothing out of the 911 Center. The locals are on their tac channel, trying to get their SWAT teams across the city, but they're tied up at the Fort Pitt Tunnel and dealing with an active shooter over at the Cathedral of Learning."

Christ, what a mess. Okay. No reason to wait for back up that wasn't coming anytime soon. "Think you can find some cover up high, hold them off down here?"

Walden pushed himself upright and nodded toward an old van parked nose out two rows in. He and Haddad made their way over to it, then Haddad helped him climb to the van's roof via a rusty metal ladder on the rear door. A polycarbonate luggage case was strapped to the top, giving him a bit of concealment, although it wouldn't give him much protection.

Lucy cursed Raziq for taking their last ballistic vest with him. Walden's blood smeared against the van's white paint, almost making her think twice. They could just cut and run, abandon the 911 operators. She shook her head. Of course they couldn't. By the time Haddad returned, she had the Tahoe's engine running.

"Where to?" he asked.

"The roof. It's the only exit they won't have covered."

The Tahoe's tires screamed as she gunned it past Walden's perch and up the ramp, spinning the wheel hard, barely keeping the tires on the ground as she circled the parking levels. She wasn't worried about the noise—she wanted the men on the roof to know they were coming. That would give Jenna a chance to move into position.

It was all up to Jenna. Which could be the riskiest part of Lucy's plan.

———◆———

ADRENALIN SPIKED THROUGH Morgan's veins. This was the moment she lived for, stepping into the dark unknown. Exhilarating. Intoxicating. Liberating.

Everything could go right—in which case, she'd end the night with blood on her hands—or everything could go wrong and she'd end up worse than dead: boxed up in a steel cage. Like her father.

Finally Nick's Ford Explorer pulled out of the VA parking lot and turned her way. She tore a few strands of blonde hair loose from the wig's braid, glanced down at her torn jeans, rubbed the scrape on her knee until fresh blood seeped from it, pulled her fleece jacket so it hung crooked. Perfect damsel in distress. No way he'd be able to resist.

His headlights came closer. She squinted, trying to preserve as much of her night vision as possible. Just as he began to accelerate down Washington Boulevard, she stepped out from the guardrail and into the path of his oncoming car.

CHAPTER 14

JENNA JOGGED UP the concrete steps to the roof as quietly as possible. Not that she could hear her own footsteps over the alarms echoing through the concrete structure, the ringing in her ears, and the roar of her pulse.

Typical Saint Lucy. Planning a suicide mission, not worrying if the rest of the team was ready to get themselves killed. Duty, honor... all those fancy words Lucy loved to wave around meant nothing when it was your ass on the line.

She paused to change hands holding her rifle. Shook feeling back into the hand that had been gripping it so hard it'd gone numb. It wasn't exactly standard issue for a Postal Inspector, but what her bosses didn't know... Besides, after what happened last month when Morgan almost killed her, she wasn't worrying about rules, not when it came to survival.

She had to live. Otherwise Morgan won.

And she had to save Lucy.

Not out of any sense of duty or heroics. Lucy was her one shot at getting Morgan. Lose Lucy and Morgan would cut and run and Jenna would never have another chance at catching the psychopathic bitch.

Sick, sick, sick, she knew. But it was all she could think about. Painful and addictive like worrying a loose tooth or picking at a scab.

She forced her thoughts in another direction: Raziq's surrender.

Idiot. "Let my wife and son go free," Raziq had shouted, calm as if he was in charge. Like he'd been during every conversation with Jenna. Smug, superior, condescending with that slightly British accent that she just knew had to be faked. She didn't understand why David liked the guy so much, was willing to go the extra mile and put his career on the line for Raziq.

Was Raziq so confident he really thought the cartel would let his family go, much less let him live?

What would they do to him?

What would they do to *her?*

She arrived at the roof. Paused and listened. Pushed the steel door open a crack. The top of the elevator housing was beside the door, giving her some cover. She sidled out, peered around the corner. One man at the far corner, manning a rifle aimed at Lexington Avenue toward the entrance to the communications center beside the garage. He'd left his back totally exposed.

Jenna sighted her rifle. She could take him right now. Everything over before Saint Lucy arrived.

She could hear the Tahoe racing up through the garage. The man didn't turn around. No way he couldn't hear that unless he was deaf.

She hugged the wall and carefully stepped around the corner so she could see the rest of the roof. Her target wasn't deaf. He was protected by a second man standing in the shadows, ready to ambush the Tahoe as soon as it reached the roof.

Jenna shifted her aim, using her ACOG 6x sight. The man was wearing body armor but his head was unprotected. She exhaled, pulled the trigger, and he was down.

The sniper spun around. She shifted to aim at him. The Tahoe roared into sight. Jenna's shot took him in the neck, above his body armor. He crumpled to the ground as Lucy and David jumped out of the Tahoe, Lucy pausing to pick up the AK-47 and ammo from the first shooter.

"Nice work," David told her.

His words made her flush with pride, remembering when her grandfather had taught her to shoot clay pigeons. She'd practiced hard, wanting to earn his praise—he was the only adult who'd ever given a damn about her and she'd do anything for the man. Including growing up to take a job she was totally unsuited for. Funny thing, what love made you do.

She shook free of the memory and bent to examine the cartel sniper's rifle. Two guns and ammo for both, that should hold off the bad guys for a while, buy her some time. Plus she had her service weapon, a SIG Sauer forty caliber.

"I still don't understand how you guys are getting into the 911 Center," she said, looking dubiously at the gap between the roof of the garage and the roof of the Comm Center. "You're not thinking of jumping that in the

Tahoe?" If so, Lucy had watched way too many James Bond films.

"No. Not the Tahoe. Just us." Lucy joined them, the first shooter's radio held to her ear as she listened to the chatter from Zapata's men. "I don't speak Spanish. Do you?"

"No," David answered. "Urdu, Farsi, Arabic."

"Give it to me." Growing up in LA, Jenna was fluent in Spanish. She took the radio and listened. "They're getting ready to storm the garage. You guys better get going while I get into position." She placed her AR-15 on the ledge and sighted through it. She had a good angle on the garage exit where Zapata's men were assembled behind the cover of an SUV. Couldn't see past the smoke and flames of the tanker fire to the south. She'd have to set up the second rifle a little farther down the wall, facing the other direction, to aim at anyone coming through the garage entrance.

David carried the cartel sniper's rifle across the roof and helped her set up her second position. "Do you have your service weapon?"

She pulled back her jacket to show him the SIG Sauer holstered at her hip. "Why?"

"Save a bullet for the end. Don't let them take you alive." He squeezed her shoulder and left to join Lucy.

Jenna's sight blurred, her gut heaving, her mind filled with images of what the cartel would do to a female federal agent. She'd read about DEA agents caught south of the border, the way they were tortured. The cartel delighted in sending their families videos and body parts.

The sound of gunfire coming from below shook her back into the here and now. She sighted her rifle on her first target and pulled the trigger. For some reason the memory of the first man she'd killed filled her vision for a brief moment. That first kill. Last month. Never would have happened except for Saint Lucy.

She blew her breath out and focused on her next target.

———◦———

PITTSBURGH RADIO PATROL CAR UNIT 3435: DISPATCH, DISPATCH DO YOU COPY? I REPEAT WE HAVE AN ACTIVE SHOOTER AT THE SCHENLEY ACADEMY ICE RINK. CIVILIANS FLEEING A FIRE INSIDE THE RINK, COMING UNDER GUNFIRE FROM AN UNKNOWN SNIPER AT THE EAST ENTRANCE. I NEED BACK UP. DISPATCH ARE YOU THERE? WHERE ARE YOU, YOU SONOFABITCH? I SEE HIM, HE'S ON THE HILL, EAST SIDE. OH SHIT, OH SHIT, I'VE BEEN HIT. CODE 3, CODE 3. OFFICER DOWN, OFFICER DOWN. DISPATCH, WHERE ARE YOU, DISPATCH?

CHAPTER 15

MAD DOG LED Andre to the detached garage behind
Kujo's. Once Andre was beyond the claustrophobic
echoes inside the house, he realized that not all the
gunfire he'd heard came from video games. He stopped
on the flagstone path beside a pile of trash and
abandoned lumber scraps leaning against the back porch
and listened hard. Automatic gunfire coming from
several directions.

He turned and looked down the alley that separated
Kujo's from its closest neighbor. A faint orange glow
smudged the sky to the southeast. Another one to the
west. Fires. Big fires.

"What the hell is going on?" he demanded.

"Get inside," MD ordered, opening the door and
holding it for Andre with a mocking half bow.

The garage had originally been a carriage house. It
was brick with a high, slanted roof. Maybe a hayloft?
Leaded windows filled the space on either side of the

door. The wide sliding door for cars or horses was on the opposite side of the building, facing the rear alley.

Andre took all this in, not appreciating the sturdy craftsmanship that had gone into constructing the carriage house as much as he was noting escape routes and sight lines.

Several overhead lights lit the open space. There were no cars or horses or carriages here now. Just a kerosene heater, a cot, some shelves with jars and cans and rags, and a workbench littered with tools, poorly kept, some coated with rust.

Darius and Giselle waited inside. Giselle now wore an overcoat belted tight around her waist. Nothing else except her heels, from what Andre could see, but at least Darius hadn't dragged her naked into the cold. Class act, that Darius.

Huddled on the cot shoved against one of the brick walls was a Middle Eastern woman dressed in a long black skirt and jacket, a headscarf wrapped to cover most of her face. She clutched a baby against her chest and kept her eyes averted. The baby was a few months old, big enough to resent being swaddled; he struggled with his blanket, but other than making a few whimpers of frustration, he was silent.

"What's going on here?" Andre asked. "Who are these people?"

Darius leaned one elbow against the workbench and reached for Giselle with his other hand. The girl immediately joined him, fitting her body against his as he wrapped his arm around her waist. "A welcome back present."

Mad Dog snickered at that, obviously in on the joke.

"Andre, meet Fatima Raziq and her son, Ali. You already know his father."

The sounds of the house, the bass line from the music seeping through its windows, the laughter and shouts of men enjoying themselves, the shrill shrieks of women faking pleasure, even the gunfire from outside, they all faded from Andre's awareness. Leaving him to focus on this, the real battle.

The woman didn't move her head but raised her gaze to meet Andre's. Pain and fear collided as she saw his face. Normal reaction, didn't mean he was used to it. Wasn't sure he'd ever get used to being a monster.

"Please," she said, her voice trembling. "You know my husband? Please tell me. Is he safe?"

Darius made a mock face of sympathy and clucked his tongue. "Oh, look at that. Poor thing is worried about hubby. Tell her you're going to take care of him, Andre. Tell her you're gonna take care of *everything*."

Andre glared at Darius. His instinct was to go for his weapon, but the woman and child were between him and Darius. Plus Mad Dog stood behind Andre guarding the door. "What do you want?"

"Not what I want." Darius smiled. "What you want. You want to kill them. Just like Raziq killed your men, massacred those schoolgirls, burned you alive." He paused as if short of breath. "Now's your chance."

Crazy. The man had gone completely off his rocker. Andre tried to buy some time to sort all this out. "I can't kill them. Not now. Too many witnesses saw me come here."

"Sure you can. We're all friends here, aren't we?" He glanced at Giselle and Mad Dog who both nodded earnestly, MD barely containing his laughter.

Some friends. Andre was so glad he could provide them with endless entertainment at his expense. "My fight is with Raziq. Not them."

Darius drew his gun, aimed it at Andre. "Sure about that? Last chance."

Andre could kill him. No sweat. But no way he could get both Darius and Mad Dog before one of them shot the woman and baby. He had no idea why Raziq's family was here, but he couldn't take a chance.

Instead, he took two steps to reach Darius. Giselle gave a gasp and tried to squirm away. Darius held her tight. He and Andre engaged in a staring match. Andre pressed Darius's weapon, a Smith and Wesson .357 Magnum straight from the movies, against his own heart.

"I'm not interested in your last chances. I've had plenty of those." Andre's mouth was dry, turning his voice into a low rumble. Darius was unstable at the best of times. He could do it. He could end Andre here and now. And who was to say that would be a bad thing? Not Andre. Not his men. Not the schoolgirls filling his head with their screams day and night. "Go ahead, pull the trigger. You're the one who said you needed me. I still don't know what for."

Giselle laid a hand on Darius' arm. "No. Darius, don't."

Darius jerked his arm, sending Giselle sprawling across the room towards the door. "Shut your mouth."

Andre didn't move. Neither did Darius' gun.

Darius' eyes narrowed as if he'd stared at the sun too long. "Maybe I was wrong about you. Maybe you lost more than your looks over there in that desert." He reached into Andre's pocket, taking the Beretta then lowered his own weapon. "How about I let you all get acquainted? We got a little time before the fun starts."

"What fun?" Andre demanded as Darius and Giselle went out the door. His only answer was Mad Dog's snicker as he slammed the door shut and locked it from the outside.

———◆———

"HOW FAR ACROSS do you think that is?" Lucy asked Haddad, eyeing the roof of the communications center and trying not to look down into the darkness between the two structures.

Haddad squinted. "Ten feet down, eight feet across."

That didn't sound too bad. They backed up to get some running room. Jenna was busy covering the street, firing off two rounds in quick succession. Now that Zapata had Raziq, the 911 operators wouldn't have much time.

Hell, they might already be dead. She might be risking her life, her team's lives, for nothing.

She closed her eyes for a long moment. Nick and Megan's faces floated before her. She opened her eyes and they vanished.

"You're not afraid of heights, are you?" Haddad asked.

"Not heights. Just falling."

She pushed off, sprinting across the rooftop, Haddad behind her then passing her. Show off. He vaulted onto the retaining wall, using his momentum to leap across the void, still in the air when she hit the edge and had to commit to flight.

Stupidest thing I've ever done. She thought about calling Nick as she left the ground. Too late now. And what would she say? *Sorry honey, I have to pass on The Nutcracker because I'm going on a suicide mission?* No. That'd never do.

I love you. I love Megan. I love Mom. I'm sorry.

That's what she'd say. But Nick knew all that already. So she swallowed unshed tears—just adrenalin, she told herself—ignored the ice in her belly, hung onto the Remington with one hand and the AK-47 with the other, and let gravity do its job.

———◆———

THE HEADLIGHTS FROM Nick's SUV blinded Morgan as she waved her hands for him to stop. Brakes squealed as he swerved past her and then pulled over on the gravel along the side of the road. He jumped out. "What happened? Are you okay?"

His voice was pitched high and she knew she'd frightened him. Good. A little adrenalin did wonders to cloud men's judgment.

"I'm sorry, I'm sorry." She ran to him, favoring the leg with the scraped knee. "I wrecked my bike and don't have my cell and my folks are going to freak because I was supposed to be home ages ago, and—" She finished with a tiny, pathetic sob. "I need help."

He scrutinized her in the dim light. "Are you hurt?"

"No. Just a few scrapes and bruises. But my bike—" She pointed past him up the road. "It flipped over the guardrail and I couldn't get it. Please, can you help?"

He considered. The road was empty. No other Good Samaritans coming to help. "Of course. Hop in."

They got into the SUV and he put it in drive.

"I'm Nick. Nick Callahan. What's your name?"

"Megan," she answered. "Megan Fisher."

He glanced over at her with a smile. "My daughter's name is Megan."

Of course it is, idiot, Morgan thought as she smiled back. The people who thought they could read people—shrinks, counselors, social workers, priests, cops—they were always the easiest to fool. Overconfident. Thought they had all this insight into the human condition.

Until they met Morgan.

"That's nice," she answered. "How old is she?"

"Thirteen—going on thirty." He chuckled at the tired cliché.

"I remember when I was that age," she continued in her oh-so-worldly-yet-naive persona. "I thought I had all the answers. Hated being told what to do or how to do it."

Such a lie. When she was thirteen her father let her kill for the first time. He didn't tell her what to do or how to do it. He let her choose for herself. She glanced at her hands in the dim light from the dashboard. It had taken days to get all the blood out from under her fingernails. When she closed her eyes, she could still hear the man's whimpers turn to a throaty gasp... followed by silence.

Silence she had created. God, the power, the exhilaration!

"That's our Megan," Nick said. "Stubborn, independent, and way smarter than either her mother or I. Makes it hard to know where or how to set boundaries."

She glanced at Nick. Relaxed, confident that he knew where he was going and what waited for him there. So very, very wrong. He thought he was in control.

Wrong again.

"I think it was just up there. Where that graffiti is on the guardrail." She pointed out the window. He pulled the car onto the side of the road. Reached across her to open the glove compartment and take a flashlight from it. She leaned forward so her breasts brushed his arm, just to see his reaction.

Nick didn't even seem to notice. He stepped out of the car and shone the flashlight over the embankment. "I see it. It's down a ways."

"Okay if I use your phone to call my dad? He worries," she asked as he stepped over the guardrail.

"Sure. Go ahead." He was focused on keeping his balance on the overgrown embankment.

While Sir Galahad fumbled in the dark for her bike, Morgan got busy in the SUV. First she downloaded spyware onto Nick's phone. Same program she'd loaded on Jenna's phone. For just twenty-nine bucks a month, paid for with a stolen credit card, of course, she'd have ears on Nick's surroundings, access to his GPS, voice mail, and texts.

Next she shimmied out of her bra and took a pair of wadded up unwashed panties from her coat pocket. She rubbed both along the steering wheel to pick up traces of Nick's DNA, shoved the panties into the crack between the rear seat cushions and the bra into the compartment on the console between the front seats.

A few of her actual hairs scattered over the rear seat followed by her *piece de resistance*: she flicked open her knife and sliced her pinky, smearing the blood across the black leather of the rear seat and door handle. Debated leaving a palm print in blood on the window—the poor, helpless victim pounding against it in desperation—but decided it was too clichéd. She was already reenacting every mean girl adolescent fantasy of punishing an unavailable older man. Besides, the cops had her prints on file somewhere and she didn't want to make things too easy.

The only question remaining was: would she leave Nick dead or alive?

CHAPTER 16

HADDAD HIT THE roof with a tuck and roll, quickly coming to his feet, M4 at the ready. Lucy kept her knees bent like her tactical instructor at Quantico had taught her, body relaxed, going with momentum, but weighed down with ammo and with both hands full, her landing was more of a tuck and sprawl.

She wasn't quibbling. She was alive and, other than a jarring thud through her shoulder as it hit, unhurt. Haddad helped her to her feet. She felt old. She suddenly envied Nick his ability to work out everyday with his patients.

The sounds of Jenna's rifle from the garage roof punctuated their steps as they ran to the door.

"Unlocked," Haddad said, opening it and listening. No sounds from inside the stairwell.

Lucy wasn't surprised. "Smokers." She kicked her toes through a pile of cigarette butts to the side of the doorway. Saved them the hassle of breaking in.

"Admin offices are on the top floor." She gave Haddad the layout as she watched Jenna disappear from sight, moving to her second rifle. Three quick shots in succession and she was back. Only now there was gunfire aimed up at her. Jenna grabbed her rifle and hunkered down behind the retaining wall as bullets ricocheted off the concrete around her. "The 911 Center is on the second floor. Ground floor has a meeting room, public reception, a few offices."

"Should we clear top down?" Haddad asked. It was protocol but would mean wasting time going through each office.

Lucy tried to force her focus onto the task at hand, but she couldn't help but worry about Jenna. She glanced back over to the garage. Jenna had moved a few feet away from her original position, barely in sight.

Zapata was smart; he would have had his own men clear the top floor and herd all the hostages together. With the snipers on the parking garage, there was no threat to them from above, so no need to waste men on a rear guard.

"No," she decided. "We head straight for Zapata's men and the hostages." They began to head down the stairs as quickly and quietly as possible.

"Think he was bluffing about a bomb?" Haddad whispered.

Lucy didn't bother answering. Nothing they could do about it if he hadn't been.

As they rounded the first landing, Lucy radioed Jenna, keeping the volume as low as possible. "Any chatter from the Zapatas that would help us pinpoint their location?"

Lucy had left the cartel radio with Jenna since Jenna spoke Spanish.

"No. They aren't talking."

"Walden, how're you doing?" Lucy asked.

"Walk in the park." A short burst of gunfire punctuated his words echoing between the radio and the space between the two buildings. "Could use more ammo. Sooner rather than later. These guys just don't know when to quit." Another three shot salvo.

She wished she could tell him help was on the way, but given Zapata's diversionary tactics that would be a lie. "Any word from the outside world?"

"Cells down more than they're up, but from the radio, sounds like the locals are taking a beating all over the city. Tactical units deployed, but too much ground, not enough men."

"What's the weather like on the street? It'd be nice not to evacuate into the middle of a firefight." *Or ambush,* she didn't add. Of course, they might all be blown up before that could happen.

"Jenna's taking care of the guys on Lexington. It's the ones inside the garage I'm dealing with now. Sneaky buggers, came in from three sides." Which meant he was surrounded unless Jenna could back him up.

She keyed the radio to get Jenna's attention. "Jenna, did you copy? Walden needs support."

Two more shots, but these came over the radio. Jenna. It was a few seconds before she answered. "I'm on it. There's no more men visible on the street, but I'm not sure if all the vehicles are clear."

"Good work." Lucy turned to Haddad. They'd reached the 911 Center. "Now or never."

Again Haddad waited for her lead. She didn't know what his problem was; obviously his tactical experiences in Afghanistan should have made him the one deciding on strategy. Yet he was content to leave the decision making to her. Lucy wondered if she needed to worry about him having her back. Too late now.

He took the flash-bang she handed him and moved into position to lob it through the door. She'd go in low; he'd go in high.

Lucy crouched low, cracked the door, listened. Nothing. No crying, no muffled screams, no talking, no footsteps, no clank of weapons. Not good. It was either a massacre or an ambush.

"Go," she whispered to him.

He pulled his arm back, ready to deploy the grenade, when she realized she'd been smelling something more than gunpowder. She glanced down and saw that a clear liquid had trickled beneath the door and puddled around her shoe.

"Wait, wait!" She didn't bother keeping her voice down as she leapt to stop Haddad.

"What?" he yelled. She'd already blown their cover. He braced against the cinder block wall, waiting for the inevitable gunfire.

It didn't come. He shook his head as if clearing his thoughts. "What the hell?"

"Gasoline." She pointed to the fluid seeping beneath the door.

"Shit." He safed the flash-bang and returned it to his pocket. "Careful now, no sparks," he coached as she gingerly cracked the door once more, checking for trip wires. None.

Lucy let her breath out and opened the door the entire way. They stepped into the communication center. The stench of gasoline inside was strong enough to make her eyes water. But there was something else as well: blood.

Workstations were grouped throughout the auditorium-sized room: fire, EMS, local police, county. Each operator's desk had three large computer monitors. The front of the room held a projected image of Pittsburgh with markers for the various emergencies that plagued the city tonight.

There were sixty desks: sixty operators responsible for the more than one hundred police and fire/EMS agencies scattered around Allegheny County. Sixty men and women who listened day in and day out to their neighbors' cries for help, of panic, of fear.

Most of the visible desks were vacant. A few had bodies slumped over them.

Lucy took a step. Her shoe squished. The carpet was soaked with gasoline and blood. Haddad moved to the right as Lucy moved left, clearing the spaces between and under the desks. No obvious threats. Just silence broken by the hum of computers.

She lost count of the number of bodies she found face down over their keyboards or fallen to the floor. At the final row of desks she spotted six more bodies on the floor near the main door as if they'd tried to escape. She hurried over, checked them for life. Nothing.

"They must have doused everything with gasoline on their way out," Haddad said. "Otherwise their weapons would have lit the fumes."

"Why go to the bother if they have a bomb?"

He shrugged. "Maybe it's not a very large bomb and they wanted to make sure there was a big enough fireball in here to destroy any evidence."

"Or to tie up more of our resources as we work to identify the victims." She glanced at the nearest body, thinking about the World Trade Center attacks and the lengthy recovery process after. Not to mention the grieving process that still hadn't ended. How long would it take Pittsburgh to recover from tonight's events?

To the left of the main entrance was a door to another room that stood ajar. No signs of tripwires or anything that would ignite the gasoline fumes. She pushed the door open.

Behind her, Haddad made a gasping noise and turned away. Lucy wished she could. Dozens of bodies were scattered throughout a cafeteria-style break room. The way they were clustered, the shooters must have brought them here in groups, Lucy thought as she scanned the room. The scent of blood was mixed with the scent of gunpowder and the damp scent of fear. Somehow the smell was worse than the crime scene at Raziq's house earlier. She choked as she tried to swallow, her mouth too dry to produce any saliva.

Eight bodies slumped in one corner, out of sight of the door unless you closed it and turned to look to your extreme left. Another dozen or so beside them, facing away from the door. Some had fallen face down, some leaned against their neighbors, all on their knees. The ones closest to the door must have realized what was coming; they were turned in every direction. Maybe they'd even tried to fight back.

"Sons of bitches executed them." She didn't realize she'd spoken out loud until the echo of her voice circled the room, filling the hollow silence.

Now she knew why the shooters didn't bother blocking the stairwell door.

A groan came from somewhere in the mass of bodies nearest her.

God, was someone still alive in here? Lucy froze for a moment, not even sure where to start with the overwhelming number of bodies.

"Haddad, get in here!" She shifted the Remington to her other hand, slung the AK over her shoulder, and reached for the nearest body. A woman. No signs of life. She pushed it aside. It rolled to the floor with a sickening thud, blood smearing against the linoleum.

Blood slicked her hands, smeared her arms and body as she moved one corpse after another. Her fleece top stuck to her, glued to her skin by the Kevlar and sweat. She felt fever-slicked and flushed as she urgently worked.

"Lucy, David!" Despite Lucy's radio being turned down, Jenna's shout made Lucy jump. "They're leaving. Not just leaving—running. You need to get out of there, now."

Haddad came in behind her. "Lucy, stop. They might have booby-trapped the bodies. As concentrated as these fumes are, it'd only take a spark for this place to go up in flames."

Who thought like that? Lucy hesitated. Leaving would be the smart option. Another moan sounded from the pile of bodies. Hell with that.

"What are you doing? Come on."

"Someone's alive. I heard them."

A man's hand grabbed her ankle. Lucy gasped, then turned to push another man's body off him. Haddad bent to help her. "Holy hell."

The man on the bottom of the pile was one of the sheriff's deputies. Large, muscular, at least six-four, two-fifty pounds. His face was pale, eyes closed, as he struggled to breathe. Blood stained his khaki uniform shirt in several spots, more pouring out with each gasp.

The man opened his eyes. Looked right at her. He opened his mouth as if speaking but the only sound that emerged was a low groan.

"Did you hear me?" Jenna's voice came over the radio. "You need to get out of there!"

"We heard, we're coming out," Haddad told Jenna.

"Now. Hurry."

Lucy worked her arm under the man's shoulders and raised him to a sitting position. He gasped in agony, blood speckling his lips, eyes rolling back as he stopped breathing. She quickly lowered him once more. His eyes fluttered. His chest heaved as he began to breathe again. With each breath more blood pulsed from the wounds across his chest.

"He's too big," Haddad said. "We'll never make it with him."

"Shut up and help me." No way in hell was Lucy leaving him here to die.

"There's no time." He yanked her to her feet, half dragging her away from the man. "We need to go. This whole place is going up."

Lucy struggled free and rushed back to the man. A stream of frothy blood and a rattling noise escaped from his mouth. His eyes were vacant.

She felt for his pulse, refusing to even consider the possibility that he was dead. After everything that had happened, someone had to live, she had to save someone.

"No. No—" A tear smeared her vision until she blinked it away.

Haddad pulled Lucy to her feet once more. She felt sick to her stomach, her throat burning with bile as he hauled her out the door.

Lucy caught her breath and ran after Haddad to the stairwell, her eyes tearing. From the gasoline fumes, of course. She wasn't crying. No way. Fire Exit, the sign above the door promised. She hoped it wasn't lying.

Haddad pushed her through the door as if he didn't trust her not to go back to try once more to save a man now beyond saving. She ran down the stairs, Haddad so close behind he practically tripped over her heels.

They sprinted down to the exit. An alarm sounded as they pushed through the door and found themselves at the rear of the building. They raced across a service road. On the far side, four dumpsters sat behind a shoulder-high cinderblock wall.

Lucy dove behind the wall. As she landed, her ears popped and the air was squeezed from her chest as a blast shattered the night.

———•———

TROOPER 4: INCIDENT COMMAND, THIS IS STATE POLICE HELO, TROOPER 4. WE'RE RESPONDING TO CITY UNIT 3435'S CALL FOR ASSISTANCE. ACTIVE SHOOTER VERIFIED. WE ARE TAKING FIRE FROM A

SNIPER UNDER COVER, COULD USE SOME
GROUND BACKUP. WHAT'S THE ETA?

NIMS INCIDENT COMMAND: NO UNITS
AVAILABLE AT THIS TIME, TROOPER 4.
PLEASE KEEP SHOOTER ENGAGED UNTIL
CIVILIANS ARE CLEAR.

TROOPER 4: COPY THAT. WE SPOTTED THE
OFFICER DOWN. HE'S TWENTY FEET WEST
OF HIS VEHICLE. NOT MOVING. REPEAT
OFFICER DOWN, NOT MOVING. CIVILIANS
STILL IN AREA AND TAKING FIRE.

NIMS INCIDENT COMMAND: WE'RE TRYING
TO CLEAR A UNIT TO RESPOND, TROOPER 4.
PLEASE STAND BY.

TROOPER 4: WE'RE HIT, WE'RE HIT.
BREAKING OFF CONTACT WITH SHOOTER. I
THINK WE CAN MAKE IT DOWN. PREPARE
FOR HARD LANDING, MAP GRID....

NIMS INCIDENT COMMAND: TROOPER 4
YOU'RE BREAKING UP. REPEAT LOCATION.
TROOPER 4 DO YOU COPY?

CHAPTER 17

JENNA STEERED THE Tahoe down the corkscrew ramp of the parking deck. She couldn't remember the last time she'd felt this exhilarated, this alive. Better than sex. At least the drunken, oblivious sex she'd been having lately.

At first she'd forced herself to think of the men she shot as targets, not human beings. It was them or her. So she shot at one, then another, then another, with a precision that would have made her grandfather beam with pride.

Each kill brought a rush of satisfaction, each miss a surge of fear.

Missing gave her opponents time to regroup and take aim at her. Soon she was drawing fire from two sides, bullets spitting shards of concrete as they ricocheted past her.

Her aim got worse as she took fire from below. Fear blurred her vision, made her hands tremble. Then she'd gotten angry. Began envisioning each target as her favorite teenaged psychopath: Morgan Ames.

Exhale, aim, squeeze. Morgan was dead. Repeat.

By the time she finished, Jenna was so juiced with adrenalin and the thrill of surviving that she was disappointed when she could find no new targets living on the streets below.

Then came Lucy's order to help Walden. She'd scooped up her AR-15, the long gun she had the most ammo for, and ran for the Tahoe. As she turned the Tahoe around she wondered if, when she talked to Morgan again, she should thank her. Without that hatred to center and focus Jenna, she never would have lived long enough to protect the others.

Weird feeling. Like she owed Morgan anything. She didn't. Not after what that bitch had gotten away with.

Fury flooded her again. She arrived on the first floor of the garage. She burst out of the Tahoe, rifle raised and ready. The van Walden lay on top of was in the center of the floor, giving him a clear aim of both the exit and entrance. But two shooters were converging on him from the rear of the garage, moving to get a clear shot at him.

The ramp had brought Jenna out on the same side of the garage as the shooters. They turned to aim at her. Too late. She took out the nearest one with a single shot and Walden managed the second. Then she spun to evaluate the threats from the front and side of the garage. One man made the mistake of showing his head above the Suburban blocking the garage entrance. It was the last mistake he'd ever make.

There was another man beside him. She fired again but her shot went wide, pinging off the side of the SUV.

The radio Lucy had taken from the cartel shooter on the roof crackled to life. Jenna realized she and Walden were the only ones left alive in the garage.

Jenna covered the ground between her and Walden, using the parked cars and concrete pillars as cover. "Where'd everyone go?"

"Not sure," he said, facing away from her as he covered one side of the garage. "They just took off."

"There was something on their radio but I missed it." She turned the volume up and listened. "They're calling all their men out of the 911 Center."

"They're going to blow it. Warn Lucy."

Jenna called in her warning. No answer. Then finally, David responded. "We're coming out."

"Hurry."

"Help me down," Walden said. Jenna climbed up the ladder to the van's roof. Walden had propped himself up behind a luggage container but there was a pool of blood below his calf. She awkwardly helped him balance on one leg as he climbed down to the ground. He sat down, leaning against the van with a sigh. "It opened up again."

"Hang on, let me re-wrap it." She took the gauze from the combat medic pouch he handed her and added more layers, wrapping them tight. As soon as she finished a ribbon of red bled through.

The building shook. Jenna threw herself on top of Walden. There wasn't a lot of noise; instead a wall of hot air hit them followed by a low boom not unlike thunder.

New car alarms screeched from all around, adding to the pain in Jenna's ears. She looked up then quickly covered her head once more as a light fixture came loose from its mooring and crashed down on top of the car next to them.

More sounds of broken glass and the whine of metal buckling. Then everything froze, as if the building was taking in a deep breath. No, it wasn't the building trying to breathe, it was Jenna. She blinked hard, fought to clear her ears. She felt like she was underwater, all her senses fuzzy.

She looked at Walden. Walden looked at her.

"You okay?" he asked. She could barely hear him but it was easy enough to read his lips.

"I'm fine." She rolled off of him. "I'm going to check on Lucy and David." Her voice echoed inside her head. Then her ears popped. The blare of the car alarms made her wish the underwater feeling would return.

Debris littered the floor of the garage: glass shards, a side view mirror knocked loose by a fallen light fixture, fist-sized chunks of concrete. Dust roiled through the open walls of the garage on the Lexington Avenue side. Jenna tucked her chin into her neck, covered her mouth and nose with her hand, and squinted her eyes.

There was a three-foot retaining wall between the garage and the service drive behind the 911 Center. Most of the dust came from the front entrance of the 911 Center on Lexington Avenue. If Lucy and David had made it out the back, they might be okay.

The walls on this side of the 911 Center were mostly intact, although the windows had all been blown out. Cinders, pieces of paper, singed plastic floated down. Flames etched the darkness, reaching through the second floor windows, greedy for oxygen.

"Lucy," she called, picking her way over the rubble. "David!"

No answer. At least not that she could hear over the damn car alarms and the ringing in her ears. She spotted a body on the ground near an overturned dumpster. Lucy.

As Jenna ran across the broken pavement Lucy groaned and rolled over. Her nose was bleeding, her chin scraped. She sat up, a bit unsteady, brushed debris and garbage from her body. They were lucky the concrete enclosure for the dumpsters was there, it had shielded them from most of the blast.

Lucy slowly climbed to her feet and seemed otherwise okay. Behind her was David. He sat on the ground, hands cupping his ears, gaze unfocused. Given how close they were to the blast origin, they probably both had lost their hearing momentarily.

Lucy staggered around in a circle then focused on Jenna as if just noticing her. "Walden?" Her voice was too loud, shouting. She began coughing before she could ask anything more.

"He's okay. Leg's bleeding and I can't get it to stop. We need to take him to a hospital. You guys should get checked out, too."

David grabbed hold of the dumpster and pulled himself up. "We need to find Rashid. I should have never let you compromise my mission."

He was yelling at Lucy. Jenna doubted if he even knew how loud he was. Lucy lurched towards him, her balance still off. "One man or sixty civilians? Do the math!"

"Fat lot of good we did them. They're all dead."

"What else was I supposed to do?" She spun on her heel, teetering, then spun back. "And what the hell is wrong with you? You're the only one with military experience. All your FAST missions in Afghanistan. All that intel Raziq has been feeding you. Why didn't you or he or the damn DEA know about the cartel and its plans?"

"He did the best he could. The man's lost his entire family—"

"For all we know the man may have *killed* his entire family!"

David stared at her, his face flushed. He stumbled toward her, one hand tightened in a fist although he didn't raise it. "Bullshit! He saved my life. He just lost everything. That man—" He sputtered to a stop, at a loss for words. "That man is my friend. He loves his family. You think he, what, sold them out to the cartel for money? You think he let his daughters be butchered so he could make a few bucks? You are one heartless bitch!"

Jenna stepped between them. "We need to get Walden to a hospital. I think the Tahoe is drivable, just a few dents. Let's go."

David climbed over the rubble and headed toward the Tahoe. Lucy watched him, a scowl on her face, both hands on her hips. "Idiot."

"You should cut him a break," Jenna told her. "There's a good reason he let you take the lead tonight."

"What?" Lucy clapped one hand to her ear, eyes wide. Jenna wondered if it was because her ears had just popped or if it was because Lucy just realized just how far she'd fucked things up tonight. Jenna tried not to gloat, but she couldn't ignore a twinge of satisfaction at seeing Saint Lucy reduced to human fallibility.

"Did he tell you about Afghanistan?"

"Don't shout, I can hear you. Yeah, Raziq pulled him out of a burning building, saved his life, whatever."

"David suffered a traumatic brain injury. It was months before they let him return to work. Raziq may have saved his life but he couldn't save the Marines who were with him. Don't you think you'd think twice about leading people into danger if the last time you did you got seven of your friends and a bunch of innocent girls killed?"

Lucy stopped. Stared at Jenna as she wiped the snot and dust and blood from her face with the back of her sleeve—about the only part of her parka that wasn't coated in blood. Jenna hated to think of what they'd found inside the 911 Center, but however bad it was, Lucy didn't have the right to play the holier than thou card with David. Not that that would ever stop Saint Lucy the Judgmental.

Lucy sniffed. Started walking again but this time more coordinated. They climbed over the retaining wall into the garage and caught up with David and Walden. Most of the car alarms on the ground floor had died. It was weird, Jenna almost missed them wailing in time with her pulse. But at least she could finally hear herself think.

"Now what?" Walden asked as David helped him to his feet.

Lucy was silent. She probed her scalp beneath her thick, dark hair, her fingers coming away with blood that she wiped on her vest before anyone but Jenna could see.

"Now we go after Rashid," David said. "Like we should have from the start."

"Where?" Walden asked.

"I say we get to a hospital," Jenna said. For like the third time. Why was it no one would listen to her?

Lucy paced, her gaze darting from dead body to dead body. "What do we know about the Rippers?" she asked, gesturing to the last man Jenna had killed and his gang colors. "Why are they working with the cartel?"

"Partner with the Zapatas and they'll drive out any competition," David supplied. "You'd be the last man standing."

"Plus they know the territory," Walden added. He hobbled to the Tahoe's passenger side door, opened it, and sank down into the seat. "Could be a help when you're from out of town. And you get to use their foot soldiers, saves bringing in too many of your own men."

Lucy nodded. "And if you had valuable hostages, the safest place to keep them would be—"

"In the middle of territory you or your partners controlled," David finished for her. "You think Fatima and the baby are with the Rippers?"

"If so, that's where they'll be taking Raziq."

"Pretty big territory," Walden argued.

"I can narrow it down," Jenna chimed in. Silence as they all looked at her. Finally she had their attention. "I tracked down the threats and the letter bomb to a few blocks radius."

"How'd you do that?" David asked. "You've only been on the case a week."

Honestly, by working practically nonstop—except for the few hours she could escape Morgan's surveillance and go out at night. She didn't tell him that. "I combined the areas where the physical letters were mailed with CC TV and traffic cam footage, weeded out the international

ISP addresses—a bunch of false trails you'd already followed—and used GIS along with a program Taylor lent me to find the ISPs that were local. They're all unsecured wifi that center on Ruby Avenue. But the undetonated device was the jackpot. A former gang banger with a Juvie record used that exact same bomb making signature when he was active eight years ago."

"Let me guess," Walden said. "He lives in Homewood."

"His grandmother does. It's the only address we have for him. Right in the middle of the Ruby Avenue ISPs I traced."

Haddad leaned forward. "Are you talking about Andre Stone?"

"Yeah, that's him. You know him?"

"He was one of the Marines I worked with in Kandahar. The guy was burned in the same explosion that almost killed me and Rashid. When he came to at the hospital he said it was Raziq who'd set up the ambush that killed his squad. But of course that was impossible. I think the blast scrambled his brains."

"Does Stone have any ties to the cartel?" Lucy asked.

Jenna shrugged. "None that I saw. But I wasn't looking for anything as big as this."

They all were silent for a moment as the enormity of the destruction surrounding them sank in.

Lucy nodded to herself as if making a decision. "Jenna, you take Walden in the Tahoe," Lucy ordered. Back to normal. "Give me your car keys. Haddad and I will take the Mustang."

"Like hell you will," Jenna protested.

David looked up, a sullen look on his face. "You and me? Where to? I'm not heading back to the Federal Building. I don't care if you do outrank me."

"I'm not giving up on Fatima and the baby." Lucy said it as if daring anyone to challenge her.

"Or Rashid," David put in.

"Or Rashid. We'll check out the Rippers' headquarters on Ruby Avenue. And this alleged bomb-maker's granny's house."

His mouth dropped open. Then he closed it again. "Okay, then. That's more like it."

CHAPTER 18

To Lucy's dismay, Jenna had insisted on Haddad being the one to drive her Mustang. His driving was worse than ever. Jerky as if his mind drifted along with the car and he needed to pull them both back on course.

Lucy rolled down her window, inhaling the fresh, cold air. Sirens provided a constant background noise, surrounding them, but none were close. Helicopters zigzagged overhead. More news copters than law enforcement, unfortunately.

Because of the roads the Zapatas had blocked around the Communication Center, they'd been forced to go through a parking lot then wind their way along narrow residential avenues. For a Friday night the roads were eerily quiet. On many blocks the only signs of life were the holiday lights and the flickering of TV screens glimpsed through windows.

Haddad turned on the car stereo. Instead of music, there was the tone of an emergency broadcast alert. "We repeat, Pittsburgh and surrounding areas are under emergency curfew. Please remain off the streets and stay in your homes until further notice. 911 calls are being handled on a priority basis. Road closings include Parkway East and West, I-79, Fort Pitt Bridge and Tunnels, both inbound and outbound..." The list went on and on followed by event cancellations.

Word was out. Pittsburgh was under siege.

Haddad turned the radio down as the message began to repeat itself. Lucy gulped in air through the window, trying to settle her stomach. Her jaws clenched, activating her TMJ, pain spiking into both ears. She had a metallic taste in her mouth she couldn't get rid of—the aftertaste of adrenalin.

The feeling of panic reminded her of last month when Morgan's father had taken her. He'd used a stun gun on her, knowing exactly where to aim to cause the greatest amount of pain. She'd almost surrendered. Almost given up.

That weakness haunted her. She hadn't told anyone about what happened in the back of that van—not Nick, not the FBI counselor, certainly not her boss or anyone on her team. The official report skimmed over those moments of terror in dispassionate bureaucratic terms: *Subject overpowered this agent, removed her service weapon and cellular communication device, and restrained her with handcuffs in the back of subject's van.*

Too bad she couldn't translate her nightmares into equally dry language.

"I didn't get his name." She broke the silence first.

Haddad almost ran them into the curb. "Who?"

"The deputy. I couldn't read his name. His badge was smeared with blood."

Silence. "Someone will know."

"Sixty families." Despair colored her voice. "I should have listened. When you said the Zapatas would think nothing of murdering civilians. As soon as that tanker blew, I should have evacuated the Communications Center, called—"

"Called who? Zones Four and Five were down. All the rapid response teams, county, local, even our guys, were running around the city trying to put out fires and stop tunnels and bridges and hockey games from being blown up. Who were you going to call?"

He had a point. But it didn't make her feel any better. "I'm sorry about Raziq. I shouldn't have said what I did."

"You wanted someone to blame and he's an easy target. I get it." His tone was bitter. As if he'd been on the receiving end himself.

"Why take his family? Why make things so complicated?" Lucy asked. She knew the cartels used kidnapping to extort money and favors, but those were simple transactions that ended up with most of the victims dead whether the ransom was paid or not.

They didn't need all this elaborate staging. Killing the girls first, setting an ambush timed to the bombing of the Communications Center... It felt like too much, over the top, even for a cartel trying to create shock and awe. Diversionary tactics. "Why not just take him on the quiet? What do they really want?"

Haddad's answer was grim. "Maybe they want to make an example out of him. Victor Zapata has perfected the art of terror. You know how he disposes of bodies he doesn't want found? He takes them to a field, has his men prepare them like they're butchering a cow, then feeds them to his very own flock of vultures."

She didn't believe it for a moment. "No way. That's just what he wants you to believe. Building himself into a legend."

"Nightmare is more like it. But it's true. I saw it. All caught on a surveillance camera. They drive up and the vultures start gathering. Hundreds of them. Just watching and waiting. I have no idea how he trained them, but it's spooky to watch. His men slice open the bodies, take a sledgehammer to the skull so the birds can get to the brains, then they signal the vultures." He shuddered. It took him a moment before he continued, "Ten minutes later, there's nothing left."

Lucy hugged herself against a sudden chill but she didn't close her window. She needed all the fresh air she could get.

"That might work in Mexico, but it's not going to work here," she said with a bravado she didn't feel.

"I wouldn't be so sure about that."

"You really believe that? A Mexican drug cartel could come into a US city like Pittsburgh and just, just *own* it?"

"Like I said before, all they need is one night, a few hours, and a little help from the media to win." He nodded to the radio. "Which means we've already lost."

She let that sink in. Exhaustion weighed her down and she struggled against it. "I guess the only question is, are we going to let them get away with it?"

For the first time since she'd met him, he smiled. "Hell no."

They pulled onto Fifth Avenue, heading north towards Homewood. Despite the curfew, she was surprised there was no traffic on the major thoroughfare. Of course, given how widespread the cartel's attacks were, people would have no idea which roads would be safe. But this road led past Zone Five's station house. Surely there'd be some first responders using it.

Haddad turned to look at her. "Why didn't you send Jenna with me? Because you don't trust me? Or maybe you don't trust *her*?"

Lucy didn't tell him the answer to both questions was yes.

"Did you see a lot of," she searched for words, "this kind of thing when you were in Afghanistan? Like what happened to those schoolgirls the Taliban killed?" *Like sixty innocent civilians slaughtered.*

He didn't answer for a long time. "We were mainly search and seizure," Haddad finally said, his voice distant. "The Marines took care of clearing any militants before I went in. But yeah. I saw a few IEDs go off. You don't get used to it, not really. You just kind of block it out. Say to yourself: I'm not dead, therefore everything's okay. Then something *does* happen to you or guys you know and—" He trailed off, his hand going to the scar on his forehead. "Suddenly everything's not okay. And you wonder if it will ever be okay again."

She blew her breath out. It was exactly how she felt after last month. It was why she'd never talked to anyone about it: talking made it real and she'd much rather deny it ever happened.

The cell lines were jammed, but she kept dialing until finally she got through to Nick's phone. Straight to voicemail, again. She was surprised he hadn't called or texted, asking her where she was.

"Hey, it's me." She hesitated. She couldn't bring herself to let him know she was headed into the worst neighborhood in Pittsburgh searching for the leader of a violent Mexican cartel, her backup a DEA agent with a personal agenda.

"I'm sorry. I need to cancel tonight. I'm sure you saw what's happening." In the side view mirror flames danced behind them. "Do me a favor and stay home. I promise I'll make it up to you tomorrow." If she lived that long. Shit. He was going to hear the panic in her voice if she wasn't careful. Nick was good at listening. Sometimes too good. "Love you. Bye."

She hung up before she blurted out a warning for him to be careful. Funny, usually it was Nick telling her that.

Haddad was taking advantage of the lack of traffic and driving faster than the posted limit by a good fifteen miles an hour. They rounded a slight curve leading past the Port Authority bus garages and approached the tunnel under the railroad tracks and Busway. Too late the Mustang's headlights caught the hulking silhouette of a dump truck stopped inside the tunnel, its lights off.

"Look out!" Lucy called out.

The truck was angled to block both lanes. Haddad slammed on the brakes. The Mustang skidded, bounced over debris in the road, ended up sideways, the edge of the truck bed scraping along Lucy's door, metal shrieking.

"What the hell?" Haddad shouted, hitting the horn out of frustration. The noise echoed between the walls of the tunnel.

The truck was obviously deserted, left as a roadblock. Its hydraulic bed was elevated, the top edge wedged against the low hanging ceiling, its payload of broken concrete, rebar, and other construction debris emptied all over the road.

"Back up, turn around," she ordered. The Mustang's wheels spun as he shoved the gearshift down. "That's neutral."

Haddad cursed and rammed the car into reverse. Rocks pinged against the windshield as bits of brick and stone bounced against the Mustang. The wheels spun then caught, bouncing them over the debris scattered across the pavement.

"You said this was the quickest way into Homewood," Haddad said as he finished the U-turn.

"Turn right." She told him.

"You mean left. We need to take Meade down to Braddock."

"Too close to the 911 Center. They'll have it shut down."

He slowed the car. "So where are we going?"

"You want to catch them, don't you? Just turn. Now." She pointed to the sign that read: NO ENTRY. BUSES ONLY.

He took the turn so fast the momentum threw her against the car door. They hugged the concrete barrier, ascending the on-ramp in a steep semicircle, and ended up on the Busway. It was a two-lane highway crossing the heart of the city—and without traffic since the buses would have been sidelined because of the emergency.

She felt sorry for all the commuters left stranded in the December night, but buses made for easy targets to carry bombs. Too risky to keep them running.

Lucy shivered and rolled up her window, not liking this change in her thinking. She grew up near here, had jumped at the chance to bring her family back here, raise her daughter here. Yet now she was thinking of the city as the enemy, its inhabitants targets or terrorists.

If you thought that way, Homewood was the perfect place for a cartel to plant roots. Only a few blocks north of where they were now, it could have been an Afghanistan war zone in comparison to the quiet street where the Raziqs lived. Homewood was already so dangerous with the rival drug gangs fighting for turf that school buses wouldn't enter and firefighters and EMS responded only with police escorts.

She understood what Haddad meant about the main war being a psychological one. A fight for emotional dominance.

Even though she was a trained and seasoned professional, even though she'd risked her life on the job, hell, had even killed a man, even though she wouldn't be on the front lines of the urban warfare sure to follow tonight's events, she still wondered if she would stay in Pittsburgh. She had her family to think of—would she risk them just for her job?

If she couldn't help thinking that, how many others would also hesitate? Pittsburgh already had a shortage of police and first responders. How many would stay to face an enemy who wouldn't think twice about targeting them and their families?

Suddenly all the news of the bloodshed and violence in Mexico felt very close to home. She'd promised Nick she'd avoid high-risk field operations. And she'd meant to keep that promise, she really had. But who could have predicted something like this?

Haddad gunned the Mustang. He seemed to have gotten a new surge of energy now that they were getting close to Raziq—or at least to where they hoped Raziq was. "How do we get off this thing?"

"Up ahead, there's a ramp down near Brushton Avenue."

"Ready to go take on Pittsburgh's nastiest gang? Along with the Zapatas?"

Lucy finished reloading their weapons and shoved all the spare ammo into her pockets or the ones on Haddad's vest. "Sure. Nothing better to do on a Friday night."

He gave a grunt that sounded like something from a war movie. But that's where they were headed. Into war.

———•———

MEDCONTROL 3RMC: ATTENTION, ATTENTION. THIS IS THREE RIVERS MEDICAL CENTER. WE HAVE A CREDIBLE BOMB THREAT, REPEAT A CREDIBLE BOMB THREAT. REQUESTING CODE GRAY IMPLEMENTATION. WE NEED ALL AVAILABLE AMBULANCES TO TRANSPORT CRITICAL PATIENTS AS WE EVACUATE. ALL INCOMING TRAFFIC BOTH EMERGENCY AND NONEMERGENCY TO BE DIVERTED TO PRESBYTERIAN. WE ARE EVACUATING THE MEDICAL CENTER. PLEASE ADVISE WITH

ETA of police and ambulances. Angels 1, 2, 3 are starting evacuation via helicopter.

Angel 1: Medcontrol, we are lifting off from Three Rivers, destination Presbyterian. Five souls on board.

Medcontrol 3RMC: Copy that, Angel 1. Angel 2 prepare for landing as soon as the pad is clear.

Angel 2: Roger.

NIMS Incident Command: Medcontrol we have two State Police helos headed your way to aid with the evacuation as well as their Bomb Squad.

Medcontrol: ETA?

NIMS Incident Command: Fourteen minutes out. Proceed with evacuation but if you find any suspicious objects do not approach. Repeat, do not approach.

Medcontrol: Understood.

CHAPTER 19

POLICE CARS, EMS, and fire trucks choked the northbound lanes on Braddock, heading towards the 911 Center. Too little, too late.

Thankfully Jenna and Walden were headed south. All they had to worry about were a few civilian drivers dawdling as they rubbernecked, trying to figure out what all the commotion was about and which way was the safest to get home.

Some genius had turned all the traffic lights on the main streets flashing amber, leaving the secondary roads congested, but keeping traffic moving for first responders. Jenna made good use of the Tahoe's lights and siren.

Walden monitored the NIMS channel as well as the local police frequencies. Jenna figured it was a good sign that he was thinking clearly enough to help despite the blood that had saturated the pressure dressing again.

"Three Rivers is evacuating," he told her just as she was about to turn down Penn Avenue toward the medical center. "We'll need to go to Presby. Zone Five is still pinned down by snipers. Local SWAT is on scene. Bomb threats all over the city: hospitals, synagogues, college dorms, even a high school hockey tournament."

"They had all spring to study our playbook on that," Jenna replied. Right before finals, Pitt University had been plagued with bomb scares. There'd been over a hundred evacuations requiring multi-agency responses before they ended. Not her case, the FBI had taken the lead.

"Hell, maybe they're the ones behind those."

"Testing us?"

"Gathering intel," Walden said. "It's what I would do. Face it, we're up against an opponent who's just as smart, just as well-armed, and better funded than we are."

"And with no paperwork to file or regs about not letting civilians get caught in the crossfire."

"Exactly. The more civilians panicking the better, as far as they're concerned."

She glanced over at him. "Which means we haven't seen the worst of it yet."

Before Walden could answer, he finally got through to the FBI offices on his cell phone. "Taylor, it's me. Go to the training channel on your radio before this call gets dropped."

He switched to the radio and waited a beat. Then Taylor's voice came through. "I'm here. Greally is deploying us." He sounded excited, his voice cracking with adrenalin.

"Is Greally there?" Walden asked. John Greally was the Special Agent in Charge of the FBI's Pittsburgh Field Office.

"Walden. What's the situation?" A second man's voice came through, older and calmer than Taylor's.

Walden gave him a quick rundown on what had happened at the 911 Center. "A DEA agent, David Haddad, ID'd the subjects who bombed the Communication Center as members of the Zapata cartel. They're working alongside a local gang, possibly the Ruby Avenue Rippers. Lucy and Haddad are following a lead into Homewood."

"They left the 911 Center?" Greally didn't sound too happy about that. It was definitely not protocol to leave a crime scene and mass casualty site unsecured. Especially not on a night when first responders were coming under fire.

Damn, not even Saint Lucy had thought of that. "Sir," Jenna said, "No one could have survived that blast. And Walden was shot. He needed medical attention."

"We neutralized all the subjects in the area," Walden interrupted, his voice managing to match Greally's administrative calm. As if they hadn't almost gotten shot and blown up and burned alive.

Jenna steered them onto the Parkway West. Traffic was light at first.

"I don't think you understand," Greally snapped. "No US city has faced anything like this since 9-11. We have to clear every bridge and tunnel before we can re-route civilians, evacuate multiple targets—"

Suddenly a sea of brake lights filled both lanes of traffic between the Tahoe and the entrance to the Squirrel Hill tunnel. There was no traffic coming the other way through the tunnel. They must have closed the tunnel, probably checking it for bombs. She didn't hesitate, immediately steering the Tahoe onto the shoulder's rough washboard pavement. Walden grimaced in pain as his leg bounced against the dashboard.

"We think these operations are following the pattern set by the 2008 Mumbai attack," Greally was saying. "Locating their base of operations could be crucial to stopping them. How definitive is this lead Lucy is following?"

She glanced at Walden. Pretty damn tenuous, if you asked her. At least the part about the Ripper's HQ. Jenna was certain she'd found her bomber in Andre Stone.

An idea occurred to her. Why couldn't they find the cartel the same way?

"Sir, if the Zapata's base is in Homewood, I can find them."

Walden stared at her.

"And just how the hell would you accomplish that, Galloway?" Greally's voice whipped through the radio.

"They wouldn't be relying on cell communications. Too unreliable with the towers overloaded. And radio is too easy to intercept; they'd save that for team members during an operation. Just like we do when we're in the field."

"Go on."

"They must be using secure satellite communications. If so, we might be able to track them." Unfortunately there were a ton of variables and not a small amount of luck involved. But hell, if she could find Andre Stone in the haystack of leads David had given her, why not Zapata?

There was a long pause as Greally weighed the possible risk to civilian lives if he allocated a handful of agents to work this tangent. "What would you need?"

"Just give me Taylor," Jenna said. "He can support me from the Federal Building with the High Tech Computer Crime resources."

Taylor's muttered complaint about being pulled from the field was cut short by Greally. "You got it. Make sure you coordinate with Lucy. And keep me informed. We're setting up a Command Center here. The governor is mobilizing the National Guard, so let me know as soon as we have a hard target."

They passed the rest of the stalled cars and reached the entrance to the tunnel. The mountain loomed overhead. Two lanes had been carved through it going in each direction. As Jenna suspected, there was a cop car pulled across both lanes. Probably another one out of sight at the entrance on the other side of the mountain.

Cars were honking, blinking their high beams at the lone transit cop blocking their path. He looked tiny sandwiched between the yellow glow of the tunnel lights behind him and the blinding glare of the headlights before him. He stalked over to the Tahoe, one hand resting against the butt of his service weapon.

Walden reached across Jenna and flashed his credentials. Good thing because Jenna doubted her US Postal Inspector badge would carry much weight.

"We're going through," she shouted over the din, using her best impression of Lucy. "I've got a wounded agent here."

The cop hesitated, glancing at the empty tunnel as if worried one SUV might bring the mountain down. "I was told not to let anyone in until the bomb squad gave the all clear."

"Well, now you've been told differently. Out of the way." Jenna gunned the engine.

The cop jumped back, motioned them past, unleashing a new spate of angry shouts and car horns from the civilians. Jenna sensed growing panic from the crowd and wondered if it might not be safer to simply let them pass through the tunnel rather than risking a riot.

The Tahoe roared through the empty tunnel, its lights and siren creating a weird strobe effect against the polished white tile walls. The sounds of the horns faded behind them.

It was an eerie feeling traveling through the empty tunnel. What if there was a bomb? She shook the thought aside. Where would the Zapatas strike next? "Mumbai, that was like a dozen men?"

"Ten," Walden answered. "Held the city hostage for three days."

"At first it was like this? No one knowing who was in danger or who wasn't, where to go, what place was safe…"

He nodded grimly.

"Three days."

"Over a hundred dead."

They cleared the tunnel and sped towards Oakland.

"In Mumbai," Taylor's voice came through the radio once reception returned, uncannily following their line of thought, "the terrorists had an operation center across the border in Pakistan. They communicated via smart phones, taking photos of high profile targets, giving and receiving orders via text. Even Googled maps and used nav satellite data to coordinate attacks and evade the police."

"That's a lot of assets in one area," Walden said. "Do you think the Zapatas would keep their command center here in the city?"

"That's my point. Jenna, your intel might be leading you into a trap."

Not her. Lucy had assigned Jenna ambulance duty. But he had a point. "If so, Lucy and David Haddad are about to spring it."

CHAPTER 20

ANDRE LOOKED OUT the garage window. Mad Dog and one of his men stood guard outside the door. The large sliding door on the back wall didn't have any windows but Andre was certain there'd be men watching the alley as well.

Mexicans, Rippers, Gangstas, and Raziq. Recipe for a bloody disaster that could turn Ruby Avenue into Kandahar—with folks like Grams caught in the middle. He hoped Callahan got her to safety before the shooting started.

Come home to Pittsburgh and the only person he could trust was his shrink. Had to be a lesson in that. But Callahan had done right by Andre so far. No way the VA was paying him for all the time he'd spent making house calls, setting up his hare-brained remote treadmill therapy sessions, checking in on Andre during his burn clinic visits. The Doc had always been there when Andre needed him, despite Andre's best efforts to push him away.

Callahan would keep Grams safe. Andre just had to believe that and focus on the job at hand. Getting himself and Raziq's family to safety before Darius unleashed whatever hell he had planned for Ruby Avenue.

They'd taken Andre's pistol, but left him with his waist pack. And everything here in the garage to work with. He wondered about that. Simple overconfidence? Or did they really not think he posed any kind of threat?

Wasn't like Darius not to have a Plan B. And a guy to take the fall for him should anything go wrong. Andre had a feeling that was his role in this game, just like it had been when he was a kid running errands for the Rippers. *Don't worry*, Darius would say. *You're under age, cops can't do shit to you, you get caught.*

Maybe Darius was counting on Andre's loyalty to the Rippers. Maybe that was why he'd left him with the cellphone. He dialed and redialed. Nothing was getting through. Not 911, the Doc, even Grams. *We're sorry all circuits are busy. Please try again.* Must have something to do with the fires.

He stared at Fatima and the baby, assessing his options now that he had two civilians to protect. The baby stared back then crinkled up his little round face and began screaming.

Andre took a knee, bringing himself to Fatima's eye level. "*Assalamu alaikum.*" He hoped his pronunciation was close; it'd been over two years since he'd used the greeting.

Fatima bobbed her head in a shy nod, still not making eye contact as she patted the baby's back. "*Wa alaikum assalam.*"

"You have a beautiful baby. What's his name?" Andre kept his voice soft, hoping the baby would respond, quiet down.

"Ali."

"How old is he?"

"Seven months."

Now for the tough questions. "Are you okay? Did they hurt you?"

She shook her head, angling her body away from his as she tried and failed to calm the baby.

Why wouldn't the kid stop crying? "Is something wrong with him?"

She looked down at the infant, not up at Andre. "Your face. It scares him."

Idiot. Of course it did. Even babies knew enough to be frightened of monsters. "I'm sorry."

He stood, turned his back, fished his mask from his pocket, and struggled to slip it on. Hard to do without a mirror to help. He had to realign it twice before it felt close to fitting properly. "Better?"

Her expression said no, yet she nodded. "Thank you."

"We're going to get out of here." He hated making promises he couldn't keep, but he needed her calm. "Tell me what happened. How did you end up here?"

She stood, jostling the baby against her hip, angling the baby so he faced away from Andre. Finally the baby quieted, clutched her arm, and drifted asleep. Poor thing was probably exhausted, the way it'd been screaming. "Our driver didn't take us home. He said my husband was waiting for us. But when he stopped, they—" She glanced toward the door. "Men, black men, they killed him. Made us come with them. Come here. Please, is my husband safe?"

The irony behind that question choked Andre to silence. Yes, Raziq was safe—as long as he stayed away from here, from Andre. Raziq was safe while his wife and child were in Andre's hands.

He nodded. "As far as I know."

She looked at the phone in his hand. "Please. You call? Ask him to come get us?"

Andre hesitated. Raziq was the last man on Earth he wanted to have a civilized conversation with. His business with Raziq was anything but civilized. Maybe that was why Darius had left him his phone—Darius wanted him to lure Raziq here. But they could have done that themselves, made Fatima call, set up a meet.

His eyes burned as he tried in vain to make sense of it all. Finally he simply handed her the phone, let her dial then put it on speaker. Wouldn't you know it, Fate smiled and the call went through, first try.

A man's voice said, "Raziq residence."

The woman jerked and shoved the phone at Andre. "Rashid Raziq, please."

"Ah, what is this in reference to?" The man talked fast, his voice pitched high with excitement. He sounded young, like a kid.

"His wife would like to talk to him."

A pause before the man responded. "Who is this?"

"Doesn't matter." Andre was getting impatient. Where the hell was Raziq? "Put Raziq on."

Another pause. "He's not here. Could I speak to Mrs. Raziq?"

Andre turned to Fatima. She was flushed, shaking her head no. "Mina," she whispered. "I want to talk to Mina. My daughter."

"Is her daughter there? Mina? She'd like to talk to her."

"You sick bastard. What's your game?"

What the hell? Andre took the phone off speaker and raised it to his ear, moving a few steps away so that Fatima couldn't hear. "I don't know who you are or what's going on, but I hope you can help. Mrs. Raziq and her son are being held against their will. They're in a garage behind 411 Ruby Avenue. If her husband or daughter is there, it would be a comfort for her to speak with them."

"Are they okay?"

"So far."

"Who are you?"

What did it matter? "Just call the police. In the meantime, could she speak with her daughter?"

"I am the police. And her daughters are dead, if you don't already know that."

Andre froze, his entire body tensing. "What happened?"

"How about you tell me."

Andre realized the cop was stringing him along, probably trying to trace the call or something. Fine by him. He wanted them found, sooner the better. But the cop sounded beyond stressed. His voice was high-pitched, rushed, like he was a kid left on his own for the first time.

Young. He sounded young. "Look, I'm just an innocent bystander trying to help out. I don't know anything."

"We'll see about that, Andre Stone."

"Good for you, you can read caller ID. Now what are you going to do about getting this woman and her baby out of here?"

"Where are you again?"

"I told you. Ruby Avenue. Ripper hangout called Kujo's."

Another pause. "Ripper territory."

The man was an idiot. Why did he make Andre repeat everything? "Yeah and they're gearing up for war. You'd better send SWAT."

"Are you nuts? Do you have any idea what's going on?"

"What the hell are you talking about?"

"Cops all over the city are under attack," the kid's voice raised in anger. "Fire and EMS, too. We lost Dispatch, we lost 911, hell, the phones are only working half the time. We can't even save our own people, in our own station houses, much less make it to Ruby Avenue."

Shit. The fires. Darius must be behind them. But what was his end game, attacking the cops? That was suicide. "You talk like there's a war going on."

"That's exactly right. War. And you, my friend, are smack dab in the center of enemy territory."

"So who are you sending?"

A long pause. "I'm sorry. There is no one to send. No one's coming any time soon." The anonymous voice sounded genuinely sympathetic. "I'll try to put a call in, maybe get a car over to you. But for the time being you're on your own."

"A single car?" One cop up against Rippers cranked up and ready for war? "Don't bother. They'll be massacred."

"Best I can—" The call was dropped. Andre stared at the handset, unwilling to face Fatima and tell her her children were dead. Or that no one was coming to save her.

He was Raziq's wife and son's only hope. Laughter from his dead squad roared through his brain.

Andre had long ago figured out any god up there was a joker with a wicked sense of humor, but this was taking things too far.

"Please," she said. "My husband, he is coming?"

"Uh, no. He's been detained," Andre adlibbed.

"Mina, my daughter?" Her eyes were tight with worry and he knew she knew something was wrong. How could she not after what she'd seen tonight? Hijacked, a man killed in front of her, held hostage.

He sat down beside her on the cot. She shrank away. He hesitated, not sure where to look or what to do with his hands. He shouldn't touch her, he knew that, but how could he just blurt out that her kids were dead without at least taking her hand?

Finally he simply looked her in the eye and said, "I'm sorry. That was the police at your house. Your daughters are dead."

———◦———

CHANNEL 2 BREAKING NEWS:
AS THE HOLIDAY SEASON IS UPON US,
PITTSBURGH IS EXPERIENCING ANYTHING

BUT A SILENT NIGHT, HOLY NIGHT. IN AN UNPRECEDENTED MOVE, AUTHORITIES HAVE IMPOSED AN EMERGENCY CURFEW ON THE ENTIRE REGION.

A SPOKESPERSON FOR THE MAYOR'S OFFICE TOLD CHANNEL 2 THAT UNIDENTIFIED GANGS WERE RESPONSIBLE FOR THE SPATE OF BOMB THREATS AND SHOOTINGS. SHE IMPLIED THAT DRUGS MIGHT BE INVOLVED AND REASSURED THE PUBLIC THAT THE LOCAL POLICE HAD MATTERS UNDER CONTROL.

"AGAIN, WE WANT TO MAKE SURE EVERYONE UNDERSTANDS THAT WHILE WE HAVE THINGS UNDER CONTROL, WE DO ASK THAT EVERYONE IN YOUR VIEWING AUDIENCE RETURN HOME AND STAY THERE FOR THE DURATION OF THE EMERGENCY. POLICE WILL NEED ROADS CLEAR OF ALL CIVILIAN TRAFFIC IN ORDER TO RESPOND AS FAST AS POSSIBLE. WE APOLOGIZE FOR ANY INCONVENIENCE BUT WE'RE SURE THAT THE CITIZENS OF PITTSBURGH WANT TO HELP US DEAL WITH THESE ISOLATED INCIDENTS AS QUICKLY AS POSSIBLE."

CHAPTER 21

"WHAT'S THE PLAN?" Haddad asked Lucy as they turned off the Busway.

"I was hoping you had one," she said only half jokingly. Two of them against Lord only knew what kind of opposition and civilians in the mix. "Turn left here."

"Is this even a road?" he asked as they bounced over pavement that was more dirt than macadam. They passed an auto body shop, a line of graffiti painted corrugated metal-walled buildings on one side and a faux-Tudor house, condemned and sagging off its foundation, on the other.

"Believe it or not, it's called Finance Road." They swerved to avoid an abandoned tractor-trailer covered in graffiti.

"Alley is more like it." The Mustang took a pothole hard and he slowed down marginally.

"Small enough I'm hoping the Rippers won't bother with it. It will take us right to the bottom of Ruby

Avenue." She rolled down her window again as they passed the Morewood Terrace public housing units. It was quieter here. No sound of gunfire, the sirens all in the distance. Go figure: on a night where the rest of the city had descended into chaos and destruction, its most dangerous neighborhood was an oasis of peace.

There was definitely something wrong with that picture.

Pittsburgh would never be the same after tonight, she realized. Police presence in high-risk areas like Homewood, the North Side, Oakland, and the Hill would be intensified, diverted from low risk patrol responsibilities. Homeland Security would probably get involved, given Zapata's narcoterrorist designation. The CC TV initiative that had stalled would be placed front and center, until most of the city's populace was monitored.

The city's already strained budget would struggle to meet the new demands for protection against gang warfare. Lucy guessed that lower priority line items: social services, public transportation, nonessential police units like the bike patrol, parade unit, river patrol, school program... would all be curtailed or canceled outright.

The media would have a field day with it. Pittsburgh's psyche, its pride in emerging from the smoggy haze of its steel industry origins to become one of "America's most livable cities," would be forever scarred.

All because of a handful of men in a few short hours.

"Do they have the roads blocked off to keep us out?" she asked Haddad. "Or to keep everyone here in?"

He didn't answer, concentrating on avoiding the assortment of garbage cans, abandoned vehicles, and incongruous random objects—a kitchen oven, a wheelbarrow, a sleeping vagrant—that blocked their path and turned the narrow alley into an obstacle course.

As they approached Ruby Avenue, Lucy tried her radio. Nothing. The antenna had snapped off. No wonder it'd been so quiet. Dumb, dumb, dumb. She should have monitored communications instead of mooning over Haddad's Afghanistan deployment and calling Nick. She blew her breath out in frustration. She knew better. The emotions that had swept over her after what happened at the 911 Center were clouding her judgment. She couldn't let it happen again.

"Your radio working?"

"Here." He reached inside his vest and handed it to her. "I turned it off to save the battery since we had yours."

"Broke mine at the Comm Center." She clicked his on and listened to the latest on the NIMS channel. If anything the chaos and confusion had multiplied. Then she switched to the training channel. "Galloway, Walden, come in, this is Guardino."

A few moments later Taylor answered. "Hey, boss. Good to hear from you."

"Taylor. Tell me you have good news."

"For everyone else in the city, no joy. But I was able to trace that guy Andre Stone's phone—all the cell companies are being super responsive given the level of emergency. He's at 411 Ruby Avenue. Place called Kujo's."

"The Rippers' HQ."

"That's why it's good news. Jenna thought it would give you one target instead of two."

Lucy didn't like it. Too pat. But it was their only lead. "Jenna, you there?"

"I'm here." The sounds of a hospital could be heard in the background.

"How's Walden?"

"He'll be fine. The doctors have to operate, repair a vein in his leg, so he'll be here overnight."

At least he'd be safe.

"Taylor, any luck with Raziq's phone? A location on that would help."

"Last location on his phone was on Lexington, at the 911 Center. They must have ditched it because it hasn't moved from there. Jenna gave me the plate on the Escalade you saw. It's a rental. Traffic cams tracked it to Ruby Avenue, but there's no cameras on Ruby, sorry."

Haddad stopped the Mustang. They'd reached Ruby Avenue. All roads led here.

"Good work. Anything else that could help us before we head in?"

"We need more intel," Haddad put in, craning his head to look up and down the street.

Given the chaos disrupting the city tonight, Lucy thought they were damn lucky to get what they had already. Then she had an idea. "Taylor. Can you call your buddies over at the Air National Guard and see if they can help with a helicopter?"

"They're already dispatched. So are the Staties. Boss, we're fielding calls for help all over the city. There's just no one left."

She heard the strain in his voice. Nothing like the frustration of being on the ground in the middle of this mess. "How about one of those drones they used during the last Presidential visit?"

"Good idea. Those babies can read the warning label on a packet of cigarettes in your pocket. I should be able to feed you real time data once we get one up."

"Make it happen. In the meantime, we'll keep an eye out for Andre Stone, look for Raziq and his family, and see if we can find Victor Zapata while we're at it. Anything else you guys want while we're out and about?"

"Pamela's isn't far, I love their homemade macadamia nut brownies," Taylor said, his grin almost audible.

"Any chance for some backup?"

"I can get there but I'm not sure how long it will take me," Jenna said.

"Get here as fast as you can. But be careful. The gangs are blocking the roads—they might have more snipers out there as well."

"No problem, I can do stealth mode."

Right. With her looks, the only place Jenna'd pull off "stealth" would be on Project Runway.

"We'll tell you where to meet us. Until then we're going radio silent."

"You got it, boss." Taylor clicked off.

Lucy gathered her breath and turned to Haddad. "Head up Ruby Avenue, past Kujo's, see what we can see. Then we'll decide on the best approach."

Haddad nodded and made the right hand turn onto Ruby Avenue.

In some ways this neighborhood mirrored Raziq's in Point Breeze North. Closer to the Busway were the more commercial properties. As they drove away from it, they passed vacant lots where empty houses had been torn down by the city in an effort to curtail squatters and criminal enterprises. Then another of the Terrace public housing projects: 1970's-era ugly yellow brick single story duplexes crammed together. They were supposed to be less conducive to criminal activity than high-rise units, but she doubted it. A few charming Victorians, most of them brick but a few wood frame, stood among condemned houses and boarded-up stores.

The first vehicle they spotted was idling at a cross street. Lucy tightened her grip on her Remington. Then relaxed. It was a white church van driven by two nuns, complete with short, navy colored veils. As the Mustang drove past, the nuns looked just as startled to see Lucy and Haddad as they were to see the nuns.

"Slow down," Lucy said as they reached the base of the hill. Five brick row houses, each with its own individual flare when it came to ornamentation and trim, filled the block to their left. On the right side of the block there were several single-family frame houses that looked well cared for despite their crooked fences and sagging gutters. "Kujo's is two blocks up the hill. On our right."

"What's that church at the top?"

"Holy Trinity."

She wished the Mustang were another color. Black would have been nice, because as they began up the hill the number of people on the street—all men, all armed— went from zero to a dozen.

"That's it," she pointed to a red wood frame Victorian that had vehicles, mostly SUVs, triple-parked out front, almost completely blocking the road. A makeshift safety perimeter, Lucy realized.

Metal shutters covered the windows and men with machine-pistols patrolled the porch and stood on the roof on either side of the chimney. No sign of Victor Zapata's Escalade, but they couldn't dawdle long enough for Lucy to get a look at all the SUVs' plates.

Loud rap music boomed from the house, making Lucy wonder if anyone else actually lived on the block or if they'd long since been driven out by the noise.

"Can't see anything with those shutters. Keep going to Holy Trinity. We should be able to find a place to hide the car near there. Then we can come back on foot so we won't be so obvious."

Haddad drove up to the top of the hill and circled the block containing Holy Trinity church. There were a few lights visible in the convent behind the high stone wall that surrounded the compound. No lights visible in the church. So much for churches acting as sanctuaries in times of need, Lucy thought. After investigating as many clergy-related child abuse incidents as she had, she'd grown cynical about all religions.

They found a service drive on the block behind Ruby Avenue and backed into it, facing out so they could make a quick escape if they needed to.

They got out of the car and did a quick inventory and weapons check. Lucy's parka was long enough to conceal her ballistic vest and the Remington. Thankfully the parka was black, which hid the blood covering it, although she couldn't do anything about the smell. Haddad's overcoat was even longer, easily hiding his vest and M4. They both had their pistols and spare ammo. They were as ready as they were going to be.

"You sure about leaving the car?"

"It's too obvious. And it's not like it offers a lot of protection against automatic weapons."

"Times like this, I wouldn't mind driving a Humvee," Haddad muttered.

"Times like this, I wouldn't mind being bored to tears by *The Nutcracker*." She smiled, imagining Nick sitting in front of the TV, feet propped up, cat on his lap and dog by his side, snoring as he waited for her to come home. She closed her eyes for a second, letting the feeling sink into every fiber of her being. Nick and Megan were why she did what she did.

No way in hell she wasn't going to make it home to them, she vowed.

———◆———

MORGAN GLANCED OUT the window of the SUV to check on Nick's progress. He'd wrestled the bike up the embankment and over the guardrail. Now he was crouched down, examining the front tire.

Perfect. His prints would be all over the damn thing. She reached for his phone, took a deep breath in, and got ready for her performance. 9-1-1, her fingers pressed. The irritating tone of a busy signal answered.

What the hell? 911 couldn't be busy. They *had* to answer.

She tried again. Still busy.

Stabbed the digits one more time. This time there was a recording: *We're sorry, all circuits are busy at this time. Please try your call again. We apologize for any inconvenience.*

Inconvenience? Her plan depended on that 911 call coming from this phone, linked to this location, at this time. Recorded, irrefutable evidence.

She threw the phone down, wanting to scream.

Nick rapped on the window. "You okay?" he asked. "You look upset."

She stepped out of the car. "Just thinking how pissed off my dad will be that I wrecked my bike."

He carried the bike to the rear hatch. "It *is* a nice bike. But I think he'll be glad you weren't hurt."

Together they loaded the bike into the back. "Yeah, I guess. It was a birthday present. More money than he and mom could afford, but I really wanted it. I feel a little guilty now. Should have been more careful."

Nick slammed the hatch shut. "Let's get you home before they have time to worry. Where to?"

She gave him the address of the vacant house off Lincoln Avenue she'd appropriated, just a few miles from where they were. They drove there in silence, Morgan trying to decide how to get her plan back on track— invite him inside, ambush him there? Send him off and then call the police? Vanish and leave an anonymous tip?—and Nick thinking whatever boring thoughts normal people thought.

Morgan's father would have relished the abrupt derailment of a plan. He lived for the thrill of being totally out of control. At the whimsy of fate, he called it, often using an unexpected obstacle as an excuse to let loose with a frenzy of violence. *Taste the danger*, he'd sing to Morgan, his eyes wide with bloodlust.

But it was always Morgan who had to clean up after him when he tempted fate—and the police—with his rampages.

She understood the thrill—like him, she needed more and more intensity just to feel *anything*, like constantly sharpening a scalpel to cut through thick scar tissue.

It was as if her blood was electric, constantly simmering, needing fire, more fire, hotter fire, to finally boil so hot it burned. There was no greater hell than sitting, doing nothing, all that electricity buzzing in her veins and nowhere to go, nothing to do, knowing the next blaze would need to be bigger, brighter, bolder to get that same thrill.

Her father's thrills centered on sex and violence, an insatiable thirst that made him reckless and got him caught. Morgan wasn't like that. Maybe it was because she was a girl—no, not a girl, she'd met girls her age and she was nothing like them. She wasn't even like the older ones in high school or college although she could pass for one of them easily. She knew the right things to say, the right way to arrange her face and hair and clothes, understood their need to skirt the edge, thirsting for whatever would make them feel good: sex, booze, drugs, good grades, bad grades, taking risks, wielding power, acting out, acting like angels...

To Morgan they were all the same shade of beige. Boring. They'd never understand what a true thrill was: absolute, total control over someone else. Dominance. Manipulating their life, their future, every moment, every breath, every day until their death.

Better than sex—or so she assumed. She had a feeling she might never know for sure. Sex didn't interest her, not after what she'd seen. She had no intention of ever lying down, letting any man or woman control whether or not she felt pleasure.

The power Morgan felt—like when she'd decided if Jenna Galloway lived or died, or now, as she controlled Lucy's husband's destiny without either Lucy or Nick even knowing—*that* was Morgan's idea of a climax.

No blood, sweat, or tears involved.

Well, at least not hers.

Nick pulled into the driveway of the empty house she'd directed him to. He came around to her side of the SUV first, opened her door for her. Such a gentleman.

"Just park it by the garage," she told him as he lifted the bike from the back of the SUV. "Thanks again."

"Aren't you going to ask me in?" he said. "You wanted something more than a ride home, didn't you?"

She blinked. Startled. And it took a helluva lot to startle Morgan. "Excuse me?"

"You didn't have to go to all that trouble. Really, a phone call would have worked just as well."

Her fingers tightened on her knife. "What are you saying?"

"I'm saying it's cold out. Let's talk inside." He smiled at her, which only confused her even more. It was a gentle, fatherly smile. As if he knew exactly what she was thinking but still cared. "The disguise is quite good. But you made a mistake using my daughter's name, Morgan."

CHAPTER 22

FATIMA PULLED HER scarf around to cover both the baby and her face. A shrill wail escaped her as her body crumbled in on its self. The high-pitched noise warbled through the room, her shoulders heaving, body swaying, joined by the baby's shriek.

Andre wanted to comfort her, bundle her into his arms, pat her shoulder, anything to ease her pain. But all he could do was watch.

She shuddered to a stop, tears streaking her face. *"Inna Lillahae wa Inna Elaihae Rajae'uon."* Her voice quivered and broke as she recited the words over and over. Andre had no idea what they meant, but they seemed to comfort her.

She sat up, the head cloth falling free, and made soothing noises to the crying baby. Then she moved her eyes to gaze up at Andre's face. Bold move for a woman from her culture. But he understood. She was desperate.

"I'm going to get us out of here," Andre promised. Suddenly all his fear vanished. Didn't matter what the hell he looked like or how weak his body was. He was goddamned Dog Company and he had a job to do.

She met his gaze warily. Then nodded a fraction of an inch.

Good enough. Andre got to his feet and turned to the tool table and shelves to see what he had to work with.

Tin of black powder. Assorted sizes of PVC pipe. End caps. Wire. Darius said he needed Andre's bomb making skills, but clearly he'd already built some bombs on his own. Even had Andre's favorite special ingredient: highway flares.

Seeing all the bits and pieces they'd used to create their masterpieces when they were kids brought back memories. It'd never been about bombs or destruction— not for Andre, not until the Rippers recruited him and he couldn't say no without risking Grams. Back when he was young, it'd been about creating.

Beautiful, bright, colorful lights. Loud noises that were a call for attention, like a symphony gearing up for a concert. One year, he'd even held a fireworks display for the folks on Ruby Avenue—folks who never got to go to the official one down at the Point. He still remembered all that clapping and *ohhs* and *ahhs*. The rush of pride that for one night he'd been able to make everyone forget where they were.

For him creating fire was like painting or sculpting. He molded it, formed it—there was nothing to be frightened of. Fire was his partner. Maybe that lack of fear was why he'd rushed into the flames back in Hajji

Baba, only to emerge to find his men gunned down in an ambush.

In a warped way the fire had protected him from death, even as it had molded him in its own image. Something dangerous, something people should be frightened of. Out of control.

He shook the tin of black powder. Nearly empty. Useless if he wanted to build a bomb, but a bomb wouldn't help things. What they needed was a diversion.

He emptied a mason jar of nails, grabbed a few foam Sheetz cups from a pile of trash on the floor, shredded them into the jar, then poured kerosene from the space heater over the foam.

"What are you doing?" the woman asked.

"Jellied gas, the Brits call it." He carefully stirred the melting Styrofoam to evenly distribute it. "Napalm. Well, its bastard cousin."

She gasped. "You want to burn us alive?"

"Believe me, lady, playing with fire is the last thing I'd enjoy." The smell of the kerosene and melted foam burned his nostrils and scratched at the back of his throat. Flames dancing in delight, searing his flesh. Memory cramped his stomach with nausea. But if they were going to get out of here he'd need to renew an old acquaintance.

Fight fire with fire.

Or, in Darius' case, crazy with more crazy.

————◆————

JENNA TRIED NOT to feel guilty about leaving Walden at the hospital, but secretly she was elated. Yeah, it sucked for Walden to be left behind, but he didn't need her to babysit. She re-loaded her AR-15 and SIG Sauer, pocketed the rest of her spare ammo—not as much as she'd like, but not as if she had time to go shopping for more—hopped into the front seat of the Tahoe, weapons close at hand, and set the radio in the front cup holder.

"What's my fastest route?" she asked Taylor.

"Use your lights and sirens, take the bus lane up Fifth," he directed.

"I thought Fifth was blocked," she said as she pulled out of the ER parking lot and turned down the hill.

"It is, but not until you get up past Penn. I'm going to have you turn before then."

"Just don't land me in the middle of a traffic jam."

"If we can get you out of Oakland, traffic looks clear." He paused. "Weird. Traffic cams look like the residential areas are quiet but there's now a new surge of people heading towards the bombsites in Squirrel Hill and Point Breeze. You'd think they'd be going the other way."

"Lookee-loos," Jenna diagnosed. "Steer me clear."

She followed his directions, weaving through back streets and sometimes down alleys seemingly at random, encountering little traffic. The streets Taylor led her through were peaceful, quiet. With the cell towers' overcapacity, not even Morgan could get through to disturb her.

It'd been weeks since Jenna had felt this relaxed.

How sick was that? Headed into a gang war was more calming than her day-to-day existence juggling work and Morgan? She shook her head. She was leading one fucked up life, thanks to Saint Lucy. And to Morgan, the girl-wonder-psychopath.

Taylor's voice crackled through the radio, interrupting her thoughts. "Okay, here's where it gets tricky."

Jenna straightened, at full alert. "How so?"

"Looks like the only route not blocked is Frankstown Avenue."

"Why would they block everything except that one road?" Jenna asked.

"I'm guessing it's their escape route."

"I think the SWAT guys call that a fatal funnel."

"Not much I can do about it," Taylor said apologetically.

"So you want me to navigate through a crowd of gangbangers? Thought you were supposed to be some kind of a genius."

"Hear me out. It looks like they only left a few men to guard it," Taylor said.

"Really? And how accurate is your data?"

"No traffic cams there, so all I've got is satellite imagery from twenty minutes ago." He quickly added. "It's the best I can do."

"What about that drone Lucy asked you about?"

"They're still getting ready to deploy. It will be at least another ten-twenty minutes before we get any images. Do you want to wait? It's your call."

Jenna thought. She knew the smart thing to do would be to wait. But she was Lucy and David's only back up. Twenty minutes could mean life or death. Besides, she was the one who'd found Andre and maybe the cartel's command center. It was only fair that she be there during the takedown.

"Give me the route. How tough can a couple of Rippers be?"

———•———

MORGAN HELD THE front door open for Nick. He didn't hesitate crossing the threshold. Didn't seem alarmed that she was behind him. Was he a fool? He hadn't seemed like one in the sessions with Jenna that she'd overheard.

He looked around the living room of the pseudo-Frank Lloyd Wright split level. "The people who live here—"

"I didn't kill them. If that's what you're asking." She gestured for him to sit in one of the leather chairs grouped around a coffee table. "Why? Would that have been a deal breaker?"

He gazed right into her eyes. Not many people could do that. "Yes."

His nonchalance was irritating. "Don't worry. They're visiting their kids in Florida." She sat down. Finally he did as well.

"You're not afraid of me. Why aren't you afraid of me?" She was genuinely curious. Usually she didn't really care about what was going on inside anyone else's head. But Nick intrigued her.

"Why should I be?"

"You said you knew who I was. Then you know I've killed people. Lots of people." Three. Nothing compared to her father's total, but three more than the majority of the population had.

"I know you've killed. For your father."

She frowned, not sure she liked his implication that her father had some kind of control over her actions. But it had certainly been more than *with* her father. "Do you think I can't kill without him?"

"I know you can."

"You should be afraid."

"You have no reason to kill me. It's not in your best interests. And you're smart enough to put your own safety ahead of a few seconds of cheap, meaningless thrills."

"You think life is meaningless?"

"No. Not at all. I think life is precious. Sacred even. I think the momentary excitation you get from taking it is meaningless." He took a deep breath, his gaze traveling up to the vaulted ceiling as if in deep thought. "Your father. He was out of control at the end, wasn't he? Chasing that adrenalin rush without a care for his well being... or yours."

He was right. Too right. Morgan didn't like that. She was used to being the only person in a room who saw the whole truth. "I'm not my father. Who's to say what I might enjoy?"

His gaze locked onto hers and he crossed his legs, getting comfortable. "You're right. You're not your father. And you've his experience to learn from. That puts you ahead of the game."

Silence as he waited.

"Does Lucy know?" Morgan asked. The question came half out of pride, half out of shame. Why couldn't she stop watching Lucy and her family? If she wanted revenge she should have just taken care of them all ages ago. She told herself she was waiting, wanting them to suffer. That was a lie. They weren't suffering. They weren't scared.

They were… happy.

"Of course she does. Megan spotted you too. Until tonight, I've been the only one without a Morgan sighting."

"It's not a game!" She jumped to her feet.

He shook his head slightly as if chiding himself. "I didn't mean to imply it was. I was making fun of myself. When I'm with my patients I'm usually the most observant one in the room, but compared to Lucy and Megan—well, let's just say they run circles around me. It's hard coming home and being treated as the absent-minded professor."

There was just enough bitterness in his tone to let her know he spoke the truth. "Your IQ is higher than Lucy's."

He gave a one-shouldered shrug. "IQ isn't everything. Look at you. You haven't had formal schooling but you're brilliant. Anyone who could hack into a database and find my IQ, who could elude the authorities as long as you have—"

"My father used to say that the University of Life was the only school worth attending." Again with her father. Whose footsteps she really didn't want to follow, not leading right into a jail cell. If Morgan had one goal, it was to never be caught like he had been.

Then why was she so obsessed with Lucy and her family? With taunting Jenna? Risking everything playing these games when she could be half way across the country doing whatever she wanted? She had to be nuts, because she couldn't understand this compulsion. And she wanted to. Needed to. So she could regain control of her own life.

"Don't you want to talk? Analyze me, fix me? Isn't that what you shrinks do?"

"I don't want to change you, Morgan. I'm not going to try to fix you. You are what you are."

She squinted at him, suspicious. "You don't think I need therapy?"

He chuckled. "Only thing therapy would do is fine-hone your acting skills. So, no. I don't consider you a good candidate."

"You think I'm hopeless, then. Beyond redemption." Anger spilled over into her voice. Usually she didn't feel emotions, not this strongly, but Nick's calm Zen-like demeanor and refusal to cower before her was infuriating.

"Not hopeless. I wouldn't say that. You have a remarkable intelligence. Abundant talent. Why would I think that's beyond redemption?" He seemed honestly concerned about her answer. As if he cared.

Had to be an act. No one cared. Not her mother. Not her fathers—either of them. Never had. Never would. It was just Morgan against the world.

The only problem was... deep down inside, she wanted more. She wanted what Lucy's daughter got without asking; she wanted to belong, to be part of something bigger. Even though in the end she knew she'd ruin it. She couldn't help herself. It was in her nature.

"You ever hear the story of the scorpion and the frog?"

He nodded, a smile playing across his face, making him look younger. "You're saying that because of your nature you can't change."

"Something like that."

"Seems an awfully abrupt conclusion to make. After all, scientists and philosophers have been arguing about nature versus nurture for centuries. You've made up your mind after what, thirteen years on this earth?"

"Fourteen," she corrected him. Wondered why she did—usually she encouraged people to believe her lies. Anything but the truth. That she guarded, kept for herself. Not with Nick. Which made him dangerous. Almost as dangerous as Morgan herself.

"You think I can change? Stop being a sociopath? Prove it. Tell me how."

"I didn't say that. I believe there are some traits hardwired into our brains."

"Like sociopathy?" She'd read every book available on the subject, taken Hare's test, probably knew more about it than he did—hell, she lived it, saw up close what her father did. She was the world's expert on sociopaths.

"Like sociopathy. Brain scans on young children who grow up to be sociopaths show aberrant anatomy and activity, particularly in the amygdala and prefrontal cortex."

"I know." She waved her hand impatiently. "I've read Wallace and Raine."

"But you want to know what it means for you, Morgan Ames."

"Yes." She narrowed her eyes at him, slid her knife from its sheath. "Tell me the truth. If I'm going to be like my father and this," she twisted the knife to reflect the overhead light, made the shadows dance across its polished blade, "is all there is, then I want to know. Now."

To her surprise, he brushed off his knees as if they'd just finished tea and crumpets, and stood. "I'm sorry, Morgan. But I have a patient who needs me and I don't have the time tonight." He smiled at her, a gentle smile that crinkled the edge of his eyes. Not made up. Genuine. He meant what he was saying. "Call me if you want to talk. But I think you know the answer already."

She feinted with the knife. He ignored her, reaching into his pocket for his car keys. "Take care of yourself."

He walked to the door, opened it. Morgan ran after him, still holding the knife. "No," she shouted. "Don't go. You can't go. I won't let you."

He turned back, said in a sad voice, "There's your first lesson. You need to know when to let people go. Trust that they'll come back, be there for you."

"You said I'm not your patient but you talk like I'm, I'm," she struggled for a word, "a friend?" Hated that it came out as a question. She was the one with the knife. She held his life in her hand. Why couldn't he see that?

"No. Not a friend. You haven't earned that right yet." He went down the steps and got into the car, leaving her there. Alone. Holding a knife with only her own blood on it.

"Good luck," he called as he backed out of the driveway.

Morgan let him go. She felt both powerful and wistful as he drove away. Her finger caressed the blade. She could have had so much fun with him.

Still could. She went inside and activated the spyware she'd inserted onto his phone. Less than a minute after leaving her and he was calling some patient, acting like she didn't even exist.

She listened as he left a message, saying he was on his way. The knife blade glinted in the glow of her laptop's screen, mocking her. He never mentioned her. Not even to boast about his good deed for the evening. As if he'd forgotten all about her already.

He was alive only because of her mercy. Yet it was as if nothing had even happened. She should have known better. Her father always said, no good deed went unpunished.

She slumped in her chair, trying to imagine how the night would have felt if she had killed him.

Nothing. No thrill at the thought. Just… nothing.

Kill a man, save a man… it didn't matter. It was all meaningless.

CHAPTER 23

LUCY AND HADDAD crossed through the alley beside
Holy Trinity to reach Ruby Avenue.

"Let's try around back." Lucy kept the Remington at
the ready, holding it down by her side where her parka
covered it. No one seemed to notice as they circled
behind a house and slid into the brick-paved alley leading
behind Kujo's.

The houses bordering the alley had either privacy
fences or garages as their rear property border, making
the alley feel claustrophobic. Three houses ahead, SUVs
facing both directions blocked each end of the alley.
Kujo's. Armed men gathered between the vehicles,
leaning against a garage, an old converted carriage house,
huddled against the wind, sharing a smoke. There were
no windows on the garage, at least not on the side she
and Haddad approached from.

The house beside Kujo's had a flat-roofed garage
along the alley. On this side of it was a large maple.

Hugging the shadows, and moving slowly so as to not attract the attention of the men behind Kujo's, she and Haddad made it to the tree. Lucy handed Haddad her shotgun. He crouched and gave her a boost up into the lowermost fork of the trunk. From there it was an easy shimmy out across the branches until she could see into the yard behind the Ripper's headquarters.

No shutters on the windows at the back. Lights blazed from every room and she could make out the silhouettes of naked women and of more men with guns. The yard was empty except for broken pieces of lumber and a pile of trash near the back porch. The carriage house had lights on as well but she was at the wrong angle to see inside. Two men stood guard in front of its door, whetting her curiosity. The small building would make an excellent place to keep hostages. Easily defendable, easy for the Rippers to escape from.

She retreated until she had a good view of the SUVs. With her night vision monocular she could read the plates. One of them was Zapata's Escalade. Bingo.

Lucy climbed back down, accepting Haddad's help to get her to the ground silently. They backed out of the alley and around the corner before speaking.

"Zapata's SUV is there. And there are people under guard in the carriage house," she reported. "Two armed men on the house side."

"And three more in the alley. How many inside the house?"

Lucy shrugged. "At least a dozen, maybe more. Women as well but only the men had weapons that I could see." Or clothes for that matter.

"So the odds are what, ten to one?"

"If we're lucky."

They were both silent for a long moment. But neither mentioned retreat. Lucy thought about it, thought hard about it, fear knotting her gut. Then she remembered the photo of Fatima and her family. The hope in Mina's eyes, the laughter in her little sister's.

"We can't let the bastards get away with it," she finally said. It was the only answer she had, the only way her job, her *world*, made sense. The only way she could face her husband and daughter when she got home.

"From the tree you can get onto the neighbor's garage roof," she told Haddad. "You cover the men in the alley and slow down any reinforcements from the house. I'll take care of the two at the door. In and out, easy as pie."

His smile had nothing to do with pleasure. More like greeting fate. His game face. For the first time since they'd met, Lucy liked the man. "Sounds like a plan."

———•———

FRANKSTOWN AVENUE HAD definitely seen better days. Vacant lots overgrown with weeds, abandoned service stations and stores, brick single family homes that had broken windows and rusted cars in their front yards. No Christmas spirit here.

Jenna slowed the Tahoe at Finley. The street was empty. A block ahead the road dipped beneath train tracks, going through a narrow stone tunnel. It was a perfect place for an ambush.

"Don't suppose you've got eyes on me yet?" she asked Taylor.

"Sorry, no. They had to divert the drone to help Zone Five. Figured the drone would be the best way to spot the snipers so they can get their wounded out."

Okay. Injured police officers took priority. Still. "I don't like the looks of this tunnel up ahead. There's no movement, but it would be a great place for an ambush." Hell, it was so dark in the tunnel there could be a whole fleet of Rippers waiting and she'd never know it. She grabbed the AR-15 and used its sights. There was enough ambient light for her to verify that there wasn't any movement. And definitely no vehicles. Finally, some good news.

"Last images I have show a black SUV parked on the north side of the tunnel," Taylor reported. "I couldn't see anyone on the ground."

Jenna turned her lights off, put the Tahoe in gear, opened the windows on both sides, and angled the AR-15 so she could grab it fast. Her SIG Sauer she kept in one hand, steering with the other. "Okay, boys, let's see who's chicken."

She barely let the brake out, the Tahoe gliding down the block almost silently. Gunfire sounded—maybe two, three blocks away. Better cover noise than the crickets.

Initially she'd planned to race past the Rippers' vehicle. But she didn't like the idea of having them at her back. When they made no sign that they had spotted her, she stopped the Tahoe at the tunnel's entrance. Leaving it idling, she crept out, sidling through the shadows, her SIG at the ready.

The tunnel smelled of dust and diesel exhaust. She pressed her back to the stone wall on the north side. Her coat would be ruined, but she'd worry about that later.

At the far edge of the tunnel a stone wall sloped diagonally down from the train tracks above to the street level. Behind it a few trees provided a bit of cover. She knelt beside the wall, peered between the trees, and spotted the SUV. Music came through its open windows and the interior was filled with a faint glow from the instrument panel and their cigarettes. Two men in the front, each with a Mac-10 machine pistol resting on their windowsills. No one in the back.

They were talking, laughing about something, looking at each other and away from her. She took her cue and ran at a crouch below their eye line, making it to a tree a few feet away from the passenger side of the car.

She raised her SIG, took a few deep breaths. The men were so close she could smell their cigarettes. Not men. *Targets.* Just like at the 911 Center. Targets. That's all.

Exhaling, she stood and fired two quick headshots into the man nearest her. His Mac-10 clattered to the ground as his grip relaxed, making Jenna jump. The man in the driver's seat fumbled to turn his weapon around but was too slow. Two more shots and he was dead as well.

She grabbed both guns then raced back to where the Tahoe waited, leaving the dead men behind.

"I'm clear," she radioed Taylor, marveling at how normal her voice sounded. She'd just executed two men. Christ, she could go to prison if anyone found out. After all, they'd been armed but no clear-cut threat. She didn't even identify herself or give them a chance. Panic trembled along her nerves, making her hands shake and her vision dance as she drove.

"Did they give you any trouble?"

"Drove right past, they didn't even notice," she lied.

"Maybe they weren't Rippers after all. About time we got lucky. Okay, let me give you the route to Lucy. You're about six minutes out."

"Sounds like a plan." Jenna swallowed hard, her mouth dry. Yet her eyes kept tearing up, forcing her to blink fast to see the street before her. Not tears, just dust from the tunnel.

At least that's what she told herself.

———◆———

"THIS IS CHANNEL 4'S EYE IN THE SKY WITH EXCLUSIVE FOOTAGE OF THE MASSIVE DAMAGE TO THE ALLEGHENY COUNTY 911 COMMUNICATION CENTER IN POINT BREEZE. AS YOU CAN SEE, MOST OF THE WINDOWS HAVE BEEN BLOWN OUT AND THE FRONT WALL OF THE BUILDING HAS BEEN VIRTUALLY DEMOLISHED BY WHAT WITNESSES ARE CALLING A HUGE FIREBALL. FLAMES STILL RAGE INSIDE THE BUILDING AS FIREFIGHTERS WORK TO CONTAIN THE BLAZE.

"AUTHORITIES AREN'T COMMENTING YET ON THE POSSIBLE CAUSE OF THE EXPLOSION BUT MINUTES BEFOREHAND A PROPANE TANKER WAS INVOLVED IN A TRAFFIC ACCIDENT AT THE INTERSECTION ADJACENT TO THE COMMUNICATION CENTER AND WAS ENGULFED IN FLAMES.

"Unverified reports of gunfire have also been received but so far authorities aren't commenting as to their accuracy."

CHAPTER 24

ANDRE CLIMBED A rickety wooden ladder leading to the loft above the garage. He needed a good vantage point to launch his firebombs from. The stale air tickled his nose even though it'd probably been a century since any hay was stored here.

At the front of the loft a pair of windows faced the house. He opened one; it swung in and up to a hook waiting to hold it. Nice. He glanced down. He could drop down on the two guards at the door if he wanted to. Not his plan, but it was good to have options.

On the alley side was an identical window. It gave him more resistance than the first window, but with a few sharp tugs, it finally opened. He stood beside the opening in case any of the men below looked up. There were two SUVs, one on either side of the garage, parked to block the alley and facing away from the house. Positioned for a quick getaway. Three men stood guard in the middle— at least they thought they were standing guard, though they were holding their weapons like they were loaves of bread and sharing a smoke.

It was an insult to expect men like that to last more than a few seconds with a Dog Company Marine.

To his surprise, he found himself humming as he climbed back down the ladder, ignoring the newfound aches as his muscles and scar tissue stretched. He hadn't done that since before the Marines. An old song his grams had enjoyed, "Summertime" from *Porgy and Bess*.

Fuses for delayed detonation were always a challenge, but he found what he needed scattered among the materials on the workbench, augmented by a few choice items lifted from the trash. Waste not, want not.

He divided the napalm into two glass soda bottles, set the fuses, found a long-handled BBQ lighter, and turned back to Fatima.

"I'm going to launch these from up in the hayloft and go out the alley." He nodded to the ladder leading up to the floor above.

She hugged the baby closer. "You're leaving me?"

"No. No. I'm going to create a diversion, then I'll escape." Her eyes widened in fear. "I'll take care of the guards outside and open this door," he pointed to the door to the alley, "for you. Then we leave. Together. Understand?"

She nodded. "We'll find my husband?"

He sucked in his breath, looking away. "Yes. Then we'll find Raziq. Get ready. Okay?"

"Okay." A tentative smile. Best he could hope for.

He carefully took the firebombs up the ladder to the hayloft. First, the house. He lit the fuse and heaved the bottle out the window, aiming for the trash near the porch.

The glass shattered and flames whooshed through the darkness with a gratifying energy. The men below shouted and ran toward the fire.

Andre didn't waste time watching them. He ran to the alley-side window and aimed his second firebomb at the SUV farthest away. He could have simply thrown it at the group of men below him; it would have taken them all out, they were that close together, but he didn't have the heart. The thought of watching them burn, smelling that smell, hearing those screams… it didn't matter if it was life or death, he just couldn't do it. Besides, he couldn't risk starting a fire that close to the door Fatima and the baby would need to exit through.

Instead, as they looked toward the SUV now on fire, he dropped on top of the nearest man. A quick elbow to the throat and he had the man's gun, a Mac-10. Before he could turn it on the other two, one of them dropped.

Andre whipped around as a second shot cracked through the air, taking care of the final guard. The shooter was above them—ah, the neighbor's garage. A man jumped down from the roof and came running down the alley. It was David Haddad, the DEA agent Andre had worked with in Kandahar.

"Haddad," he called as he unlatched the large sliding door. "The hell you doing here?"

The DEA agent whirled, raising his weapon at Andre. "Drop the gun!"

Andre placed the Mac-10 on the ground and kicked it behind him so that it skidded towards the side of the garage. "Whoa, friendly, friendly. It's me, Andre Stone."

Haddad hesitated. "Stone?"

Right, the mask. "In the flesh, so to speak. There's a woman and baby inside. Help me get this open."

Haddad hesitated then nodded. Together, they heaved against the door, sliding it open. Andre rushed inside just as the front door to the garage opened and a dark-haired woman ran through it, shotgun raised. Fatima cowered against the wall, twisting to protect her baby.

"Put that down, you're scaring her," he shouted to the woman. "Fatima, it's okay. Come with me."

"This is Andre Stone," Haddad told the woman.

She jerked her chin in a nod. "Lucy Guardino. Thanks for the fireworks," she told Andre. "Let's save the reunions for later." She slammed the front door shut. Gunfire immediately shook the small building. "Go. I'll cover you."

Fatima stood frozen. Andre reached for her arm but she jerked away, crying in fear.

"Come on, come on," Haddad yelled, moving to cover their retreat from the alley.

"Fatima, we have to go. Now," Andre said, trying to keep his voice calm. He reached for her again. Ignoring her fear and grabbing her arm, he jerked her out the door.

The dark-haired woman, Lucy, followed them. She'd just crossed the threshold into the alley when the front door burst open. Four men with guns swarmed into the garage followed by Darius and a short, slender Hispanic man in a suit.

Andre ignored them. Because there was another man with them. Rashid Raziq.

He dove to the ground, grabbed the Mac-10 he'd dropped earlier. Raised the weapon, ready to shoot, wanting to shoot. Just as his finger slipped from the trigger guard onto the trigger, Fatima and the baby crossed his line of fire.

———•———

As JENNA HEADED towards Ruby Avenue, her phone rang. The call came in labeled Nick Callahan. A favorite number for Morgan to spoof once she'd learned about Jenna going to see Nick for counseling. Jenna almost ignored it, really was in no mood to coddle the adolescent psychopath, but knew better than to piss off Morgan.

"Hello, Morgan."

"He made it so easy," she said with a sigh that Jenna couldn't tell was real or faked. Who was she kidding? Morgan didn't have any real emotions.

"Morgan, what did you do?"

"Is this how you people live? Walking around so… exposed? He looked right at me, Jenna. Right at me."

Jenna clenched her fist around the steering wheel and fought to control her breathing. Who was it? One of the guys she'd met during the last month? Had she been the one to lead them to a killer? Or was it someone off the street, an innocent bystander? "Tell me what happened."

"Vulnerable. You're all so vulnerable. And you don't even see."

"Morgan—"

"Relax. I couldn't do it. It just wasn't fun anymore. Not like with my father."

Morgan's father. There was a role model—a sadistic serial killer specializing in kidnap, rape, and torture. A man who schooled his children to follow in his footsteps, make Daddy proud.

"You didn't do it. Why not?" Jenna tried to reel the girl in. She didn't tell Morgan that tonight was probably the one night she could get away with murder. Like Jenna just had. No. She was nothing like Morgan. Those men had to die; they would have killed Jenna. It was self-defense. Killing them might have saved dozens of lives down the line.

Another sigh. A pause as if Morgan was uncertain—but Morgan was never uncertain. The girl was the most determined, confident person Jenna had ever met. And that included Saint Lucy. "I'm not sure why I didn't kill him. I felt—empty. Like why bother? It wasn't going to give me what I needed. Not like it did for my father."

"Maybe you need something else to focus on."

"Don't try to shrink me, Jenna." Morgan's tone had an edge to it.

"I'm not. But," Jenna hesitated. She hated this, these mind games, giving Morgan a glimpse inside her soul. "You sound like you're at a crossroads."

Another pause. Damn, she'd pushed too hard. Jenna was certain Morgan was going to hang up, change her mind and go kill again.

"I see politicians on the commercials, read about rich bankers and CEOs. They get it. They're like me. But you people… you're all so blind." Morgan's tone was filled with emotion that sounded genuine.

Granted it was disdain mixed with confusion, but it reminded Jenna of her own emotional turmoil when she was about Morgan's age. Her grandfather—the only adult she'd ever trusted or respected—had died, leaving her with parents who couldn't stop bickering or using her to hurt each other long enough to give a damn.

"I could be anything," Morgan finished with a note of triumph. "There's a whole world of you... sheep... out there and I could do anything I wanted and none of you could stop me."

Now she sounded like a toddler out of control, searching for boundaries that weren't there. No, not a toddler. A normal, out-of-control teenager. Just like Jenna had been at her age. Damn, where was Lucy when Jenna needed parenting advice?

The police radio crackled in the background, reminding Jenna of how many people might die tonight. Yet here she was, talking a psychopath through an existential crisis.

How much time and effort had she wasted on Morgan already? Was it worth it?

Not when facing what could well be the last night of her life.

"I have to go, Morgan."

"No," Morgan snapped. "You know the rules, Jenna."

"Sorry, kid. You're going to have to play your sick games with someone else. I've got work to do. You wouldn't understand. People are dying. They need my help."

Jenna hung up, feeling free to take a deep breath for the first time since last month. She pressed down on the accelerator, blowing through a red light, streetlights rushing past, blurring at the edge of her vision. Places to be, things to do, people who needed her.

Despite the smudge of fire appearing above the rooftops, the howl of sirens coming from every direction, the staccato bursts of gunfire heard in the distance, Jenna couldn't help but smile. She had no idea why. It was as if her body and mind had been scoured clean. No, emptied, that's what she felt. Empty. But in a good way. Kind of like the feeling Morgan had been trying to describe.

As if anything was possible.

CHAPTER 25

IF ANDRE HADN'T been counting on him to get his grandmother to safety, Nick would have pulled over on the side of the road and puked his guts out.

As it was, all he could do was swallow bile and work to stop his hands from trembling. He tried to do a breathing exercise, like the ones he used for his patients, but all he could think of was the blood on Morgan's knife. Bright red. As if it was fresh.

It could have been his.

One wrong word, one wrong look, that's all it would have taken.

He'd felt fear before, of course. But it was always fear for others' wellbeing. For his patients, like Andre, who'd been verging on full-blown agoraphobia and clinical depression when Nick first met him. For Megan, when she was sick a few months ago. Fear for Lucy every damn day she strapped on her gun and went to work.

Tonight was the first time he'd ever come so close to being killed.

He fumbled for his phone, trying to call the police again. Morgan was far too dangerous to be allowed to wander the streets. All he got was a busy signal.

She'd surprised him. More impulse control than he'd expected after hearing about her violent upbringing. She reminded him in some ways of Megan: trying so hard to act like an adult, yet no clue about who she really was or wanted to be.

At least he'd been able to help Morgan think twice about following in her father's footsteps. Otherwise, he doubted he would have left alive.

He tried calling Lucy but the call was dropped before it connected. What was up with the damn cell towers? The weather was clear. As he approached Homewood he realized the streets were empty of cars. And a lot of helicopters flew overhead.

Lincoln Avenue was blocked near Route 8, an eighteen-wheeler lay on its side, sprawled across both lanes, but he was able to circle through the side streets to Ruby Avenue. He turned off his Garth Brooks CD and listened. Gunfire. Andre had said something was going to happen tonight.

Nick tried Lucy one more time. Circuits busy. Damn. If she was home, she'd be pissed—they'd already missed the curtain on *The Nutcracker.* Usually it was Lucy who made them late for events. He frowned. She was not going to be happy when she heard why he'd missed their date night. Talk of Morgan Ames always brought out the mother-bitch side of Lucy.

She was kinda sexy when she bristled with over-protective energy, but he'd never tell her that. It was one of the few secrets he kept from her.

He toyed with the idea of adding one more to the list; maybe not telling her about his encounter with Morgan. After all, it'd ended just fine.

No. He'd do what he always did and tell her everything. She'd do what she always did—get upset, then grow quiet and do whatever needed to be done to protect him and Megan. Probably send them and her mom away on a vacation that she'd find an excuse to back out of at the last minute. Anything to clear the way so she could hunt Morgan on her own.

She'd wanted to do that last month, had even hired a private security firm. Both he and Megan had rebelled at the thought of living the rest of their lives patrolled and restrained and secured. Lucy had reluctantly given in. Now Nick was glad—it had probably saved some poor bodyguard's life.

Still deep in thought but feeling calmer, he pulled up to Andre's house, the middle one of five quaint brick row houses. A faint ripple of light could be seen through the curtains in the front window. He ran up the steps and rang the bell. "Esther, it's Nick."

A few moments later a woman using an elegantly carved wooden cane opened the door. She was slight of build with gray hair in tight curls and a wide smile. Esther was virtually blind, ravaged by diabetes, but fiercely independent. And despite her infirmities she still baked the best homemade apple cake Nick had had since he left Virginia.

"Nick! What a surprise. Come in, come in. Join the party."

Party? Nick closed the door behind him as Esther hobbled down the hall, past the front parlor, and into the dining room.

"Be sure to lock that, now," she called over her shoulder. "Bad times out there tonight."

"What?" He glanced up the steps. No lights on upstairs that he could see. "Did Andre make it back yet?"

The front parlor was dark, the thick drapes pulled tight—first time he'd ever been here and seen the drapes pulled shut like that, no lights on. Esther had enough sight remaining that having lights on helped her navigate more easily.

"Andre sent me to get you," he said as he followed her.

He walked down the hall and turned into the windowless dining room sandwiched between the parlor and the kitchen at the rear of the house. Esther's hospital bed was against the kitchen wall. The heavy oak pocket doors to both the front room and the kitchen were both shut. The antique table that usually featured a lace runner and pair of silver candlesticks had been pulled out from the far wall and transformed into mission control.

Five women, all in their sixties and seventies, sat around the table, each with their own laptop. Several also had cell phones and were busy texting. Two others had earphones on and were listening intently to broadcasts from their computers.

"Got another fire. The old shoe store on Bennett," one of the ladies with earphones reported. "And looters at the East Liberty Target."

Fingers typed furiously.

"Fifth's blocked as well," said another into her computer. A woman's face was on it. They were Skyping, Nick realized. "Sister Agnes, did you copy? Looks like Frankstown is your only open route."

"I'm on it," the woman on the computer screen said.

Nick turned to Esther. "What's going on?"

"Tweeting and texting. Someone's got to let folks know where the latest trouble is."

"Trouble? You mean the Rippers?" Andre had said he was worried about the Rippers threatening Esther, but glancing at the map on one of the computers there were red highlights over most of the city. Except Homewood. That was funny. Usually Homewood was known as one of the most dangerous areas of the city. Strange for so much to be happening around it. "And the nun?"

"Nuns. Sister Agnes and Sister Patrice. They've got the van out, picking up folks and bringing them back to Holy Trinity for safekeeping. So far we've been spared but we don't know how long that will last."

"We're their eyes and ears," one of the other ladies said. "Margot, there's another bomb threat. This one at the Federal Building."

"Esther, Andre asked me to take you somewhere safe." Then the lady's words registered: *another* bomb threat?

"Nick." Esther reached over, finding his arm, trailing her fingers down to pat his hand. "Nowhere's safe in this city. Not tonight."

Tires squealed in the distance. At least Nick thought it was the distance. The row house's thick walls and doors muffled the street sounds. It wasn't until gunfire crashed through the upstairs, the sound of glass breaking and wood splintering echoing through the house, that he realized they were right outside.

He tried to cover Esther's body with his own, but she pushed him off. "I am not about to die a coward. Not at the hands of a bunch of no good drug dealers."

A second salvo of bullets drowned out the rest of her words.

———◆———

HEY GUYS, ANYONE ELSE HAVING TROUBLE WITH 911 TONIGHT? MY DOG'S BEEN GONE THREE DAYS NOW, COULD USE SOME HELP #PGH911FAIL

#PGH911FAIL @JOEPIZZA HEAR YOUR PAIN MAN, COPS DON'T CARE JACK 'BOUT WORKING MEN TRAPPED BY THEIR FASCIST CURFEW

@STEELERLUVER: BROKE DOWN ON PARKWAY WEST NO HELP FROM COPS NO HELP FROM 911 WTF DO WE PAY TAXES FOR? #PGH911FAIL

F*&IN COPS WON'T ANSWER DAMN PHONE NEIGHBOR PARKED IN FRONT OF MY HOUSE, MOVED MY PARKING CHAIR CAN YOU BELIEVE THAT SH%$??? WHAT'S THIS CITY COMING TO? #PGH911FAIL

@PROUDGRANNY REPORT OF SHOOTING PENN CIRCLE EAST ANYONE CONFIRM? STAY SAFE OUT THERE #PGH911FAIL

CHAPTER 26

LUCY SAW ZAPATA enter the garage with his men. Raziq was with him. She raised her shotgun almost without thinking. Zapata was unarmed, but God, she'd never wanted to kill anyone more in her life. All she could smell was the stench of innocent blood; all she could see were the bodies of slaughtered civilians piled high at the 911 Center.

"Drop your weapons," she shouted. She and Haddad were outnumbered and probably outflanked, but it was worth a shot. "Give us Raziq."

Before the men could respond, Fatima and the baby crossed into the line of fire.

Shit, shit, shit. She lowered her gun. The others still had her in their sights but obviously they wanted Fatima alive. She backed away.

"Fatima," the man in the mask, Stone, shouted, shoving Lucy aside as he scrambled to his feet. "No. Don't go."

Haddad slid the heavy wooden door shut, blocking their view. The men on the other side opened fire. Lucy threw the bolt to latch the door. Then she turned her Remington on Stone. "Give me the gun."

"Damn it. Why did she go with them?" Stone asked, ignoring her demand, but not resisting when Lucy yanked the Mac-10 from him.

"We've got company," Haddad shouted. An SUV had appeared at the far end of the alley, down the hill. "Let's go." He grabbed the door of Zapata's Escalade. "The keys are in the ignition."

"No," Lucy said. "We need to track them. Leave your phone."

She used the Mac-10 to shoot the tires of the SUV facing away from the Escalade. Making Zapata's choice of getaway vehicles easy. When she turned back, Haddad had his phone out and was slipping it under the cargo mat at the rear of the Escalade. He slammed the hatch down.

Together with Stone they ran up the alley away from the approaching SUV. Shots flew above them but they were out of range of the machine pistols. Angry curses followed as the men were blocked by the other SUVs near the garage. Once they were a few blocks up the alley and out of sight of the men following, they climbed onto a trash bin and jumped over a privacy fence into someone's back yard. Stone stumbled a bit on the climb over the fence, but otherwise kept up with them.

Lucy wasn't sure about Andre Stone. He'd been trying to help Fatima and the baby escape, yet he'd almost shot them when they ran to Raziq. Haddad said Stone blamed Raziq for his injuries. Maybe Stone had been using Fatima and the baby to lure Raziq into the open where he could kill him? Had this been some kind of elaborate trap, using the Rippers and Zapata to spring it?

No. Zapata obviously was the leader. Why was Stone there, then? What was his role in all this?

Her head hurt just thinking about it. She had a nice goose egg on the side of her scalp, but the bleeding had stopped. Unfortunately after each adrenalin surge faded, she found more bruises and aches to catalogue. What was really painful, though, was finding Raziq and his family only to lose them again.

Waving the others back, she used the house as cover to observe the activity on Ruby Avenue. The house appeared to be empty—an old yellow brick single-family home with newspapers covering the windows and a convenient collection of overgrown rhododendron surrounding the front porch that they could use for concealment.

Lucy motioned the two men forward. They sat behind the bushes. Cars and SUVs raced past them coming from Kujo's two blocks south: the Rippers out hunting.

Lucy watched through her monocular. "No sign of Fatima or Raziq in any of them. Hopefully that means they're in the Escalade." She radioed Taylor to track Haddad's cell.

"No problem," he replied. "Give me five and we'll be live. I see you found Stone. Or at least his phone. Is he in custody?"

She pulled away from the others, retreating to the shadows of the backyard, and lowered the volume on the radio. Stone didn't act like he'd heard, but who could tell for sure? Not with that mask hiding his face from her. She clicked the mic, reminding Taylor this was an open channel. "Not quite. Did you learn anything more?"

"Won't tell you how, but got his discharge summary from the VA. They list Post Traumatic Stress and Traumatic Brain Injury due to Concussive Force as part of his diagnoses qualifying him for disability. Plus third degree burns over 34% of his body and whole bunch of surgeries."

Lucy didn't want to know what firewalls Taylor had breached to get that info. "Anything else?"

"Yeah. I've been looking at footage from the 911 Center. The bomb used was pretty small as far as destructive capacity. We're not talking Oklahoma City here."

"Explains why they added the gasoline vapors to the mix."

"The fire ball definitely magnified the damage. Point is, Stone could be your guy. None of the bombs he built as a kid were very big—more fire and noise than actual blowing things up."

"Is this coming from ATF?" She couldn't believe they were already on scene and not helping out elsewhere in the city.

"No. As soon as the fire was out, everyone was deployed elsewhere—except a squad of police cadets left to secure the scene."

"Then where did you get footage from?"

He chuckled. "TV news copters. Plus cell video from the cadets. They were so excited about being able to help. Rookies."

Like he wasn't still a rookie himself. Lucy looked up. She remembered helicopters overhead as they drove through Point Breeze, but although she could see the lights of a few in the distance, there were none nearby. No news worth covering here on Ruby Avenue, they thought. How wrong they were.

"Let me know as soon as that cell moves," she told Taylor. Gunfire sounded. Maybe a few blocks away. "How fast can Jenna get here?"

"She's there already. Been making a wide loop of the area. Says most of the Rippers left their HQ, just a few left behind to guard it. Hasn't seen Zapata or Raziq."

How the hell was Jenna driving around Ruby Avenue without the Rippers spotting her? True, the Tahoe's windows were tinted and Lucy hadn't seen a working street lamp since they arrived, but still, it was a big risk. "Have her drive to the corner of Ruby and Felicia. We're at the yellow brick house on the corner."

"Will do."

She returned to the bushes where she'd left the others. "He'll radio when he has anything. In the meantime, our ride is coming."

"What if Zapata doesn't use the Escalade? We should have stayed and kept eyes on him," Haddad told her.

Right, with both the Rippers and Zapata's men after them. She understood his frustration, but she'd made the right call.

A car turned down the side street, heading towards them, slowly, passengers on both sides holding large flashlights, scanning the area.

They all flattened on the ground. When it was safe again, Haddad sat up and turned to Stone. "Why were you there with Fatima? Do you know where they were headed?"

Stone said nothing at first. The faint moonlight reflected from his eyes; the rest of his face was hidden by the fabric of his mask. It was very unsettling. Two eyes alive in the shadows of his hoodie.

Then he nodded. "I'll tell you everything. But first you have to make sure my Grams is safe."

Jenna slid up beside them in the Tahoe, her lights off. They hopped in, Lucy in the back with Stone, Haddad up front.

"Where to?" Jenna asked.

Stone answered before Lucy could say anything. "Turn left on Ruby, head over the hill, down three blocks. That's my Gram's house."

———◆———

"PEOPLE ARE DYING." Jenna had said. "They need my help."

Jenna acted like Morgan didn't understand what that meant, like she didn't care.

Of course, she didn't. Why should she? What had "people" ever done for her?

Besides, she was a sociopath. She didn't have to care. She couldn't.

It was like having a permanent excuse to get out of gym class.

Or a crutch. Morgan didn't like that. Yes, she could get away with murder—but if she did, she wanted it to be because she was smarter, cleverer, because she deserved to, not because some part of her brain was wired wrong.

Or wired right. Her father said they were the superior beings. Predators. Of course they had to hunt. It was their nature, being higher on the food chain, the next link in human evolution.

Look how he ended up. Self-destructing in a most spectacular way. All because he couldn't deny his primal impulses, his blood lust. Now he was caged in a six by eight cell, like a zoo specimen.

That was Morgan's idea of hell. She'd kill herself before she ever let that happen. Only question was: who would she take with her?

No, no, no! She screamed, the shrill noise echoing through the empty house. She wanted to hit something, someone. But she restrained herself. She was better than that. Better than her father.

She hoped.

No. She *was*.

Well… at least she wanted to be. Nick was right. She was smart enough, strong enough to go another route than the one her father had chosen—but she needed to learn so much more if she was going to succeed.

There was nothing Morgan hated more than failure.

She grabbed her laptop, pulled up the spyware on Jenna and Nick's phones. Jenna was on Ruby Avenue, driving down the same street where Nick was stationary. That was strange. What were they both doing on Ruby Avenue, this time of night?

Jenna had said something about lives needing saving. She'd sounded rushed and excited—and had the nerve to hang up on Morgan. Something must be happening, something big that Morgan missed while she was dealing with Nick.

She opened up a new tab with Pittsburgh Police radio calls streaming live, another one linked to a local news channel. Flipped back and forth between them, enjoying the hyper-stimulation as she pieced together what was happening.

The entire city was under attack, police stations bombed, snipers, fires at hockey games, civilians killed, helicopters down. Mesmerized by the chaos, she surfed from site to site watching jerky cell phone videos of the destruction, reading Tweets, listening to news anchors all breathy and thrilled at being the center of the nation's attention as they pronounced it "the night Pittsburgh died."

Morgan grabbed her laptop and car keys. No way in hell was she going to miss out on the fun.

CHAPTER 27

"I TOLD YOU," Esther said as soon as the shooting slowed enough for them to hear anything. "Nowhere is safe tonight."

"Who is that out there?" Nick asked. His voice sounded abnormally loud and a bit more panicked than he would have liked. He took a deep breath. "Why are they shooting at us?"

The women around the table looked at him as if he were daft. Or particularly slow. All he felt was shock.

"This is Ruby Avenue," one of the women said. "Home of the Rippers."

"They don't need no reason," chimed in another.

"Call 911," Nick said.

The women laughed. "911 don't work here best of times."

"Won't do no good," Esther said. "Not tonight."

"Maybe someone from the church?" Nick suggested. "You could text or Skype the nuns, ask them."

"I'm not bringing the Sisters into a middle of a gunfight."

She had a point. "Just see if they can help." He grabbed his own cell phone and dialed Lucy.

"Are the Rippers behind this crime wave y'all are charting?" Nick asked, gesturing to the map on the laptop and the never-ending stream of police calls coming from Esther's headphones.

"Them and some Spanish, best we can tell," Esther said. "Blew up the 911 Center, shooting at police stations, trying to blow up bridges and tunnels."

"All hell broke loose," one of her friends said solemnly.

"But why here? What do they want from you?"

Loud knocking at the front door echoed down the hall. Nick was glad for the sturdy construction of the row house and the fact that since it was the middle unit, it only had windows front and back. The dining room was probably the safest place in the house.

The knocking repeated. "Sorry 'bout all the fuss, Miss Esther," a man called. He sounded like he was fighting off laughter. "But we needs you to come with us."

"Ain't going nowhere with you Mathias Maddoc! You just try and make me."

"Esther, don't agitate them," Nick said.

"It's my house. I'll agitate whomever I please," she snapped.

"Want me to shoot them, Esther?"

Nick spun around. The quiet lady in the corner had fished a large revolver out of her bag. He grabbed it from her, ignoring her arched eyebrow in rebuke.

"No one is shooting anyone." He turned to Esther. "Why do they want you?"

"Probably something to do with Andre. He used to run with the Rippers when he was young."

"Yes, but—" Nick trailed off, not wanting to let Esther know the Rippers already had Andre. Which answered his own question. Damn, he was getting thick. They wanted her as leverage to force Andre to kill that man.

Maddoc pounded on the door. "Just come out and talk, will ya? I promise, Miss Esther, nothing's going to happen to you."

"Like I'm going to listen to you after you shot out my upstairs!"

Nick handed his phone to the woman he'd taken the gun off of. "Keep dialing that number. If someone answers, tell them Nick needs help and bring it to me, okay?"

She smiled and nodded.

"Okay. Is there another way out?"

"Just the backdoor. But just because they're Rippers don't mean they're stupid. They'll be watching it," one of the other women answered.

"And we're not leaving Esther."

"How about the basement? It's got to be more defensible than here." The women looked at each other and nodded. "Why don't you ladies help Esther down to the basement and I'll try to buy us some time."

They grabbed their laptops and purses and moved through the door to the kitchen.

Nick craned his head out into the hall and looked down towards the door. Not an ideal negotiating position but he'd just talked his way out of an encounter with a sociopathic killer, so why not? After all, he'd read all the hostage negotiating texts, had even contributed a few chapters himself.

He studied the pistol. Revolver. Simple enough that even he could handle it. Although despite Lucy's best efforts, he was not the best shot in the world. Should he leave it with the women to defend themselves?

No. He *was* their defense. The weight of that realization made the gun feel heavy in his hand. Not only was he responsible for the safety of Esther and her friends, but he had to somehow stay alive long enough for more help to arrive.

Not going to be easy. He glanced down the hallway towards the front foyer. Lucy always said to take the high ground and put your back to a wall. Should he make a dash for the steps, make his stand there? He'd have an excellent shot at the front door, but if they came in the back he'd be blind and out of position.

The middle of the hallway was the only place where he could cover both entrances. He'd be in direct line of fire of anyone coming from either direction. Damn, how did Lucy make these decisions? He'd been standing here almost a full minute and she usually only had split seconds before acting.

Clearly the gun wasn't the answer as much as a last resort. He positioned it on the floor beside the front door where he could reach it quickly. If it came to that.

"Mathias," he called out as soon as he saw the door to the basement shut with the ladies safely on the other side. "Let's talk. I think I can help you."

———— ✦ ————

LUCY NODDED TO Jenna. "Go ahead. Turn around and drive down Ruby. But slowly. Anything looks off, get us out of here."

Jenna craned her head to take a look at Stone. "You caught my bomber. Way to go."

"Bomber? I haven't done anything," Stone protested.

"Then you won't mind letting me take your waist pack and search you for weapons." Lucy grabbed a pair of flex-cuffs from her vest and held them out for Stone. "Put your hands out."

"Look, lady—"

"That's Supervisory Special Agent Guardino," Haddad snapped in a tone Lucy hadn't heard from him before. "She's securing her position, Stone. Cooperate, Marine."

Stone blew out his breath. "Yes, sir. But I'm on your side."

He slid his hands into the plastic restraints. For the first time Lucy got a good look at the scars left from his burns. She pulled the restraints over the cuffs of his jacket so they wouldn't bite into his skin. Once he was secure, she took his waist pack, handed it to Haddad to examine then patted him down for weapons. All she found was a folding knife, which she pocketed.

They crested the hill above the Rippers' HQ. Jenna stopped the Tahoe. "We got trouble."

Lucy leaned forward, expecting to see Rippers coming at them from Kujo's. Smoke hung above the house and there were still flames visible at the side of the house. Product of Stone's firebomb. Two Rippers stood guard at the front porch. Other than that, the place looked deserted.

She glanced farther down the hill. Two blocks down, several SUVs gathered in front of a group of row houses. Their headlights silhouetted two men with machine pistols aiming at the center house.

"That's my grams' house," Stone said. "You have to help her."

Lucy used her monocular to get a better look. The Rippers had only shot the upper floor's windows; the first floor appeared intact. Then the front door opened. A man dressed in gray sweatpants and a navy fleece jacket appeared. He stepped into the glare of the headlights, arms held open and wide, hands empty indicating that he wasn't a threat. White, about six foot with reddish-blond hair.

Nick.

———•———

TROOPER 4: ALLEGHENY TOWER, ALLEGHENY TOWER, DO YOU COPY?

ALLEGHENY AIR TRAFFIC CONTROL: COPY, TROOPER 4, GO AHEAD.

TROOPER 4: HAVING TROUBLE GETTING THROUGH TO INCIDENT COMMAND. CAN YOU RELAY MESSAGE THAT WE'RE FINE, NO NEED TO DIVERT ASSETS TO ASSIST?

ALLEGHENY AIR TRAFFIC CONTROL: TROOPER 4, CONFIRM YOUR STATUS.

TROOPER 4: DOWNED BY MECHANICAL
FAILURE BUT OTHERWISE A-OK

ALLEGHENY AIR TRAFFIC CONTROL: ROGER
THAT, TROOPER 4. GLAD TO HEAR IT. WILL
RELAY TO NIMS INCIDENT COMMAND.

CHAPTER 28

NICK.

Lucy's instincts took over. Fury and fear exploded in a surge of adrenalin. She lowered her monocular. Turned to Stone. He straightened, not liking the look in her eye. Smart man.

"What's happening? What did you see?"

She raised her Glock, held it at Stone's throat. "Want to tell me what my husband is doing surrounded by Rippers with guns? At your grandmother's house?"

Her voice was low, calm. Jenna jerked around. "Nick's there? Why would—"

"Shut up," Lucy said. "I'm waiting for Mr. Stone's answer."

To his credit, Stone didn't flinch from her gun. She wished again that he wasn't wearing the mask, but his eyes narrowed as if he was puzzled. "Nick? Doc Callahan is your husband?"

"Tell me exactly what's going on here. Fast."

"Callahan is my shrink. He comes out, we workout together, he and my grams chat, she feeds him apple cake and cookies and shit. He calls it therapy. I don't know. The VA set it up."

Nick had mentioned a Marine with severe burns. Hadn't mentioned making house calls to the most dangerous neighborhood in Pittsburgh.

"What's he doing here tonight?"

"We were jogging, talking on the phone. He heard the Rippers grab me, ask me to kill this guy I knew in Afghanistan."

"Rashid Raziq."

"Right. Anyway, the Doc heard it all through my phone. I asked him to call the cops, make sure Grams was safe—knew the Rippers would go after her to make sure I cooperated." For some reason he suddenly relaxed. "I should've never doubted him. He really came through for me."

"That's what Nick does." She lowered the Glock. "Haddad, get as close as you can and keep an eye on Nick." She handed the DEA agent her monocular.

"Rules of engagement?" Haddad asked.

"They're gang bangers holding a gun on an unarmed man. Take them out if they make a move against him." She would have preferred to just shoot them on sight but no way could she risk Nick while he was out in the open. What the hell was he thinking?

Haddad slipped out of the SUV. Lucy tapped Jenna on the shoulder. "Find me a way to that house, out of sight of the Rippers."

"Best way is head a block south and turn," Stone said. "There's no alley in the back, but you can go through the

Guzman's back yard to Grams'. Nothing but a few bushes between them."

Jenna made the turn. Lucy closed her eyes for a moment, wishing there was a way she could stay and keep eyes on Nick herself.

"How would the Rippers approach?" she asked Stone.

He thought for a moment. "If I was them, I'd have a man at the back porch—it's the only rear exit. Force anyone inside out the front."

"And if I need to get inside?" Might not come to that. If Nick was smart enough to go back inside, she and her team could take care of things, clear the streets. But she needed as much intel as she could get.

"The porch door is solid, you'd need a ram. But there's a basement window under the porch. You might fit through it. Or she might," he nodded to Jenna. "No way I can, though."

"You? You're not going anywhere."

"I'm a Marine. That's my grams. And Nick's my friend. Let me help."

He sounded sincere. But Lucy couldn't take the risk. "No. You stay here." She reached across him and zip-tied his bound hands to the door handle. "Jenna, let's go take out the Rippers in the back." She keyed her radio. "Haddad, what's the situation out front?"

"They're still talking. Whatever your husband's saying, he's got them laughing, relaxed. If you can get to a vantage point inside, I think between us we can take them down. Or maybe lure them inside, take them prisoner? They might know where Rashid is."

It was the best idea he'd had all night, but lousy timing. "Only after we have Nick and the woman safe."

She and Jenna left the Tahoe backed into a driveway across the street from the Guzman's, Stone's backyard neighbors. They crept through the darkness towards the house backing onto Stone's. It was a small single-family bungalow. Christmas lights and ornaments scattered over the lawn but they were turned off. Curtains in the front window shut with only a faint crack of light shining through. Lucy motioned Jenna to the left as she went around to the right. The backyard was tiny, a swing set and sliding board plus assorted shrubs filled it. No signs of any Rippers.

Lucy kept her Remington at the ready and stayed low as she headed for the shoulder-height boxwood hedge forming the rear property boundary. Jenna was right behind her, scanning the way they came, making sure no one snuck up on them from behind. Lucy pulled a branch aside. There was a lone Ripper sitting on the back porch steps of Stone's house, weapon across his knees.

She beckoned Jenna close and whispered, "Good news. Their manpower must be depleted with all the action throughout the city. There's only one."

"About time."

"Bad news is there was no way to cross the backyard without him spotting me. We'll need to bring him to us. If I get him close, can you take him out quietly?"

Jenna grinned. "Got just the thing. Give me a minute." She turned and ran back towards where the Tahoe was parked. When she returned she was holding a stun gun. "Never leave home without it."

Once Jenna was set, hidden in the shrubs, Lucy used her shotgun to rustle the branches in front of her. It took a few tries and she'd almost given up when finally the Ripper noticed and sprung up. Lucy wondered if he'd been sleeping. If so, he was wide awake now. If she wasn't in a hurry it would have been funny to watch him hold his gun like in the movies, waving it from side to side as he approached.

She waited. Finally he began poking the branches with his Mac-10. When he got close enough it was an easy matter to grab his wrists and haul him through the bushes. He flew off balance, tripping over his own feet. As soon as he was on their side, Jenna stepped forward and used her stun gun, dropping him.

Once Jenna had him restrained, Lucy sprinted to the house. Now all she had to do was get inside, get Nick inside, and take care of the Rippers out front without them sending for the cavalry.

The back of the house was quiet. She found the basement window Stone told them about. Took a calculated risk that the walls of the house between her and the Rippers on the street would muffle the noise, and smashed the glass with the butt of her shotgun.

As she reversed the gun, ready to clear the glass with its barrel she heard women's voices. "Stop right there," one of them said loud and clear. "We don't want to hurt you, but we will."

Lucy rolled away from the window, grabbed her flashlight and, reaching at an angle so she wouldn't expose herself to any gunfire, looked into the basement. A bunch of old ladies, holding gardening tools and hammers and… a laptop?

"FBI," she whispered into them. "Are you ladies locked in?"

"No. We're barricaded in," one of them said.

"Wait." Another, holding a claw hammer and looking like she meant business said. "Show us your ID."

"How many white girls not the police gonna come 'round here with a shotgun?" a third argued.

Lucy didn't have time for this. "Could one of you open the back door so I can escort you to safety and get my husband out of here before those Rippers out front decide he's not as funny as he thinks he is and shoot him?"

———•———

THE REDHEAD RETURNED alone and took up a position in the driveway, guarding the SUV.

Andre couldn't help but stare. Stunning was the best word he could come up with. He wasn't usually attracted to white chicks, but she had this look in her eye, like there was more than just good looks going on. It was the same look he saw when he looked in the mirror while putting his mask on. Haunted. Wary. Vulnerable.

And hating it. He wondered where her scars were—certainly not anywhere obvious. Guessed in some ways that probably made them worse than his kind.

He stretched his hands to roll down his window. "So, what's your name?"

All that got him was a flick of her gaze and a curt, "Jenna Galloway."

Andre didn't give up that easily. Besides, there was obviously a helluva lot more going on here than he knew about and he figured it was about time someone let him in on the secret. "I know Haddad is DEA. And I'm guessing Miss Supervisory Special Agent Lucy is FBI,

given the stick up her butt." That earned him a smile.
Nice. He'd like to see more. "Are you FBI as well?"

"Nope." He waited. "US Postal Inspector."

"Okay. Wasn't expecting that. You out here with a
sniper rifle because someone forgot to put a stamp on
their Christmas cookies?"

She leaned down to stare straight into his eyes.
Favored him with another smile, but this one reminded
him of Darius. Predatory. "I'm here to fry your ass for
sending threatening letters and a bomb through the US
Mail, Andre Stone."

———— • ————

LUCY HAD JUST gotten inside the house when her radio
buzzed. "You might want to get out here," Haddad said.
"We have ourselves a little situation."

"On my way." She turned to the three ladies who'd
left the basement to let her in. "Why don't you ladies stay
downstairs until I let you know it's safe to come upstairs."

They looked ready to argue, but she didn't stay there
long enough to listen. She hadn't heard any gunfire from
out front, but still panic dug its claws in, eroding her
concentration. A few deep breaths, reminding herself she
wouldn't do Nick any good if she wasn't focused, and she
was at the front window.

Peering around the edge of the heavy drapes she saw
Nick sitting on the porch steps—good grief, could he
have chosen a worst tactical position?—talking earnestly
with a young Ripper and a middle-aged woman while a
second Ripper stood behind them, laughing.

259

There was a new vehicle on the street, a white van with Holy Trinity Outreach painted on the side. And two nuns standing beside it. Plus several elderly men and women craning their heads out the van's open side door.

Holy heck. No wonder Haddad hadn't described the "situation." How the hell could you? First things first. Securing the Rippers.

"Where are you?" she radioed Haddad.

"Right behind the closest SUV. You missed the screaming match. The lady clocked the kid with her purse and things kind of went sideways from there."

"Can you subdue the older Ripper?" The one laughing at his friend's predicament. That was the Ripper still holding his Mac-10 at the ready, although he had it pointed down at the ground. The kid being yelled at had his weapon dangling from his finger as if he'd forgotten it.

"No problem. I've got a good angle."

"Make your move as soon as I come through the door." She inhaled deeply, the house was cold—all that air coming in from the shattered upstairs windows—but smelled like Christmas, all pine needles and cinnamon. No Christmas tree that she could see, but there was a balsam garland hanging above the drapes. Focus. There were too many civilians out there and too many weapons for her to mess this up.

She moved to the door, kicked a revolver out of her way—what the hell was that doing there?—raised her shotgun, grabbed the brass doorknob. In one fluid motion she yanked the door open and pushed through the heavy grated screen door onto the porch.

"FBI. Put the gun down and show me your hands," she called to the young Ripper. Behind him Haddad made his move, grabbed the other Ripper's weapon with one hand as he jammed his pistol into the man's neck. Within seconds he had his target prone on the ground.

One down. But her target surprised her—or rather the woman he was arguing with did. She lunged in front of him. "Don't you shoot. He ain't done nothing wrong."

Then Nick stood. Directly in Lucy's line of fire. "Nick, get down."

He ignored her. "Now, Miss Larimar, no one's going to shoot anyone. But we really need Jadon to put his guns down. You don't want anyone to get hurt, right?"

Lucy moved down the porch steps, past Nick. The two nuns ran up to the older woman. Damn. Just what she didn't need. More potential hostages between her and the kid with the gun. Haddad glanced up from where he was restraining the first Ripper. The kid had backed up against the SUV, blocking any shot the DEA agent might have had.

"Lucy," Nick said in his therapist's tone. "Let me."

Like hell she would. But he touched her arm and whispered, "Trust me."

It went against all her training and instincts but she nodded. Didn't relax her grip on the Remington or move her aim away from the kid's head—the only part of him visible beyond the three women who'd gathered in front of him. He was tall, taller than Nick's six feet, and towered over them.

Nick had been able to keep the Rippers talking and not shooting for the time it had taken her to get here, she told herself as he walked forward. At least he stayed out of her line of fire this time.

"Jadon," he said. "You don't want your aunt to get hurt, right?"

The kid—and despite his size, he was only a kid, maybe fourteen, tops—shook his head. "Just go away. Leave us alone and things will be fine."

"There's been a lot of killing tonight," Nick continued in that same hypnotic tone. "But I know you didn't have any part of that."

"I didn't. I didn't kill no one. All I done was shoot some windows." The kid was practically in tears.

"We know that. But holding a gun with innocent people like your aunt and the sisters here, well, that makes it hard for people to believe you."

"Jadon." The middle-aged woman, his aunt, grabbed his arm. "I won't let no one hurt you. Now do as he says and let go the gun."

The kid nodded, his entire body trembling as he stared at Lucy. Then her Remington. Then back again at her face. "Okay. Okay."

He thrust the Mac-10 at Nick. Lucy ran down the porch steps and reached the boy as Haddad rounded the front of the SUV. They turned him to face the SUV, Haddad standing guard as Lucy searched him, taking a chrome-plated 9mm from the pocket of his baggy jeans and a switchblade from his high-top.

"We're clear," she said, finally able to take a deep breath. Then she turned to Nick. "What the hell were you thinking?"

CHAPTER 29

OF COURSE JENNA got stuck ferrying the three gang-bangers and her mad bomber. Along with David. Although she wasn't sure riding in the van with a bunch of nuns and old folks was any better. At least she had her man, Andre Stone. Chalk up a win for the Postal Service.

Saint Lucy hadn't deigned to reveal her holy vision to the grunts on the ground. Just told Jenna to follow them to Holy Trinity.

She followed the nun's van up Ruby Avenue, now suspiciously empty of traffic, cars, and Rippers, to a big gothic church surrounded by an eight-foot stone wall. The van stopped before a pair of wrought iron gates, which swung open after the nun driving punched a code in a keypad.

Jenna peered up at the church. Their headlights revealed wide wooden doors arched at the top. Over them was a ledge lined with gargoyles. And towering over everything, a squared off bell tower. Charming. But she liked the thick wall behind them, not to mention the solid construction. It would take an army to break through these walls. They could hide up here until reinforcements arrived.

The van led them around to the rear of the church where there was a second small stone building. It was squat and unadorned, two stories high with a plain wooden door. Jenna parked beside the van and waited until the nuns had the old folks unloaded and had led them inside the smaller building, which she guessed was the convent. She wondered where the priests lived.

Lucy and Nick were the last out of the van. Lucy looked more uptight than ever. Nick was smiling but Jenna had no idea why. Maybe just to piss Lucy off.

Jenna got out of the Tahoe. Their prisoners were all restrained and would be safe enough with David inside. "What's the plan?"

Lucy glared at her. Great. There was no plan. Saint Lucy winging it on almighty inspiration. Again. Same holier than thou attitude that almost got Jenna killed last month.

Nick glanced from Lucy to Jenna and back. Stopped smiling and opened his mouth to intervene, but Lucy cut him short with a glance.

"We'll find somewhere to secure the prisoners," Lucy said. "Then question them."

"Question them? What about?" Jenna asked.

"Where Zapata took Raziq and his family. There's still a chance they're alive." Lucy turned to Nick. "I'll need your help. We don't have time to waste."

"Help with what?" he asked.

"If they know anything, I need them to talk fast."

"Lucy." He leaned in as if he'd misheard her. "You seriously can't expect me to help you extract information from these men. First of all, it takes time to develop rapport, observe their emotional states. Second of all, one of them is just a teenager. Third of all, they have a right to counsel—or have you forgotten about a little thing called the Constitution?"

Way to go, Nick, Jenna cheered silently. Nice to see someone stand up to Saint Lucy.

Lucy's eyes closed for a moment. Funny, Jenna usually forgot she was taller than Lucy. But right now Lucy looked exhausted, tiny in comparison to Jenna's five-ten. Her face was filthy, grime mixed with blood, that godforsaken parka stinking of gasoline and gunpowder and more blood, hair matted with sweat.

Then she inhaled and opened her eyes.

The power of Lucy's glare made Jenna look away, pretend to check the straps on her vest. Nick didn't budge, somehow faced Lucy. Lucy no longer looked exhausted or small or weak. Shoulders straight, chin high, eyes blazing. She looked fierce.

More like batshit crazy and intent on getting them killed. But no way was Jenna going to tell her that.

"I haven't forgotten," Lucy said in a low voice, each word measured as if she was saving her breath for something important. "I also haven't forgotten about two young girls who should be asleep in bed instead of lying on a slab in the morgue. One of them had her hands cut off and then was burned alive. And the monster behind that also had sixty innocent civilians executed. I saw them, Nick. I was the last person who saw them. Before the damn building exploded and now their families will be lucky to take home a few scraps of DNA to bury."

"Lucy, I didn't—"

"No. No. You want to know why I need these men to talk now. I'm going to tell you. Let you decide the right thing to do. Because all I know is that Zapata has those little girls' mother, father, and baby brother in his hands. Want to guess what he'll do to them, Nick? Want to guess how long it will be before he starts? How about how long it will take for him to finish?"

Finally Lucy blinked. Jenna swore there were tears on her cheeks, but it was hard to tell in the dim light. Nick reached his hand out but Lucy spun on her heel and walked away, her footsteps jerky as if she strained to carry something heavy.

Jenna felt sorry for Nick. He was a civilian and didn't deserve to get dumped on by Lucy's messed up shit.

"You don't have to help her," she told him. "She's out of control. There's no way those people are still alive. She's just too damn stubborn to give up."

For the first time ever Nick glanced at Jenna with disapproval. After all their sessions together, him listening without judgment to all her dirty secrets, it stung.

"She can't give up. Ever," he said. A touch of regret crept into his voice. "Even if it means risking everything."

Everyone was more like it, Jenna thought as Nick sped after Lucy.

Jenna planned to stay right here, safe and sound behind these very nice and very thick stonewalls. No way in hell was she following Saint Lucy on another hopeless rescue mission.

———•———

MORGAN HATED FEELING lost as much as she hated losing. Even worse was being lost in a neighborhood where she didn't feel like she had the upper hand on anyone she encountered.

The major roads had been blocked, forcing her to take side roads she had no clue had even existed. She was distracted, listening to the news, alternating between Nick and Jenna's GPS tracers, eavesdropping on their conversations, scanning the dark streets lined with terrace-style public housing units arranged around cul-de-sacs that she'd turn down only to find herself trapped at a dead end. Faces staring at her from windows, a few young men venturing out onto porches or sidewalks, knowing her for not belonging.

That she was used to. Different. Outsider. Beyond ken.

But being looked at like prey? Weak? Vulnerable? Screw that.

She finally pulled into a funeral home's parking lot, easing the stolen Honda into the shadows behind the crematorium. She didn't feel nervous or skittish, not like a normal person. Rather it was that electricity singing in her veins, begging for release.

Only problem? Until now in her life, release meant blood.

There had to be another way. Something that would give her the same strength and purpose Lucy had. Or Nick. Hell, even Jenna had found the guts to hang up on Morgan when there were lives at stake.

Jenna had said people needed her. That's what Morgan wanted. To feel needed. The power of saving lives—couldn't that be just as strong as the power of taking them?

She double-checked the GPS signals. They'd moved but were still together, just a few blocks up Ruby Avenue. She plugged the address into her nav app. Not too far, she'd almost made it without knowing. Okay, okay. She'd play the game, give this a try.

Starting the car and pulling out onto the street with a destination, she felt better. Calmer, in control.

For now.

———•———

"HEY, HEY, HEY, HOMES, THIS IS RAPCAT COMING TO YOU LIVE FROM GANGSTALAND. WE GONNA BE ROCKIN' TONIGHT, YO. ALL YOU RUBY AVENUE RIPPERS OUT THERE, YOU ARE R-I-P, HEAR ME? Y'ALL CAN GO F-YOURSELVES CUZ GANGSTAS MAKIN' OUR MOVE AND WE'RE GONNA OWN YOU BITCHES BY MORN. THAT'S RIGHT, FOOLS. FIRST WE GONNA CAP YO BOYS, THEN WE GONNA FUCK YO HOS, THEN WE'LL DANCE ON YO GRAVES, AH-YEAH..."

CHAPTER 30

NICK CAUGHT UP with Lucy in one of the church's side chapels. Candles blazed in red glass votives, creating the illusion that she was covered in blood. He shuddered, shook free of the image, and went to where she sat in a pew, staring into space.

Funny that she'd run here. He was the one who made it to Mass with Megan most Sundays. Lucy found every excuse not to go—she'd lost her faith a long time ago and hated looking like a hypocrite to Megan. At least that's what she said. There was more—with Lucy there almost always was—but even after all these years he still wasn't quite sure what. Wasn't sure if she knew herself.

"Long night." He sank onto the seat beside her. She said nothing, just blew out her breath and rested her head on his shoulder. He wrapped his arm around her, pulled her close.

They sat in silence in the candlelight. Then she straightened, pulling away from him. "It's not over yet."

She pushed up to her feet just as the door opened and a Middle Eastern man in a long coat and camouflage bulletproof vest entered.

"DEA Special Agent David Haddad," Lucy made introductions. "This is my husband, Dr. Nick Callahan."

David nodded to Nick. "Taylor says the Escalade hasn't moved. He has the drone over the Ripper's HQ. Place looks deserted. We lost them."

"So our only chance is if one of the Rippers knows where they took Raziq."

"I say we start with Stone. Man's nuts enough to send a bomb through the mail and turns out we have an in." David looked at Nick and said in an accusing tone, "We know you're his therapist, Dr. Callahan."

"Why would you think Andre Stone had anything to do with this?" Nick had seen two men besides Jadon and the other Ripper, Maddoc, in the Tahoe but with the tinted windows hadn't recognized Andre. "You have him shut up with your other prisoners? Let him out. Now. He's not a Ripper and he had nothing to do with any of this."

"I'm afraid everything points to him, Nick," Lucy said.

"No. You don't understand. The Rippers grabbed him off the street. Held him prisoner. Said they wanted him to kill someone—Raziq. That's the guy they kidnapped, right?" His words tumbled over themselves as he rushed to put the pieces together and make his case without violating confidentiality. He could divulge information to prevent harm to others. No more. "They threatened his grandmother—that's why I was at Esther's house. Lucy, you need to get him out of there. Lord only knows what the Rippers will do to him."

David stared at Nick like he was crazy. No matter, Lucy was listening. "Haddad. Bring Stone here. But keep him in his restraints."

David left. Nick turned to Lucy. "I can't tell you much—confidentiality. But I promise you, Andre has nothing to do with this. I'd stake my life on it."

She gave him a wry half-smile. "You already did, coming here tonight. Why didn't you tell me you were making house calls to the most dangerous neighborhood in the city?"

"Because you would have looked at me exactly the way you are now."

"And you yell at me for taking risks."

"I was doing my job. Just like you."

She winced. "Guess I deserve that one. Anything else I should know?"

He almost told her about Morgan. Wasn't sure why he hesitated. Unlike with Andre there were no confidentiality issues. But was this the best time? Lucy was in the middle of a desperate plan to find a family and rescue them before it was too late. The city was engulfed in violence. Last thing she needed was thoughts of Morgan distracting her.

"Who are you people and what are you doing here?" a man in a priest's black shirt and white collar called out from the other side of the church. The rectory must be there, Nick realized. The priest was old, in his seventies, with shaggy white hair and five-o-clock shadow. His clothes looked rumpled as if he'd fallen asleep in them. "Get those guns out of my sanctuary."

Lucy was glad for the priest's interruption. Once they explained the situation, he agreed to allow them the use of the basement classrooms below the rectory. She retreated downstairs to wait for Stone and Haddad, leaving Nick to soothe the priest's concerns.

The room was cinderblock, painted yellow with bible quotes and crayon-colored pictures on the walls. There were several tables surrounded by chairs, a desk, and most importantly to Lucy, a blackboard. Not as nice as the large whiteboard in her office at the Federal Building, but good enough.

She started with a timeline. Fatima and the baby's departure from Cranberry at one end, Mina and Badria's time of death, the ambush at the 911 center, attacks on Zones Four and Five, and finally seeing the Raziq family alive with Zapata on Ruby Avenue. She radioed Taylor who helped her add in other major events like the bomb threats, the shooter and fire at the hockey tournament, the bomb at Three Rivers, the downing of the State Police helicopter, and several more shoot outs between the Rippers and the police.

There were other events: riots, car accidents, looting. But she focused on ones that appeared to be Zapata's work.

"Boss," Taylor said when they were done. "I'm not seeing a pattern here. And, hate to say it, but you're the only one who has seen any signs of a cartel. All of the bodies we've recovered have been wearing Ripper colors."

"Any taken alive?"

A pause while he double-checked. "No."

"So the thinking is, what? A gang dependent on the drug trade decides to thoroughly piss off every law enforcement agency in Western PA all in one night? Never thinking of the repercussions? The Rippers are finished. They'll be dismantled in a month, probably less. Homewood will be on permanent lockdown, Ruby Avenue will have more police per block than any other street in the nation. What's the end game here? And why target Raziq?"

"Haddad got threats as well, don't forget. Although," he paused, "he's also the one who actually ID'd Zapata." Taylor enjoyed playing devil's advocate—a role she usually had Walden for, but she had to admit Taylor had a point.

Haddad disagreed. He'd walked with Stone in just in time to overhear Taylor. "Are you calling me a traitor?"

"Just exploring all the options," Lucy said. She didn't have time to coddle his sore feelings. "Taylor says there's no evidence of cartel involvement in any of tonight's events."

"Bullshit. We saw Zapata take Raziq. That's evidence enough."

Lucy waved him quiet, peering at the time line. There was no obvious pattern, yet it was all too well-coordinated for there not to be. She just had to figure out what Zapata and the Rippers wanted...

"I still don't see why Zapata would target Raziq," she muttered.

"Maybe because he's a fraud."

She whirled around. Stone stood behind her, as focused on the board as she had been. "What do you mean?"

"He burned down that school in Hajji Baba. Killed all those girls."

Haddad took a step toward Stone. "Why do you blame Rashid for Hajji Baba and not me? After all, I was in command. I led the mission."

Stone frowned. "Why should I blame you? You were just as taken in by him as I was."

"You still believe he arranged the ambush that killed your squad?"

"I know it." Andre gestured with his bound hands in frustration. "There were two explosions that day. A small one, barely enough to knock you out. And a second, larger incendiary bomb that conveniently went off after Raziq got you out."

"Of course. The second was designed to get anyone who responded to the first. Rashid risked his life to save me."

"Then why did he tell me you were still inside when you were already out? And why did he send my men into that ambush while I was caught inside the fire, supposedly saving your ass?"

Haddad sat on one of the tables, stunned. "That's impossible."

"You were out cold. How would you know?"

"But all the witnesses—"

"Paid off by Raziq. Don't you understand? The man played you a fool from the beginning. All those drug stashes he led us to? Setups to eliminate his competition.

Rashid Raziq was the biggest drug smuggler in the province. And we did his dirty work for him."

"You were burned and had a head injury. You've got it all mixed up, Stone. Your subconscious mind scrambled the timing so you wouldn't feel guilty about your men getting killed."

"If that's so, it sure as hell didn't work." Stone's shoulders hunched then dropped in resignation. "All I know is what I know."

"You're wrong." Haddad shook his head angrily. "I don't believe you."

"No one does. But it's the truth. His men set that ambush and gunned down my men. He set that IED that almost killed you and burned down that school. The man is a killer."

"Why? If he's the monster you say he is, why go to all that trouble? He could have kept on doing what he was doing, no one would ever have known."

"Maybe it's my fault—I was asking questions, talking to his men. Maybe he was worried someone said the wrong thing. Or maybe he saw it as a chance to get you to owe him one so he could pave his way to make more money, move to America, open up new routes for his operation. After all, that's exactly what happened, isn't it?"

"Of course. I sponsored his move here—he had a price on his head over there. But as for more money, no. We paid some moving expenses, a couple months' consultancy fees, that's it. And if he wanted to start a drug operation here, why in the world would he choose Pittsburgh of all places?"

"Raziq chose Pittsburgh?" Lucy interrupted.

"Yes. He was very specific. Said he wanted a safe place to raise his family. Now does that sound like the drug kingpin you've described?" Haddad's tone turned to one of pity. "You're wrong about him, Stone. Dead wrong."

Both men stared at each other, neither yielding. Lucy had no idea who to believe but she remembered her initial impressions of Raziq and his home. Contradictions at every turn.

"Let's focus on the present," she suggested. "Stone, where were you today from two pm on?"

"He was with me," Nick said as he walked into the room. "Or with people from the VA."

"I had a clinic appointment with my surgeon," Stone said. "The van picked me up at one, but the surgeon was running late, so I didn't get out of there until around two thirty. Then I picked up this gizmo from Callahan." He raised his wrist to display a heart rate and GPS monitor. Nick had one just like it; Lucy had given it to him last Christmas. "After that the van took me back to Grams' house."

"And then Andre and I were on the phone together as we both ran. Until the Rippers picked him up. You can check my cell records and the GPS monitor from the watch." Nick stared at her as if daring her to accuse Stone of killing Raziq's daughters.

"So you're not my killer. What about the threats?"

Stone shrugged. "No idea what you're talking about."

Haddad wheeled on him. "We traced email threats and letter threats sent to both Rashid and myself. They all came from Ruby Avenue. And there was a letter bomb that matched your signature."

"I'm being set up. Darius, he's a shot caller for the Rippers, he's the one who taught me to make bombs when I was a kid. I added my own special touch, using road flares, but he knows that." He turned to Nick. "You heard him, Doc. He said he wanted me to build a bomb for him. But when he put me in that garage with that woman and baby, everything I would have used was already there——" He slumped against the wall, shaking his head.

Lucy wished again that he didn't have the mask on; it was so hard to read his expression. Was he faking?

Nick obviously didn't think so. He moved to Stone's side, stood so he could make eye contact with him. "Andre. What is it?"

"All the bomb making stuff in the garage——I touched it. You guys will find my prints all over it. That's why Darius locked me up there. He needed my fingerprints and DNA and shit. Plus I made some napalm, those fire bombs that helped get us out of there. You can test my hands. I'll have shit all over me. I'm screwed three ways from Sunday."

Lucy stared at him. Something in her wanted to trust him. But she had to be sure. She grabbed her phone. The classrooms had functioning Wi-Fi, good. "Taylor, show me a map of all the disturbances the Rippers or Zapatas were behind tonight."

The screen filled with a map of Pittsburgh covered with red dots. The only clear area was Homewood. It had a single red dot: the site of their shoot out with the Rippers at Kujo's.

"Now clear all the bomb threats that were unfounded." The density of red dots lightened. "Clear the 911 center and the attacks on Zones Four and Five."

"Why?"

"Because those make strategic sense. Same with the bomb at Three Rivers and any direct attacks on police. Okay, now take out the bombs found at synagogues and mosques." Suddenly the map was almost totally clear. Except for two red dots overlapping in Highland Park, near the zoo. "What are those?"

"Fire and active shooter at the Schenley Academy ice rink," Taylor told her. "Took down a police officer and a State Police helicopter. Civilians rescued the officer but we've lost contact with the Statie."

"An ice rink?" Why did that bother her so much? Lucy stared at the red dot until it blurred. "Was there a game or practice?"

"High school holiday tournament. Huge crowd, lots of panic. We got lucky. No civilian casualties."

"Oh my God," she whispered, immediately glancing up at the ceiling as if the priest above could have heard her. "Special Agent Haddad, you're right. We need to find Raziq."

CHAPTER 31

AS SOON AS the FBI agent, Lucy What's-her-name, said that, Andre knew he was doomed. She believed Haddad, not him. He turned to Nick, trying to find words to convince someone she was wrong.

"Dr. Callahan," she said in a tone that would have made his old drill sergeant smile. "Move away from the prisoner."

Christ, now she thought he'd take the Doc hostage or something? What kind of monster did they take him for?

The kind that would butcher two little girls.

Callahan didn't move. Lucy took a step towards him. Haddad raised his M4. Aimed at Andre. Good God, what were they doing? The Doc was just a civilian.

Andre pushed Callahan behind him, out of the line of fire. "He has nothing to do with this."

For the first time since he'd met her the FBI agent smiled. She motioned to Haddad to lower his weapon. The DEA agent looked as confused as Andre felt.

The Doc stood beside Andre, glaring at the FBI agent for a long moment. His shoulders were hunched and his face flushed. Angry. Andre had never seen the Doc angry before. "Lucy—"

She shook her head at the Doc as if giving him a warning. If Andre didn't know they were husband and wife, the way they exchanged an entire conversation in a single glance would have told him for sure.

Lucy stepped forward and took Andre's hands in hers. She flicked a knife open and cut him free of the zipties. "Sorry about that, Stone. I had to be sure. You're a hard read."

Her tone was gentle, almost admiring. He shook the feeling back into his hands, touched his mask. "Yeah, you should see my poker face."

Callahan was the only one who smiled at that. Then he got serious again. "Andre, she knows nothing about our sessions. And I can't tell her anything."

"He never does." Lucy rolled her eyes. But he could tell she was proud of the Doc. "I didn't even know he was making house calls. I thought all this workout therapy was on the treadmills at the VA."

Haddad interrupted. "We're running out of time here."

Lucy nodded, her expression turning business-like once more. "I know. Mr. Stone, do you know the three Rippers we captured at your grandmother's house?"

"The older one, Maddoc, yeah. He's a bully. Darius' enforcer. The two others, I have no clue."

"Think you can get Mr. Maddoc to tell you where they took Raziq?"

He thought about it, shook his head. "No. And neither can you. There's a reason his street name is Mad Dog. Guy's stubborn as hell, meaner than a pit bull, and more than a little crazy. He'll never rat on Darius."

"This Darius, he was keeping Raziq's family for Zapata. Do you think he'd be with Zapata and Raziq now?"

He had no clue who this Zapata dude was, but he knew Darius. "Hell yeah. He talked like he was getting ready for a big payoff. No way he'd let his moneymaker out of sight."

She sat on the desk. Not just leaned against it, flat out hauled her butt up there and pulled her legs up to sit Indian-style, like a little kid. Was quiet for a moment, but didn't stop staring at Andre. Not his face, though, his body... no, his watch.

"Mr. Stone—"

"Andre. I ain't no Mister." And he wasn't no Sergeant, not anymore. "It's just Andre."

She nodded, locked her gaze on his. Looked a little sad. "Andre. How would you feel about getting out of here? Taking us to Darius?"

Callahan interrupted. "He already told you he doesn't know where Darius is."

Haddad turned to the Doc. "Maybe he's lying. Maybe he's holding out on us."

Lucy was silent, staring at Andre, waiting for his answer. He raised his left hand, glanced at his watch. She gave him a half-smile and a nod.

"I'll do it."

"Do what?" Haddad asked.

Callahan figured it out first. "No. Andre—"

"Too late, Doc. I said I'll do it."

"How closely can you track a GPS watch?" Lucy asked the guy on her radio.

"Five foot radius in the open air. Inside a building, I can give you horizontal position but won't be able to give you a vertical one."

"And you'll give us live time video via the drone?"

"Yep. Colonel Adamson cleared it. I'm afraid there's not much more in the way of backup available. If you can give me time once we have the location I can try to pull a few bodies."

"I thought you said things were quieting down out there," Haddad said.

The guy on the radio grew sober. "We lost Zone Five. SWAT teams were storming the sniper positions and they," he swallowed hard enough that it echoed through the radio, "the Rippers took them out. Rocket-propelled grenades."

Silence. Andre and Haddad exchanged glances. Firepower like that, they were going to lose a lot more men tonight if they couldn't find Zapata and stop this.

"Any luck tracing their command center?" Lucy asked.

"No. Closest I've been able to narrow it is somewhere in Homewood, Highland Park, East Liberty, or Larimar. Wherever it is, they have it on the move."

Probably in a van or RV. Something that wouldn't be noticed—maybe a tractor trailer. That's what Andre would use.

Lucy frowned. The Doc stepped over to her, didn't touch her, just stood closer. She gave him a grim smile. "Any more bad news?"

"The riots and looting have spread. Not to mention the Gangstas seemed to have figured out that this would be a good night to eliminate the competition. There's a whole gaggle of them headed your way."

"Taylor, as always, you're the sunshine of my life."

"Sorry, Boss."

She turned to the men before her. "Gentlemen, it looks like we have our work cut out for us. And time is growing short."

Andre began taking his mask off. He remembered Mad Dog's look of revulsion mixed with fear and pity when he'd seen Andre without it before. He could use that now.

The Doc turned to his wife. "Lucy, there has to be another way."

She unfolded her legs and jumped to her feet. "Is there any medical reason why he can't do it?"

"Besides the fact that they'll kill him?"

Andre stood tall, his mask off, and faced the Doc. "You said I needed to take control of my life. This is me, doing what I want, when I want, how I want." Callahan opened his mouth to protest. Andre kept going before he could say anything. "My last mission didn't end up so good. I need a chance to make it up to my men."

He knew Callahan didn't agree, he could see it in the Doc's eyes. But still, he nodded his understanding.

Andre turned to Lucy. "Just let me say goodbye to my grams first."

She nodded. "Of course. We'll need a few minutes to set up a jailbreak. And I want to talk to the other Rippers, just in case they know something." Her tone made it clear she wasn't counting on it.

"Doc, you'll see that Grams is taken care of, if—" No need to say what the "if" was.

Callahan nodded. "Yes, of course. But Andre, don't think that way. You're coming back."

Andre shrugged. Callahan walked with Andre out the door and up the steps.

"I'm serious," the Doc continued. "If they wanted you dead, they would have killed you already. And Lucy, she's the best. I'm not just saying that, honest. She won't stop until she has you and Raziq's family safe. You actually remind me a little of her."

"Pig-headed," Andre quipped, gesturing with the mask still in his hand.

The Doc's chuckle was a second late in coming. "Yeah. Something like that. Anyway, all you need to do is buy her time."

"It's okay, Doc. Really. This is what I'm the best at. I'm just a grunt from Dog Company, but I'm the best goddamn boots on the ground grunt you'll ever meet. Now, let's go find my Grams."

"She's going to be pissed as hell."

Andre's one regret. "Yeah. I know. That's why I'm bringing you along."

CHAPTER 32

JENNA DECIDED THAT Saint Lucy had officially gone off her rocker when she heard the plan. David was okay with it, as long as it meant he got Raziq and his family back safe and sound. Jenna had no idea what Andre Stone thought—although it would be his ass on the line.

She and David ferried the three Rippers down to the rectory's basement, keeping the two kids in one room and isolating Mad Dog in the other. She left David interviewing the kids while she went to get Stone. Lord only knew what Lucy was doing, she was holed up in the Tahoe now parked out of sight behind the convent, working with Taylor.

Jenna crossed the small courtyard that separated the church from the convent. The clouds had cleared, the stars were out, a brisk breeze gave the air a pleasant crispness. The scent of smoke only added to the homey atmosphere. No Morgan, not since Jenna had hung up on her earlier, no drunken revelry that she'd regret in the

morning, no need to constantly look over her shoulder…
why couldn't it always be like this?

Because Saint Lucy had another windmill to tilt at
and Jenna couldn't let her and David go in alone.
Despite his guilt-ridden fixation on Raziq, David was a
good guy. She wasn't about to let Lucy get him killed.
And she still needed Lucy alive if she was ever going to
get her hands on Morgan. Although somehow that
fantasy just didn't have the power it once had.

She was tired, so tired. Of playing games with
Morgan. Of never measuring up to Saint Lucy's
standards. Of feeling so goddamned all alone no matter
how many men she fucked.

Jenna sighed, her breath steaming the air in little
wisps that blew away like birthday wishes. She entered
the convent where one of the nuns pointed her to a small
sitting room where Stone sat with a little old lady. He
had his mask off and for the first time Jenna saw the
extent of his injuries. Jesus. No wonder the guy was off
his rocker. To live through that only to find out your men
had all died? And then return home and look in the
mirror at the evidence of your failure every day?

It was a lot like the way she felt knowing she'd let
Morgan get away, free to torture and kill and do
whatever she damned well pleased. Jenna couldn't let the
bitch get Lucy because that meant Morgan won. It
meant Jenna was a failure.

God, life would be so much easier if Lucy had just let
her pull that damned trigger last month.

Nick stood in the corner of the room watching Stone
with the same fatherly look he often gave Jenna. Like he
was watching a kid ride his bike down a steep hill for the

first time without training wheels. Funny, she'd never thought about him actually caring about other patients the way he cared about her. It made her feel not so special.

"We have to go," she said brusquely, interrupting Stone's little goodbye party. Petty, she knew, but they really did need to get started.

Stone leaned forward and whispered a few words into the old lady's ear, then kissed her on the head as if she was a child. She gripped his arm, finally released him.

"Come home to me, child," she called as they left the room. "I love you."

Nick stayed behind, taking Stone's place, patting the old lady's arm.

"That's your grandmother?" Jenna made conversation as she led him back outside. "She going to be okay?"

"She's tougher than most Marines I know, so yeah." He glanced over his shoulder one last time as the door shut behind them. "You the one I'll be wrestling the shotgun from?"

"Yeah. Lucy thought it might look more realistic if you tackled me instead of Haddad." They walked around behind the convent to where Lucy had parked the Tahoe. She held a finger up for them to wait, finished talking with Taylor, and joined them.

"Andre, Taylor has the software for your watch loaded onto all of our cell phones and he'll be tracking you as well, so we'll all know where you are at any moment. If you get into trouble and need us to come in heavy, just take the watch off. We'll know as soon as we lose the signal," Lucy said.

"What if they take the watch from me?" he asked.

"They'd only do that if they suspect something, which would mean you need us to get you out." Lucy opened the Tahoe's hatch and grabbed the only weapon left inside: a shotgun loaded with nonlethal beanbag rounds. "Be sure you're the one who grabs the shotgun from Jenna and fires at her. If you can, miss in a way that Mad Dog can't see where the shot went. If you can't, hit her in her vest."

He turned to Jenna. "You okay with that? These things pack a punch."

Nice of someone to ask. Jenna rapped her knuckles against the ceramic plates of her ballistic vest. "I'm tougher than I look."

He returned her smile. In the dim light, even with his smile twisted and crooked, something about his eyes gave her a glimpse of the man he was before. She thought she would have liked to have met that man.

Lucy double-checked that the load was non-lethal. She practically vibrated with adrenalin. Jenna was surprised her hair didn't stand on end from all the energy spilling out from her. Now wouldn't that be a sight?

Lucy gave Jenna the shotgun and continued her briefing, barely taking a breath between sentences. "Either way, Jenna will fall so Mad Dog won't be able to see the wound or the lack of blood. Then you guys run. I left the van out front—"

"No way he'll want to take that piece of crap," Stone said. "Too easy to follow."

"Exactly. So you'll go through the pedestrian gate and head out on foot. My hope is that he'll grab the Escalade we left at Kujo's. If not, take any vehicle. I don't care as long as he's convinced that he needs to take you to Darius before we catch you."

"Don't worry. I can make it happen."

From where she stood behind Lucy, Jenna gave a small shake of her head. She couldn't believe the guy was going along with this crazy, jacked up plan. It was suicide.

But then again, she couldn't believe she was either. Lucy was going to owe her big time after this.

———◆———

As JENNA SHOVED Andre down the stairs beneath the rectory, Andre could hear Lucy and Haddad arguing inside the classroom. They'd put the two kids in the bathroom and barricaded them inside, leaving Mad Dog in a second, smaller classroom behind the first. Where hopefully he heard everything.

"I have him dead to rights on threatening a federal agent, terroristic activities, kidnapping, and felony assault," Lucy yelled. "He's mine."

"No way. I'm the one he threatened, it's my call," Haddad returned. "We let the locals pick him up for murder. I'm not letting those two little girls' deaths go unpunished while he serves time in the federal system. Pennsylvania has the death penalty, I say we let them use it."

"C'mon, you really think he'll last a week in prison? Looking like that?"

"I want him going down for murder."

Andre stumbled. Haddad's voice dripped with ice. Guy was telling the truth—he really, really wanted whoever killed those girls punished. If it went down the way Lucy had said, Andre couldn't blame him.

Jenna shoved him past the door to the first classroom where Lucy and Haddad continued their argument.

"Make it look good," she whispered. She reached to open the door. He could have taken her then, but the timing didn't feel right. He needed Mad Dog prepped first. She pushed him inside the room, slammed the door behind him, and locked the door.

The room was set up for younger kids. No desks, just tiny chairs on a foam rug covered with cartoon characters. Walls lined with plastic bins of coloring supplies, finger paint. And Mad Dog. Sitting on a desk shoved into the corner, hands restrained behind him, yet somehow he looked as cocky as he did when he'd grabbed Andre off the street earlier.

"They got a hard-on for you, dawg," Mad Dog drawled.

Andre looked over his shoulder at the closed door. Lucy and Haddad could still be heard shouting at each other, now arguing about who out-ranked who.

"Sonsofbitches setting me up for murder," Andre said. It wasn't hard letting traces of both fear and venom leak into his voice. The emotions were honest. "Say I killed a couple of girls. Tried to blow up some DEA agent. They're talking the fuckin' death penalty, man."

"Too bad we can't do something about that."

Andre slumped against the wall. Conscious of Mad Dog watching him, he raised his ziptied wrists to wipe the sweat from his forehead.

"What happened to your mask?" Mad Dog asked.

"Bitch took it. Said I'd best get used to showing my face cuz they won't let me have it in prison." Andre looked over his shoulder at the door, letting a touch of fear show.

"They kept your hands in front."

"Had to," Andre said off-handedly. "Can't reach behind my back. Scar tissue." He frowned, hard. Pushed off the wall and paced to the door. Tried the knob. Locked. Spun and paced the other way. "I can't go to prison. No way. And murder? I didn't kill no one."

"Like they care. You say anything about Darius?"

Andre jerked his chin up, stared at Mad Dog. "No. I'd never rat. You know that. Could've given Darius up last time I got caught, but didn't." His shoulders sagged and he spun back to the door. "Besides, what was I supposed to say? That I couldn't be killing those girls because I was helping you guys plan to kill someone else?" He kicked the door so hard it shook. "I'm fucked!"

"Chill, homes."

Andre ignored him. He paced in a tight circle, his breath coming in heaving gasps that almost bent him double. "Fucked, fucked, fucked. No way out." He stopped suddenly, faced Mad Dog with wide eyes. "MD, they're gonna kill me. I got to get out of here. Now."

Mad Dog looked at him with a combination of pity and cunning. Almost there. Andre finally fell against the wall, wheezing, face buried in his hands.

"Andre, stop it. Hey." Mad Dog got to his feet and kicked Andre's thigh. "I said stop it. You do everything I say and I'll get you out of here."

Andre didn't look up. "Really?" he moaned through his hands. "How?"

"First of all stop your bellyaching. It's embarrassing."

Andre wiped his face, lowered his hands.

"Find something you can use as a shim. Get me out of these damn things." Mad Dog waved his bound hands at Andre.

A few minutes later, with the help of a paperclip Andre found on the floor, they both had their hands free.

"Now what?" Andre asked.

"Now you fake an asthma attack. I'll get the guard in to get your inhaler."

Andre nodded and began to fake wheeze and cough loudly. Mad Dog kicked on the door. "Help! Hey, he's dying here. Needs his medicine. You all got to get him his medicine!"

A moment later the door popped open and Jenna stepped in. "What's going—"

Andre lunged and twisted her gun from her grasp as Mad Dog tackled her. As soon as Mad Dog rolled clear of her body, Andre fired the shotgun, missing Jenna by inches—but Mad Dog's back was to her, so he never knew. The shot thundered through the basement.

"Shit, dawg. I said to hit her, not shoot her," Mad Dog grumbled as they ran down the hall.

"Stop!" Lucy shouted behind them. She fired her gun as Andre and Mad Dog sped up the stairs. They pushed through the door and ran into the courtyard.

"Take the van?" Andre asked when Mad Dog hesitated. Damn, it was hard to lead a man without him knowing it.

"No, stupid. Too slow. This way." Mad Dog spotted the pedestrian gate and sprinted for it just as Lucy and

Haddad burst through the door behind them, firing at them.

Callahan came out the convent door, blocking Lucy and Haddad's path. Andre spun and aimed at him. Pulled the trigger and nothing happened.

"Damn, I'm out!" He threw the shotgun to the ground with a clatter.

Lucy and Haddad waved Callahan back, but it slowed them a little. Enough to allow Mad Dog to reach the gate.

Andre grinned in the darkness then followed Mad Dog. About time he got to take the fight to Raziq. As he ran, footsteps pounding against the pavement, he swore he heard his squad cheering him on.

CHAPTER 33

AFTER ANDRE VANISHED into the night, Lucy checked her phone. His signal was easy to follow. She walked past the convent, heading towards the Tahoe, and Nick joined her.

"I'm coming with you," Nick said in his "you can't talk me out of this" tone. "He's my patient."

Lucy turned to him, had to swallow her initial, adrenalin-fueled response. Fake gunfight or not, there was no way to avoid triggering the flight or fight reflex. After a deep breath in and out, she was able to answer him in a steady tone. "We've reports that the Gangstas are headed this way. I need you to stay here, keep everyone safe. Watch over these people."

"Then you stay, too." He stretched to his full height, shoulders back so his chest appeared broader. There was nothing like a firefight to create a testosterone spike. "At least that way, I'll only have Andre to worry about."

Not even on the menu. She needed to know he was safe—or as safe as she could make him. "Nick. These people need you. Really, it's the best way you can help." Besides, she was not about to let an untrained civilian put himself in danger—or worse, distract her so they both got killed. "You're not coming. That's final."

His forehead furrowed with anger. "You think I'm a liability, don't you? Lucy, is that what you've always thought?"

God, not now. She and Nick seldom argued much less fought—but when they did, they tended to be knock-down-drag-'em-blow-outs of fights. Fast and loud and furious.

"This isn't the time or place. Let's talk later when we're both calm." Damn, she was using her hostage-negotiation voice. Nick hated when she did that.

"Don't treat me like a child or one of your two-bit criminals."

She reached a hand out to him but he shrugged it off. Jenna waved to her from the Tahoe, *hurry up*. But she couldn't leave Nick. Not like this. She grabbed both of his wrists, wouldn't let go even when he tried to jerk his hands away. Pulled him so close her face would fill his vision—which had probably narrowed to a small circle thanks to the adrenalin pumping through his system. "Nick. I love you. I want you safe. I would give anything to stay here with you."

He pulled back, lips twisted into a scowl. So not her husband, Mr. Zen-calm. But then, he'd never been in battle conditions before. He'd come close, a few months ago when Megan had been threatened, but Lucy had dealt with the actual danger.

Since then, small fractures had splintered through their marriage. Hearing about her job, reading about it in the news, was a hell of a lot different than seeing it and knowing all you could do was stand helpless on the sidelines.

Now Nick was in the middle of a war. And it was all too clear he wanted a chance to fight. "I can take care of myself."

"I know that. That's why I'm trusting you to take care of these people. There isn't anyone else I would trust to do that."

His expression softened. "I just—I can't let you go back out there. What if something happens to you?"

She kissed him. Hard and deep, not releasing the pressure until he relented and some of the tension eased from him.

"I'll be fine. I promise." He knew she never made a promise she couldn't keep. Neither of them pointed out that this promise was one she had no earthly control over. "But I'll be more fine if I know I don't have to worry about anyone here." Anyone including Nick.

He was still irritated, but nodded. "Okay. Give me a gun."

She handed him her backup Baby Glock and a spare magazine. He took it clumsily but held it without aiming at anyone. Nick had always been a bit passive-aggressive about having weapons in their house, much less actually using them. She'd never called him on it before, had let him hold the moral high ground, because, well, Nick almost always had the moral high ground in their relationship. He always put family first, even over his patients, while Lucy couldn't honestly say that about her job.

"God, you look so sexy right now," she told him in *sotto voce*.

He grinned and with a flash of bravado, pulled her close, bending her back in a dramatic dip as he kissed her. "You'd better keep your promise and come back in one piece. Because I'm expecting one hell of a date night to make up for missing the ballet."

Laughter burbled from her, driven by relief. Whatever happened, he'd be okay—they'd be okay. Knowing that, she could face anything.

——◆——

THANK GOD FOR spyware, Morgan thought as she idled outside the gates of Holy Trinity. Otherwise she would have never been privy to Lucy's plan.

Who was this Andre Stone that Lucy was using as bait? And this Raziq family they were trying to rescue? It was clear Andre didn't trust the father, yet he was willing to put his life on the line for them.

What could be so important about them on a night like this when people were dying all over the city?

Interesting. She especially liked the part where they were going to track Andre back to whoever had orchestrated the city's bloodbath. Zapata. Him she'd like to meet.

She'd initially planned to simply watch through her binoculars. But when the gang guy and Andre made their break and came running down the street right towards her, how could she resist joining in on the fun?

The whimsy of fate, her dad's voice echoed through her mind. That and the fact that she'd strategically parked downhill from Holy Trinity. If she was a prisoner intent on escape, she'd turn to run downhill, not up.

Morgan unlocked the Honda's doors, turned her lights and turn signal on as if she'd just gotten into the car and was driving away. She made sure her bag was on her side of the car, right at hand between her seat and the driver's door. It looked like a purse but it was much, much more, holding everything she needed: duct tape, two stun guns, pepper spray, wire, compact Smith and Wesson .38 revolver, lock picks, three stolen cell phones, cash, and, of course, her beloved knives. Surgical steel, freshly sharpened.

She pulled from the curb, timing it so she almost hit the first man running, and lurched to a stop. She rolled down her window, one hand on her .38, just in case, and called, "I'm so sorry. I didn't see you!"

Before she could finish he'd raced around to the passenger door and jumped in. His partner, Andre Stone she assumed, hopped in the back. "Drive, bitch!"

——— • ———

ANDRE TOOK HIS eyes off Mad Dog for a second, that was all, while he checked their flank, and next thing he knew there was a screech of brakes and Mad Dog was jumping into some white girl's car. Girl had to be about the unluckiest person on the planet, choosing this street on this night to get lost on.

Only way to keep her safe was to hop in after Mad Dog. Like he needed one more civilian to worry about.

"How about I drive and we ditch the chick?" Andre suggested from his place in the backseat.

The girl hunched over the wheel, gripping it so tight they'd need a crowbar to pry her loose. Plus she was speeding up Ruby Avenue, the little Honda bouncing like a trampoline with each pothole.

"Chill, I got this," Mad Dog said, sounding like he was enjoying himself. "You get down back there, can't afford to have anyone see your ugly face."

No way. Andre needed to see where they were going. Not to mention what Mad Dog was doing to the girl. He already had his hand on her thigh, kneading her leg through her jeans like he owned her. Shit. Maybe it was for the best that she was driving—at least he couldn't rape her.

It was what would happen to her once they arrived that Andre was worried about. How was he going to take out Mad Dog with Darius and who knew how many Rippers and cartel guys there?

If he left the girl alone with Mad Dog at least he'd have a chance of finding Fatima and the baby, completing his mission. No, he couldn't risk her life. He'd just have to take his chances with Darius and anyone else waiting for them.

Might finally get his wish and re-join his squad. Funny, the thought didn't really have the appeal it had a few hours ago. Like he had something worth living for.

That thought scared him more than the idea of dying.

CHAPTER 34

LUCY DROVE. AMAZING how being behind the wheel made her feel so much more in control. Of what she wasn't sure because it was obvious to everyone that her "plan" could have been better labeled a "wing and a prayer." But it was the only chance Raziq's family had.

Jenna sat in the back giving directions from her laptop and talking with Taylor. Haddad had shotgun—literally, holding Lucy's Remington and keeping an eye out his open window.

"Taylor says they jumped into a gray Honda. No ID on the driver. It was reported stolen three days ago."

Lucy frowned. "There's no way they could have arranged for a getaway car."

"Maybe one of the Rippers followed us after we picked them up?" Haddad suggested. "Was waiting for them?"

"Figures the bad guys would be two steps ahead of us," Jenna said. "They're headed west on Frankstown."

Lucy stepped on the accelerator and turned left onto Frankstown Avenue. She wanted to stay out of sight of Andre's vehicle but didn't want to be too far behind in case he needed backup. "Ask Taylor if he's having any luck locating Zapata's control center."

The sound of automatic weapons fire came from not far away.

"See anything?" she asked Haddad who had her monocular in addition to the shotgun.

"No vehicles approaching."

"Taylor says it's Gangstas," Jenna reported. "They torched Kujo's and have begun to raid the projects, looking for Ripper stash houses."

Lucy hated to think of driving away, leaving civilians to fend for themselves, but she could only be one place at a time. "Anyone coming to help them?"

Jenna was silent. Lucy interpreted that as a big fat "no."

She kept driving, turning onto Liberty. A police car sped past going the other way, but other than that, traffic was nonexistent, although there were a lot of vehicles double-parked, choking the street from its normal four lanes down to barely two.

More sirens and the rumble of helicopters came from the south. "That's the new Target on fire," Lucy said. Haddad swiveled to look out the window. Flames danced across the skyline.

"Looks like they got Whole Foods as well," he pointed to a second, smaller fire.

An entire neighborhood's hopes for revitalization doomed in one night.

"Turn north onto Highland," Jenna directed.

"Where the hell are we going?" Lucy wondered.

"Wherever it is, they planned well," Haddad said. "This area is covered by Zones Four and Five. Once they were gone, there was no real police presence."

"Except the police tied up at both station houses."

"Until the Rippers took them out," Jenna added. "With freakin' RPGs." She didn't sound too happy about the prospect of facing that kind of superior firepower. Lucy couldn't blame her.

Taylor's voice squawked excitedly from her radio. "Boss, I know where they're going."

"Where?"

"The Highland Park Zoo. It's perfect. Tons of empty land, easy access, and with Washington Boulevard blocked no one will be driving nearby. Think of the possibilities—"

"What makes you so certain?" Not that she didn't trust Taylor, but sometimes his imagination went a little wild.

"I flew the drone ahead of the Honda, trying to map out their possible route and the zoo was the only place that made sense. Then I sent it around at treetop level and guess what I saw?"

"Taylor—"

"An RV with a satellite antenna. And going into it was Rashid Raziq."

"Rashid?" Haddad twisted in his seat and reached for the radio. "Are you sure? Was he okay? Were Fatima and the baby with him?"

"He was alive and walking. Couldn't tell much else. One guard with him. Carrying what looked like an AK-47."

So Raziq was a prisoner. Still, Lucy couldn't shake her doubts about the man. Too many contradictions, too many coincidences—like Zapata targeting the hockey tournament where Mina's boyfriend was playing. No evidence, but enough to make her anxious.

"Taylor, send us a map of the zoo and mark exactly where that RV is. Keep an eye on it—if it moves, we need to know." They could track Andre via his GPS while using the drone to watch Raziq.

Lucy hit the gas pedal. Maybe this plan wasn't such a crapshoot after all. Maybe she really could save Mina and Badria's family. The two girls deserved much more—like their killer caught—but it would be a start.

MD, THE GUY with the gold on his teeth spelling out his initials, directed Morgan to the zoo's employee entrance off Lake Drive. Two men stood guard. MD stuck his head out the window and they opened the gate. Morgan had never been to the zoo before. She hadn't realized it was surrounded by forest—you'd never know you were in the middle of a city.

They passed through the gate. There were amber lights lining the narrow street. To their left was a large glass building with a wavy roof. The sounds of an elephant trumpeting drifted through MD's open window.

His hand rubbed against her crotch and he asked her, not for the first time, "This how you like it, bitch?"

She'd decided that MD stood for Must Die.

Happy to oblige, bitch. In addition to the toys in her purse she had a wicked little switchblade hanging from a chain around her neck and another, larger one clipped to the small of her back. If good ole MD got any more friendly she might not wait until they arrived at their destination.

Andre had tried his best to distract MD, asking him questions, pointing to the fires in East Liberty, pretending to spot cops and telling MD to get down.

Morgan had been impressed by his volunteering to help Lucy—although she'd wondered if he had some kind of death wish. She'd also taken note of the bond he and Nick shared and had even been a little envious of the way he and his grandmother cared for each other.

But watching him trying so hard to protect her—especially as he was more than clueless about who or what she was—well, that was too precious for words.

She'd do her best to keep him alive, she decided.

She indulged herself in a little shiver of delight. It reminded her of that moment before she'd stepped in front of Nick's car earlier tonight—that exhilarating feeling that anything was possible. This being a hero was kind of fun. Maybe Nick was right, there were better ways to channel her talents.

MD laughed, thinking her shudder was amorous in nature. Oh yeah, she just couldn't wait to get up close and personal with him. Give her a few minutes and she'd have his heart in her hand.

They came to a crossroads. An Escalade was parked below a street sign. Lions and tigers and aquarium to the left. Bears to the right. And straight ahead the African Painted Dogs.

"We get out here," MD announced.

Morgan gave a little shriek that she hoped sounded like she was terrified. In reality she was trying to decide which animal species would most enjoy snacking on MD's heart.

CHAPTER 35

ANDRE GOT OUT of the Honda on the passenger side. He stood, blocking Mad Dog's door, hoping the girl would take a hint and run. She turned the car off, took her time getting out, even grabbing her purse and carefully arranging it over her shoulder. Like they'd just arrived at a restaurant for a date or some shit.

Mad Dog shoved his door against Andre. Leaning his weight against Mad Dog, Andre looked over the hood of the car and met the girl's eyes.

She winked at him. What the fuck?

Mad Dog pushed the door again, harder. Andre stumbled back. When he looked up, the girl had vanished into the shadows.

"Shit, where'd she go?" Mad Dog shouted. "Andre, you idiot."

"No time for that," Andre said. "I killed a fucking fed, man! We've got to find Darius and get the fuck out of here. Now."

"Chill. Darius will take care of you. He's right over there." Mad Dog pointed past the Escalade down the path to a food stand lit up in the darkness. "Right across from the bears. Don't fall in, let them eat you."

"Aren't you coming with?"

"Nah. Gotta a hot date with some white pussy." Mad Dog hitched up his jeans and strolled toward the bushes surrounding the aquarium where the girl had disappeared.

Andre blew his breath out in frustration. The girl was gone, he had to focus on finding Fatima and the baby. He checked his watch. Working just fine. He jogged toward the food stand.

The bears were in pits to his right. They must have missed dinner because they made snuffly growling noises as he passed. He moved to the other side of the trail. Another elephant called out in the distance. At the end of the path, on the other side of the food stand, was a huge pyramid shaped glass building. The sign pointing to it said "Primate Habitat" and had pictures of monkeys and apes on it.

Andre had almost reached the food stand when he pulled up short. This side of the trail was lined by a chain link fence. Rustling came from the other side accompanied by strange high-pitched chirping. Like a dolphin's song—only it was coming from the high grass and bushes.

The rustling grew louder. Andre scanned the darkness beyond the fence. Yellow eyes flicked in and out of sight. He started jogging again, passing a sign that read "African Painted Dogs" and had a picture of a dog with a long snout and large, saucer-like ears.

They didn't look or sound like any dogs he'd ever met. Andre figured any dog that could survive the wilds of Africa probably wasn't one he wanted to meet. He took another two steps towards the food stand when he heard another noise. Not the weird chirping dogs, not this time. This time the noise was distinctly man-made.

The sound of a shotgun shell being chambered. From behind him.

"Glad you could make it, Andre," Darius said as two men flanked Andre. Darius still wore his fancy designer suit. Giselle trailed along behind him, but even in the faint yellow glow of the lights lining the path Andre could see she now sported a black eye and split lip. She cut him a sidelong gaze and he had the feeling he was somehow to blame for her beating.

Darius caught her looking at Andre and grabbed her wrist, yanking her almost off her heels. "What you looking at, bitch?"

Andre let Darius' men pat him down. They didn't bother with his watch.

"Where's your mask?" Darius asked.

"Lost it." Andre fought to remember to play his role. Hard to do when anger lit through him like a wildfire and all he wanted to do was haul off and plant Darius on his ass, give him a taste of a good old fashioned beat down. "I need your help. Mad Dog and me, we shot a Fed, killed them. They're gonna be looking for us. He said you had a way out of the city without the cops knowing."

Darius squinted at Andre as if deciding whether to trust him or not. Then he nodded. "Come with me."

Andre and the guards followed Darius and Giselle the rest of the way towards the food stand. It was a small rectangular building. Wood siding and a metal roof covered with fake thatching, like it was supposed to be out of Africa or some bullshit like that. Round metal tables with attached benches surrounded the entrance.

At the table farthest from them sat Fatima, holding her baby close.

———•———

HOLY TRINITY'S BELL tower was square, open on four sides with a narrow catwalk around its perimeter. It was only three stories high, but since the church was on the top of the hill and faced down over the city, it felt much taller.

Walking its perimeter Nick felt like an ancient Centurion, guarding the Roman Empire. Silly, he knew, but he never would have dreamed that he'd be standing in a tower, looking out over a city at war, holding a weapon, and responsible for the lives of over a dozen people.

Every day he listened to his patients recount their stories of their war—and he prided himself on not just empathizing with them but really seeing each story as a separate, unique, individual war. All of them woven together added up to nothing remotely like the fiction the media twisted "war" into, but it was the individual perspective he was most interested in. Each person's private story of what being a soldier fighting for their country meant to them.

What a jackass he'd been, thinking he understood anything! And Lucy, God, she must think him an idiot. All those times he lectured her on being safe and not taking risks and putting her family first.

The gun, small as it was, was heavy in his hand. He'd tried carrying it in his pocket but it was too hard to pull out fast and too easy to accidentally slide his finger on the trigger. He didn't dare let it go or put it down—what if he needed it and it was out of reach? What if he was looking in the wrong direction, missed the danger? What if something happened and he wasn't fast enough, smart enough, good enough to deal with it in time?

Every automatic thought and anxiety he taught his patients to conquer now held him hostage. He used all the techniques he knew, but under the pressure of adrenalin and responsibility they failed.

His nerves jangled with agitation, he felt at once on edge and drained, jittery and exhausted. Just holding on to all the paradoxes of emotion surging through him sapped his energy. But he couldn't give in to fatigue. He had to stay alert.

He continued his endless pacing, cataloguing dangers.

East: new fires, several blocks away, accompanied by gunshots. There were cars now on the roads, weaving through the neighborhood. Gangstas on the prowl.

South: the fire at the Rippers' clubhouse had spread to neighboring houses, both empty, the sisters had told him. Otherwise Ruby Avenue was quiet.

West: two large fires in East Liberty. Helicopters buzzing all over, their blinking red lights and the occasional high-powered spotlight breaking through the haze of smoke.

North: a large blaze where the Zone Five police station and fire department training center had been bombed. Rocket-propelled grenade—RPGs his patients called them. Helicopters circled the destruction.

His city was dying. And his wife was out there somewhere.

Footsteps sounded on the steps below him. He whirled, brought the gun up—and almost shot Sister Patrice. Nausea washed over him as he lowered the pistol. Forced himself to unclench his hand and set it on the wall. "I'm sorry, Sister."

She smiled, forgiving him. Despite the long night, she still looked refreshed, her navy slacks sharply creased, white blouse crisp, navy veil falling in unwrinkled folds to her shoulder. He couldn't tell her age; he often had that problem with nuns. Why was it priests always looked older than they were but nuns younger?

"I brought you a fresh thermos of coffee and some cinnamon buns straight from the oven." Hell was breaking loose under their feet and the nuns were baking? No wonder Lucy had lost her faith. Or maybe that was a reason to keep the faith. More paradoxes his mind couldn't hold together.

"Thank you." His voice had a tremor. Hard to talk when your teeth were clenched. He had a new appreciation for Lucy's chronic TMJ symptoms. He had a feeling that after tonight he would see a lot of Lucy's world in a different light. If only, please God, she made it back to him alive. See, there was that Faith again. Only maybe it was more like foxhole religion.

"Is there anything you need before we go out?" Patrice asked.

"No. I'm fine—wait, go where?"

She pointed to the east. "We got word there are families trapped in the Terraces." The public housing a few blocks over. "Gangstas breaking in, terrorizing them, looking for Rippers and drugs."

"You can't go out there," he protested.

"They don't have a way out. We'll pick them up in the van, bring them back here where they'll be safe."

"No, Sister. You can't. You need—" He picked up the gun. It felt very small, no protection against what was going on out there. Better than nothing. "I'll come along. Guard you."

She shook her head as if chiding a child who'd gotten his catechism wrong. "No, Nick. You stay here. Bringing a gun will only make things worse."

"But—no. You don't understand. The Gangstas will kill you. You need protection."

Her smile was both patient and forgiving. She said nothing, simply touched the cross around her neck, its plain silver glinting in the faint moonlight.

To think he'd once accused Lucy of magical thinking. Sister Patrice vanished down the steps as he stood, holding the gun, torn between racing after her and staying to watch over the people she was leaving behind.

Finally he ran after her, the gun clutched tighter than ever in his hand.

———◆———

NO SIGN OF Raziq or Zapata. Andre slowed his steps as they passed the tables. Darius looked back. "Hurry up."

The two goons stayed at his side. He needed to help Fatima get out of here—but doing that meant sacrificing his chance to be extracted. Once he ditched the watch Lucy and her team would have no idea where he was— or their real targets, Raziq and Zapata.

Was he seriously going to blow the op to save the family of the man who'd massacred his men?

The watch was off his wrist and in his hand before he even had a chance to answer his own question.

Sorry guys, it's the right thing to do, he thought as he turned one way, startling his guards and diverting their attention, while tossing the watch onto the grass in the other direction.

"Where are we going?" he asked to cover his movement.

He wasn't really expecting an answer, wasn't even sure if it was worth continuing with the act. Darius looked back over his shoulder. "You were Dog Company in the Marines, right? That's what they called you?"

What the hell did that have to do with anything? "Yeah. So?"

They came to a fork in the path in front of the large glass pyramid that was the Primate Habitat. Darius turned left.

"Then I guess you could say you're going to a family reunion." The smile he shot Andre revealed both rows of teeth. If you shook hands with a man smiling like that, you'd count all your fingers after. "Only you're the main course." Darius laughed. The sound would have been at home among the hyenas except Andre didn't see any on display. Instead the nearest sign said African Painted Dogs.

"Cut the joking, Darius," Andre protested, staying in character even though he knew it was useless.

"No joke, Andre." Darius strolled down the path as his men prodded Andre with their guns, forcing him to follow.

"Dog meat" had been his drill sergeant's favorite name for his recruits. Andre could only hope Lucy and her team got here before that became literal.

CHAPTER 36

LUCY AND NICK had taken Megan to a special nighttime event at the zoo when they first moved to Pittsburgh. It'd been a fun way to see the animals—the darkness made walking among the wildlife feel exciting and exotic.

When she'd pulled up the map of the attacks on the city earlier, she'd noted the lack of activity surrounding Ruby Avenue but had totally discounted the huge swath of land bordering the Allegheny River where the zoo was located. She had to admit it was a brilliant strategy, using the zoo as a staging area. Low priority as a target of concern to law enforcement, no one would think twice about any activity at night, easy access to the river, major highways, and all parts of the city.

"Andre just drove in through an employee entrance," Taylor reported. "They have guards on the gate, so I'm going to route you to a spot nearby where you can climb over the wall."

"We're not going to end up in the lions' den, are we?" Jenna quipped, her voice high-strung and nervous. Gearing up for action.

"No. You'll be between the bears and the gate. So try to stay low and quiet."

His directions took them off road and out of sight of the guards. Lucy parked the Tahoe alongside the eight-foot high concrete wall.

They hopped out, grabbed their weapons. "Raziq was spotted here, in front of the aquarium." Lucy pointed to a spot on the map displayed on her phone. "Secure him, destroy their operations center, and then once you're clear, join me. I'll be following Andre's signal."

Haddad said nothing, just nodded. Jenna cleared her throat. "What if the mother and baby aren't with Raziq? Should we keep looking for them before we take out the command center?"

Lucy had thought about that. No way was she giving up on Fatima and the baby—but she had a responsibility to Andre to keep him safe. And she had to consider the rest of the city. "No. Cutting their communications takes priority. That's our best hope of stopping any further attacks they have planned. Last thing we need is a three-day siege like in Mumbai."

Jenna nodded. She and Haddad climbed to the top of the Tahoe and then over the wall. Just as Lucy was getting ready to follow, Taylor broke radio silence.

"Lucy, I just lost Andre's heart rate monitor," he said in a breathless whisper. "That's the panic signal, right?"

"Give me the coordinates." Lucy hustled up onto the Tahoe and over the wall. If Andre's watch stopped broadcasting, it meant he'd either found Fatima and the baby and was ready for them to come in… or he was dead.

———•———

JENNA LAY ON her belly in the tall grass at the edge of the wide paved path leading around the zoo. David lay alongside her, scouting the RV with Lucy's night vision monocular. "No guards on the outside. Lights on inside, but I can't tell how many people are in there."

"How do you want to work this?" She slung her AR-15 behind her and drew her SIG. The RV was too small for the rifle to be useful.

"We set up on each side. I throw a flash-bang in through the main door and you go in the driver's door. Meet in the middle."

Except in a RV the "middle" was about six feet away. She didn't like the idea of firing weapons in such close quarters. "Just make sure you don't shoot me."

"Make sure you don't shoot Raziq," he cautioned her.

Shit, that reminded her. "Can we use a flash-bang if the baby's in there?"

He hesitated, glanced through the monocular one more time, obviously re-thinking his plan. "You're right. We'll have to just chance it without. Go in, neutralize any of Zapata's men, grab the friendlies. Once they're out, we'll take care of the communications equipment."

She nodded. "Signal?"

"I'll toss a pebble at you when I'm set to go."

A nicely timed cloud slid over the moon and she used its concealment to sprint across the path to the driver's side of the RV. The driver's door was unlocked; she hoped the main door on David's side was as well.

A pebble flew over the RV's hood and landed at her feet. She yanked the door open and jumped up onto the driver's seat, weapon raised and aimed towards the men in the rear compartment just as David crashed through the main door.

"Federal agents. Hands where we can see them," he shouted.

Jenna covered the two men sitting at the table directly behind the driver's seat. They looked up over the computer equipment filling the space between them, surprised. One made a move for a semi-automatic pistol on the table but Jenna shook her head at him and he raised his hands high instead.

On the far side of the door, Raziq sat on a sofa across the room from David. Beside Raziq was a Hispanic male who had a laptop propped up on a chair in front of him. He looked at Raziq then at David and finally raised his hands.

"Rashid," David said, relief lowering his voice. "It's good to see you, old friend. Wait outside and we'll go find Fatima and the baby."

Raziq looked shocked. He sat for a moment. Jenna wanted to prod him, they didn't have a lot of time here. What if one of Zapata's men stumbled by?

Finally he stood and gave David a smile and a nod. He seemed choked up, as if he didn't trust his voice. Jenna could understand that. She remembered how overwhelming her emotions had been when she was captured and rescued last month.

Raziq took the three steps needed to reach David at the door. David moved forward to keep his man covered and give Raziq room to go out the door. Raziq stumbled, bumping into David.

The gunshot was so loud in the confined area that Jenna reacted instinctively, aiming her weapon at each of her subjects. Neither had moved. She whirled to take care of the guy on the couch. She fired twice at him, but he was already on the ground. Had David shot him? How did she miss that?

No, David was down, on his knees, and Raziq held his M4.

Then Raziq took his other hand from his pocket. Holding a small pistol.

That's when she saw the blood spraying from David's mouth as it opened and closed, no sound coming.

As her mind tried to process all the contradictory information, Raziq whirled on her, raising the M4.

"Drop it," she shouted, still not sure who'd shot David. The man on the floor behind Raziq? No, he was climbing to his feet. It couldn't have been Raziq... but...

She caught movement from the two at the table and spun around. Just in time for the one closest to her to hit her on the side of her head with his pistol butt. The pain was like getting struck by lightning: flashing, blinding, overwhelming.

She tried to fight it but the man hit her in the face followed by a sucker punch to the gut. Slumped against the back of the driver's seat, she felt fingers pry her SIG Sauer from her hand.

"Keep her alive for questioning," she heard Raziq say. Then everything went black.

CHAPTER 37

MORGAN HAD NO idea what kind of bushes these were—
evergreen with short, flexible needles, and light colored
berries—but they were perfect for her needs. Tall enough
to hide her, short enough they wouldn't force MD to go
around them, thick enough that they'd obscure MD's feet
as he pushed his way through them.

She grabbed the wire from her bag. Her father had
kept it for a variety of uses: garrote, bindings, restraints,
leash… tripwire.

As soon as the trap was set, she crouched and waited.
It was only a few moments before MD's clodding
footsteps could be heard.

"Here pussy, pussy," he called in a voice he must
have copied from a porn flick. "Come to daddy."

She rustled the bushes beside her when he began to
head in the wrong direction.

"Come out, come out. I won't hurt ya. I promise. Hand to God. But those other guys, you don't want to run into them. Stop playing games and come out—"

He tripped and fell onto his face in front of her. Quick burst of the stun gun and she had his wrists in wire, duct tape over his mouth. His legs flailed around as she flipped him over, so she sat on his belly, right over his diaphragm, making it too hard for him to breathe to fight her.

He stared up at her, eyes showing white all the way around. Fear fought with fury in his expression. She waved her favorite knife, a wicked eight-inch Spyderco, before his eyes then slid it to press against his throbbing carotid artery. Fury vanquished, only fear remained.

"Whisper quiet now," she told him. "Don't want to make Mommy mad, do you, MD?"

Idiot began to shake his head. She held her knife hand steady, letting him nick himself against the finely honed blade. A drop of blood slipped across the steel.

"Careful now, sweetie. All you need to tell me is one thing then we'll be all done. Okay?"

He didn't nod, just blinked slow and hard.

She peeled the duct tape away slowly. "Where will they take Andre?"

"Andre? How do you know Stone?"

The knife bit into his flesh. More blood, a satisfying trickle. Superficial vein, but he didn't know that. He gulped hard, his Adam's apple pushing against her knife hand.

"Answer me."

"Uh, uh, probably to the building beside the dogs. Darius had me scout it for him. It's behind the food joints, long cement building."

"How many men are here?"

He started to shrug, remembered in time and froze, shoulder half-cocked. "I dunno. Mostly all Zapata's men. I think I'm the only Ripper Darius trusted to bring with him."

She shook her head sadly at the tone of pride in his voice. Poor thing actually thought he'd been chosen. From what she'd gathered from listening to Jenna and Nick's conversations, Zapata was setting the Rippers up as Judas goats. She pressed her lips close to his, sealed the kiss as her blade slid home.

With practiced ease she pushed his head away from her, arterial spray leaking onto the dirt beside him. She cleaned her blade on his jacket sleeve then moved through the bushes, hunting.

She came out on the trail in front of the aquarium. There was an RV parked in the middle of the path. The door opened and she pushed back into the bushes, out of sight.

Two men dragged Jenna out of the RV. She sagged between them, unconscious. Behind them a third man in a suit jumped out and followed.

Blade in hand, Morgan followed cautiously. Now she had two to save. And more to kill.

Who said being a hero wasn't fun?

———◆———

DARIUS AND HIS goons took Andre behind a large privacy fence, through a door marked: Private, No Public Allowed, to a long single-story cinderblock building with a metal roof topped with more fake thatching. It had a wooden door and no windows on this side, just a few open slits as wide and high as a cinderblock up below the roofline.

A wire mesh fence extended from each front corner, creating an enclosure that included the building. As they approached, two of the strange chirping dogs gathered at the fence line, watching them.

Andre hoped it wasn't because they were hungry for dinner.

Inside it stank of rotten meat and ammonia but it was clean, with whitewashed walls and a cement floor. There were a few naked light bulbs hanging from the ceiling of the long central corridor. There were stalls on each side, like for horses, except they had cinderblock walls and thick wire doors with sturdy latches. Cages for sick animals, he guessed. Bales of straw lined the corridor outside each enclosure, ready to be spread inside for bedding. At the opposite end of the long, narrow building was another door, this one leading out to the dogs' fenced-in enclosure.

They walked him past eight stalls, four on each side, until they reached the final ones. Darius opened the cage door and motioned Andre inside. He tensed, ready to fight it out here and now, but one of the guards placed the muzzle of his gun at the base of Andre's skull.

"We don't really need you alive anymore, Andre," Darius said in a tone of mock sympathy.

Andre gauged the odds. Better to wait, give Lucy and her people more time. Maybe catch Darius off guard. He relaxed his fists and strode into the enclosure. The guards, Darius, and Giselle stayed outside the wire, watching him. This cage and the one opposite were different than the others, he noticed. On their rear walls was a sliding metal grate; an exit for animals to return to their exhibit. Above it an observation window.

There were a few bales of straw stacked against the wall, so he took a seat and waited. Just had to distract Darius and his goons long enough for Lucy to find Fatima and the baby.

Darius leaned against the wire mesh door, staring at Andre with a look of smug satisfaction. "You are one stupid piece of shit, Andre. Just want you to know that before you die."

Andre was damned tired of being treated like a zoo specimen. "You think you're so smart? No way in hell are you or the Rippers surviving this partnership you have going with Zapata."

Darius stepped forward and backhanded Andre. The blow stung, but it barely registered on Andre's pain scale. A few months of torture in a burn clinic and a few dozen surgeries would do that to you.

"The Rippers are dead," Darius said. "They just don't know it yet." He tapped Andre's temple, hard as if checking to see if his skull was hollow. "Zapata is big business, Andre. You wouldn't understand."

"Try me."

"It's all about the bottom line. Which includes keeping my new partners happy."

"Partners?" Andre frowned. "You *are* working with Raziq. But you killed his daughters."

"Did I?" Darius gave him a look that was both condescending and amused. As if Andre was a trained animal performing beyond expectations. "Time we're done, cops gonna think it was you, Andre. You picked the wrong time to come home, dawg."

"So why all this other shit? Blowing up police stations?"

"Not us. The Rippers," Darius said. He sounded proud about betraying the men they'd grown up with. "See, I learned something while you were gone. Anytime the streets got bloody the old ma'ams would raise holy hell and the cops would come running."

"Yeah, so?"

"Did you know the police department publishes an annual manpower and budget report?" This time Darius tapped his own head. "Where you think they get those extra cops? They take them from other areas like the rivers and docks." He threw up his hands, beaming in delight. "Raziq and Zapata saw it as well. They realized Pittsburgh was a perfect fit. So we whipped up the perfect storm. A neighborhood ready to explode. A vicious gang wanting to prove themselves top dog. And you, our fall guy, a dangerous former gang member obsessed with Raziq and bombs."

Andre knew Zapata and Raziq were the brains behind tonight's events. What did they get out of this? It definitely wasn't business as usual, not even for a Mexican cartel. No, not business. Military. Where everything depended on… "Supply lines. This is all about supply lines."

"Bingo. Maybe you're not so stupid after all."

"You want to control the distribution channels. The rivers." He looked up at Darius. "Barges. That's why they chose Pittsburgh. That was Raziq's job. Setting up a system of barges to smuggle Zapata's drugs up and down the East Coast."

"That and helping the DEA eliminate our competition in both Afghanistan and Mexico."

Our? Andre spotted the flaw in Darius' thinking. "You keep saying 'our' and 'we.' What makes you think Zapata is going to let you live now that you've done his dirty work for him?"

Darius narrowed his eyes. "We're partners. He needs me."

"Really, Darius? For what? Your keen fashion sense?" Andre knew he was asking for trouble, but he had to keep Darius engaged, stall for time.

"Hell, yeah," Darius laughed, snapping his cuffs. He gestured to Giselle who'd been watching from behind the door. From the worried look on her face, she'd come to the same conclusion that Andre had: that if Darius was disposable, so was she. She sidled to join Darius, her gaze locking onto Andre's, pleading. As if he were in any position to save them.

He tried one last attempt to reach Darius, breach his wall of denial. "We should make a break for it now. Get out of here before it's too late. Grab Fatima and the baby, use them as bargaining chips with the cops."

"Nice try, Andre. But I ain't buying." He nodded to the two guards. "Take his shirt off, hold him down."

Andre thought of struggling but there was no way he could take on all three and he didn't want to give Darius the pleasure. So he stood tall, waving the guards off as he unzipped his hoodie and shook free of it. Underneath he wore his fitted long-sleeved compression garment. He tore the Velcro fasteners open, pulled his arms out of the sleeves, and let it drop to the floor.

"Didn't know you were into guys, Darius." He couldn't resist the taunt.

The two guards stared at his scars. Some were surgical straight lines. Some looked like the doctors had taken a cheese grater to his skin—those were from the skin grafts. Some of the scars were pitted down to the muscle—the burns. And some were bulging worm-like pink fleshy ugliness—hypertropic, the docs called it. His skin had healed but had gone overboard, like it was on steroids and wouldn't stop heaping up on itself even after the wound was covered.

"Damn, that's ugly," Darius said. He was smiling again. Andre couldn't wait until he had the chance to wipe that smile from his face. Darius had his hand in his pocket. When he took it out he had a switchblade. He clicked it open. "Hold him down."

The two guards pinned Andre against the cement block wall. Darius flicked the blade twice across Andre's belly. Not too deep, just enough to draw blood. The skin was so thick there and the nerves so damaged, Andre barely flinched. Darius didn't like that.

Frowning, he looked over his shoulder and shouted, "Giselle, go get me the gasoline."

CHAPTER 38

LUCY MOVED THROUGH the trees along the side of the path as quietly as possible. She hit a chain link fence at the outer edge of the bear enclosure. The air was filled with a musky odor. Animals moved restlessly on the other side of the fence.

Skirting the fence, she ended up on the trail between the aquarium at one end and the Primate Habitat on the other. Across the path was a food stand with its lights on; a neon slice of pizza looking garish against the fake grass thatch roof. Two men lounged at a table, backs to Lucy.

They stood guard over a woman holding a baby. Fatima.

No sign of Andre. What had they done with him? She double-checked the GPS position on her phone. The food stand was definitely where Andre's watch had stopped sending his heart rate signal.

She'd promised him the cavalry, but he'd have to wait until she got Fatima and the baby clear. Then she realized that was exactly what he wanted. That's why there was no sign of a struggle, no sign of a body. He'd dropped the watch here so she would find Fatima.

Good intentions, but it wouldn't help her find Andre. If he was still alive.

"Taylor," she whispered into her radio. "I've spotted Fatima and the baby." How the hell was she going to get mother and child over the wall? Shit. She'd have to hide them for the duration. "I'm going to take them to the Primate Habitat exhibit for safe keeping."

"Okay, Boss. I'm still working on reinforcements. Washington Boulevard is completely shut down after the bombing of Zone Five, but I've got a squad of National Guardsmen coming in across the river. They should be there in about fifteen, twenty minutes, barring no nasty surprises."

This whole night had been chock-full with nasty surprises, why should they stop now? "Tell them to clear the bridge first. It would be a good place for an IED."

"They're on it. Can you wait for them?"

Lucy studied the situation. The men were relaxed; they were no immediate threat to Fatima and the baby. But she'd feel better with the two safely out of the line of fire. "I'm going to move them now," she told Taylor. "That will leave the coast clear of civilians once Haddad and Jenna get Raziq."

"No word from them."

She almost missed his transmission as the sound of a gunshot rang out from near the aquarium. Both men jumped to their feet, one grabbing an AK-47 from beside him, the other holding a pistol. The man with the pistol sent the first man down the path towards the disturbance as he took up a position guarding the front of the food stand, keeping Fatima behind him.

As soon as the first man passed her position and the remaining guard was looking in the opposite direction, scanning for trouble, Lucy sidled across the path. The fake-thatch canopy provided some nice, deep shadows. Hugging the food stand's wall, she came in behind the remaining guard.

There was only one chance to get this right. She couldn't risk the noise of a gunshot, but hopefully he wouldn't know that.

Fatima had turned her body to face the wall, cradling the baby between it and her, giving him as much protection as possible. Lucy crept past her, closer to the guard. He wasn't much taller than she was. He was kind of skinny, too, so if it came to close-quarters combat she might have an edge. But it would be far, far better to end this quickly and quietly.

The guard paced in the other direction a few steps, staring into the wilderness behind the fence. Strange chirping noises came from there. The African dogs, she remembered from her previous visit.

The man stepped back from the fence. She got a glimpse of his face. He seemed afraid of the dogs; he was making the sign of the cross. He took another step back and she was close enough to pounce.

She leapt forward, jamming the muzzle of her Glock against the small of his back, shoving him against the fence. "Drop the gun," she whispered. He let the pistol fall to the ground. "Don't move."

As fast as possible without dropping her guard, she checked him for more weapons, taking a spare magazine of ammunition and a folding knife from him. He wore a jeans jacket over a hoodie. She restrained his hands behind his back with a flex-cuff. Carefully crouching low enough to retrieve his pistol, an anonymous nine-millimeter, she pocketed it then turned him around.

Fatima had pivoted to watch. Fear narrowed her eyes as she hunched her shoulders protectively around the baby.

"It's okay," Lucy whispered to her. She glanced over her shoulder. No sign of the second man. But he'd be back soon, she was certain. She shoved her captive behind the counter and inside the food stand's prep area. Looked like Zapata's men had made themselves at home, leaving hot dogs, hamburgers, and pizza scattered over the countertops.

Lucy grabbed a dishtowel, tied it as a gag around the man's head with the drawstring from his hoodie, and pushed him into the walk-in pantry. She restrained his ankles with flex-cuffs. Then she locked the door and ran back to Fatima.

Men's voices came from the direction of the aquarium. Lucy grabbed Fatima's arm. "We have to go. Now."

———◆———

THE ROOM WAS total darkness. Jenna's mind felt blurry, like a car windshield that refused to defrost no matter how high you turned up the fan. Slowly awareness returned. She sat on a wooden chair, arms and legs bound to it by zipties that bit into her flesh.

Her body ached, someone had used her as a punching bag—oh yeah, that would be the guys who'd jumped her. She ran her tongue over her teeth, all there, but there was blood in her mouth and her jaw was sore. Her ribs hurt when she breathed, but at least she was breathing. Her gut ached like she'd been sucker punched but no pain below, no feeling of… she hadn't been raped.

She shook the thoughts from her head and tried to produce some saliva. A bright light clicked to life, aimed at her face, blinding her. Shadows crowded all around her and she realized there were men standing in them, watching her.

"You have to make her talk," one of the men whispered. Raziq, the bastard. "We need to know if we are compromised."

Another man whispered back. "Leave it to me. Go, get ready."

A door opened, allowing faint light to momentarily invade the room. Jenna took a quick inventory. Cinderblock walls, wooden shelves with large, white pill bottles on the far wall, a small metal desk to one side with a stack of notebooks on it. A man sidled out and the door closed again before she could see anything more.

"I'm a federal agent." She tried to shout but her mouth was so dry it came out more like a croak. "Let me go. I'm a federal agent."

"Yes, we know." A calm voice came from the shadows. Accent Hispanic, but not very thick. Invisible hands scraped a chair forward until it faced hers. Moments later a man in an elegant black suit sat down in the chair, crossing his legs, his head hidden by shadows.

The man had to be Zapata, but there was no way in hell she was going to let him know that she knew who he was. The less he knew about what they knew, the better.

"Who are you?" Jenna asked after the silence became unbearable. "My name is Jenna Galloway, I'm a federal law enforcement agent. If you let me go—"

The man laughed, cutting her off. "Why should we care if you're a *federale*?" He leaned forward as if confiding a particularly tasty morsel of gossip. "Do you know what we do to *federales* in my country? We cut off their hands and feet while they're still alive and give them to their family to bury. When we're done with the rest of the body, we drag it through the street behind our trucks and sew their faces onto soccer balls."

"What do you want?" Tears mingled with her words. They hadn't made any demands. That couldn't be good. It meant she had nothing to bargain with.

The man sat back, staring at her as he lit a cigar. "Do you know what my favorite bird is?"

Jenna wasn't sure she heard the bizarre question correctly. He arched an eyebrow and nodded at her to answer. "I don't—uh—the eagle?"

"No. No. Not the eagle. The vulture. Such hard workers. Yet they are maligned for doing their job. Just like I am. I do a job. I supply a need. I give my customers good value. But I am hunted down, cursed, treated like a dog in the street."

He paused but Jenna had no idea what to say to that.

What would Lucy do? The thought almost made her laugh. Saint Lucy would have taken them all on, no doubt, using her superpowers of persuasion to get them to let her go, maybe tie themselves up in a nice gift package while she was at it. Saint Lucy wouldn't have gotten caught off guard in the first place.

Jenna was no saint. "Let me go," she told him, anger and fear making her voice shrill. "There's the death penalty for harming federal agents in this country."

Zapata nodded, his cigar bobbing. "*Sí*, in my country as well. But, you interrupt. I was telling you about the vultures."

"I don't care about the—" From behind her, a man's hand jerked her chin down with a brutal twist and slid a knife between her teeth, silencing her.

"It is rude to interrupt. Back home I have a special place. Home to my vultures. And Carlos," he nodded to the man behind her, "he is a very special man. A butcher. First it was cows and pigs, but now he has an expertise. We bring the bodies to my fields where the vultures live. Dozens, no hundreds, of them. They watch and wait— they know what's coming. Carlos, he prepares the bodies just so. Slices open rib cages so the vultures don't have to work to reach the heart and lungs, pulverizes bones so the vultures can suck out all the marrow, cuts off the heads and crushes the skull until the brain is exposed.

"Then we stand back and I call the vultures. They come like that." He snapped his fingers. "And they eat and eat and eat. All in a few minutes. Then, whoosh," He flicked his cigar ash into the air; it vanished into the shadows. "All gone. Nothing left but a few pieces of bone to use the sledgehammer on. Dust to dust in a matter of minutes. All because of my vultures."

She closed her eyes, trying to hide from the image Zapata painted. She'd heard about a DEA video that had captured a scene like he'd described—had dismissed it as urban legend. DEA cowboys telling tall tales. But Zapata wasn't lying. It was true. All of it.

He jerked his chin at Carlos who removed the knife. Jenna dared swallow again, tasting blood from where the sharp blade had pressed against her tongue. She had the sudden need to pee, strained to focus on not suffering that indignity.

"I need to send a message to your *federales*. They need to understand this is now my city. Not theirs. But first you will tell me: who else knows we're here?"

He looked so earnest, so much like a damn bad movie villain, that she couldn't stop the laughter that burbled from her, blood speckling her spittle. "You don't scare me. There aren't any vultures in Pittsburgh."

He chuckled along with her. The laughter was cathartic, purging some of her fear—but not her anger. Good, she'd need that.

"You are correct, *chica*. But there are other, terrible ways to send a message." Carlos' palm grasped the top of her head, his fingers forcing her eyelids open. Zapata regarded his cigar as if it was inferior quality. Then he put it out. Against the back of Jenna's hand.

She couldn't help but scream. Zapata merely smiled. Jenna forced herself to swallow, it was the only way to stop the scream, focused on her breathing, trying to block out the pain.

"This is the message I will send. We will be leaving soon in a helicopter. You will accompany us. At least for the first minute of flight." He paused, one eyebrow lifted. "What do you think your corpse will look like after falling eight hundred feet?"

Jenna stared at him. The man was insane. She remembered her briefings about the Mexican cartels and their inhuman brutality. Sadistic pigs, she'd thought them at the time. It hadn't seemed at all real, as if all those decapitated bodies, those tortured men and women were fictional characters, not real life flesh and blood people.

This was the twenty-first century. They'd eradicated smallpox, cured polio, been to the Moon and Mars and beyond. Even after what she'd seen tonight, what Zapata described—no, it didn't feel real.

Zapata stared at her, his smile revealing his teeth—all of them. He just kept smiling. And she knew it was real.

Her only hope was if Lucy found her in time. Jenna screamed, shouting for help, for mercy, for God.

Victor smiled. "Pray all you want, *chica*. God is not here. Only me."

CHAPTER 39

AT ESTHER'S, NICK had been able to hold off the Rippers by playing the fool. He was a white man, clueless, in the wrong place at the wrong time, and to them that was hilarious. Plus, they'd been in no rush. They knew they had the upper hand: Esther was in the house and wouldn't be able to leave without going through them.

If it hadn't been for the nuns arriving with Jadon's aunt, Nick might have ended up dead.

The Gangstas would be an entirely different matter, he thought as he rode in the back of the white church van with Patrice and Agnes. The Gangstas had come roaring into Ripper territory looking for war only to find the enemy had already left. All that pent-up anger and adrenalin needed an outlet. Right now they were taking it out on the innocent civilians the Rippers had deserted. Nick could get them to turn their attention to him instead, but it might have deadly consequences.

There had to be another way. Not the gun—the Gangstas' guns were bigger, faster, badder than Nick's little pistol. What was left?

Lucy knew how to deal with men like the Gangstas. She always said that the trick to catching criminals, whether street thieves or serious predators, was the same: give them what they want but don't let them take it.

What did he have that the Gangstas wanted?

They arrived at the Morewood Terraces. Surrounding the parking lot, giving the housing project the shape of a three-leaf clover, were circular grassy areas, each with nine single-story, two-family brick duplexes crowded shoulder to shoulder around the perimeter. They reminded Nick of Conestoga wagons circled against a common enemy.

There was no breathing space between buildings— one unit's windows opened directly into its neighbor's. Back in the seventies when they were built he was sure the designers thought them a step up from high-rise public housing. But if Nick had been planning an experiment on overcrowding and its negative impacts, he wouldn't have had to go farther than the Terraces.

As soon as the van stopped, porch lights flicked on and doors opened. Sister Patrice jumped out, leaving Sister Agnes behind the wheel with the motor running. Women and children, elderly men, two sheepish teenaged boys prodded by older women, shoulders hunched as if trying to make themselves look smaller than they were, all came pouring from the buildings, clutching pillowcases and gym bags and shopping bags with possessions.

Nick got out as well, opened the side doors so people could get in. There was no way they'd be able to take everyone in one trip.

The first group was still several yards away from the van when the first shots rang out. The *tat-a-tat-a-tat* of a machine pistol. The people barely flinched. They simply froze, staring down at the ground.

"Look at the rats fleeing the fire," a man said, emerging from the shadows. He was dressed all in black, including a black ball cap with a large G on it. More men dressed similarly also stepped forward—all holding guns. "No one goes anywhere 'til I get what I came for."

Sister Patrice urged her flock to keep moving. "Ignore them." She turned to face the Gangstas. "There's no need to bully innocent women and children."

The leader took two steps forward, staring her down. "Think I won't shoot a nun? Think I give a shit about your God? Think again, lady."

He raised his gun. Nick's stomach clenched in anticipation. The Gangsta was going to execute Sister Patrice. He was sure Lucy would have had some brilliant tactical maneuver but all he had was himself.

Nick strolled forward into the no man's land between the Gangstas and the civilians. "Maybe I can be of assistance?"

The Gangsta glowered at him, eyebrows hunched together, mouth tight. Nick smiled at him. Behind him, Sister Patrice kept the people moving to the van.

"You lost, white boy? Know what we do to folks like you around here?"

Nick's smile didn't falter. "I know what you want." He paused. "I know how to get it for you."

The Gangstas laughed, but their posture relaxed. "You know nothing."

"I know the Rippers deserted these people," he raised his voice so that everyone could hear him. If this was going to work, he'd need help from the people on both sides of the guns. "They ran out on them, left them unprotected. They also left behind some product of value to you."

The last was a guess, but the Rippers didn't seem forward thinking enough to have emptied every stash house—besides, where would they put it? Not like they could carry it with them as they rampaged throughout the city. Nick had the feeling tonight wasn't supposed to go the way it had, that the Rippers had started something that got out of control.

He was betting his life on it.

"Where is it, then?" the Gangsta leader demanded.

"What's your name?" Nick asked. Behind him Sister Patrice loaded people into the van, but Nick had to play a long game—one vanload escaping wasn't going to help the folks left behind. "I'm Nick."

"He's Tee-Bo," someone behind him shouted.

"Pleased to meet you, Tee-Bo."

"Cut the bullshit, white boy. Where's the stash?"

Ahh… the million dollar question. He could feel the people behind him tense, ready to dive for cover. Curtains fluttered in windows all around the Terrace. All eyes on Nick.

"If you give me one minute to discuss that with my friends here," Nick said. "I'll get you your answer. But you have to promise me that when you get what you came for, you'll leave these people in peace and not come back. Do I have your word on that, Tee-Bo?"

Tee-Bo raised his gun. Nick's cheeks grew icy and his heart pounded in his ears as he waited for the Gangsta to pull the trigger.

But all Tee-Bo did was use the pistol to scratch between his shoulder blades. "You give me the Ripper's stash and I leave, that's it?"

"You leave and don't come back." Nick let his Virginia accent creep into his conversation. A southern accent made every negotiation feel a little more civil. "On your word of honor as a gentleman."

One of Tee-Bo's men snickered at the last. "Tee-bo ain't no gentleman."

Tee-Bo whirled at that, aimed his gun at the speaker. "No one asked you, mo'fucker. We trying to have a civilized discussion here. Why you go ruint it?"

The speaker looked down. Scuffed the ground with the toe of his shoe. "Thought the dude was joking, is all. Playing you."

Tee-Bo turned back to Nick. "You playing me, white boy?"

"No sir. We both want the same thing here. I'm just trying to facilitate the process."

The Gangsta thought for a moment. "Guess I have nothing to lose. Go on, you've got one minute. I'm counting it down." He raised his gun, pointed it at the civilians behind Nick. "You don't give me what I want after that, I start shooting. The kids first."

———◆———

AT FIRST, FATIMA balked at going with Lucy. After what she'd been through today, Lucy totally understood. "I'm with the FBI. Here to help."

Fatima nodded and moved a little faster. "My husband?"

"David Haddad and other agents are getting him out. But we're a bit outnumbered, so I'm going to need you and the baby to hide for awhile."

"Where?" She looked around, one hand cradling her baby's head against her shoulder. The baby must have just eaten; he was groggy, eyes drooping. "Where is safe?"

Nowhere, was the honest truth. Lucy pointed to the large glass pyramid up the hill ahead of them. "In there. Here," she handed Fatima her phone, "take this. That way we'll be able to find you when the coast is clear."

Fatima faltered, looking up at the building towering over the trees before them.

"It's the best way," Lucy urged. Together they ran up the path into the trees. The trail took a few curves as it climbed to the Primate Habitat.

They emerged onto a large clearing where several branches of the paved footpath converged. On the far side were the steps up to the entrance to the Primate Habitat. But that's not what stopped Lucy.

What stopped her was the State Police helicopter neatly parked in the center of the clearing. Trooper 4 the call sign on the tail read.

She'd found the Staties' downed helo. Only it looked perfectly undamaged. As did the man in the flight suit coming around the nose towards her. He was inspecting the helicopter, hadn't spotted them yet, but he would any second.

"Run," she told Fatima. "I'll find you inside. Hide and stay quiet."

"But, he's a police——"

"Go, now." She shoved Fatima towards the steps as she swung the Remington over her shoulder and into her hands.

Fatima ran with the baby. The movement alerted the pilot who whirled and drew his weapon. He spun, aiming at Fatima's back.

Lucy raised the shotgun. "I'm FBI," she shouted. "Lower your weapon."

He shifted his aim to her. His first shot went wide. She didn't give him a chance for a second one. The blast from the Remington echoed through the trees, drawing shrieks and squawks from the animals within hearing distance. She'd loaded the shotgun with slugs, solid projectiles, rather than buckshot. She was about ten yards away from her target, and at that distance she rarely missed.

She didn't this time either. The pilot staggered back against the helicopter. Lucy checked her perimeter, no one coming yet, and raced over to his body, kicking his weapon out of his hand. No need to worry. Not with the fist-sized hole ripped through his chest.

CHAPTER 40

SOMEONE—ZAPATA, ANDRE assumed—shouted down the hallway in Spanish. The guards left. Didn't even wait for Darius' permission. Well, now. That said a lot about the pecking order around here. Darius may have thought he was trading up, but it was pretty damn obvious he was low man on the Zapata totem pole.

Andre almost made a break for it when Giselle arrived, but Darius had the gate shut behind her too fast. She staggered under the weight of a three-gallon can of gasoline she carried with both hands. Darius held his .357 Magnum on Andre, motioned to him to turn to face the outside wall. The blood steamed down Andre's belly thick enough that it left a stain on the thick Plexiglas window.

"Unlock the gate," Darius ordered. He meant the animal gate that took up the lower half of the wall below the observation window. Andre had a feeling he knew what was coming and tried to decide which option would be worse: fire or dog meat.

But an exit was an exit. Andre pulled the latch open. The metal gate swung free in both directions, the only thing holding it shut was Andre's foot braced against it. It was a three-foot square—he could easily make a break for it. Had a feeling Darius hoped that he would.

The wild dogs weren't far; he could hear their snuffling and chittering in the enclosure beyond the gate. Excited by the scent of fresh blood.

"Giselle, get the lights," Darius ordered.

The fenced in area beyond the window lit up as overhead spotlights came to life. Three dogs were caught in the beam. They must have been used to it, because they didn't run to hide in the shadows. Instead, they raised their snouts, their strange over-sized ears cocked at attention, and strolled forward. Four more dogs emerged from the darkness to join them, chirping and calling to each other as they created a perimeter, ready for an ambush.

"I checked them out," Darius told Andre. "These dogs have an eighty percent kill success. Lions only have a thirty percent. Eighty percent, that's gotta be a helluvalot higher than any damn Marine's."

Damn impressive, Andre thought, studying his opponents. In profile the dogs' heads looked a lot like German Shepherds, if you ignored the over-sized saucer-shaped ears and the curious markings that did indeed look like they'd been painted on. Their bodies resembled greyhounds, lean and hungry looking, like the dogs he'd encountered in Afghanistan, although he was certain the

Pittsburgh zookeepers kept this pack well fed. In fact, he was counting on that.

A wire fence about twenty feet away separated this enclosure from the main dog exhibit. Which meant that his fastest escape route would be by moving to the front of the building and getting over the fence there. He could do that. Absolutely.

Andre turned to face Darius. One last chance to see if there was another way out of this. If he could get the gun away from Darius... but, no, Darius stayed just far enough away that it would be suicide even trying.

"Gonna give you a choice, dawg." Darius let out a weird choked-down giggle. Like he was drunk or high or something. Enjoying this that much. He grabbed the gasoline from Giselle, almost knocking her over. She clung to the gate behind Darius, staring at Andre as if expecting him to save her.

Darius kept the pistol trained on Andre as he swung the gasoline around, dousing the straw bales that stood between him and Andre. He set the gas can down. Took a silver-plated lighter from his pocket. "You can choose the fire or take your chances with the dogs."

Giselle edged out through the gate but didn't shut it. Was she holding it open for Darius? Or Andre?

Andre decided he'd rather face a pack of wild dogs than gamble on a crack whore. "Already beat fire once," he taunted Darius. "Reckon I'll try the dogs this time."

Giselle's expression turned from pleading to anger. Her eyes went so wide he could see the whites around them. She shook the cage door hard. What did she want from him? Not like his burning to death could save her from Darius.

"I was hoping you'd say that." Darius stood poised to strike the lighter if Andre reneged. "Go on. Let's see what you got."

Andre didn't wait. He crouched down, his muscles stretching, and lunged through the dog-door. He slapped his hands against the ground, pushing himself to his feet as quickly as possible once he'd cleared the opening.

The dogs didn't growl. Just that strange chirping that could have been crickets. But they were obviously communicating, re-arranging themselves as if they each had their own job. Kind of like his squad. You had your 203 gunner with his SAW, your guys with M4s, your point man, your Sergeant.

He stared at the dogs, picked out the one who seemed to be their leader as he scanned the area for possible weapons. There were no rocks or sticks in sight. He kept his back to the wall, edging past the observation window.

Darius thumped on the window, obviously disappointed with the action. "Get in there and fight them, Andre," he shouted. "You don't, she's dead."

Andre swiveled his gaze to see what Darius was talking about. Darius stood at the window but held his gun aimed at Giselle who still stood at the door. She looked around her, realized there was no escape. Even if she locked Darius inside the cage, he could shoot her through the holes in the wire. Plus, Zapata's men controlled the building.

"Come here and watch your boyfriend fight for you, bitch," Darius called to Giselle, gesturing with his free hand. "Get your ass over here now or I'll kneecap you. Won't be no great loss. You're no good for anything unless you're flat on your back anyway."

"Wait," Andre shouted. The dogs' ears swiveled at the noise. Their leader took a step forward, chest pushed out. "Don't hurt her. I'll do it."

He stepped away from the wall. The dogs moved to circle him, but they kept a wary distance. Andre looked over his shoulder to check Darius' reaction. He had his face pressed against the window, motioning with his pistol for Andre to keep going.

Giselle backed away from Darius. Tears streamed down her face, ruining her makeup. As soon as she got to the other side of the gasoline-soaked bales of straw, she took her rhinestone encrusted lighter from the pocket of her trench coat.

"No!" Andre lunged towards the window. Darius realized something was wrong and turned to look just as Giselle closed the gate. She thumbed down the striker. The lighter flared to life. She threw it through the wire, into the cage. Flames engulfed the small room.

The dogs fled. Darius' screams filled the night. Andre flung the dog door open, got down on his hands and knees and tried to reach Darius. God, the smell. How could he have ever forgotten that smell? The heat coming from inside the cage made the sweat on Andre's torso sizzle and pop like oil in a skillet.

Darius grabbed onto Andre's arm. But instead of letting Andre pull him free of the inferno, he tried to yank Andre inside with him. Giselle shrieked. Andre could barely hear her over the roar of the fire.

The cage had become a mass of blazing red flames and black smoke. Flames traveled around the wire mesh door. Andre pulled away from Darius, had to slap out flames that had found his sweatpants. Black smoke billowed from the small opening. The heat was unbearable. Finally he rolled away.

That's when he heard the other screaming. From the front of the building. He couldn't tell if it was a man or a woman, it was choked off too fast.

Andre climbed to his feet. Every instinct in his body screamed at him to run, follow the dogs to safety. But Giselle was still in there. She'd just saved his life. He couldn't leave her.

He stumbled around the corner to the rear door. It was unlocked. The knob was warm but not so hot that he couldn't hold it. He braced himself against the wall, knowing the sudden increase in oxygen would feed the flames. This was suicide, the tiny sane portion of his brain whimpered. He was going to die in there, eaten by flames.

He remembered the pain, remembered how it felt when he couldn't save his men. Then he opened the door.

———◆———

LUCY KEPT THE helicopter at her back as she edged towards its nose, scanning the area for a second pilot. She checked on Fatima's position. The mother and child had made it to the top of the steps leading into the building. Footsteps came from behind Lucy. She whirled.

Rashid Raziq emerged from the trees. "Fatima," he called. "Stop! Where are you going?"

Fatima yanked the door open and vanished inside the Primate Habitat.

"No, it's me," Raziq shouted. "Bring Ali back. Come here."

Lucy registered several things at once. Raziq was alone. No guards. And he had a semi-automatic pistol in his hand.

"It's Special Agent Guardino, Mr. Raziq. Lower your weapon," she shouted, stepping out into the open.

Raziq stopped, staring at her in surprise. He could have shot her, he could have turned and escaped into the trees. But instead, he cut across the clearing, racing up the steps after Fatima and his son.

The helicopter blocked her path. She ran around it, following Raziq. "Stop," she shouted. He didn't even look back as he ran into the Primate Habitat.

Lucy clattered up the steps after him. She grabbed her radio. "Taylor, I'm pursuing Raziq into the Primate Habitat. He's armed."

"Armed? I thought he was our hostage."

"We thought wrong." All those contradictory impressions Lucy had about the man... damn, she should have listened to her instincts. Who else but Raziq would have targeted the hockey tournament where his daughter's illicit boyfriend was playing? Although he could just be in shock after escaping from Zapata. Either way, she needed to find him. "Give me a location on Fatima, she has my cell."

"Hang on. She's moving to the west, northwest. I can give you GPS coordinates—"

"Not going to help." She had no map. Lucy remembered that the primate exhibit featured a spiral walkway around the perimeter, climbing higher and higher into the jungle canopy allowing visitors to view the animals through glass walls. West meant Fatima was climbing it clockwise. "Keep an eye on her. I'm going in."

She pushed the glass doors open. A pneumatic sliding door was on the other side. Beyond it an eerie darkness. The doors swished shut behind her and she could smell the ozone and pungent plant life of the jungle habitat. Birds and insects called to each other, mixed in with the chatter of chimps and monkeys.

Strangely shaped shadows crowded the path that twisted and turned so you wouldn't realize you were on a simple curved ramp climbing into the heart of the jungle. The only lighting came from tiny red lights lining each side of the path.

She stepped into the shadows, pushing a large palm frond aside. This was madness. Raziq could be hiding anywhere and she'd never see him or hear him from the path. She closed her eyes, took a deep breath, adjusting to the strange environment. What would she do if she were him? What did he want?

What he'd wanted all along. Same as she did: Fatima and the baby.

He wouldn't hurt them. No, he'd eliminate the competition: Lucy.

She opened her eyes and instead of searching for Fatima, she scouted for the best place for an ambush.

———•———

MORGAN STOOD BENEATH the roof overhang of the cinderblock building the men had taken Jenna to. There was an opening above—not even a window, more for ventilation than anything else. But it was large enough to allow her to hear Jenna's screams.

Not that Morgan cared. Not in the traditional sense. She knew that. In fact, part of her brain was busy trying to figure out what techniques they might be using, anticipating when the next scream would come. But that didn't mean Jenna didn't matter to her, that she wasn't concerned.

After all, Jenna was *hers*. It was as if these men had stolen from Morgan.

She didn't like that. Not at all.

She was about to make her move on the two men guarding the door when a shotgun blast in the distance got their attention. They took off at a run and the coast was clear.

Morgan entered the building, quickly oriented herself. It was some kind of animal kennel, caged enclosures on either side of a long hallway. Jenna was inside a room at the front, behind a solid wooden door.

No more guards inside although there was a woman at the far end of the corridor near another exit. She was watching something inside one of the cages and didn't even notice Morgan.

Morgan held her knife at the ready and knocked on the door. A man answered in Spanish. She knocked again, this time more urgently.

The door opened and a large Hispanic man looked out, his focus on the space above Morgan's head. By the time he looked down, her blade had already pierced his heart.

Tall men were the easiest; her short stature put her at the perfect angle to stab up below their ribcage, give the blade a little wig-wag to slice the ventricle, and pull it back out, releasing only the tiniest drop of blood on the surface.

He blinked, dropped something to the floor behind the door, and staggered back a step. Morgan shoved him the rest of the way inside the room. He fell to the floor. The other man in the room, a man in a suit, leapt to his feet, swearing in Spanish, reaching for a gun inside his jacket.

Too little, too slow. Morgan used the stun gun on the man. He slumped back into the chair. She took his pistol, stunned him again for good measure, then used her wire to tie him to his chair.

She closed the door, picked up the item the big guy had dropped—a small blowtorch—and finally turned to Jenna.

"You look a mess," she told Jenna as she cut through the zipties holding Jenna to the chair. It wasn't a lie. Jenna's one eye was swollen shut and already turning purple. Her nose was bleeding and more blood came from her mouth.

But that was the least of her injuries. They'd used the blowtorch. Not on Jenna's skin, no, that would be too predictable.

They'd burned off Jenna's hair—the shoulder length, thick, auburn hair that Morgan had always envied. The stench of burnt hair saturated the room and blackened locks curled around Jenna's feet and clung to her clothing.

They hadn't done more than to raise a few blisters on Jenna's scalp. Morgan tried to imagine what it would have been like: painful and terrifying, fire so close to your face yet out of sight, unable to anticipate when they'd put it out, where they'd start it next. For a woman, a most effective technique, she decided.

"Morgan," Jenna opened her good eye and gasped. "What are you doing here?"

"I'm here to save you." Morgan surprised herself, the pride that came with those words. She had to admit, it did feel good. Felt right, somehow. Better than she'd ever felt with her father.

She sliced through the final ziptie restraining Jenna. "Can you walk?"

Jenna bobbed her head in a nod. She raised a hand to her scalp, grimaced in pain as it touched a particularly angry red area. "Is it bad?"

"Better than being dead."

"Why'd you let him live?" Jenna stared at the man in the suit who was starting to stir.

"We might need a bargaining chip. Who is he?"

"Victor Zapata."

Morgan had thought as much.

Jenna pushed herself out of the chair and stood wobbling. "Give me your knife."

"We need him alive to get out of here." This was how emotions got you in trouble.

"Give me the knife, Morgan. Make sure the coast is clear," Jenna ordered. Morgan glared at her, but handed her the switchblade.

Morgan turned and cracked the door open. Black smoke billowed in. "Jenna, we've got to go."

A man's shriek, high-pitched like an animal's, cut her off. Morgan whirled to see Jenna pulling the knife blade from Victor Zapata's left eye. Blood and fluid gushed from it and he kept screaming and screaming.

Morgan felt torn between approval—the man deserved everything he got—and disapproval—Jenna was supposed to be one of the good guys, not someone like Morgan. More smoke pushed into the room. Morgan coughed. Jenna raised the knife, considering her next target.

"The place is on fire, Jenna." Morgan grabbed Jenna's arm. Why was it that Morgan always had to be the sensible one?

Together they made it out the door and to the hallway. The temperature had risen dramatically in the few minutes since Morgan had entered. The whole building was like one big brick oven.

They'd only staggered a few feet when Jenna collapsed, gasping for air. Morgan dropped to the ground as well, hoping there'd be fresh air down low.

"Giselle," a man called, his voice bouncing off the cinderblock walls.

"Help," Morgan shouted. "Help us."

She pushed Jenna along the floor, trying to crawl to the door. Were they going in the right direction? How far was it?

Just as she was sure they were hopelessly lost in the thick smoke, a man reached down and grabbed her.

"Jenna," she gasped, surprising even herself. Being a hero didn't mean going all soft and sentimental, did it? "Help Jenna."

CHAPTER 41

NICK HOPED THE Gangsta was making an empty threat when he said he'd shoot the children first, but Tee-Bo's body language and expression appeared truthful.

The people who hadn't made it into the van gathered around Sister Patrice as if she had an invisible shield activated by the rosary beads in her hand. The van was filled with the youngest children and their mothers. Even Patrice's seat was taken up by two little girls, faces pressed against the front window, crying, pointing to an elderly man in the crowd.

More Terrace residents had come to their doors, watching warily. Nick turned to the people, seeking out the two teenagers. "You all know what he wants and where it is. We don't have much time."

"Ain't no snitches," one of the teens said angrily. The elderly woman beside him elbowed him in the stomach. Hard.

"The Rippers will know it was us," one of the men said. "We can't risk that."

"They won't know who talked," Nick argued. "I'm not even sure they'll be back at all. After what they did tonight, the police, FBI, DEA, you name it, are going to be after them."

"Hah." A woman in her thirties spat at Nick's feet. "Police. Not like they fuckin' cared before. Why bother now?"

He glanced at Patrice. She helped, saying, "The Rippers went too far. They attacked the police. Killed some. The police aren't going to let that go unpunished."

"So as usual, we're the ones paying the price."

"This is your only chance. We're running out of time."

The crowd shifted, grumbled, but no one made eye contact with Nick.

"All I need is the unit number. Won't you give me that to save the lives of your children, your grandchildren?"

The elderly man belonging to the girls in the van spoke up. "1778. That's the one you want."

The others looked at him in surprise, the teenage boys with anger. Nick walked back to Tee-Bo. "I have the location. You let this van full of people drive off safely—a gesture of good will—and I'll give it to you."

"Nah, man. You give it to me now and we'll see how much good will I have after."

"You gave me your word of honor. As a gentleman. Wouldn't want to let all these people know your word isn't worth anything." Nick held his ground, meeting the Gangsta's gaze. "I expect a business man like yourself protects his reputation above all else."

Finally Tee-Bo relented. "Okay, okay." He laughed as if this were all a joke, not innocent lives they were gambling with. "You pretty hard-assed for a white boy. You win. We play it your way."

———————◆———————

WHEN THE SMOKE and heat first hit Andre, it felt as if his windpipe had squeezed shut. Eyes watering, vision useless in the haze, he wheezed and gasped. He flailed from one side of the hall to the other, banging against the cage doors, trying to find Giselle. Where the hell had she gone?

No sign of Giselle. Instead, he tripped over two bodies near the front of the building. A woman and a girl. He tried to gulp in a breath but couldn't. His vision danced with red spots as he grabbed the girl's arm.

"Help Jenna," she whispered.

Jenna? The sexy redhead? Had those been her screams he'd heard, not Giselle's?

Andre wasn't sure he could get his own body to the door, which seemed an impossible distant away. *Move it, Sarge,* his men called to him. *Show them what makes a Dog Company Marine.*

He dragged the girl and Jenna with him to the door. One foot forward, then the other, one more, and again… Lungs burning, head spinning, he heaved against the door. It didn't open.

He wanted to quit. But then he heard his old drill sergeant. *Only time a Marine quits is when he's dead.*

Right. And he wasn't dead yet. He dropped the girl's arm to pull the door open instead of pushing against it then grabbed her again. He stumbled out into the night, dragging them with him.

The cool night air was like a woman's caress. Soothing his irritated airways, he was able to relax and breathe in. Another breath and his vision cleared. His chest still felt tight, but it was as if his asthma had closed his throat in time to protect him from inhaling too much of the smoke. He heaved in a few more breaths then pushed himself to his feet. Smoke roiled through the open door, flames licked at the top of the doorjamb, reaching for the fake thatching. The girl was coughing but sitting up. She couldn't speak, but motioned to him to help her with Jenna.

He waved her aside and lifted Jenna in his arms. What had happened to her hair? Zapata. Fury gave him strength he hadn't imagined he possessed. Together with the girl they staggered down the path.

"Thank you, Andre," the girl said. She was the one from the car, he realized. But how the hell had she known his name?

———•———

LUCY TOOK HER time, acclimating her senses to the weird twilight and raucous noises. Instead of following the path, she stepped over the boulders lining it onto moist ground that was soft beneath her feet. There was a display of exotic foliage, thick enough to hide a man, just up ahead.

Approaching it from what she hoped was Raziq's blind side, Lucy crept through the brush, quietly, gingerly pulling back branches, weaving her body through them. Stalking her prey.

Raziq's dark suit blended into the shadows but the dim lights made his white shirt collar and cuffs stand out all the more. He crouched about ten feet in front of her and to her left, ready to pounce on anyone coming down the main path.

Lucy stepped towards him, moving past the final dwarf palm standing between her and Raziq.

"Put the gun on the ground and raise your hands where I can see them," she instructed, her voice raised over the jungle noises but sounding strangely calm and normal.

He hesitated and she thought she might have to shoot him. There was still a chance he was an innocent victim in all this. He could have escaped, stolen a weapon, gone after Fatima and the baby. But Lucy wasn't taking any chances.

Raziq carefully lowered his gun to the ground. He stood up straight, hands on his head in the universal posture of surrender.

"Lie face down on the ground," Lucy instructed him. "Arms spread out to your sides."

He complied. "All I want is my son."

She grabbed a flex-cuff, restrained him then searched him, no other weapons. Hauling him back to his feet, she said, "Okay, let's go."

He stood, head flung back and shouted, "Fatima! Bring Ali here. This instant!"

She nudged him onto the path. "Shut up and walk."

"You need to be nicer to me if you want to live through this night," he said as they followed the trail out the main doors. "I'm your only hope."

Okay, that put him squarely on the side of the bad guys. Lucy had known there was something wrong about Raziq. She wondered how far he was involved with Zapata. Was so tired it was hard to care, as long as she had him in custody and Fatima and the baby were safe.

She prodded Raziq down the steps to the bottom. Stopped him there to radio Taylor an update.

"The Guard unit just breached the front gate," he said. "They'll be there in a few minutes."

Gunfire sounded from the east. That should keep Zapata's men occupied. "I'll wait here, make sure no one tries to escape in the helicopter."

She'd just pocketed the radio when Andre staggered out of the trees. He carried Jenna in his arms.

"Andre, what happened?"

He shook his head as if there was too much to explain. Jenna looked awful—her hair was gone, her face and head swollen with bruises and blisters. Christ, what had Zapata done to her?

"Any sign of Haddad?" she asked.

"No," Andre answered as he lowered Jenna to her feet. She appeared stunned, but was able to stand on her own.

"He's dead," Jenna said. She coughed and cleared her throat. "Raziq shot him. He killed David."

Lucy turned to Raziq. "Killing a federal agent. That's the needle."

Jenna jerked up, her gaze swimming around, past Lucy, taking in the helo then Raziq. She lunged at Raziq, clawing at him. Andre pulled her away before she got close. Raziq spat in her direction.

"Shoot him, damnit!" Jenna screamed.

"She can't," Raziq said. "I'm too valuable. No one can touch me."

Lucy ignored him. She'd love to shoot the man, he deserved to die, but as much as she was tempted, she couldn't. Not and look Nick or Megan in the eye ever again.

"Saint Lucy," Jenna sneered, fists futilely pummeling Andre's arms restraining her. "Do you have any idea how many men I killed tonight? Just to save your scrawny butt. How about Walden? Or David Haddad? And how many men did you kill, Lucy? Have you even fired your weapon, you miserable coward?"

Lucy stared at her in shock. She was obviously traumatized. What had Zapata and his men done to her? "Jenna—"

"Don't 'Jenna' me, bitch. You sit on your high horse, so judgmental, talking about justice this and justice that. But you're just a coward. Too chicken to deliver that justice you preach about. Well, I'm not." She spun free of Andre. Before he could grab her, she flew across the space between them, aiming a knife at Raziq.

"Jenna, no!" Lucy stepped between Jenna and Raziq. God help her, the look in Jenna's eyes. It was as if Jenna wanted to kill her as much as she did Raziq.

"Out of my way, Lucy." Jenna's voice was so hoarse it barely sounded human. Her hand that held the knife shook. Hell, her entire body trembled with fury.

"No. Jenna. You can't."

"I can and I will. Get out of my way."

"Give me the knife." Lucy reached her hand out.

Jenna hesitated and for a heartbeat Lucy thought she was actually going to stab her in order to get to Raziq.

Andre grabbed Jenna from behind and the knife clattered to the ground.

"Get her out of here," Lucy told Andre. "I'll deal with this." She nodded to the helo, the pilot's body, their crime scene, her prisoner… God, what a mess.

"Don't worry," he said. Lucy had the feeling he was talking more to Jenna than her. "I'll take care of everything."

He half carried, half led Jenna away, looking over his shoulder and meeting Lucy's gaze as if wanting some promise from her. What kind of promise she wasn't sure. That the trauma Jenna had suffered had been worth it? That everything would be okay, the city would heal? That Raziq would rot in prison for the rest of his life?

Lucy wished she could make any one of those promises. But she couldn't.

Raziq looked up at her from where he sat on the steps and laughed. "Americans. No stomach for business. That's why Zapata and I made such a great team. Look what we did to your precious city. All in one night."

Lucy stared at him, speechless. Did he have any idea how many people had lost their lives tonight? For what? Money? Power? What could possibly be worth all this?

He continued, "You think you're impervious, you're protected. Hah. You're all weak. Vulnerable. And now you're scared. Because if we did this to you, anyone can. And they will. After tonight, none of you will ever be safe again."

"Neither will you, Raziq. Any idea what they'll do to you in an American prison?"

"You can't send me to prison. I know too much. I'm too valuable. If the cartel can't pay me for what I know, the US government will." He shrugged. "What do I care where the money comes from?"

She almost vomited, she was so disgusted. "Your wife cares. Or she will after I have a little chat with her. You'll never see your son again."

His eyes narrowed. "You can't do that. I ask for my son, I get my son. Why do you think we went through all this, this drama?"

Lucy crouched down to his eye level. "I think you wanted it all. The money Zapata promised you, freedom to spend it, and a son to be proud of. Your daughters were collateral damage. Getting rid of them was part of the price Zapata paid for your services, wasn't it?"

"Badria, no. She was unfortunate." He actually managed to sound contrite. "But the other—" He spat at Lucy's feet. "It was worth it. To hear her scream, beg for mercy, for forgiveness. Ungrateful whore."

A sinking feeling made Lucy's gut go cold. She'd suspected the truth but to hear him boast about it... She smelled smoke. Worse, burning flesh. Like what she'd smelled when she'd first entered Raziq's house. "You were there. You're the one who watched."

He smiled. "Of course I did. It was my honor sullied, my right to see her punished."

Sonofabitch. She looked away, her chest tight, making it hard to breathe. Her gaze fell on Jenna's discarded knife beside her.

"After Zapata's men were done with her, I'm the one who lit the match," Raziq said. "You should have heard her scream."

She could do it. She could end the bastard here and now; no one would ever know.

Lucy grabbed the knife. Raziq laughed again. "You can't do it. Typical woman. Typical American. No taste for blood."

"Maybe not." She folded the knife shut and pocketed it. "I prefer the taste of justice."

She turned away. Just long enough to regain her composure without him watching, searching her for any sign of weakness. A tiny moment of privacy. She scrubbed her face with one hand, trying to remember what it felt like not to be exhausted. Thought of Nick and Megan. Took a breath. Reminded herself that she was alive—and nothing Raziq said could change that. She had won.

Behind her she heard a small, choked cry. Lucy whirled, gun in her hand. Morgan Ames stood over Raziq's body. His throat was slashed, blood still gurgling as it spilled onto the ground.

"Morgan! But why, how—"

Morgan coldly cleaned her blade on Raziq's coat hem. "Because there are monsters even worse than my father." She stood, glanced over Lucy's shoulder where sirens filled the night. "We're even now."

She ran off, vanishing into the darkness before Lucy had a chance to do more than watch. Unless she wanted to shoot Morgan in the back.

Lucy looked down at Raziq's still body. Swallowed against a wave of bile and disgust. He wasn't worth it.

CHAPTER 42

"WHAT I DON'T understand," Lucy said to Nick as she drove his Explorer across the river and turned towards home, "is what Morgan was doing there in the first place."

They'd left Jenna and Andre at the hospital, being monitored overnight for smoke inhalation. Andre had refused to leave Jenna's side. Lucy thought he would be a good influence on Jenna.

Walden was out of surgery and going to be fine, according to the doctors. The Guardsmen used the zoo's fire-fighting equipment to put out the blaze before it spread. They found Zapata's body along with those of two other men and a woman. No animals injured, they'd been proud to report. Best of all, they'd found the zoo's nightshift workers locked up in the main staff office. Only one security guard had been killed. After what she'd seen at the 911 Center, the news had seemed like a miracle—after all, Zapata had no reason not to massacre them all.

All Lucy could think was that he'd been holding onto them to use as hostages if his plans fell apart. Made her smile to think that she and her team had spoiled that for him.

Fatima and the baby. That had been the hardest thing—telling her the truth about what her husband had done. Lucy still wasn't sure the mother had taken it all in. The poor woman was isolated, couldn't even give Lucy the name of anyone to call other than her friend in Cranberry. There was no way she'd be able to make it there with the roads still shut down. In the end, at Nick's suggestion, she'd left them with the sisters at Holy Trinity.

She'd saved Fatima and the baby, she'd caught Mina and Badria's killer... yet, given the enormity of the destruction, the price paid for those small successes, she knew she'd failed. The backlash of adrenalin fleeing left her feeling hollow inside. As if she'd lost something important tonight and she wasn't sure if she could ever get it back again.

Taylor had already dug up evidence of the State Police pilot's bribe. Sold his soul and his helicopter to Zapata for a mere fifty thousand dollars. Documents in the helicopter revealed that he was supposed to fly Zapata and Raziq to an isolated farm in Maryland, from there they would have begun a leisurely cross-country trip to Mexico by car while the authorities were busy blocking the airports.

The names of the 911 operators massacred were beginning to be verified. The press was calling them Pittsburgh's Martyrs. Lucy still didn't know the name of the deputy she'd failed to save, but she vowed that when she did, she'd find his family. Tell them everything.

Other than a few isolated incidents of looting, the city was calming down. Enough so that after her initial debriefing she was granted permission to escort their "civilian witness" home.

"I know Morgan wasn't following me," she continued when Nick remained silent. "Jenna said she's been stalking her, but that doesn't explain how she knew to be at Ruby Avenue at the right time waiting in a car. Or how she knew who Andre was."

Nick cleared his throat and shifted his position. Did he have any idea how guilty he looked?

"Nick. I'm not an idiot. Just tell me."

He blew his breath out. God, he looked exhausted. She almost regretted pushing him, but she needed to know Morgan wasn't a threat before she let Megan come home. From the girl's parting words, she didn't think there was a problem, but she'd underestimated the teenage psychopath before.

"I was the idiot," he finally said. "I was driving to Andre's when she appeared in the road. I almost ran her down. Said she'd wrecked her bike, needed help. I didn't recognize her at first—she had a wig and colored contacts—and when I did it was too late."

"Wait." She hit the brakes and pulled into a Sheetz. She bypassed the gas pumps and stopped the car along the side wall of the convenience store where they would have privacy. "Morgan Ames was alone with you? In this vehicle? What happened? Tell me everything."

As he explained, including a bone-chilling account of his time alone with the killer in her house, Lucy searched the car and presented Nick with the trophies left by Morgan.

At least he didn't try to feign surprise at the obvious story told by Morgan's underwear and blood left in his car. But he didn't look angry either. More… disappointed.

"She didn't go through with it," he said.

He didn't know about Raziq. Or about the expression on Morgan's face when she slit Raziq's throat—or rather, the lack of expression.

"Are you really defending her?" she demanded. She loved him for his empathy; it was what made him so good at his job. But couldn't he turn it off for one damn moment? "Do you have any idea what she could have done to you? Not just rape charges. She could have staged something much, much worse—set you up for murder." But even that wasn't the worst thing she feared. She had to suck in her breath just to find the strength to say it aloud; hoped she wasn't tempting Fate. "Nick, what if she killed you?"

He hung his head, didn't look at her. "I'm sorry."

"That's it? You're sorry?" Anger and fear forced her from the car before she could say anything else. She stomped around the corner and into the convenience store, grabbed two large coffees, a half dozen Krispy Kremes so fresh they were still warm, a can of lighter fluid and a Zippo.

When she returned to the Explorer, Nick leaned against the front bumper, watching for her. She handed him the food, threw Morgan's underwear onto the pavement, doused them with lighter fluid, and lit them on fire. As they burned, she wiped down the seats with wet-naps left over from their last BBQ take out, added those to the small pyre. "Did she touch anything else?"

"She used my phone."

Lucy held out her hand. Nick placed his phone in it. Lord only knew what kind of spyware Morgan had planted on it. She could be listening to them right now.

"Morgan, if you hear this, I want you to listen closely. My family is off limits. Come near them again and I will hunt you down and I will end you. Final warning. Goodbye."

She removed the battery and SIM card. Tossed the SIM card in the tiny blaze and stomped on the phone's case.

"Lucy, don't you think you're over reacting?" Nick said. "I can get a new SIM card without you destroying—"

She whirled on him, feeling dizzy and breathless and more out of control than she had all night. God, she hated when he got all Zen-calm and reasonable on her. "Nick—"

To her surprise he immediately threw up his hands in surrender. More than that, he stepped forward and wrapped his arms around her, containing the wild energy that made her entire body quake. She tensed at first, but slowly let herself relax into his embrace.

"I'm sorry," he said. "I'm so sorry. You're right. I should never have underestimated her. I'm sorry."

After she quieted he released her to stare at her appraisingly. "Anything else you want to burn? The car's contaminated, we could torch it."

Lucy shook her head, finally laughed. It came out shaky and nervous, but it was a start. A first timid step back to normalcy. "Who are you and what have you done with my peacenik husband?"

He smiled one of his sloe-gin smiles that started at the corner of his mouth and spread across his face. "I guess maybe tonight I got a taste of war. It made me appreciate what you face everyday. I'm sorry if I make your job harder."

Lucy's mouth opened. She shut it. It fell back open again. He'd never said anything like that before.

She covered by grabbing her coffee and the donuts and getting back in the car. Nick joined her and they sat in silence, indulging in a double-action sugar and caffeine rush.

Nick broke the silence. "I am going to ask you for one thing and if you can't do it, you need to tell me now. I need you to be honest with me."

Silence. She fidgeted, waiting for his question, unbuckled, re-buckled, unbuckled her seat belt and let it zip back into the roller. "About what?"

"No. That's what I'm asking for. Honesty. Don't sugarcoat the truth. If you're headed into a dangerous assignment, tell me. Because if something," he looked away, made a choking noise, "ever happens to you, I need to know. I need to be... prepared. For Megan's sake, as well as my own. She deserves that, I deserve that."

No argument there. She blinked hard, not sure which words were the right ones, the ones that would fix everything. Damn, she was so good with words at work, could negotiate any situation. But with Nick... She gave up on words and instead simply lay her hand over his and squeezed hard.

He didn't return the squeeze. "You caught your bad guys. Sometimes I think—I worry—that you care more about that than you do about yourself. About keeping yourself safe. You could have been killed out there tonight."

She blew out her breath. Her job. The paradox their relationship revolved around as if it were their own personal sun. "I don't give a damn about catching the bad guys, Nick. Not the way you mean it, like it's some kind of competition. What I care about is keeping you safe, keeping Megan safe, keeping people like Andre and his grandmother safe. And yes, I'll risk my life if that means saving innocent civilians. I never, *ever* do it without thinking of you and Megan and what it would mean if I fail. But I can't let that stop me."

Just like David Haddad didn't let it stop him. Damn. She was dreading that phone call. Telling his wife and family what happened.

"I'm not asking you not to do your job," he said in a low tone. "I'm just asking you not to treat me like I'm an outsider. One of those civilians you have to protect."

"You want me to share." Hard to do when she was constantly compartmentalizing her private life and her work life. Something that was getting harder and harder to do. That was becoming exhausting, actually. Maybe he had a point.

"I want you to share." He centered his gaze on her. Usually she loved it when he did that. It made her feel like the rest of the universe had vanished, leaving only the two of them. But this time there was a new distance between them. A distance it was up to her to cross.

"You're right." She turned his palm over and brought it to rest against her heart. "I'm sorry."

Slowly, just as the first rays of morning light crept over the rooftops surrounding them, he smiled. The same wide smile she'd fallen in love with over fifteen years ago.

She unbuckled his seat belt and leaned forward to kiss him. "Thanks for the great date night."

His chuckle vibrated through his body into hers.

"Your mother was so excited when I came up with the idea. Although of course, she was most excited about taking Megan for the weekend," he said, his voice lighter, back to the Nick she woke up to every morning, who stood hip to hip beside her while brushing teeth or doing dishes, who heard her unspoken fears and chased them away with a kiss.

Honesty. "About that. You should know. I hate the ballet."

His eyes crinkled as he laughed. "I know that."

"But—*The Nutcracker?*"

"Lucy. Being in *The Nutcracker* when you were young was the last time you and your mom and dad did anything as a family before your dad got sick. The last time as a child when you felt truly safe. You've been so distant from me, from Megan, since last month, I wanted you to remember that feeling. What it meant, feeling safe."

She blinked hard, but not hard enough to hold back her tears. "Last month—you knew?"

He shook his head sadly. "No. All I have are fears and middle of the night bogeymen and wild guesses. Want to tell me about it?"

The tears were streaming so fast now that she had to wipe her nose on the sleeve of her fleece top. Back at the zoo she'd thrown away her filthy parka, never wanting to see it again. Her Glock was in evidence. The only thing marking her as an FBI agent was the badge out of sight in her back pocket. Probably a good thing. Big, tough FBI agent. Blubbering like a baby. Nick reached across the seats and pulled her into his arms.

"It's okay, Lucy. You can tell me anything."

Visions of being trapped with Morgan's father, the pain, the sound of her voice breaking as she tried not to scream, fought to not give in, not to give him any satisfaction… they all came rushing back, drowning her until she couldn't catch her breath.

But this time Nick was there to pull her back from the panic. He held her tight and finally, finally she told him everything.

And she knew that in the end, nothing could ever come between them again. With Nick she'd always be safe. She'd never have to hide the truth.

EPILOGUE

Two days later

ANDRE LET HIMSELF into Jenna's building and climbed the steps up to her loft, his arms full of grocery bags. The woman seemed to live on diet cola and wilted lettuce, no wonder she was so damn skinny.

As he rounded the final landing, he saw Morgan coming out of Jenna's apartment. She spotted him and laid a finger to her lips. "She's sleeping," she whispered.

Morgan had told Andre she was seventeen, but sometimes she seemed much younger—and sometimes she seemed much older. He still couldn't believe the way she'd taken on Mad Dog and had rescued Jenna all on her own. She'd stopped by the hospital with flowers but Jenna had been with the doctors, so she'd left those with Andre. Jenna had cried later when she'd read the card. It said, "I'll always be there for you."

Andre wasn't sure that they were happy tears, if Jenna was reassured because until then, no one knew if

Morgan had made it out of the zoo alive, or if Jenna's tears were caused by something else.

He had a feeling it was the something else. Jenna wouldn't talk about who Morgan was, why Morgan was in her life, but no doubt about it, the girl was dangerous.

He carefully set the bags down to free his hands. He didn't have a weapon and wondered why his first thought was that he might need one. After all, the girl was barely five feet tall; he could pick her up with one hand.

Andre stared at Morgan. Morgan stared back. Her eyes reminded him of a few guys in his company. Guys who'd gotten too damn used to killing—and too damned good at it.

"Relax, Andre. I'd never hurt her. Or you." She smiled, revealing her teeth.

He wasn't reassured. "Why the hell would you say something like that?"

She nodded to his hands. He looked down, realized they were clenched into fists. He'd shifted his weight to balance evenly on both feet. A fighting stance.

To his surprise, she laughed and stood on tiptoe to kiss his cheek. "I like you, Andre. Take care, now. See you soon."

She skipped down the steps before he could do more than raise a hand to touch his cheek. The spot where she'd laid her lips was scar tissue, he couldn't feel anything there, yet his skin still felt flushed.

Weird, weird girl. He wasn't sure what the best way to handle her was. Maybe Callahan would have an idea. He picked up the bags and turned to let himself into Jenna's loft.

Jenna was standing there, watching Morgan disappear down the stairs. Sleep lines creased her face but they couldn't disguise her wistful expression. Like she maybe wanted to run after Morgan—or run away from her?

Without saying a word she turned and went back inside the loft, leaving the door open for him. "You sure that girl is your friend?" he asked as he set the bags on the counter.

Jenna locked all the locks on the door and leaned against it for a long moment. Her shoulders were slumped and he worried that she was crying again. But her voice was clear when she said, "My grandfather used to say you get the friends you deserve."

"What's that supposed to mean?" But he had a feeling he knew. Like he'd once upon a time deserved friends like Darius and Mad Dog.

He was putting away the groceries when he heard the hushed slap of her bare feet on the hardwood floor behind him.

"You want anything?" he asked Jenna without turning around. He still hadn't gotten his mask back or replaced his long-sleeved compression garment. He felt a bit naked walking around without them—and more than a bit shy around Jenna. He wished he could figure out why—he'd had no problem talking to the cops or even going to the grocery store. But Jenna...

She wrapped her arms around him from behind. He jerked, startled, but she didn't let go. Instead she rested her chin on his shoulder. "I want a whole lot. Think you can give it to me?"

"Jenna—"

She dropped her hands and stepped away. "I get it. I'm damaged goods."

"God, no." They'd spent almost every minute of the last two days together until he'd left this morning to check on Grams and move her into her new room with the sisters at Holy Trinity.

He'd told Jenna things he never thought he'd tell anyone, not even the Doc. She'd listened and told him about her childhood, about her grandfather, the judge. A letter bomb had left him in a coma. Jenna had helped to take care of him, even though she was only twelve, had been there when he'd finally died.

She hadn't talked about Zapata yet. But they had plenty of time. He hoped.

"Are you sure about this?" He turned to face her. She was beautiful. What could she ever see in him?

She met his gaze and nodded. "What do you say, Marine? Ready to go the distance?"

He wasn't sure. Well, he was. But... his nerve fled him and he resorted to his age-old defense: warped humor.

"So yeah, we can be like fire and ice, ice baby." He did a rap tattoo in the air with his hands.

She stared at him. Andre was sure he'd lost her for good. Part of his brain chided himself, the rest of him felt relieved. So much less pain this way. After all, her burns were minor, they would heal, and her hair would grow back and she'd be gorgeous once again. Why would she want to hang out with a freak like him?

Then she grinned, patting the air around her head as if her hair was still there. "You making fun of my naturally curly red hair?"

The nurses had trimmed all the hair she'd had left so it wouldn't interfere with the burn ointment and bandages. She'd been lucky, just first and second degree burns; once the blisters healed, she'd be fine.

"I don't see any red hair. All I see is glistening white."

"So then you're calling me frigid?" Beneath her scowl a smile flitted in and out of view. "Cold as ice? Is that it?"

"Aw jeez. It's ironic. Humor. If I have to explain it to you, it's not funny."

Now the smile fully emerged. "Oh. Ironic. Like a black guy who's mostly not black anymore? More like a jelly bean, one of those pink and black speckled ones."

Wow. She got his warped humor and it didn't bother her. Small miracle right there. But that was just the first barrier. There were plenty more standing in their way. Like what lay beneath his clothing. Up close and personal, actual touching—no one, not a doctor or nurse, had been able to do that without a flinch or a shudder.

"Maybe we could be jelly belly and spice?" She sidled up to him. Close. Real close. "I'm spice. Obviously." As she spoke, she unbuttoned his shirt. Exposed the new stitches zigzagging across his belly alongside the old scars. "And you're jelly belly."

Jenna stopped and looked for a long moment. He sucked in his breath and couldn't let it out again for fear of scaring her away.

"I got plenty of spice myself," he finally joked, giving her a chance to escape without either of them being hurt. Not too bad, at least. "And don't you be dissing my six pack—well, five and a half pack. Ain't no jelly there."

She didn't flinch or shudder or faint. Instead she slid her hands along the scars covering his belly. He almost ran but was too damned stunned by her touch to do anything.

He was the one who shuddered. Not because it hurt. No. Because it felt so damn good, he was afraid he might cry. *Pull it together, Marine.*

Then she tilted her chin and kissed him, full on, not trying to avoid the scar that made one corner of his mouth bulge and dug a crater into his chin. It was the muscle flap that had rebuilt his lips. The surgeons did it so he could feed himself, but now he was so damn glad they had.

Finally he had to breathe. He pulled away a little, giving her space, still half-expecting her to bolt. She didn't move, her gaze locked onto his.

She trailed her lips across his, following the scar that ran down to his collarbone. The skin was sensitive. It tingled at her touch. Felt good.

Her smile grew wicked. "How about those old fashioned pink and white candies that had black licorice on the inside? What were they called? Good 'n plenty?"

It took him a moment before he could answer.

"Good 'n plenty? Yeah, I can do that." He tried to keep a straight face, play into the humor that had saved him so many times in the past, but ended up looking at the ceiling, blinking back tears.

"Shut up," she told him as her mouth returned to his.

A good Marine always obeys orders. And Andre was a damn fine Marine. "Ma'am, yes ma'am."

Lucy's Back!
And She's in the Fight of Her Life...

AFTER SHOCK

As head of the FBI's Sexual Assault Felony Enforcement Squad, agent Lucy Guardino has made a name for herself bringing the lowest of lowlifes to justice: rapists, serial killers, pedophiles—she's faced them all down with her signature grit and determination.

Today is different for Lucy. Because the man who has taken her prisoner has promised Lucy three things: that before this day is over, she will be dead; that someone in her family will also die; and that he always wins.

Trapped inside her worst nightmare, Lucy faces a ruthless killer as he plays Russian roulette with the lives of those she loves. Wounded and unarmed, how can Lucy defeat a psychopath who doesn't play by any rules?

AFTER SHOCK is a heart-pounding, lightning-paced thrill ride that will leave readers breathless as they root for the ultimate superheroine next door.

CPSIA information can be obtained at www.ICGtesting.com
Printed in the USA
BVOW02*0609020616

450361BV00001B/2/P